D1448970

TIPTON

Praise for
TIPTON

"A work of biblical resonance and personal depth, *Tipton*'s exodus and promised land are found within the American home front of World War II. We are led on this journey not by bearded patriarchs, but by a band of irrepressible youths yearning to overcome their own histories and open a space for the heart. At times in prose and at times in poetry, these voices offer insight into fractured lives and landscapes that have become our own."

Kevin McFadden, author of *Hardscrabble*

"When World War II arrives, Alice Williams, a young housemother at the Tipton Home in rural Oklahoma, sees a chance to reunite with her husband. But will she find the love she wants—or will she be leaving love behind in Tipton? From the stark vistas of Oklahoma to the green fields of Virginia, from the depths of the Great Depression to the optimism of post-war America, *Tipton* traces the changing fortunes of its characters against the timeless landscape of the human heart."

Jane Freimiller, author of *A Year of Reading, A Month-to-Month Guide to Classics and Crowd-Pleasers for You or Your Book Group*

"Hilary Holladay's debut novel is an eloquent achievement. Set in rural Oklahoma and Virginia in the late 1930s and continuing into the war years, with much of its action swirling around Alice Williams, the complex heroine of the story, *Tipton* presents a sepia-toned world of characters whose lives, while initially apart from, are drawn increasingly into the cataclysms of the larger, darker world. Holladay's gifts as a poet are on display in her uses of precise, even exquisite detail. Friendship, the search for identity, coming of age, class, the effects of war, and the power of love are rendered new by Holladay's imagining, and *Tipton* leaves us with its own hard-won truths."

David Daniel, author of *Six Off 66*, *Reunion*, and *American Pastime*

"Hilary Holladay has written a big story, alive with the twists and turns of real life in its unpredictability, pain, and delight."

William McCranor Henderson, author of *I Killed Hemingway*

TIPTON

A NOVEL

Hilary Holladay

KNOX ROBINSON
PUBLISHING
London & New York

KNOX ROBINSON PUBLISHING

34 New House
67-68 Hatton Garden
London, EC1N 8JY
&
244 5th Avenue, Suite 1861
New York, New York 10001

First published in Great Britain and the United States in 2014 by
Knox Robinson Publishing

ISBN HC 978-1-908483-72-0
ISBN PB 978-1-910282-24-3
ISBN EB 978-1-910282-25-0

Typeset in Trump Mediaeval

Printed in the United States of America and the United Kingdom

www.knoxrobinsonpublishing.com

In memory of my grandmother,

Helen Warren Holladay

TIPTON

Contents

Fields of the Fatherless

1

In the fall of his fourteenth year, in 1938, Ross Gentry made his first close friend. He and a half-dozen other boys were picking cotton when a pickup truck came up the long dirt driveway at the Tipton Home. After the truck's occupants had a brief conversation, a boy emerged carrying a cigar box. The truck went off in a cloud of dust, and the stranger watched for a moment before approaching the field.

"Say," he called out, "do you fellows know where I could find Mr. and Mrs. Jenkins?"

Ross, who was closest to the orphanage's main building, set down his sack of cotton and began walking across the field. "Are you moving in or just visiting?"

"Well, it depends who you ask and what time of day you ask it." The boy looked about Ross's age. "My father is dead and my ma is sick. I was with my grandparents, but they can't keep me no longer. My ma will take me back when she's able."

"What's in the cigar box?" Ross motioned for the new boy to go with him up the walkway to the front door.

"All my worldly possessions, that's what. A comb, a toothbrush, a pair of socks, and my father's belt buckle."

"His belt buckle!"

"From the belt he used to whip me with. It's my bad-luck charm."

His name was David Moore and he, too, was fourteen. His arrival meant that the Tipton Home suddenly became a much more enjoyable place to live. He was a fast runner and good at every sport he tried. With David as instigator, the children began playing softball or kickball just about every afternoon. His curly blond hair blew back from his forehead as he ran from base to base with a zeal and determination that sometimes made Ross laugh with delight. The little boys and girls, the ones not yet in school, especially loved him. They dissolved into peals of giggles when David chased them around the big front yard. Just when he was within touching distance, he would stop in his tracks, widen his eyes, and take off in mock fright while waving his arms and yelling.

Like the other children at the Tipton Home, David hadn't had an easy start in life, and sometimes Ross glimpsed him looking preoccupied and sad. But never for long: his natural buoyancy propelled him back into action, and everybody became more outgoing when he was around. It occurred to Ross that David had a touch of stardust on him. It was not the stardust of future fame, though, but of something Ross couldn't quite put into words. The closest he could come was the stardust of goodness.

Ross shared David's love of sports and games, but he was more studious and inwardly turned than his new friend was. In recent months, Ross had become self-conscious about his appearance. No matter how much he ate, he felt he always looked raw-boned and underfed. He had big ears and big bony hands. His thick brown hair was his best feature, but Mrs. Jenkins always cut it too short over his ears. His brown eyes were almost black and had a bottomless, unknowable quality, even to him. Sometimes he looked in the mirror and wondered if he were an Indian. He had the capacity for pensive silences that he associated with the Indians who worked at the orphanage during harvest season. He didn't know anything about his mother or his father—he had been left at the Tipton Home when he was an infant—and had no idea who or what he really was.

Every Fourth of July, a newspaper photographer took a group picture during the annual picnic at the Tipton Home. It was an old and imposingly large brick house with white columns and several wings, with white clapboard siding, attached to the back and sides. There were upwards of forty children in residence, and for the picture, everybody lined up on the porch steps. Mr. and Mrs. Jenkins and the housemothers stood in the back, the teenagers were in the middle rows, and the little children were in front with Dusty, the dog, in the center. The Jenkinses ordered a framed copy and added the new photo to a lineup on the dining room walls. Each time a new picture went up, Ross would linger after a meal and have a long look. In the first picture in which David appeared, nearly a year after his arrival, he and Ross stood side by side in the middle of the group. Like all the other boys, the two of them wore overalls and long-sleeved cotton shirts, but David was in railroad stripes that caught the eye. He aimed his winning, dimpled smile right at the camera, while Ross looked slightly down, his brow furrowed against the sun. Below them were all the younger kids. The little girls wore flowered or plaid pinafores. They had bowl haircuts, their bangs cut in a neat line across their foreheads. The little boys looked like miniature farmers in their overalls. The children's expressions ranged from open smiles to mild stoicism to purse-lipped grimaces.

The state officials who occasionally toured the Home could look at the photo all day long and never guess the children's stories: the towheaded Hall sisters, Caroline and Mandy, holding hands in the front row, whose parents had been killed when their car stalled on a railroad crossing; skinny Billy Moxley, standing off to the side, the only survivor of a house fire; dark-skinned Abe Walker, whose mother died in childbirth shortly after his father was lynched in Texas. No one came to Tipton for a happy reason, and when Ross looked at the photos he thought of how much pain each child had endured.

David was better off than many, since he expected to return to his family, but he had suffered, too. His father was a mean drunk who whipped him regularly for small infractions—not hanging up his coat, not appending "sir" to every sentence he uttered. The day after the pauper's funeral the town had scraped together, his mother set the old man's leather belt on David's bed. "You should have something of your daddy's," she said. David stared at the belt, his old enemy, and said nothing. "It's all that's left of him," his mother continued, "so let it be a lesson to make more of yourself than that." He had kept the buckle, polished it up, and buried the frayed belt in the backyard.

His mother, frequently sick but not mortally ill, had a young daughter at home, in a little Oklahoma town three hours northeast of Tipton. She had barely two nickels to rub together, but every few months, she sent David a pair of red socks she had knitted. "Just in time," he said when he opened a package from her as Ross watched. "These are at the end of their natural life." He untied his shoes, peeled off a pair of red socks worn through at the toe and heel, and balled them into a knot. Ross laughed when, without even aiming, David tossed them over his shoulder and into a wastepaper can halfway across the room.

They had adjacent beds in the older boys' dormitory hall. That night, after David fell asleep, Ross found the new socks tucked inside David's shoes. He rolled them into a ball that he tossed at David's face. "Hey!" He threw the socks back at Ross, who then hurled them across the room at Earl Parham, reading a comic book by flashlight. Within a minute, a dozen boys were awake and laughing. Earl's flashlight beam followed the socks from bed to bed. The object was to keep them away from David, who scrambled to his feet and ran around the room crying out in a stage whisper, "Give 'em back! My ma made those." David was laughing along with everyone else, but Ross noticed that he went silent when the socks landed on Dennis Delmarvin's bed.

Dennis was a handsome, hard-eyed boy who had resented David's athleticism and popularity from the beginning. Until David's arrival, he had been Tipton's best ball player and fastest runner. Early on, he had challenged David to a two-mile race around the cotton fields. After he lost in a sprint to the finish, he spat on the ground at David's feet. The other boys looked on in dismay but David, acting as if he hadn't noticed, stuck out his hand to his rival. For a split second, his hand hung in the air as

Dennis, his eyes glittering with anger, turned on his heel and walked away. If the other boys thought less of Dennis after that, they didn't say so: he was nearly six feet tall, lean and muscular, and short-tempered. Everybody was a little scared of him.

The sock game didn't interest Dennis Delmarvin. He rolled over on his stomach and put a pillow over his head. Another boy grabbed the socks and kept things going. The game ended when one of the housemothers, Alice Williams, came in and stood framed in the light of the hallway. She was a tall and slender young woman with amber eyes and a turned-up nose. Her long honey-brown hair was usually pulled back in a ponytail tied with a bright ribbon. Over the past several months that she had worked at the Home, Ross had grown to like her kindly manner. "What's going on now," she said, a smile tugging at her mouth. "What're you boys doing now?" She was wearing a plaid flannel robe and tonight her hair was loose and flowing down her shoulders.

David stood marooned in the middle of the room and smiled back uncertainly at Alice. A stifled giggle rose up from the far end of the room. The socks suddenly arced high over David's head and landed at Alice Williams's feet. She picked them up and slipped them in her pocket. "I'm going to put these in our lost and found box and the owner can claim them in the morning. You boys settle down or I'll go get Mr. Jenkins."

Nobody wanted that. Mr. Jenkins, with his slow voice and tendentious manner, would make the boys kneel and pray for fifteen minutes. That was how he handled uprisings. It was effective and tiresome, and the boys would rather sleep than pray. David returned to his bed and, after a few snorts and some drowsy leftover laughter, the room grew still and the boys slept.

The Tipton Home was a busy place where the children had little time to ponder the circumstances that had brought them there. Even during the worst of economic times, the orphanage succeeded as a small farm because everyone pitched in. As the children headed off to their chores, Mr. Jenkins was fond of quoting the Oklahoma state motto, "Labor vincit omnia!" The boys worked in the fields and took care of the large animals. The girls tended the chickens, helped prepare meals, and cleaned the dormitories and common areas. All the children, boys and girls alike, took turns sweeping the porch and washing clothes. The Jenkinses supervised these efforts and offered remonstrations when needed. Several young women helped them run the place in exchange for room, board, and the smallest of salaries.

After high school, which the children attended just down the road from the Home, a few of them went to college, a few joined the military, and one or two of the boys headed off to a seminary. The rest settled nearby and married quickly, intent on having the families denied them in childhood. One thing was certain: they could not stay at the Tipton Home past the age of eighteen. The Jenkinses needed room for new arrivals; this fact was impressed on the children early in their teen years.

David and Ross sometimes talked about their plans for the future. One gloriously warm day in May, they were returning the milking pails to the barn. "I can't decide what I want to do-oo-oo-ooh!" David shouted while flinging his arms out to his sides and stiffening them like airplane wings. The milk pails swung from his fists as he broke into a run.

Ross ran to catch up, his pails flung out in the same way. "Run for president."

"Naw, I think I'll just run for my life."

They dashed to the barn, their bare feet kicking up dirt, and tossed the pails inside. David turned to look at Ross, panting by his side. "What do you want to be?"

"I have a way with a hammer. I'm going to be a carpenter."

"'Cause there's so much money in that line?"

"Hah. Tell me what else I could do."

"Hey, let's be flying soldiers. We'll be paratroopers and jump out of planes!" David was running again, his curly hair blowing back from his face.

"I'm scared of heights," Ross yelled, pumping his arms to keep up with his friend.

"Just keep your eyes closed and you'll be fine."

More and more, the Tipton boys talked about going to war. Newspaper reports and radio broadcasts piqued their interest. They watched Mr. Jenkins's face sag with worry when reports of the Nazis came over the airwaves. Dennis Delmarvin boasted over lunch that he would be a general someday. "A general ass," Ross said under his breath to Billy Moxley and then immediately regretted it. Dennis glared at him and caught up with Ross outside a few minutes later.

"What'd you call me?"

"Nothing. I called you nothing."

"If anybody's an ass around here, it's you, Injun." He pushed Ross to the ground and kicked him in the stomach.

Even as he lurched to his feet and swung a punch at Dennis, Ross wondered whether the other boy knew something about his heritage that he didn't. Within seconds both of them were on the ground, hitting, grabbing, and yelling. Blood was flying off Dennis's nose, and Ross's stomach ached where Dennis had kicked him. As Dennis reared back to strike him again, Ross grabbed Dennis's leg and then an exquisite pain entered his forehead. The last thing he heard was Dusty barking in alarm. Then darkness fell behind his eyelids.

When he awoke, he was in the infirmary and it was nighttime. In a chair near his bed sat Alice Williams, reading a book by a dim lamp. "Ross! How do you feel?" She set the book aside and spoke to him softly.

"Not too good." His head throbbed and he felt emptied out. "What happened to me anyway?"

"Dennis hit you with a rock and you blacked out. We got you to wake up, and the doctor came—but maybe you don't remember all that." She continued to speak in a worried rush. "Doctor Terry put a few stitches in your forehead and said you should stay quiet for a couple of days. You might've broken a rib, and you may have headaches for a while."

He touched the bristly stitches above his right eyebrow. "Is Dennis okay?"

A look of surprise flickered across her face. "Dennis is all right, though I expect he'll be sore in the morning."

"I don't want that kid getting sore at me again."

She smiled. "Well, then don't call him General Ass again."

"I didn't call him that directly. I was speaking—generally."

"I see. Well, fighting is not acceptable here, you know that. When you're feeling better, Mr. Jenkins will want an apology out of both of you."

"He's not kicking us out?"

"Apparently not." She set her lips in a line, indicating the topic was closed. "Now, have a drink of water and I'll see about getting you something to eat."

Ross nodded his head like a weary soldier and accepted the glass she offered him. The water was cool and soothing to his dry throat.

Alice crossed the room and looked back at him, her hand on the doorknob. "Your friend David asked about you. He wanted to wait with me until you woke up, but I told him he could visit you in the morning." She paused. "He was the one who pulled Dennis off you and held him until Mr. Jenkins got there."

"I guess I don't remember that, but it sounds like something David would do."

In a few days Ross felt fine again, except for the twinges in his rib. He enjoyed the attention when the other children wanted to look at his stitches. One evening Mr. Jenkins asked him and Dennis to come to his study. Fresh from chasing a couple of runaway piglets back into their pen, Mr. Jenkins rolled up his sleeves and wiped his sweating neck with a handkerchief. Ross could see that the man was exhausted at the end of a long day but still determined to set things right. After clearing his throat as he always did before speaking, he read a few Bible passages about forgiveness. He raised his eyes between verses to look pointedly at Ross and then Dennis. Without further prompting, they muttered apologies to each other. All three of them kneeled to pray silently and then Mr. Jenkins led them in saying The Lord's Prayer aloud. Ross noticed that Dennis's voice quickly trailed off; he did not say "thy will be done" or any of the words after that.

After the stitches were removed, Ross knew the deep scar running parallel to his right eyebrow would be with him for the rest of his life. It made him look older than he was and tougher than he felt. He ran his finger along the scar and thought, *This is who I am and always will be.* In a strange way, he was grateful to Dennis for giving him a part of his identity that he understood.

When he tried to explain how he felt one afternoon when he and David were walking home from school, David stopped and stared at him. "Have I got this right? You called him an ass, which he is, and then he nearly killed you. Then *you* had to apologize, not just him. And now you're grateful to Dennis 'cause you have a scar on your face?" Ross laughed and let the subject drop. He knew David was right, but awful as the fight and its aftermath had been, he felt a strange bond with Dennis now. They had shared something—and even though it was something bad, it was real and memorable, and would forever link them.

After the evening of prayers and apologies, Dennis kept his distance from Ross and everybody else. But Dennis was always a loner, Ross reflected. With his muscular shoulders and athletic prowess, he was a leader on the playing fields but an isolated figure, quick tongued and hard to warm up to. He cared more about his own performance than anything else. David was the opposite, the sort who led his teammates to victory and then offered words of encouragement to the losers. There was nothing conceited or supercilious about David. He wore his kindness lightly, the same way Alice Williams did.

More and more, Ross found himself thinking about Alice and seeking her out when he wasn't in school or doing chores. She had stayed beside his infirmary bed for two nights to make sure he was all right and not wanting for anything. When he opened his eyes, he would see her knitting or reading her book. The second evening, while they were having a cup of tea, he asked her what she was reading. She turned the volume's cover toward him and he saw the name Emily Dickinson.

"She's a poet who lived in New England. My husband gave me this book."

Ross wanted to ask what she was doing at the Tipton Home if she had a husband. Instead he said, "Would you read me a poem?"

Alice moved her chair closer to the bedside lamp and flipped through the book. After a brief search, she read a short poem that started off, "I'm nobody! Who are you? Are you nobody, too?" Ross leaned back on his pillow and closed his eyes as he listened. Alice had a low-pitched, husky voice that made him feel warm inside. When he opened his eyes, she was looking at him expectantly.

"Well, what do you think?" she asked him.

Since he wasn't sure what to say, he asked her to read the poem again. "You read it this time," she said and adjusted the lamp so the light fell across his lap. His teachers often made him and the other children memorize poems and recite them. He had no trouble remembering the words but was shy about standing up in front of the others. Even now, he felt his pulse quicken as he looked down at the open book. He sat up straight and read the poem as best he could.

Afterwards, he said to Alice, "I like the part about the frog, but I don't understand any of it. Do you?"

She sat back in her chair and smiled ruefully at Ross. "I don't know. It's just how I feel sometimes, like I'm this little person"— she stopped to pick a thread from her sleeve—"and I could get swept off in a tornado and it wouldn't make any real difference, except maybe to my parents and Macklin, that's my husband— but they'd be all right soon enough. But then I think, that's okay, I like my life just fine, I don't need any more than I have."

Her sudden burst of speech intrigued him. He could think of no other time when a grownup had confided in him. "I didn't know you had a husband. You don't wear a wedding ring." His cheeks reddened with his boldness.

She sipped her tea before speaking again. "We couldn't afford a ring. And now Macklin's back in school, where he needs to be." She paused. "He's a long way away. But I'm sure he'll send for me, as soon as he can."

Over the next hour, Ross learned a lot about Alice Williams. She and Macklin had fallen in love at the state university in Norman, where he had an academic scholarship and she worked in the school cafeteria. By April of their freshman year, she was pregnant, much to the dismay of her parents. They quit school and hastily married. Macklin got a job as a country schoolteacher and then, before his job had even started, Alice fell through a rotten floorboard of their rented shack and lost the baby. Shortly after that, Macklin received a letter from a great-uncle offering to pay for his education at the University of Virginia in exchange for work on the family farm. The uncle lived near Charlottesville and had a spare room available for Macklin. He didn't seem to know of Alice's existence, and Macklin said his uncle probably wouldn't be willing to support both of them. Macklin wanted to be a college professor, and while he and Alice were living in the wilds of Oklahoma with no hot water and a baby on the way, he had given up on all that. Now, he had a chance again.

That was how he put it: "'I have a chance again,'" Alice said, not "'we have a chance.'" Macklin said he would send for her but only when he could afford to, and he didn't know when that would be. At the insistence of her mother, who still railed against the premarital pregnancy despite everything that had happened since then, Alice made her way to Tipton. Mrs. Jenkins was Alice's aunt, and the Jenkinses had received her without complaint and immediately put her to work. She was grateful to them for taking her in and offering her a job as a housemother.

His head throbbing, Ross watched Alice through half-closed lids as she told her story. He waited patiently when she bit her lip and stared down at her hands. At one point, as she was saying how Macklin's great-uncle hadn't known about her, she lightly tapped his arm for emphasis, and he responded with a few words of comfort. So this is how you get to know a woman, he thought: you listen to her, you say little things to keep her going, and then if you're lucky, she'll listen to you, too.

Alice did listen. She asked him how long he had been at the Home, and when he said all his life, she looked at him questioningly. He told her he knew nothing about his parents and the Jenkinses wouldn't tell him anything. When he asked whether she could help him get answers, she said she would do what she could.

As the hour grew late, Ross felt his eyes dropping shut. Alice was talking about Macklin again. He didn't want the conversation to end, but his body craved sleep. Alice rose from her chair and pulled the covers up to his chin. Looking down at him, she said, "You're kind to listen to me, especially when you're feeling poorly. Forgive me for keeping you up while I natter on."

His last memory before he fell asleep was Alice's face smiling down at him, her slender fingers grazing his shoulder. On subsequent nights, back in the dormitory quarters with the other boys, he conjured Alice's face and hands after the lights were out. He was almost sixteen and she had told him she was nineteen, almost twenty. He knew about sex and had heard about love, but he had a hard time putting his feelings for Alice into words. She was a married woman, after all, and a housemother.

For the first time in his life, he began to pray on his own, not just on command. Lying on his back with his fingers interlaced behind his head, he closed his eyes and silently moved his lips: "Dear Father in Heaven, please help me to be strong and brave, and not to hurt anybody, except the Nazis if I ever get the chance. Please help the Jenkinses have enough money and food to get us through another year. Please keep us all healthy, especially the little kids, who catch cold so easily. Forgive us for our sins, and please help Alice Williams and her husband Macklin. In Jesus' name, amen." He could never think of anything specific to ask God to do for Alice or her husband, but he figured they needed His assistance very badly. Sometimes he neglected to pray for

Macklin, since he had never met him and didn't especially like what he heard about him. But not praying for Macklin made him feel guilty. Alice yearned to be with her husband in Virginia and Ross wanted Alice to be happy, even if that meant losing her to a man and a place far from Tipton, Oklahoma.

2

Ross was not the only one who had discovered Alice's charms. Sociable and athletic, she enjoyed playing softball with the children. In this respect, she was different from the other housemothers, who went off on their own when the workday ended. With a ribbon flying from her hair, Alice ran around the bases with admirable speed and happily took the pitcher's mound if her teammates asked her to. She had a strong arm and a surprisingly raucous laugh, and the boys and girls loved it when she joined their games. With Alice on one team and Ross on the other, they played after supper on summer evenings, their games ending only when Mrs. Jenkins rang a big cow bell on the porch and beckoned them inside for evening prayers and bedtime.

One humid twilight in August of 1939, when the bugs had begun their nighttime serenade, the gang decided to ignore Mrs. Jenkins's bell and finish out the inning and the game. The score was tied, with two outs and no one on base. David was pitching and Ross was the catcher. Squatting down and positioning his glove in front of him, Ross could barely make out the children in the outfield. The ones guarding the bases had a ghostly look to them. Only David stood out, the day's last light illuminating his curly head and shining white teeth. The bugs whined and Ross felt sweat trickling down his shirt.

Alice Williams picked up the bat and took a few practice swings. She was wearing white shorts, a sleeveless calico blouse, and a pair of dusty tennis shoes. Her green ribbon was a bit bedraggled. She had been uncharacteristically quiet when the game began but seemed like her old self as she flashed a grin at Ross before stepping to the plate. Her team had been leading the game with nine runs to three, thanks to Dennis Delmarvin's powerful hitting and effortless fielding of fly balls. But then Dennis had inexplicably quit the game and wandered off behind some trees. Taking his place was Billy Moxley, who carried his yoyo with him to the far reaches of left field. Now the game was tied at nine runs each, and everything rested on Alice's slim shoulders.

She swung fiercely at the first pitch and the ball arrived, unscathed, in Ross's glove. The second ball was a foul that landed in the cornfield. Ross watched David wind up for the third pitch, his arm a blur of motion. The ball met Alice's bat with a loud crack and sailed high and far. She threw the bat down and ran hard to first base, and then harder still once she saw Kathleen O'Shea in center field scrambling for the ball in the shadowy weeds. "Throw it!" David yelled. Kathleen was giggling wildly. Finally she found the ball and heaved it toward the second baseman, sweet little Harry Foote—or Hairy Feet, as he was widely known. Harry ran to scoop up the ball as it rolled toward him. He threw it to David, who caught it barehanded and then spun around to make the throw to Ross. Alice was heading home at full-tilt, her arms pumping wildly. Everyone on the sidelines was yelling and screaming, "Go Miss Williams, go!"

Ross held his glove aloft. In the excitement and near-darkness, David threw the ball too high and Ross moved away from home plate to make the catch. Alice bore down on her goal. She dived headfirst for home plate just as the ball hit his glove.

She had won the game in the most dramatic fashion Ross had ever seen. Her teammates swarmed around her and cheered lustily. Billy Moxley even put away his yoyo so he could clap for her. Alice had scraped her forearms and blood trickled down both knees, but she was grinning and laughing as the littlest children brushed dirt off her legs.

Mrs. Jenkins was on the porch ringing her bell again. Most of the children, tired and happy, hurried along. They knew Mrs. Jenkins would have lemonade for them and would want to hear about the exciting game.

Ross and David brought up the rear with Alice between them. David congratulated her on her fantastic finish, and Ross patted her awkwardly on the back.

"You're the next Harlond Clift," David said merrily.

"Who the heck is that?" Alice asked.

"Just the greatest baseball player from Oklahoma, that's who. He plays third base for the St. Louis Browns and he's from El Reno, like me. He and I used to play catch, and now he's one of the best players in the American League. He hit thirty-four homeruns last year."

"I thought you were going to say I was the next Babe Ruth. Now there's a baseball player people have heard of."

"You mean a baseball player *you've* heard of. I think you just like the 'babe' part. We should call you Babe Alice." David was walking backward, tossing the softball as he talked. Suddenly she grabbed the ball mid-air and threw it toward the house. The two of them scampered after it like energetic puppies.

Ross followed, scuffing his toes in the ground. It didn't surprise him that two people as attractive and effervescent as Alice and David would be drawn to one another: they looked good together, like an ad in a magazine. But as he watched them flirt and have their silly fun, he felt left out and deeply lonely.

Suddenly something pelted him on the back. He turned around and saw a walnut rolling across the dirt. "*Pssst!*" came from the shadowed branches of a nearby tree. "Hey, Injun."

Ross walked back to the tree and peered up at it. A shiver of amusement mingled with irritation ran through him. "Dennis, what are you doing up there?"

Dennis swung himself down to earth in a single graceful movement. He had a lit cigarette in one hand. With his other, he reached up and removed an open bottle of beer from the tree. "Today's my eighteenth birthday, and I'm leaving tonight. I'll never come back to this wretched place." He took a long drink of beer and then offered the bottle to Ross, who shook his head no. "What, are you scared to? It's not going to hurt you, Injun. It may just keep you sane."

Ross gazed curiously at Dennis. They had rarely spoken since their fight and now Dennis was acting like they were intimately acquainted. "I know you want to get into her pants," Dennis continued, jerking his head toward the house where Alice and David dawdled on the porch, still talking and laughing. "Everybody does. But damned if that high-stepping pansy doesn't get there before you and me and everybody else."

Again Ross felt twin impulses of amusement and irritation. David was his best friend and no pansy, and he had broken up the fight with Dennis that left Ross knocked out cold. Yet just moments earlier, desire and jealousy had stirred within him. His mood had darkened and he hardly knew why. The last thing he expected was to have Dennis drop down from a tree and explain everything so crudely.

Rather than pursue such an insinuating line of the conversation, Ross asked Dennis where he was headed, if he indeed planned to leave Tipton that very night.

"I'm hitchhiking to Oklahoma City, and then I'm going to enlist in the army first thing. Or maybe the navy." he said with an airy wave of his hand, ash spilling from his cigarette. "I'd like to see the ocean."

"What makes you so sure they'll take you?" Ross said.

"Oh, they'll take me all right, Injun. I've got soldiering in my blood, and you watch, we'll be in the war soon and they'll need every palooka they can get, even you and Blondie-boy. But I'll be the one leading the charge across Europe." He raised his bottle to the stars. His Adam's apple was working up and down excitedly. "The Germans shot off my father's leg in 1918, and I'm going to avenge that outrage a thousand times over." He finished off his drink and swung the bottle backhanded across the fields. They heard it smash against a tree.

"Where's your father now?" The question was out of his mouth before he could think about it. The haggard look that appeared on Dennis's face told him it was a dangerous subject.

Silence hung between them, and Ross was aware of how alone they were. David and Alice had gone inside and the porch light was out. There was just enough moonlight for him to see the pale blue of Dennis's eyes.

He was surprised when Dennis finally spoke. In measured, hollow tones, as if reading from a script, he said, "My father lost two brothers in the war. He was a very unhappy man. He hanged himself when I was twelve years old."

"Do you have anybody else?"

"What do you think?" Dennis replied evenly, his voice his own again. He stomped out his cigarette and began doing chin-ups on a tree limb. Between exertions, he said, "I got nobody—and nothin'—and I'm gettin'—the hell—outta this nowhere place."

Ross didn't know what to say, yet the situation demanded some kind of comfort or counsel. "Dennis, you idiot," he began, "don't forget what Mr. Jenkins always says."

"Gentry, you idiot. What does Teachy McPreachy always say?"

"Just that God loves us, that's all. And that's something, you know."

Dennis once again dropped to the ground and faced Ross. "I decided long ago that if God exists, he's a bastard."

The conversation seemed over. On his last night at the Tipton Home, Dennis was reaching out to Ross, for what reason Ross had no idea, but he was doing it so clumsily and rudely that Ross had no desire to prolong the exchange. "All right, Dennis. I hope you do well in the army. Or the navy. So long."

Ross began to turn toward the house. Suddenly Dennis reached out and grabbed his hand, causing Ross to spin around awkwardly. "I'm getting out of here and I'm gonna see the world," Dennis said. "That's not too much to ask, is it?"

He pumped Dennis's hand once before pulling back. "No, of course not." He looked up at Dennis, who was staring at Ross's forehead. "You'll be a great soldier. You're tough, you'll knock 'em dead."

Dennis's mouth curved into a brief grin. "Or die trying." With that, he began running toward the road. He seemed to know that Ross was watching when he turned and yelled back from a great distance, "I'm sorry about that scar. Don't say I never gave you anything!" Then he resumed running and after a few seconds all was quiet except for the bugs and, in the distance, the sound of a wakeful rooster.

Dennis's absence went unnoticed at evening prayers and none of the boys asked about him as they prepared for bed. It was only after the lights were turned out that Ronnie Campbell piped up, "Where's Dennis?" At fourteen, Ronnie's voice was changing, so the question came out in a comical mix of high and low tones.

Since no one else had an answer, Ross sat up in bed and made the announcement. "Dennis moved out tonight. He's going into the service."

There was a pause, and then in his squeaky voice Ronnie asked, "You mean he's gone for good?"

"It looks that way," Ross replied soberly.

The room was still as the boys absorbed the news. The thoughtful silence ended when someone broke wind long and loud. The room erupted in laughter, and then someone else made a rude, squelchy sound by squeezing his hand under his armpit. Others copied. The laughter grew louder.

In due time, the door swung open and Mrs. Jenkins appeared, her rumpled figure lit from behind. She was a nervous, frizzy haired woman who was much more at ease with the younger children than the older ones. Ross wondered why she was on duty instead of Alice Williams. "Is everything all right?" Mrs. Jenkins asked, peering into the dark room but not noticing Dennis's empty bed. "Don't you boys want to get some sleep?" The group settled down. "Remember, school starts soon and you all need your rest."

She shut the door and the boys listened to her footsteps trail off down the hall. Ross was just getting ready to silently say his nightly prayer when a voice once again broke the quiet. It was Abe Walker, speaking in falsetto, doing the minstrel-show impression he had perfected for occasions of great irony: "Massah Dennis done gone and left us. Praise the Lord!" Again the room filled with laughter, and there was another round of armpit noises.

The door swung open and everyone immediately fell silent. It was Mr. Jenkins this time. He roused the boys from bed and led them in prayers on their knees. After he left, a voice spoke wryly, "Thanks a lot, Abe!" and Abe, still in character, replied, "I so sorry." A murmur of chuckles rippled across the room. Then everyone finally grew still and fell asleep.

The next day, when Mr. and Mrs. Jenkins learned of Dennis's departure, Mr. Jenkins reacted with equanimity. Mrs. Jenkins seemed relieved, even pleased, that he was gone. "It was time for him to go," she said, rising from the kitchen table in their private quarters where Ross had found them after breakfast. "He never understood what we were trying to do here. And he had a terrible temper. He frightened the younger children."

Mr. Jenkins frowned slightly. "He was a troubled boy." He stirred a spoon in his coffee and asked Ross whether the two of them were friends. It struck Ross as odd that they were already talking about him in the past tense.

"No, I wouldn't say that. He just wanted to talk to somebody before he left, and I was the last one coming inside last night. He was watching the game from up in a tree."

From behind Ross, where she was washing dishes at the sink, Mrs. Jenkins let out a loud sigh. He hadn't realized that either Mr. or Mrs. Jenkins had personal opinions about the children in their care. It made sense that they did, but he had never been privy to these conversations before. They seemed much more open and forthcoming here in their kitchen, with everyone else outside working in the fields or the barn or the laundry shed.

"He told me about his father," Ross continued.

Mr. Jenkins looked up from his coffee and Mrs. Jenkins came over and laid a hand on her husband's shoulder. "What did he tell you?" Mrs. Jenkins asked, peering intently at Ross.

"That the Germans shot his father's leg shot off, and Mr. Delmarvin lost two brothers in the war, and he hanged himself when Dennis was twelve years old." Ross felt a little ill as he gave this account. He had heard some ghastly stories about deceased parents, but it wasn't a topic that came up often. The children didn't talk much about why they were at Tipton. The Jenkinses discouraged it and the stories were always so sad. But at least Dennis has a story, he thought. He could never shake the empty feeling that accompanied his own unknown beginnings.

"I always knew he was trouble," Mrs. Jenkins murmured under her breath.

Mr. Jenkins shook off his wife's hand and rose to his feet. To her he said, "We can talk about this later."

Ross could tell they were about to ask him to leave the room. "What about me?" he blurted out. "What about *my* father? What about my mother? I've asked you before about my parents, and you've never answered. I'm sixteen. I'm old enough to know who they are—or were—and why they brought me here." He was standing up now and looking from one to the other. After his growing spurt of the past year, he was as tall as Mr. Jenkins and he towered over Mrs. Jenkins. That made it all the worse that he felt like crying. Mrs. Jenkins also looked upset. She and Ross exchanged a brief watery stare.

Mr. Jenkins put his hand on Ross's back and guided him to the door. "We'll talk another time, young man. I think you know that at the Tipton Home we speak gently to one another. We don't shout and we don't make demands."

"I wasn't shouting. I just want to know where I came from. That's not too much to ask, is it?" He realized he was repeating Dennis's question of the night before. This time he had raised his voice, and he supposed he was making a demand. Without another word, Mr. Jenkins gave him a sharp meaningful look before showing him out.

Standing near the threshold, one hand poised to knock and the other clutching a broom, stood Alice Williams. She acknowledged

Ross and then smiled at Mr. Jenkins. "Just came by to sweep your floor. I'm making my Saturday-morning rounds."

From inside the kitchen, Mrs. Jenkins called, "Never mind about our quarters, Alice. The little girls need your help in their wing. That's where you'll be from now on."

Then the door was shut, and Ross and Alice stood facing each other in the hallway. Alice shrugged and beckoned for Ross to follow her. They went out the back of the house where she dropped her broom on the ground. "Let's go up to the apple orchard," she said.

Together they headed toward a path between the cotton field and the cornfield. The sounds of the farm—the cows, chickens, and pigs, the children yelling back and forth—grew faint as they walked up a long grassy slope leading to the orchard. The sky was a cloudless blue and the air smelled good. A little rain had fallen in the night, but the ground had already dried. It would be a nice day, not as hot and humid as the day before. Alice was in a yellow dress with short sleeves. Her hair, streaked blonde from the sun, was pulled back as usual, tied with a red ribbon this time. She wore a bandage on her knee, a reminder of her bold slide into home plate. They walked along in companionable silence.

After a little while they stood in the middle of the sun-dappled orchard. The branches were filled with fat green apples that would begin turning red in a few weeks. The grass was lush in the spaces between the trees. They sat down in a shady spot, with Alice leaning against a tree trunk and Ross beside her. He listened to the birds calling back and forth as Alice gazed down the slope toward the Home.

"Do you like coffee?" she asked suddenly.

"I've never tried it. It smells good, though."

"I wish I'd brought a cup with me. It would help me wake up. I didn't sleep very well last night. I got in some trouble with my aunt, you know." She wiped a strand of hair from her face and turned to Ross.

"Because you scored a homerun and made a lot of kids happy?"

Alice smiled. "In a word, yes. Aunt Muriel told me my behavior was unbecoming for a housemother. She said I shouldn't play softball, I shouldn't wear shorts, and I shouldn't take my job here for granted. And as you heard, I've been demoted to the little girls' wing. If I don't shape up, she and Uncle Dale'll send me back to Boise City."

She had said so many surprising things that Ross needed time to sort through them all. *Muriel and Dale*, he thought. He had never imagined Mr. and Mrs. Jenkins having first names. In their previous conversations, Alice had always referred to them simply as her aunt and uncle. They were growing more vivid and unpredictable, especially after his recent encounter with them in their private quarters. But he didn't want to talk about them. "What do you mean, Boise City?"

"It's where I'm from, Ross—you know that. Where the air is so thick with dust most of the time you can hardly breathe."

Alice had told him in one of their first conversations about her hometown of Boise City. It was in Cimarron County at the western end of the Oklahoma Panhandle. Alice was an only child. Her father sold farm equipment and her mother was a piano teacher, but not many people wanted piano lessons in a place best known for its dust clouds, and the farmers in Cimarron County mostly got by with the equipment they already had.

Ross waved his hand impatiently. "I know where you're from. But why would Mr. and Mrs. Jenkins send you back there? You're the best thing that's ever happened to the Tipton Home."

Alice tilted back her head in laughter and then hugged him lightly around the shoulders. "Thank you kindly, Ross," she said, releasing him and settling back against the tree. "I wish Aunt Muriel thought so. But she doesn't like me having fun and acting like one of the kids. And with Macklin gone to Virginia, she must be afraid I'll be on her hands forever—or at least until I ruin my life all over again." Her lips turned down and sadness filled her amber eyes.

The image of Alice and David, standing close together under

the porch light, flashed through Ross's mind. He pictured Mrs. Jenkins spying them through the window and imagining the very same thing that Dennis Delmarvin had described in such vulgar terms. It made him angry in Alice's behalf, but a jealous little part of him thought she should watch her step. She had gotten carried away after the big game and openly flirted with David. It was like she was asking for trouble—and David, too. Still, Ross reminded himself, David wasn't the only one who enjoyed her company. Ross thought of her every night before he fell asleep and his heartbeat had quickened just now when she hugged him. It was in her nature to laugh and touch, to draw people near. Her husband was crazy to leave her behind.

"Do you think if you saved enough money, you could move to Virginia? Maybe Macklin doesn't write because he's embarrassed he can't buy you a train ticket."

Looking down at her lap, Alice shook her head slowly and emphatically. "I know Macklin, and if he wants me to come to Virginia, he'll say so. He's a very focused, deliberate young man. He does things his own way. It's a wonder I got pregnant, considering how carefully he plans everything. That was the one area where he wasn't so careful." She glanced up, unembarrassed, and fixed Ross with an intense look. "When the time comes for you to start using rubbers, Ross, make sure you don't use the same one twice. You'll think you're saving money, but you're not. Take it from me."

Ross returned Alice's serious look and then lay down on the grass and laughed. She laughed, too. But when he sat up, he saw tears in her eyes. He was having trouble keeping up with her quicksilver moods. "I lost my baby, Ross. The doctor wouldn't even tell me whether it was a boy or girl. He just said it might've happened anyway, even if I hadn't fallen through the damn porch. I know he thought that would make me feel better, but it didn't. And Macklin—Macklin seemed relieved. Once he found out I was pregnant, he acted like he loved me less. It was only after my father talked to him that Macklin proposed. I guess when I lost the baby, he was glad he wouldn't have another mouth to feed. But he still had a wife. So then he up and moved twelve hundred miles away from me." She wiped her nose on her sleeve and looked down the slope at the farm. "Sometimes I wonder if I'll ever see Macklin again."

Ross was at a loss for words as Alice struggled to compose herself. He thought she was better off without Macklin, but he didn't dare say that. Sometimes it seemed that Macklin was already far from her mind. But even without an absent, inattentive husband to worry about, she still had problems. He couldn't imagine a meaningful future for her at the Tipton Home, and if she left, where would she go?

For a while they sat in contemplation, deep in their separate thoughts. The birds chirped in the trees around and behind them, and a soft breeze stirred the high grass between them and the Home. As the sun rose higher and the earth got warmer, Ross felt himself growing drowsy. Normally on a summer morning, he would be weeding the garden, picking vegetables, or mucking out the horse stalls. His time in the orchard with Alice was an unheard-of luxury.

Listening to her talk, he had temporarily forgotten his own emotional upheaval. They were sitting so close that he could smell her scent: a blend of soap, flowers, and a spicy, almost peppery, aroma that was hers alone. His hand was just inches from hers.

It was from this daydream that Ross was jarred when Alice cried, "Look!" and jumped to her feet. The sky had filled with a hundred or more birds, each one pink and white and gray. Their extraordinary tails spread apart into two long narrow sections as they ascended into the air. They swooped and dived in loose formation, catching bugs invisible to all but them. Ross had seen scissor-tailed flycatchers before but never so many all at once. The splashes of bright pink beneath their wings stood out spectacularly against the sky's deep blue. It seemed they had come from nowhere, but Ross knew they must have been roosting deep in the orchard.

The birds frolicked as Alice and Ross stood together in speechless wonder. Then, as if in response to some secret sign, the flock arose high in the air and flew toward the Home before veering off and disappearing altogether. Ross turned to speak to Alice when, just beyond her, he noticed a single bird that had lagged behind. It dropped from high in the sky, spiraling downward in an acrobatic flourish, its pink feathers flashing. Then the bird righted itself and hung for a split-second about twenty feet from the ground before chasing after the rest of the flock. *A sky dance*, Ross thought. He had learned the term in his natural history class. The male scissortails typically did this dance during spring mating season—not late summer as it was now.

Alice had been looking in another direction, and Ross said nothing to her about the dancing bird. The final beautiful image had unaccountably brought David to mind. Then he remembered the day, now two years past, when he and David had run barefoot to the barn, their arms outstretched, milk pails swinging from their hands. They had talked about becoming paratroopers. Ross had confessed his fear of heights—a revelation born out of repairing shingles high on the Home's roof—and David told him everything would be fine if he just kept his eyes closed. Somehow the line, just a joke, had stayed with him. He wondered what that scissortail had seen as it toppled earthward: sky and fields, apple trees, a young woman in a yellow dress, and a skinny boy with big ears. A home for children whose parents were gone, a landscape without a single human mother or father. Or had it closed its eyes and seen nothing, with only instinct telling it to stop, hang motionless in the clear summer morning, then leave the old world behind? Maybe that same creature would return the following spring, maybe not. If the latter, would he remember Tipton and its pure blue air? Maybe the answer depended on how much pain that bird had known there—its mama or papa killed in a storm, a mate lost to illness, or just a hard season, not enough bugs. Ross's mind reeled. He felt shaken as he stared up at the emptied sky.

"I'll remember that forever," Alice said, and Ross wondered

what she had been thinking while he was lost in his reverie about the one bird she hadn't seen. But she was not going to share. "We should go back," she announced rather abruptly. "I need to help cook lunch and I bet there's a row or two of beans waiting for you to pick them."

With Ross leading the way, they went down the slope toward the Home. Alice asked him what was going on when she came upon him in the Jenkinses' quarters. He began by telling her everything about Dennis.

"Dennis made me uncomfortable at times," she replied meditatively. "I used to catch him staring at me and then he would look away and pretend he was occupied with something else. But he was so lonely and tormented that I felt sorry for him and would try to talk to him. He was like you in one respect—he didn't know what happened to his parents—well, his father anyway. He even asked me if I could find out, around the time you asked me the same thing. He said my aunt and uncle wouldn't tell him why his next-door neighbors brought him here when he was twelve years old; it was like he had been kidnapped. He figured out that something terrible had happened to his father, but he didn't know what. He was an only child and his mother had died the year before. The neighbors who brought him here moved away so there was no one who had any answers for him. My aunt always told him he was better off not knowing and to stop asking so many questions."

Ross stopped on the path and waited for Alice to catch up with him. Again she had startled him with a string of revelations. "Was it before his big fight with me that he asked you to find out about his parents?"

She narrowed her eyes as she searched her memory. "I believe it was. Why does it matter?"

"Let me ask you something else before I answer that. Did you get him the information he wanted?"

"I asked Aunt Muriel whether they kept records on all the children. At first, she was very forthcoming and said oh yes, of course they did. The state required it. They have two big cabinets full of files in my uncle's study. Then she stopped what she was doing and gave me a funny look and asked why I wanted to know. When I said Dennis Delmarvin asked me to find out, she told me not to talk to him anymore. She said Dennis had problems that I couldn't solve."

"You didn't tell me all that when I asked you to help me find out about my parents," Ross said, unable to keep an aggrieved tone out of his voice. "And then you never got back to me with an answer to my question." It was the first time Ross had ever reproached Alice about anything. It hurt his feelings to think that she had deliberately misled him.

Alice sighed. "I thought maybe Dennis was an exception and that it would be different if I asked specifically about you. And that's exactly what I did, the next time I had a few minutes alone with Aunt Muriel. We were planting radish seeds in little trays," she said, as if that detail made her account more credible, "and I asked if I could borrow your record from the file cabinet and let you read it." She paused and flashed the rueful smile that Ross had grown familiar with. "I guess that was stupid of me. She could've shown you that file a long time ago. Anyway, she refused. And it was around that time she started watching me closely. But we still got along fine until I made such a spectacle of myself last night on the softball field."

It was what you did after you left the field that got you in trouble, he thought, the image of David and Alice entering his mind yet again. "Getting back to Dennis," he said, "did he break into your uncle's study and read his file?"

Alice stopped and looked at him. "I suppose he must have. I'd told him about the file cabinets behind my uncle's desk"—there was mischief in her eyes and then alarm—"so he knew where to look."

Ross was quiet for the rest of their walk. He remembered the day Dennis had talked excitedly, even feverishly, about his desire to become a general. After finally learning about his father's suicide, from a file within easy reach his entire time in Tipton, he must have been in great pain. How had he even managed to join the others at lunch that day? And then Ross insulted him in front of the other boys.

His thoughts shifted to Alice's involvement. She had gotten to know Dennis Delmarvin and tried to help him. Ross had never seen the two of them talking, yet apparently they had done so at length. Until now, she hadn't mentioned her conversations with this odd and unpopular boy, who had beaten him unconscious. She said Dennis made her uncomfortable and Dennis's crude talk certainly didn't recommend him as her friend, but perhaps there was more to the story than what Ross knew. He racked his brain for images of Alice befriending the teenaged girls at the Home, and found none. All of her energy and attention went to the older boys, who couldn't help noticing how pretty she was. No wonder Mrs. Jenkins had moved her to the little girls' wing. Alice was a flirt and a troublemaker.

That night, lying in bed, Ross did not say his usual prayer. He ran a finger along the scar on his forehead. With all that was on his mind, he knew it would be a long time before he settled down and slept. He thought about Alice's conversations with Dennis and wondered why Dennis hadn't told her months ago about his father, the suicide. He pictured Dennis rifling through the files in the Jenkinses' study and his jaw muscles tightened when he imagined the terrible shock Dennis was in for. Then he thought of David and Alice: in his mind, they chased the softball again and again, then stood with their heads close together, their ebullient voices traveling through the dark to where he and Dennis had said their strange goodbyes. Finally he tired of that sequence and thought of how, just that morning, Alice had hugged him in the apple orchard and set his heart to racing. He remembered the scissortails flooding the sky, and the dancing bird that only he had seen. With his eyes closed and his hands behind his head, he conjured Alice's long slender fingers and then his mind drifted to the sky full of birds. His body slowly relaxed. But the image of the birds gave way to Dennis's haggard face, the sound of a bottle smashing against a tree. He touched the scar again. Just before he fell asleep, he thought: *My file is in there, too.*

3

In the remaining weeks of summer, Ross tried to avoid Alice Williams. Out of the corner of his eye, he watched her comings and goings but didn't seek her out. One day, soon after their morning together in the apple orchard, she found him in the carpentry shop and asked if he wanted to ride into town with her and Miss Boyer, the new housemother. They were going to pick up school supplies and could use an extra hand. He told her he was helping her uncle replace the sashes on the dining room windows. It was true, but his answer came out too rapidly, like a lie. She gave him a quick look and then made a smiling exit. After that, they grew awkward around each other.

Ross wasn't sure why he didn't want to talk to her, but it had something to do with Dennis. He felt bad that none of the boys had noticed Dennis's absence until Ronnie spoke up. Once they knew, they reacted with gales of laughter. The Jenkinses were glad he was gone. Granted, Dennis was not a very nice person. He was rude and standoffish, and vain about his athletic ability. But his behavior, Ross decided, must have reflected his private anguish. For so many years, he hadn't known what happened to his father and then after Alice pointed him to his file, he had lived alone with the awful truth. Why hadn't the neighbors who brought him to the Home told him his father had killed himself? Terrible though it was, it was something Dennis had a right to know. Why hadn't Mr. and Mrs. Jenkins answered his reasonable question? By not answering, they contributed to Dennis's pain.

He thought of the years he and Dennis had slept six beds away from each other, the thousands of meals they had shared, the walks through good weather and bad to the school down the road. For a while, before David arrived at the Home, Ross had occasionally teamed up with Dennis to work on projects around the property. They had replaced a fence together and, with Mr. Jenkins's help, installed a whole wall of bookshelves in the study hall. There had been a time when they talked on a regular basis. Or rather, Dennis talked and he listened. Dennis was a history buff who liked to rattle on about the Civil War and how the Confederates would have won if they'd done just a few things differently. He was particularly fond of a Confederate general nicknamed Old Bald Head.

After David's arrival, Ross stuck close to his new friend and pretty much forgot about Dennis. David was easier to be around, and he was always willing to help Ross with his carpentry projects. One time, Ross had crafted and then installed crown molding throughout the Home. It was an idea he came up with himself. Mr. Jenkins was dubious at first, but Ross promised him it would be worth the effort. After weeks of work, with five or six boys helping him until one by one they tired of the labor and only David stayed by his side, the project was finally complete. In his dinnertime remarks that evening, Mr. Jenkins waved his hand toward the molding and briefly thanked Ross and his crew. Before Mr. Jenkins could move on to his next announcement, David led the whole room in a rousing rendition of "For He's a Jolly Good Fellow" in Ross's honor. Since birthdays were not celebrated at the Home—and why was that, Ross sometimes wondered—it was very rare to get any personal recognition. He forgot his usual shyness and basked in the attention. The molding really did look good.

David had a way of making life at the Home not just bearable but fun. If he felt bad that his mother and grandparents never visited him, he did not say so. At least his baby sister wrote him letters. Ross had seen her round, little girl's handwriting on envelopes stuck inside David's schoolbooks. David sent her penny post cards in reply, and at Christmastime, he sent her and his mother a box of candy. He was a gentle person, Ross thought, and a good sport. He extended his hand in friendship and generosity, whereas Dennis Delmarvin threw punches in anger and desperation.

Ross decided he would concentrate on his schoolwork in hopes of getting a college scholarship. If that didn't work, maybe he could work as a carpenter and pay his own way. He would put Alice Williams out of his mind along with Dennis Delmarvin. For different reasons, each one of them stirred his emotions and distracted him. He cared about Alice, but her unpredictable ways kept him off balance. As for Dennis, he felt he had not been the friend that Dennis needed and wanted. Even though Dennis had beaten him up and left him with a permanent scar, something about the other boy stirred a mature pity in Ross's heart. That left only David. Maybe David's athleticism could earn him a baseball or track scholarship and they could be roommates at the state university or some place other than Oklahoma. It would be nice to get out and see a little more of the world.

It was with these thoughts in mind that Ross began his final year of high school in the fall of 1941. Everything had been going along predictably until one afternoon in mid October. Ahead of them on the driveway as they returned from school Ross and David saw a beat-up car parked near the Home. Its occupants were just emerging, stretching their legs and looking all around. A thin woman wearing a housecoat and kerchief peered up at the Home. Beside her was a wiry old man in cap and overalls. Getting out of the backseat was a girl, with rippling blonde hair. She wore a bright blue dress and an oversized cardigan sweater.

Suddenly David let out a loud whoop. "Mama! Louise!" The three visitors turned around, and the girl and David ran toward each other. David picked her up under her arms and swung her around in a circle. They were laughing and shouting as the woman hurried toward them. When she drew near, David set the girl down and grabbed the woman in a bear hug. Ross saw tears streaming down her narrow face when she broke the embrace and stepped back. "David!" she cried. "You've grown so tall, my darling son." The old man stood off to the side, his arms folded across his chest with his hands under his armpits. He eyed the others warily.

After marveling over David, his mother gestured shyly toward the old man. "This here's your new step-daddy, David. We come to take you home."

Ross had never seen someone's mouth drop open in astonishment, but that was what happened now. David gaped at the stranger before him. Then he collected himself and proffered his hand, which the man shook briefly and firmly. "Name's Pettigrew, son. Austin Pettigrew. You can call me Mr. Pettigrew for now, and after we get better acquainted it'll be Papa Austin. That's what your sister calls me."

David and his little sister traded a glance. Louise had David's fair complexion and curly hair, but the cornflower blue eyes were hers alone. Ross saw a conspiratorial glimmer in those eyes. She shrugged slightly at David, as if to say, "Don't mind this rude old man."

"Well, it's nice to meet you, Mr. Pettigrew," David said. "Oh, and everybody, this is my best friend, Ross Gentry. Ross, this is my mama and my sister Louise. You've heard me talk about them. And this is Mr. Pettigrew."

David's mother gave Ross a brief, distracted smile, Mr. Pettigrew offered a scowl of acknowledgment, and Louise's face broke into a frank grin. "Where'd you get that scar on your face, Ross?" she asked. Ross touched his forehead self-consciously but was too surprised to answer.

"Now, Louise, you know better'n that." Her mother began steering the girl toward the front steps. "Come on, David. Let's get your things. We don't have time to waste. Your papa's got work to do back in El Reno."

"And you got a barnyard to get acquainted with in the morning, boy." The old man chortled. "Your mama told me you like your baseball and your other games, but you won't have no time for that no more."

"We got a farm, David, what do you think of that?" Mrs. Pettigrew smiled up at her son and laid a hand on his arm. "Forty-two acres and a house all paid for."

Ross watched them head toward the Home and disappear inside. He sat down heavily on the front steps, his mind in turmoil. Was it possible David was leaving for good? He knew instinctively that Mr. Pettigrew was a replica of David's father—a bully who would view David as both rival and whipping boy. As much as Ross wanted his friend to be reunited with his mother and his sister, he could not imagine that David's life in El Reno would be happy. He wondered whether David would even finish high school. The old man didn't seem like he would care about education.

After a little while, the front door opened. Ross stood up as David and the others emerged with Mr. Jenkins close on their heels. "You're a fine young man, David," Mr. Jenkins was saying. "Mrs. Jenkins and I are sorry to see you leave Tipton, especially so sudden-like, but I know you're delighted to be with your family again. And we're delighted for you. You write us a letter every once in a while, you hear?" He and David stood on the porch as Mr. Pettigrew, David's mother, and Louise walked ahead to the car. Ross noticed that neither adult was carrying anything. Louise had a bundle of David's clothes in her arms.

"Oh, Ross," David said, "come back inside with me a minute. I forgot something."

Without speaking, the two boys hurried to the big room where they had slept side by side for the past four years. Afternoon sunlight slanted through the windows. Dust motes spun in the corner.

David kneeled down and pulled a small box from under his bed. He stood up and thrust it at Ross. "It's all I got to give," he said.

Ross started to lift the box's lid, but David reached out a hand to stop him. "Goodbye, Ross. I'll see you in the army. Don't forget, we're gonna be paratroopers."

David's eyes were red. Ross set the box down and hugged his friend. He could think of nothing to say.

He followed David to the porch and watched him get in the backseat beside his sister. As Mr. Pettigrew began maneuvering the car, David rolled down his window and yelled to Ross, "Tell Alice I said goodbye. And all the kids. Tell 'em I'll miss 'em!"

"Goodbye, David!" To his dismay, Ross heard his voice break. He waved as the car receded into the distance. Both David and Louise leaned out of the car and waved back, their yellow hair shining.

That evening, for the first time since his fight with Dennis Delmarvin, Ross did not have supper with all the others. He could not bear to hear Mr. Jenkins announce David's departure. He was afraid he would cry in front of the other children. When the supper hour approached, he grabbed the box that David had given him and slipped out the back door. It had been an exceedingly rainy month, but this night was dry and cold. He decided to go up to the apple orchard where he and Alice had spent a single charmed morning back in August.

Shivering in his light jacket, he settled himself under a tree and clutched his knees to his chest. Most of the apples had been picked by now, but he could smell fallen fruit in the grass around him. In the cold still air, the aroma was heavy and sweet, a little rotten. The stars were coming out, and Ross stared up at them, trying to connect them into constellations of his own making. The moon cast a faint glow over the ground where he sat. Finally he reached for the present from David. It was in a cigar box that looked vaguely familiar. Ross flipped open the lid and saw a brass belt buckle shining dully in the moonlight.

He smiled as the story came back to him: the day he and David had met, David told him the belt buckle was all he had of his late father's. "My bad-luck charm," he called it. Ross weighed the buckle in his hand. It was cold to the touch and surprisingly heavy. He thought of what David had said that afternoon: "It's all I have to give." But that was not true. David had given him friendship and companionship for four years. When he introduced Ross to his family, he called Ross his best friend. In his heart, Ross knew he had other friends. The other boys and girls liked him, after all. But David was special, and he had a terrible feeling he would never see or hear from him again.

When his teeth had begun to chatter, Ross stood up. He took one last glance at the star-filled sky and picked out Orion's Belt. The buckle heavy in his jacket pocket, he shook his head ruefully. He hurried down the path toward the Home.

As he approached the back door, he heard footsteps and laughter coming his way. Out of the darkness appeared Alice and Miss Boyer, each of them carrying a paper sack. They stopped short when they saw Ross, and Miss Boyer's laughter abruptly stopped. She was a tall, sturdy young woman whose thick dark-blond hair swung just above her shoulders. Her skin was very pink and she had deep-set, penetrating eyes. She was rumored to have money and her fancy car was proof of it. Alice had begun going out with her in the afternoons for driving lessons. Ross had the uncomfortable feeling that Miss Boyer did not like him, though he could not imagine why.

"Hey, Ross. You won't tell on us, will you? We're just going to slip into the kitchen and clean up after all you kids." Alice's eyes were bright. Standing near the two young women, Ross smelled something unfamiliar and then realized it was beer on Alice's breath.

"Alice, before you go in," Ross said, "there's something important I need to tell you."

Miss Boyer tossed her head impatiently. "You go ahead, Anna," Alice said. "I'll be along in a minute."

"Don't stay out here too long or you'll get in trouble with your aunt." Miss Boyer handed over her sack. "Hide mine, will you?"

Cradling the two paper bags, Alice rolled her eyes as Miss Boyer went inside. It was then that she saw Ross's pained expression and her face softened. "You look really upset. Come to the barn with me. It will be warmer there and the cows won't mind the company."

Ross headed to the barn with Alice. She was cozily dressed in wool coat and scarf, but he was not prepared for the cold night and could not control his shivers. "Here, Ross," she said, setting her bags down and handing over her scarf and one of her mittens. "There's no point in freezing."

He wrapped the scarf around his neck and then slipped on the soft fuzzy mitten, a little snug on his hand. The familiar warmth of her kindness spread over him. He murmured his thanks and stole a grateful glance at her out of the corner of his eye.

They sat down on milking stools in the barn, with an oil lantern casting shadows between them. Alice regarded him expectantly. Ross knew that he would have to begin. "Were you out all afternoon and evening?" She nodded in reply. "Well, then, I have to tell you that David's mother came to get him—his mother and his sister and his new stepfather—and they took him away. He didn't get to say goodbye to anyone besides Mr. Jenkins and me, but he wanted me to tell you goodbye for him, and so that's what I'm doing." Ross had not allowed himself to pause while delivering this important news. Now he took a breath. Alice was gazing at him, and once again he felt his throat tighten with tears. "I'm telling you goodbye for him," Ross repeated, his voice breaking. He was mortified by the tears falling down his face as Alice continued to look at him, her expression calm. He looked down at his lap and wept.

Alice edged forward. With her index finger she caught one of his tears before it rolled off his cheek and then touched her finger to her tongue. Ross looked up in surprise. When she held out the bottle she had removed from one of her paper sacks, he accepted it. It was the first time he had ever drunk beer. It tasted funny, but in a good way.

"It's hard when a friend leaves," Alice said, leaning against the barn wall. "Did David know his mother was coming to get him?"

"No, he would've told me. And he sure didn't know she'd remarried." Ross took another swallow of beer. "You should've seen David's stepfather, Alice. He looked like he was thirty years older than David's mother. And he wasn't very friendly."

"A mean old bastard, was he?" Alice smiled and then her face clouded over. "I'm sorry to hear that. David is such a sweet kid. He deserves better."

They sat in companionable silence. Ross listened to the cows stirring in their stalls and took in the barn's redolent smells. Alice's presence comforted him. The lantern's light flickered across her cheekbones and her slender neck. Though it made his stomach ache to think of David's absence from his life—and even worse, David under Mr. Pettigrew's rule—he was grateful to Alice, who had said just the right things. She didn't make him feel self-conscious about being so lonely and missing his friend. And if she thought of David as a "sweet kid," she wasn't interested in him romantically—something that had nagged at him for a long time. Now he knew he had been foolish, the night of that softball game, to fear that the two of them would pair off and leave him far behind.

Alice shifted her feet and Ross looked up at her. "How old is David?" she asked suddenly.

"His birthday is next week. He'll be eighteen."

"Well, he could join the service. That would be an honorable way to escape a bad situation at home."

An image of Dennis Delmarvin's face flashed through Ross's mind. He thought of Dennis's mingled anguish and elation the night he left the Tipton Home. By now, Dennis was far away, at a military base or even on a ship. "When David and I said goodbye, he said we would be paratroopers together. That's been his dream since he was a kid."

Alice chuckled. "Ross, am I right in recalling you're afraid of heights? Going to war is bad enough without having to jump from a plane."

"I would do it for David, and I would do it for our country," Ross said, sitting up and straightening his shoulders. He mustered a brave grin.

"Well, if you change your mind, I won't tell anybody." Alice stood up and took a last gulp of beer. "We should be getting back. It's time for me to check on the little girls. I don't think I can count on Anna to cover for me."

They hid their emptied bottles at the bottom of a trash barrel, doused the lantern, and headed back to the Home. The moon lit their path. Alice shivered and tucked her arm in Ross's. "Don't forget to give me back my scarf and mitten before we go inside. I can only imagine what my aunt would say if she saw you like this."

In one of the first spontaneous acts of his life, Ross grabbed Alice's bare hand with his and broke into a run. She matched his pace, and they arrived at the back door out of breath and laughing. He pulled off the scarf and mitten, and she stuffed them in her pocket before they went inside. With one last smile, Alice turned on her heel and disappeared down the hall. Ross found his way to the study room, took his books off a shelf, and slid into a chair between Abe Walker and Harry Foote. They glanced up at him sleepily. If they noticed his red cheeks or the beer on his breath, they didn't say so.

To his surprise, he received a letter from David a couple of weeks later. Mr. Jenkins handed it to him when he returned from school on a bitter-cold November afternoon. Ross saved the letter until after he had finished his chores and then hurried back to the dorm hall to read it in private. It was printed mostly in capitals, and Ross could see a few places where Ross's pencil had pushed through the page of tablet paper:

Dear Ross,

HOW ARE YOU? I HOPE YOU ARE DOING WELL AND ALL THE KIDS TOO. AND THE JENKINS!

I WANTED TO TELL YOU I'M IN SCHOOL HERE IN EL RENO. MR. PETTIGREW WANTED ME TO QUIT AND WORK ON THE FARM ALL DAY, BUT I TOLD HIM NO, EDUCATION IS IMPORTANT (LIKE MR. JENKINS ALWAYS SAID, AND YOU

SAID IT TOO) AND I AM GOING TO FINISH HIGH SCHOOL. MAMA BACKED ME UP, THOUGH SHE WAS AFRAID, AND MR. P. IS STILL MAD. BUT I AM TOO BIG AND TALL FOR HIM TO WHIP ME, LIKE MY REAL DADDY DID. I GET UP AT 4:30 A.M., WORK ON THE FARM, WALK LOUISE TO SCHOOL, GO TO MY CLASSES AND THEN COME HOME AND WORK AGAIN. NO SPORTS, BUT THAT'S OK.

WELL, GOODBYE FOR NOW AND WRITE BACK!

Your friend,
David

A sheet of pale blue stationery, folded into a small square, had fallen out of the letter onto Ross's lap. It was a second letter, written in dark blue ink in a neat, wobbly script:

Dear Ross,

David said I could write to you if I promised to be nice. But I am always nice! Well, most of the time. I am sorry I asked about your scar when we first met, it just caught my eye. You don't have to tell me about it if you don't want to. (David already told me. That Dennis Delmarvin—what a rat!)

Anyway, I want a pen pal. Please be my pen pal.

It is cold here. We have snow and more predicted. Mama is sick again but not too bad. The one I call Papa Austin makes me cook for him when she can't. I tell myself I am cooking for Mama and David. The one called Papa is 67 years old. Mama is 39. I am almost 14. You know David just turned 18.

Well, write and tell me all the news about "the home."

Your pen pal (if you want one),
Louise

P.S. David told me about the crown molding. Wow!!

He read both letters several times and then slipped them back in the envelope and into David's old cigar box, which now stayed under Ross's bed.

He was happy that his friend had written, especially since he knew that writing didn't come naturally to David. Maybe they would still end up as college roommates; that would be much better than jumping out of airplanes. Louise's letter made him smile, but it was a little sad. In his mind he could see her waving to him out the car window. She was a playful and precocious girl, but Ross sensed her loneliness. David, her ally, was finally home after four years at the orphanage. But Louise had to share her mother with Mr. Pettigrew—a tough old goat, in Ross's estimation. The old man didn't seem happy that a good-natured teenaged boy and a bright young girl were suddenly his to care for and love. And in Ross's view, David and Louise were unusual. In his few minutes with her, Ross had glimpsed the same sparkle in Louise that David had. There was an aura about them, a light around those curly blond heads.

When Ross wrote back to David a few days later, he slipped a postcard inside the envelope. The card, which had a photo of the Home on it, was for Louise, and he wanted to make sure David read it. In his small, careful handwriting, he wrote:

November 19, 1941
Hello, Louise:

All is well here at the Home. We're getting ready for Thanksgiving (tomorrow), and it will be a big feast, as always. I'm excited about the pies the girls are baking!

I gave your name and address to Kathleen O'Shea, who also lives here. She wants to be your pen pal. She is also 14 (almost 15) and I think you will like each other.

Study hard, and be good.
Your friend, Ross

He didn't think it was right to strike up a correspondence with Louise, who was so much younger than he was, and a girl. Her mother and Mr. Pettigrew probably wouldn't like it, and David might think it was strange. Still, he was not going to ignore her letter. Kathleen O'Shea was a sweet girl, and her freckled face broke into a big grin at the prospect of a pen pal. She was bright and giggly, a good match for Louise.

4

Ross's teachers said that his high grades could earn him a scholarship to the University of Oklahoma; they had been in touch with the admissions office there. Although Mr. Jenkins encouraged him to go to seminary, Ross felt it was too obvious a choice for someone as mild-mannered and studious as he was. More and more, he wanted to be around people, in the midst of things. With his teachers' encouragement, he began to feel that he had a future beyond Tipton, and his growing self-confidence attracted new friends. In David's absence, he became more sociable and popular. Sometimes he wondered whether it took David's departure to bring him out of his shell. Without David by his side, he talked to more people at school and the Home, and they eagerly responded to his overtures. In his last months at the Tipton Home, he was finally coming into his own.

Though the war in Europe had been going for two years, and Ross had always told himself he would fight the Nazis if he had the chance, he had not thought about the particulars. In recent months, he had begun to assume he would go to college in Norman and then move far away—maybe somewhere on the East Coast. The attack on Pearl Harbor forced him to think about his future differently. In the Tipton High School auditorium on December 8, 1941, he and his classmates listened in stunned silence to President Roosevelt's speech: "No matter how long it may take us to overcome this premeditated invasion, the American people in their righteous might will win through to absolute victory." When Ross heard those words, the hair on the back of his neck stood up.

That night he and Billy Moxley and Abe Walker went to Mr.

Jenkins and told him that they planned to enlist in the army as soon as possible. Listening to first one boy and then another, Mr. Jenkins looked bleary eyed with worry and concern. He warned them against the certain dangers they would face as enlisted men and told them to finish high school and see how the war developed over the next six months. He took Ross aside after the others left and placed a hand heavily on his shoulder. "This is going to be a long war, son," he said, his eyes red at the rims. "Your heart is in the right place, but don't just give your life away."

For the remaining months of the school year, it seemed as though a hush fell over the Home. Christmas came and went, with the usual donated presents from local churches filling the parlor on Christmas morning. The winter was cold but not unusually so. When spring came, and the days grew noticeably longer, the younger children did their chores quietly and without complaint. Mrs. Jenkins had to shoo them outside to play. In the evenings, Ross and the other older children listened to the radio with Mr. and Mrs. Jenkins. Everyone's eyes burned with fear and wonder as the reports came through. At night, when the lights were off in the dorm, the boys whispered about their plans. Billy and Abe had resolved to enlist the day after their graduation in June. They had begun a training regimen, and at night they discussed how far they would run the next day, how many pushups they could do.

During these conversations Ross said little. He wondered about David, who had not written again. When he thought of their boyhood plans to become paratroopers, he broke into a sweat. If he could hardly stand to walk along the roof of the Home, just two stories high, how would he manage an ascent into the sky and then a reckless plunge toward Earth? The rising and flying and jumping frightened him more than the idea of going into battle. But he had nodded when David had brought up the paratrooper plan the day he left Tipton. Ross did not want to back out of a promise to his best friend.

One Saturday morning in early June, a week before his graduation, he ran into Alice on the front porch. They had seen little of each other in recent weeks, with Ross busy with schoolwork and chores and Alice spending all of her free time with Anna Boyer. She was sitting on the swing, idly moving back and forth with her legs stuck out straight. It was nearly lunchtime and he didn't have any work to do that afternoon. Alice appeared similarly unoccupied. "Do you want to go for a walk?" he asked her.

"I have a better idea. I'll make us a couple of sandwiches and we can go to the river in Anna's car."

"She won't mind?"

"Well, if she does, I'll just tell her I needed more practice driving without her supervision." Alice's laughter trilled across the porch. She leapt up from the swing and disappeared inside.

Soon they were leaving the Home in Anna's sky-blue Packard, a sleek car with shining fenders and white-walled tires. Between them on the front seat was a bag overflowing with sandwiches, fruit, and cookies. When he asked what they would drink, she laughed and said the drinks would be Anna's treat. After that, as was their way when they went somewhere together, they spoke little. Ross looked out at the flat green and brown landscape whirling past him. How many times had he gone down this road lined with farms and fences, the trees familiar as old friends, the skinny dogs standing sentry in their front yards? It would not be long now before he left it all behind.

He glanced over at Alice's suntanned hands gripping the steering wheel. She was leaning forward, her jaw taut. It seemed she was still not a confident driver, though she and Anna often took the car out in the afternoons.

Ross still didn't understand Alice's friendship with Anna Boyer, the young housemother from Chicago. Dressed expensively and dropped off by a chauffeur who handed her the keys to the Packard, she had arrived at the Home under a mysterious cloud. Like Alice, she had a connection with the Jenkinses, yet no one knew why a young woman of independent means would stay at an orphanage. She was nearly six feet tall, sturdily built, and her thick dark-gold hair always caught Ross's eye. She should have been pretty, he thought, but somehow she was not, maybe because she was so standoffish. She had little conversation for anyone besides Alice, the only one at the Home whose company she enjoyed. One autumn evening, he watched them hit a tennis ball back and forth under a full moon. Anna had moved with startling grace, never missing the ball, no matter where Alice hit it. Shouting out a mock challenge, Alice hit the ball as high into the starry night air she could, and still Anna tracked it down and hit it back. Another time, he saw the two of them in the kitchen washing dishes and standing very close together. Alice whispered something in Anna's ear that made both of them laugh. In profile, Anna was radiant. When Alice turned back to the sink, Anna continued to gaze at her with a look that Ross, to his amazement, recognized as love.

Being around Alice made Ross happy, too. Whenever they were together, he wished he had great, important things to tell her. He had not experienced much in life, but she still cared about what he had to say. Her teasing was always gentle, as if she intuitively knew his limits. Yet her penchant for mischief nagged at him. He suspected she and Anna spent a lot of their time away from the Home drinking beer that only Anna could afford to buy. They went into town whenever they could and stayed out late on weekends. Weeks went by when Ross saw Alice only in passing. Mrs. Jenkins appeared to have given up on both her and Anna. She checked her watch and shook her head slowly when the two girls, rosy cheeked and giggling, rolled in at night. Ross wondered sometimes why they didn't get fired. But the industrious Anna got more work done in an hour than any of the other housemothers in an afternoon, and Alice was, after all, Mr. and Mrs. Jenkins's niece.

Alice turned the car onto a narrow dirt road that led to the riverbank. Ross had been to the river on fishing trips a few times every summer ever since he was a little boy. He loved going there, and it was always nice when they had catfish or striped bass for dinner at the Home—fish the children had caught themselves. In the noon sun, the wide expanse of the river flashed brightly. Before they got too close to the water, Ross took off his shoes and let his bare feet sink in the squishy ground. He could see a few fishermen on the shore a hundred or so yards away. Farther off still, a family strolled along, the parents hand in hand and three little children running along the water's edge.

After walking for a while, they found a grassy spot on a small bluff where they could place the blanket Alice had brought. From the bag Ross had carried from the car, she dug out a couple of beers and a bottle opener. "They're not cold, but you get what you pay for, Ross." She flicked a bottle top in his direction. Settled on the blanket, with food and drink between them, they began to talk. Alice wanted to know his plans.

"I'm going to the university a few weeks from now. I have a job in the cafeteria this summer and during the school year, too. Even with a scholarship, I'll still need a job."

"You're not enlisting then?"

"Billy and Abe are pressuring me to, but to be honest, I'm just not ready yet. I've hardly ever been outside Tipton my whole life. What do I know about fighting battles in Europe?"

"Nobody knows anything about war until they get there, Ross. You learn as you go. But I'm glad you're going to college—and I think you'll like it there." She paused and smiled at Ross uncertainly. "Anna said if I wanted to go back to school, she would move to Norman with me and we could get an apartment together."

Ross turned to her in surprise. "You mean this isn't goodbye?" A big smile spread over his face.

"Well, I don't know, it might be. I don't think the dean of women will take me back. She knew I quit school because I was pregnant. I'm sure she would consider me a bad influence on the other girls." Alice took a bite of her sandwich and chewed meditatively. "Besides, I have my cap set on going somewhere else. If Anna agrees to it, I'd like to track down that husband of mine. We could be in Virginia in two days."

Ross took a long swallow of beer before turning to face her. "You must be kidding."

"I've looked at a map, and it's entirely possible."

"That's not what I meant, Alice, and you know it. Unless you've been holding back on me, you haven't heard from Macklin in years. Why go after him now?"

Alice set down her sandwich and fluttered her eyelashes in mock surprise. "Why, Ross, you certainly ask a lot of personal questions. What I do with my husband is my business."

He reached out and rapped her shoulder with the back of his hand, a little harder than he meant to. "Your husband left you. Haven't you figured that out by now? You should file for divorce and be done with him once and for all."

She eyed him levelly, her nostrils flaring. A coldness had come between them. "I have a faithful heart, Ross. I thought you knew that by now. And I make my own plans and my own decisions. I don't answer to you or anyone else around here."

Her cotton blouse rose and fell as she breathed rapidly, and her voice sounded tight, as if she might cry. It occurred to him that she did have to answer to her aunt and uncle—and Anna as well, since Anna owned the car that was Alice's only way out of Tipton. He knew he should stay quiet until she calmed down, but he could not resist saying what suddenly popped into his head: "'I'm nobody! Who are you?'"

She stared at him blankly. Then a small smile lit her face. "'I'm nobody, too,'" she replied and then continued with the next two lines: "'Then there's a pair of us. Don't tell!'" Her eyes were shining and he could see that she had relaxed. "I can't believe you remember that."

"After we read that poem together when I was in the infirmary, I checked out Emily Dickinson's poems at the school library." Ross felt himself blush; he was unaccustomed to talking about poetry outside of English class.

"Well, you have Macklin to thank for your love of Emily

Dickinson. He was the one who gave me the book."

"It wasn't Macklin who read me the poem, Alice."

She looked at him speculatively and her lips parted as if she were on the verge of speaking. Then Ross saw her change her mind. She turned toward the river and resumed eating. A dramatic spray of white clouds drew her eyes and Ross's to the top of the sky. Ross watched birds diving into the river and then looping upward. He could hear the faint laughter of children. The faraway merriment underscored the quietness between him and Alice. He wondered what his life would be like without her playful smile and quicksilver changes of mood. He did not allow himself to wish for too much when he was with her, but when he imagined moving away and never seeing her again, he felt as though he were walking into an open pit whose depths of darkness he could not see.

Still looking straight ahead, Alice said, "I guess you know that David's already enlisted and on his way to basic training."

Ross's heart skipped a beat. A wave of betrayal washed over him. "How did you find out?"

"El Reno is not exactly New York City. I just addressed a letter to him, care of Mr. Pettigrew, and he wrote back soon's as he received it. He graduated from high school last week, and he's going to Fort Bragg in North Carolina. That's where the paratroopers are based. He said he'd write again once he got there." She turned to him. "You haven't been writing to him?"

Ross felt something curdle inside him as he saw her disingenuous look of surprise. He decided to ignore her question. "His mother and sister can't be too pleased."

"They're used to him being gone. And they need the money he'll make. Besides, you know David's always wanted to join the army. He's not the type to sit at a desk and study all day, and he deserves better than whatever El Reno has to offer him, which doesn't sound like much."

"He'll be a good soldier."

"I told him you had no plans to enlist as far as I knew."

Ross rose to his feet and glared at Alice, who looked startled by his sudden movement. "Why'd you tell him that? That's my business to tell or not tell."

"He asked about you. We're all friends, aren't we? I wasn't sharing a state secret—at least I didn't think I was." Alice stood up now, too, and brushed crumbs off her blouse. She continued to talk as she gathered up the leftover food. "I think he wanted you to enlist and meet him at Fort Bragg, but I reminded him about your fear of heights and said you'd probably go to college if you got a scholarship." Alice shook out the blanket they had been sitting on and folded it into a square. "You would have known this yourself if you'd bothered to write to your best friend."

Ross took his empty beer bottle and hurled it as hard as he could. It smashed against a tree trunk and for a second, the image of Dennis Delmarvin flashed through his mind. "I did write to him, Alice. He wrote to me and I wrote back, and then I didn't hear from him again. Why did you have to meddle in my friendship with him?"

"We should be leaving," Alice said, her voice low and steady and her expression wary. "Your bad temper is making me uncomfortable."

Ross followed her along the path they had taken to the river. She threw their things in the backseat and gunned the motor as they pulled onto the road. They were both too upset to speak. Ross watched the landscape streaming past his window. It was a good thing they didn't have far to go.

Back at the Home, Alice parked the car in the shady spot where Anna kept it during the summer. She edged the car under a large tree's overhanging branches, backed up a few feet, then thought better of it and hit the accelerator. The car rolled forward and bumped against the tree trunk. It was a small jolt but unsettling nonetheless.

Alice swore under her breath as Ross inspected the Packard, which had a shattered headlight. There was nothing he could do to fix it, and he was glad the problem wasn't his. "Too bad, Alice. I guess you need a few more parking lessons. You'll just have to tell Anna what happened and hope she has mercy on you." He began walking away. Over his shoulder he called out, "Or how about if I tell her for you! That's what friends are for, right?"

"You bastard!" Alice yelled at his back, loud enough for the girls working in the vegetable garden to hear.

Ross didn't care. Once he got near the Home, he veered off and began running toward the orchard. His heartbeat pounded in his ears as he ran. He was furious and sad, and for the length of time it took him to run up the slope, he wished he would never have to see Alice again.

Alone among the trees, he paced around clenching and unclenching his fists and muttering to himself. He thought about his plans for college and the people he had met on his visit to Norman. He had sat in on a class and liked the way the professor lectured. And the students were friendly; he had talked to a few of them over lunch. If he could afford it, he would join one of the fraternities they had told him about. Of course, the fraternities would be decimated now, with so many of the boys shipping off to war. Then his mind turned to David. He pictured him suited up in a bulky parachute and waiting to jump from a plane somewhere in Europe: brave and uncomplaining. The other soldiers would love him, the way everybody did at Tipton.

His mind racing, Ross allowed himself to think of Alice. Besides David, she was the person he most cared about. He could not imagine his life without her. But again and again, she startled and upset him. It seemed she was always a step ahead. By all rights, the humiliating circumstances of her arrival at Tipton should have embarrassed her. Her cad of a husband had deserted her as soon as she lost their baby. She had no means of support other than her pittance of a salary. If she had any contact with her parents, Ross didn't know of it. Yet Alice was cheerful and self-confident by nature. She had her finger on the pulse of all things at the Home. She did exactly what she wanted yet didn't lose her job.

Ross kneeled on the ground at the base of a tree. His thoughts whirled on. He remembered how Alice told Dennis Delmarvin where he could find his personal records. Dennis's rage upon learning the truth about his father had indirectly led to his attack on Ross. He ran a finger along the scar above his eyebrow. It had always bothered him that Alice was friendly with Dennis, who spoke so rudely of her behind her back. Was there something between her and Dennis? Or maybe she was in love with David, whom she wrote to with such regularity. He felt hot tears welling in his eyes.

The Monday after his graduation, Ross packed up his belongings, including the cigar box containing the belt buckle and the one letter he had received from David, and loaded his duffle bag in the farm pickup truck. Mr. Jenkins was at the wheel with Abe and Billy beside him. It was raining steadily, but Ross refused to squeeze inside the truck with the others. He climbed into the back, drew a tarp around his shoulders, and pulled his knees up to his chest. He had said his goodbyes to the children that morning. After Mr. Jenkins went out to start the truck, Mrs. Jenkins gave each of the boys a firm hug. She reminded them each to take along the pocket-sized New Testament and the sacks of sandwiches she had prepared for them. Her glistening eyes lingered on Ross, but she turned away when he noticed. No one followed them outside. Alice was nowhere to be seen.

Ross reached out a hand to brace himself as Mr. Jenkins began backing up the truck. He took a final glance at the Packard, which had not been moved since its last fitful burst of speed. They were just about to head down the driveway when a voice called out, "Wait! Don't go yet!" The truck paused, its motor idling, as Alice ran up to Ross and thrust a bulging paper bag at him. "You'll want this, Ross. Don't think too ill of me. I'll miss you." She reached a hand toward his and their fingers brushed before the truck started rolling forward again.

"Goodbye, Alice!" Ross called out, his voice breaking. "I'll miss you, too." He grabbed the bag and stuffed it under the tarp and inside his jacket. She waved to him and then just stood in the rain, holding Ross's gaze the whole time. Her hair was loose on her shoulders, and she was in her yellow dress, his favorite, though he had never told her so. Through the soaked material he could see the outline of her breasts and hips. Her figure had filled out since her early days in Tipton. He wanted to say more to her, but just as he opened his mouth to speak, she turned on her heel and headed back toward the Home.

That afternoon in Frederick, after he and a dozen other boys met with a recruitment officer and got their bus tickets to Oklahoma City, Ross sat alone in a corner of the bus station. He spilled onto a bench the contents of the bag Alice had given him. It contained two postcards and a letter, a folder containing a single typed page, a little red blanket of soft and fragrant wool, and something small wrapped up in newspaper. One of the postcards had a photo of Honolulu on it. Ross flipped it over and saw an unfamiliar scrawl:

Injun: I survived the burning of the "Oklahoma" (irony of ironies, I was assigned to that one). I am a great sailor and the major says I should go to Annapolis to be an officer. Maybe next year. For now, off to the high seas. I never get seasick. Are you taking your lazy ass to college?

Yours truly,
Dennis Delmarvin

Ross couldn't help chuckling as he read the card. Below his name, Dennis had neatly printed a military forwarding address.

The other one was a piece of cardboard cut to the size of a postcard. Ross recognized the large printing:

HI ROSS, HOW ARE YOU? I'M ON MY WAY TO FORT BRAGG, N.C. ALICE SAID YOU GOT A SCHOLARSHIP, GOOD

JOB! SEE YOU AFTER THE WAR—UNTIL THEN, LOOK IN THE SKY, FIND ME THERE!

Your friend,
David

David had not included a forwarding address. But, Ross thought, he probably didn't know what his address would be, other than Fort Bragg. He imagined his friend's glad surprise upon learning that Ross had decided to keep his promise and join David in the army. He would try to get assigned to Fort Bragg if he could. After the war, they could room together at the university. Though his stomach churned at the thought of his abrupt change of plans, Ross told himself everything would work out all right.

He picked up the little blanket and fingered it curiously. It smelled of pine needles. A scrap of paper fluttered to the floor as he held the blanket up to his face. Scooping it up, he read a brief, scribbled note: "Ross, I hope to leave here very soon for Rapidan, Virginia. See enclosed file. I hope you are not angry with me (again), but you always said you wanted to know. Love, Alice."

His mind swimming, Ross looked at the items he hadn't examined yet. When he unfolded the newspaper, a toy soldier fell into his hand. It was unpainted iron, a slender round-headed figure in a helmet. Ross weighed it in his hand and studied it. The little figure stood with arms akimbo and eyes cast upward. Somehow it reminded him of himself. He slipped it in his pocket.

He dug the cigar box out of his duffel bag and put the two cards and Alice's note in it. He had yet to read the letter and the paper inside the file folder. For the time being, he set the letter aside. The writing on the envelope looked vaguely familiar, but there was no return address and rain had smeared the postmark. He opened up the folder and placed its single, yellowed sheet of paper on his lap, on top of the blanket. It was a report typed on Tipton letterhead:

The Tipton Home
Tipton, Oklahoma

November 8, 1924

ROSS GENTRY (history unknown except for what I, Dale Jenkins, report here)

A week ago, on a Sunday night, a young girl knocked on the back door and begged us to take the baby boy crying in her arms, wrapped in a little red blanket. Muriel told her to come inside, but she refused. She also refused to tell us her name. She looked to be a half-breed: long black hair, high cheekbones, green eyes, medium height and very thin. I would put her age at seventeen or eighteen. At first I thought she was alone and then I saw a figure in the background. It was an older man, thin like the girl, with the same black hair. I took him to be her father. She was crying when she put the baby in Muriel's arms and said, "I've heard about the Tipton Home. I know you will take good care of him."

She started to go back toward the man, but I grabbed her arm and said, at least tell us the baby's name. She was sobbing and would not answer. I said, well, who is the father? She got herself together and said, "He was a gentry man. He would not want you to know his name." Then she broke free. I called after them, but she and the man ran away. It was a cold night and windy, and the baby was crying hard and loud. Muriel took him into the kitchen and we turned on the light and had a good look at him. Black hair like his mother's (I assume she is the mother) and brown eyes. He is about nine months old (so Muriel thinks). He stopped crying when Muriel rocked him and then he ate some stewed apples and a bit of bread pudding.

We dug out the crib and put it in our bedroom. He sleeps well, a very good baby. We know of no rules for babies dropped off like this. I told Muriel we should name him Ross (her late father's name) and keep him as our own. She said no, that isn't fair, his mother may want him back. But I know she'll never be back. To that Muriel says we can't just take the children we like best and say they're ours. I think she is afraid to love him (so many years after our own baby died) and I do not blame her, but this child came just to us. He grabs my fingers and Muriel's too.

Muriel says we will keep him a month or two and then he'll go with the housemothers. He will stay in their quarters until he's old enough to be in the dormitory with the little boys. She gave him Gentry as his last name. I insisted we call him Ross. When I say the name, he smiles.

November 11, 1924

Doctor Terry paid a visit and pronounced Ross healthy. I knew that already with my own eyes and ears. He eats well and is strong. Continues to sleep through the night, our little champion. May God bless this dear sweet boy.

Ross bowed his head over the page. He had always wondered how he would feel if he learned the story of his birth and his placement at the Tipton Home. Now, with that very knowledge, incomplete though it was, he felt stunned and a little dizzy. He had too many questions about his mother and father even to begin formulating them clearly. His mind went instead to Mr. and Mrs. Jenkins, and how they never let on that they felt any differently toward him than any of the other children. He was an orphan among other orphans, and the kindly couple had maintained a gentle but firm hand in rearing all of them. They were all God's children—that was what Mr. Jenkins called them—and there was never any hint of favoritism. If sometimes Mr. Jenkins wanted him to aim higher than his peers, he assumed that was because his grades were good and the teachers sent along letters commending his achievements. Mrs. Jenkins had rarely talked to him at any length. She delegated responsibilities to the housemothers and sometimes seemed detached from her young charges, perhaps because there were so many of them to care for. Her attention went mainly to the younger ones. She straightened their clothes as they headed into the dining room for breakfast and ministered to them again in the afternoons. The teenagers didn't interest her in the same way. As their adult personalities emerged, she backed off and became a little nervous around them.

It was the first time Ross had given so much thought to the couple that had housed and protected him for as long as he could remember. Mrs. Jenkins had cried that very morning as he prepared to leave, and outside the Frederick recruiting office, Mr. Jenkins shook his hand and then pulled him in for a bear hug. But Mr. Jenkins had hugged the other boys, too. Abe and Billy had been at the Home a very long time as well, and they were all going off to war. If ever there were a time for the Jenkinses to show affection, this was it.

What would his life have been like if they had adopted him and called him their son? Would he have felt safer in the world, braver, more acquainted with love? What had stopped them from taking him as their own? Ross cupped his face in his hands as he imagined that he simply didn't deserve their love—no more than he deserved his real mother's love, or that of his father, the unknown "gentry" man.

The bench and floor seemed to wobble beneath him as first one voice cried out and then another: "Come on, Ross! The bus is here." "Hurry up, Ross!"

He struggled to his feet and stuffed the blanket, the folder, and the cigar box in his duffel bag and hurried to catch up with Abe and Billy. He had the strange feeling they had been calling him for a while. Something made him glance back as he pushed the door open, but newly arrived travelers blocked his view of the bench where he had read the postcards from Dennis and David, Alice's note, and the file explaining how he ended up at the Tipton Home.

A few days later, on a bus headed south, he strained his eyes in the gathering darkness to read, for the hundredth time, the page typed by Mr. Jenkins. It was then that he suddenly remembered the letter among the things Alice had given him. That night in the barracks he carefully went through his belongings, but the letter was nowhere to be found. He felt sure he had left it on the bench in the Frederick bus station. By now it was long gone. He told himself it could not have been important, since anyone with any interest in him was already accounted for. But he could not shake the suspicion that the letter held just as much meaning as the file Alice had stolen from Mr. Jenkins's study. During the months that followed, he dreamed that he found the letter in his clothes or the cigar box or on the field where he and the other soldiers ran. In these dreams he was ecstatic, but he always woke up before discovering who wrote the letter or what it had to say.

Girls and Boys

Anna Giesele Boyer

Dusk, summertime, at the kitchen sink we stand so close
I smell the wild rose in her hair. Her breath becomes my air.
If she feels nothing, why does she press against me
whispering secrets?
Why does her tongue graze my ear.
From behind, both young yes, both tall yes, but none would say
sisters: she is willowy, lithe, and quick where I am broad of back
and German-strong.
She is the only good news from Oklahoma.
She is my idea of a song.

Watch me roll all
of Tipton into a ball
and hurl it straight
to Chicago
where it lands
with a thump
on my parents'
doorstep.

Why do they never call.
Do they love my absence more than me, the daughterless quiet of
their endless rooms—
the ticking clock, the hushed music of the streets below?
At night I conjure my mother's icy eyes when she and Father sat
me down.
Some teacher had seen a moving, curving shadow,
my hand in another girl's hair, our lips—what could I say.
I was finished with finishing school.

They packed me off to the poor relations with promise of a gift,
and yes I took the Packard and tipped the chauffeur
then watched him lope down the road whistling.
Goodbye, Chicago.
Call me angry yes, broken-hearted yes, but I am capable, fastidious,
honest in my way.

Now consider Alice, yes Alice, and the faraway ocean that sounds
in my ear when she draws near: the call of a lifetime, murmur of
laughter years from now (oh please, let it work)
when we are mature ladies lounging
amid newspapers and teacups
the Manhattan sunlight not at all displeased
with tangled bedclothes
the parakeet not minding
bare arms and bare feet
and perhaps we talk about
her Uncle Dale (onion breath)
Aunt Muriel (we kept our distance)
Dennis Delmarvin (sounded bad)
that Negro kid (the first she'd ever known)
a sky full of birds (she said they danced)
Ross that stupid Ross (apologizing to the grass he walked on)
David that stupid David (the pied piper with curls)
Tipton damn Tipton (except—)
Oklahoma double-damn with a dustbowl on top (except—)

This is how it comes to me on a summer evening
water rushing through my hands
her fingers my fingers
soap bubbles and secrets
her tongue just grazing my ear
Alice now and Alice then
if we could—
if she can.

Abraham Nathaniel Walker

A song—what else to call the howl of hounds
that chased my father through the woods at dawn
then brought him to ground on a Lubbock lawn.
Next came screams amid flames—unearthly sounds.
He had a wife and would soon have a son
yet he jumped three white women (which to choose?)
in search of rhythm, propelled by booze.
So they claimed, but who knows. They're all long gone.

A song—my first cry and my mother's last.
A midnight angel moistened the widow's lips;
into this world I came from her thin hips.
Her spirit rose from the bed and ascended into Texas.
I gasped and wept. She passed in the night.
I'm all that's left of my own birthright.

William Michael Moxley

Sometimes I smell charred wood beneath my nails.
It happens at night when I lie on my stomach,
chin on my hands, facing the barracks window.
The other soldiers sleep easily and snore.
I listen to them and watch the stars.
I've trained myself not to mind how endless it is—
the night I mean, not my life, about which: we shall see.

I'm smelling the memory of my family's last night on Earth:
my father the drinker who might've kicked over the lamp
my mother the smoker who might've dozed off
my sister Janna, who slept.
I was awake but no scream formed on my lips
and by the time I beat on their doors
I was a dragon exhaling smoke and

then a fireman found me—unconscious, alone.

Pity the nurse and doctor who had to tell me.
I remember her soft hands and his furrowed brow.
She kneeled by my bed as he turned away.
Then came the weeping aunts and uncles,
a group funeral I was too sick to attend,
and lots of talk about the Tipton Home.
They said I would be safe there, with good food.
They wanted me to smile about the food.
I turned my face to the pillow. Sometimes
the nurse rubbed my back and said not a word.
Sometimes her hands were all that kept me
from slipping out of this world and into
the smoldering darkness of home.

My first year in Tipton, I slept with one hand raised
to meet my parents and sister reaching down to me.
Imagine my surprise when they got busy in heaven.
All I heard was silence as I searched for the hum
in the air that meant they were near. I listened
in the fields, the garden, the barn, the horse stalls.
One day I banged my fists against the ground just
so I could hurt for real and begged them to come.
Alice Williams washed and bandaged my hands
and in her eyes for a moment I saw Janna:
Janna grown to young womanhood, older than I.
After that, I scrutinized every smile and stare, but no one came.
The humming was over and Miss Williams
made a face when I tried to hold her gaze.

I decided to be a child again and delighted in a yoyo
wrapped for "Tipton boy" under the Christmas tree.
My plan worked until the string broke and a war began.
Ross and Abe and I talked late into the night,

but their words slowed and they always slept.
One time as Ross spoke, I thought I heard the hum.
I leaned over and looked in his eyes, then Abe's.
Nothing. I saw nothing. While they slept
all of Europe burned in my fingertips.
I smelled the fires a soldier walks through.
I decided I really would go. I had lived this long
and there was no reason not to be a man.

Louise Larkin Moore

The last thing I expected was that you wouldn't write back.
Not with your kind eyes and shy smile.
After a week passed, I began to wonder: had I addressed it wrong?
But no, there is but one and only Tipton Home.

How could you not reply to word of my mother's death,
how could you leave that news alone.
I thought you'd understand that with her gone,
David off to war, and Mr. Pettigrew's eyes full of angry tears,
I had no choice but to point the arrow of my life toward Tipton.
I thought you'd be there to guide me along.
For now I, too, am an orphan.
I walk the fields you and my brother walked,
I spade the earth and pull the weeds.
The clouds float by and the cows murmur in their stalls.
I hear the birds you heard. The hay smells sweet.
It's not so bad and it's terrible, all at once.
The goneness of my mother is not all that makes me cry.

For if you can't find it in your heart to write—
though I know you are a busy young man, a soldier—
what does that say about the world? I always believed the world
was better than Mr. Pettigrew, better than the scarred acres
where we scratched out a life. My brother's lilting laugh,

the blur of sky as he whirled me high in the air,
the sound of your voice breaking as you told him goodbye—
I believed in that. And then my dying mother unclasped her locket
(the only jewelry she'd ever worn),
slipped it in my hands, and went completely still.

At the funeral I cried for the story that locket told
(twisted strands of her mother's hair, brittle and brown)
and for my soldier brother who could not come home.
I returned in my mind to Tipton, to the day our truck went down
the road, my hand and my brother's, and yours—all waving.
I could see layers of beauty and sorrow, sky and shadows, the
waking dream of it all.
I told myself I would write to you.
I told myself if my grandparents let me, I too would live
at the Home.

These days, Kathleen O'Shea stays close by my side.
Her freckled face is not your face, her dirt-smudged knees not
yours, but she is my friend. In the morning, she grabs my hand
and pulls me out the door and sometimes I forget how I feel
and we race to the barn laughing and shouting.
When I told her I wrote to you, she said,
Give it time, someday you'll have your answer.

The Christmas Party

1

Macklin Williams arrived in Orange, Virginia, on a cloudy and cold December afternoon in 1938. His great uncle, Minor Williams, met him at the train station. In sporty cap and tweed overcoat, the old man leaned on a brass-tipped cane and waited for the nineteen-year-old to approach him. Coming closer, Macklin recognized the piercing blue eyes that had frightened him when they first met at a funeral long ago. They talked while he loaded up his suitcases. Then he saw to his surprise that his host expected him to drive.

"We need to fetch Sorbon from Sparks's," Uncle Minor said from the passenger's seat. "Go up Main Street and you'll see him." Macklin reluctantly started the car, a Ford with red clay stuck to the tires.

"There he is," the old man barked. Macklin saw a barrel-chested Negro holding a box of groceries and waiting on the opposite side of the street. In a flash he made his way to the car and got in the backseat.

Mr. Williams introduced Sorbon Carter as the farm manager. "Turn around up here and we're headed straight home," Sorbon said. "It's about seven miles to Rapidan. You'll turn left into the driveway just past Purcell Presbyterian Church."

Macklin glanced in the rear-view mirror. The man looked to be about forty-five. He had some gray in his close-cropped hair and a few deep lines on his forehead. His breath, when he leaned forward to speak, was sharp with peppermint.

Mr. Williams and his farm manager talked intermittently as Macklin drove. Snow was predicted; the owner of Batton (a nearby farm, Macklin gathered) was in the hospital with pneumonia; the price of butter, Sorbon said, had risen three cents. The two men were very comfortable with one another and seemed barely aware that anyone else was in the car. Macklin was irritated. Would it be that hard for his uncle to ask him a question or two? Perhaps they would talk more when the farm manager wasn't around.

Turning into the driveway at Red Road Farm, Macklin gaped at the manor house perched on a hill. Upon closer inspection, he discovered that the large wooden framed house had three stories and twenty-two rooms, and there was a formal garden with a fishpond and sundial. Although the house appeared to be in good shape, the paint was peeling. Maybe Minor Williams hadn't noticed or didn't care. Widowed, his son long dead (that was the funeral Macklin had gone to), he had lived there alone for a long time.

Minor had the master bedroom on the second floor and Macklin was to have the bedroom at the opposite end of the hall. His new room was simply furnished with a narrow bed and walnut dresser, a writing desk and Windsor chair. Macklin was pleased to see that everything in the room was tidy and clean. Uncle Minor said that Sorbon Carter's wife, Regina, was the housekeeper as well as the cook. She was a small, sharp-eyed woman who greeted him with a quick nod and a penetrating look when he encountered her in the hallway.

That night, over a delicious supper that Regina had prepared, Macklin learned to his disappointment that the University of Virginia was a full hour's drive from Red Road Farm. Between forkfuls of roast beef, Minor Williams said he wouldn't pay for Macklin's education unless he lived and worked at the farm as promised. Since Macklin had no money of his own, he voiced no objections.

Further conversation with his uncle revealed that Red Road Farm comprised about four hundred acres. Minor Williams leased out large parcels for grazing cattle and growing a variety of crops. The remaining acreage only required mowing. Minor seemed to think it was a great gift that he wasn't requiring Macklin to work in the fields all day. Instead, he told him, Macklin would help

Sorbon with the horses in the early mornings and evenings. There were nine horses and Macklin had the duty of mucking out their stalls. After he learned to ride, he could help exercise them as well. They were expensive "yard ornaments," Minor said with a thin smile, but occasionally someone in the neighborhood or up in Maryland bought a horse or two. It seemed that the old man had been quite the horseman in his day. Rapping his hand on the table, he said, "Red Road Farm will always have horses." When Macklin asked whether he would get weekends off, his uncle replied that horses didn't know the difference between a weekday and a weekend.

The next morning Sorbon was already at work in the barn when Macklin arrived. The farm manager talked enthusiastically about the horses as Macklin looked around groggily. Wearing a castoff overcoat his uncle had given him, he kept his bare hands stuffed in his pockets. It was another fiercely cold day. When Sorbon directed him toward the shovel he would use, he tripped over an anvil and landed facedown with a thud. Sorbon ambled to his side and offered a hand. "You all right?" he asked. Macklin thought he saw a smile pulling at the man's mouth. He stood up without aid and looked down in dismay at his dirt-smudged pants. He was a fastidious person and ordinarily would have changed clothes right away, but that would be silly, considering the task before him.

Two weeks later, Uncle Minor came to Macklin and handed him two sheets of stationery engraved with his name, Edwin Minor Williams, Red Road Farm, Rapidan, Virginia. On one he had written in his flowing fountain-pen script, "Clothes for my great nephew Macklin Robert Williams." On the other, "A year of university for my great nephew Macklin Robert Williams." He had initialed each sheet with a spidery EMW.

"Take this one to Merton's in Orange, and the other to Charlottesville." He fixed his gaze on the young man and moistened his lips with his startlingly pink tongue. "You can use the car on weekdays, but be home by five o'clock to help Sorbon." He put twenty dollars on the writing desk and said that would pay for schoolbooks and incidentals.

That night, Macklin took a few sips from the flask he had bought en route from Oklahoma. He dozed off and the next thing he knew, his alarm clock was ringing loudly in the dark. With a groan, he heaved himself out of bed and fumbled for his work clothes. He had nine stalls to clean and a suit to buy in Orange before he drove to his new university.

When he arrived at Merton's Shop later that morning, a plump clerk emerged from a back room to greet him. Narrowing his eyes, magnified by spectacles, he seemed offended by his customer's shabby clothes. Everything changed, however, when he read Mr. Williams's note. His face grew pink and he excused himself. Macklin heard a murmured exchange and then the clerk reappeared with an older man, similarly plump and pink, close on his heels.

"I am Merle Merton," the elder said, proffering a damp hand. "And this is my son, Little Merle. I understand you're the nephew of Mr. Williams of Red Road Farm."

It was then that Macklin began to feel the power of his uncle's name. "Yes, indeed," he said, instinctively copying his uncle's way of speaking. "I've come for a new suit—no, make that two. And I need one of them ready within the hour so I can continue on my way to Charlottesville."

The elder Merton went out of his way to help Macklin select the finest materials, nicest shirts, and most expensive accessories. He took Macklin in the back to adjust the suits, one of which needed only a few extra stitches. While Little Merle folded sweaters and hummed tunelessly in the background, Macklin decided to add a coat and gloves and a red wool scarf to his stack of purchases. Mr. Merton directed his son to ring up the total on the cash register. "I'll mail the bill to your uncle at Red Road Farm," Little Merle said with a challenging look as if he thought Macklin might be an imposter.

"He'll be expecting it," Macklin said, meeting his eye and tossing a few pairs of socks on the counter. "And be sure to call when my other suit is ready." After that, he swept out of the store in his new navy blue wool suit and camel hair topcoat, with a big shopping bag under his arm and the red scarf around his neck. Little Merle shut the door behind him a little too quickly.

From there he continued on Route 20 toward Charlottesville. He had asked Sorbon that morning for directions. The farm manager had stopped carding the speckled mare and called over his shoulder, "Turn right at the end of the driveway and just keep going until you get there."

It was a hilly, winding trip, but he found the school without difficulty and parked on McCormick Road. The other students were dressed in clothes similar to his and that eased one of his worries. At the registrar's office, the note from his uncle was well received by an officious fellow who clearly recognized the Williams name. Macklin selected his classes, which began that very day, and marveled over his good fortune.

The term started off well. He had an excellent memory and a genuine appetite for learning, and his professors liked him. The other first-year men occasionally invited him to join them for supper at one of the little restaurants near the Grounds, as everyone called the campus. When he declined, saying, "My uncle expects me home," that seemed to satisfy them. Many of them knew of the Williams family of Orange County and a few seem to know, uncannily, bits of Macklin's own family history.

When he was in Rapidan, he spent much of his time in the barn. At night he ate a quiet supper with his uncle, and then, after studying at his desk for a few hours, went to bed. Often he was so tired that he fell asleep immediately, but sometimes he lay awake and thought about how his life had changed. When his mind turned to Alice and the baby they lost, he would sit up and write in his journal. Then, if he still couldn't sleep, he would reach under the bed for his flask. After a few good swallows, his mind blurred. He was not a habitual drinker, but he appreciated the sedative powers of his uncle's bourbon.

Much to his delight, he quickly made two close friends at

the university. He and Dudley Douglas began having lunch together after their Western Civilization class. Soon Chippers Hebblethwaite, a member of the tennis team, was joining them. They went to The Virginian for hamburger platters or to Buddy's for towering sandwiches, and talked about their classes, world affairs, and various love interests. Dudley was the self-assured and good-looking son of a Richmond lawyer. He was interested in state politics. His girlfriend, Poppy, was at Hollins College. Chippers, who came from Winchester, was studying art history. His family had fallen on hard times and he could barely afford college. He told Dudley and Macklin he was dating a girl named Edith Langborne who attended Sweet Briar College. Already he was thinking about marrying her.

When Macklin's turn came, he proceeded with caution. When asked about his parents, he said as little as possible. His mother was long dead, and he didn't want to talk about his hapless father, whose unfortunate life Macklin tried not to contemplate. Rather than dwell on his Oklahoma origins, he talked about Red Road Farm. He told Chippers and Dudley about the property and the horses and made them laugh when he described his acerbic old uncle. When Dudley asked if he had a girlfriend, Macklin grew uneasy. Nothing would induce him to tell his new friends he had left his teenaged bride after she miscarried their child. He hadn't risked asking his uncle if he could bring her to Red Road Farm—and in fact, had wanted a fresh start on his own, far from Oklahoma and the mistakes of his youth. For the time being, he told his friends that he didn't have a girlfriend, which was true enough.

In late February, Macklin received bad news. While he was in his room studying, he heard the telephone ring. After a few minutes, Uncle Minor called up the stairs. The old man was sitting in his massive armchair when Macklin sank down on the horsehair sofa that smelled of a recently deceased poodle. His uncle's lined face looked unusually bleak. "Son, I'm very sorry to tell you this," he said, reaching out a bony hand to touch Macklin's sleeve. "Your father passed away this morning. He had a heart attack."

His father had been in Tulsa looking for work when he collapsed on the sidewalk. After he died, it took a number of phone calls before anyone could determine his next of kin, but someone at the hospital eventually tracked down an aged cousin back home in Perkins, Oklahoma. Cousin Ned had just called Uncle Minor, though Ned had not known that Macklin was at Red Road Farm.

Minor said he would pay for the funeral and buy Macklin a train ticket home. Staring down at his knees, Macklin mumbled his thanks. The two of them then sat in uncomfortable silence. Finally Minor reached for a folded newspaper he had evidently been reading when the call came. Macklin said good night and went back upstairs. He sat on his bed and stared at the wall for a while. Then he forced himself to open one of his schoolbooks, but nothing stuck in his mind as he read the same sentences over and over. With a stifled sob, he got ready for bed and tried to fall asleep, but it was no use. He sat up and pulled his journal from the drawer in his nightstand and wrote rapidly:

I remember Father making me a rope swing the summer I turned six years old. He was so proud of it, and he pushed me high into the sky. I half wished and half feared the swing would go all the way around the tree and come back down on the other side. But it always swung back to my father's hands, and after a while he lifted me down and turned me around by the shoulders. He told me he loved me—it's the only time I remember him saying it— and I hugged him around his legs. He would have been 26 years old. He had a hard life after that, what with Mama getting sick and him never being able to keep a decent job. After Mama died, I kept my distance. He was not what I wanted to be. I never even told him I was moving to Virginia and going to college here. I think he would have been glad for me and proud, except for the part about leaving Alice behind.

He set the journal aside and lay down on his bed. It seemed like hardly any time had passed when the alarm clock rang and he had to get up and tend to the horses.

That afternoon Sorbon dropped him off at the train station in Orange. Macklin bought a ticket that would allow him only two nights in Oklahoma, because he was afraid that if he stayed away any longer his uncle might renege on his offer of an education and a place to live. He missed three days of classes, and only Chippers and Dudley noticed. When he told them his father had died, Chippers's face went pale with compassion. Dudley took both of them out for a sober lunch. At home, his uncle said nothing further about the death after one brief inquiry about the funeral. Macklin went numbly about his business. It occurred to him that he was an orphan, yet it was Alice, both of whose parents were still alive, who lived at the Tipton Home.

After the school year ended, Macklin spent his days working on the farm. He had learned how to ride, and it took his mind off his troubles to saddle up and ride around the pasture. Most of the time he moved at a trot or canter, but occasionally he let loose and urged the horse to a full gallop. Such speed was scary but invigorating. Macklin had grown more muscular since moving to the farm, and his long hours of manual labor no longer exhausted him. He helped Regina tend to the kitchen garden and enjoyed keeping it watered and free of weeds. Sometimes he took his uncle to see the doctor in Orange, but this latter chore often fell to Sorbon, whose company Uncle Minor clearly preferred.

In early July, Minor announced he was going to Richmond for a series of medical appointments. He would stay with old friends and be gone for a few weeks. Sorbon drove him to Richmond and returned late that afternoon. Macklin was cleaning the horse stalls when Sorbon pulled up in the driveway and honked the horn. A few minutes later he came up beside him and said, "Your uncle is not doing very well, Macklin. He told me about his condition on the drive down, and I think you had better prepare for the worst."

Macklin had been lost in reflection and deep in a stubborn pile of manure when Sorbon interrupted him. He said, "Do you think Uncle might die?"

Sorbon nodded. "Well, he's eighty-one years old, you know."

Macklin had not, in fact, known his uncle's age until then. He would have guessed older, late eighties or even ninety. On one unusual occasion, when they had shared a bottle of sherry, the old man told a story about burying the family silver behind his grandmother's house during the Civil War. Now, doing some quick calculations, Macklin realized Minor had been a young boy at the time. As he looked at Sorbon, he thought of how his uncle ignored him when he asked him whether he had dug up the silver after the war.

While Macklin's mind wandered, Sorbon surprised him by asking, "Do you want to come over for supper? My wife has gone to stay with her people in Mine Run while your uncle's away. I can cook us up some chicken and greens, and there's bread pudding left over from last night."

Macklin wondered what the etiquette was. Did Sorbon view him as the family scion that he, the Negro hired man, should wait on or as a mere boy unable to fend for himself? Or was this just one farmhand reaching out to another? He looked Sorbon in the eye and detected nothing but weary kindness. "All right," he said. "That sounds nice. I'll come by around six."

An ironic smile flickered across Sorbon's face. "Make it six-thirty. I've got a chicken to catch."

As the time approached, Macklin rounded the bend behind the stables and headed toward the house where Sorbon and his wife lived. It was a peaceful July evening. Sorbon had mowed the fields, and the scent of grass and wild onions was in the air. The friendliest of the barn cats, the big orange one, walked beside him and rubbed against his leg when Macklin stooped down to pet it on the head.

He was curious about Sorbon's house—the tenant house, his uncle called it. This was his first visit. He saw Sorbon open the door to the screened porch as he approached. The house was dimly lit and blessedly cool, thanks to the shade trees all around. As Macklin's eyes adjusted to the light, he saw that brightly colored cotton curtains were drawn against the heat. The house was tidy and smelled good. There were small vases of wildflowers in the sitting room and artwork on the walls. He followed Sorbon into the kitchen. On the stove a pan sizzled with chicken, and a pot bubbled with collard greens. Another pot contained boiled beets. He glimpsed a loaf of homemade bread on the counter. Two tall glasses of iced tea were already on the table.

Sorbon handed him a plate and gestured for him to serve himself from the stove. They sat down at the oilcloth-covered table and eyed one another. Then Sorbon bowed his head and mumbled a brief blessing.

"The living room is cooler, but I prefer to sit at the table," he announced by way of conversation.

Macklin nodded in agreement. It was then that he noticed a painting on the kitchen wall: a neighborhood scene, depicting several families having picnics and playing games. There were several houses in the background and lots of smiling children and dogs and cats and rabbits. The wooden frame was neatly lacquered.

"Who painted that?" Macklin asked.

"My mother," Sorbon said. "She painted all her life."

"She was talented." Macklin gestured toward the painting. "Is this scene from around here?"

Sorbon shook his head. "My mother grew up in Raleigh. Her grandfather was a mason who helped build the capitol there. He did pretty well for himself. He built a house for himself and a few others for his relatives, and the painting shows all the family places in the background."

Macklin looked more closely. He noted two brick houses and another of stucco peaking out from behind flowers and trees. "Are the houses still in your family?" he asked.

"My brother has the brick one in front, my sister has the other. Mine is the stucco, but I've got tenants in it. I wouldn't mind moving back, but Regina's from up here and doesn't want to leave." He sat back in his chair and sighed.

They ate in silence for a while. The supper Sorbon had prepared was tasty and filling, much like his wife's cooking, but Sorbon had a heavier hand with the saltshaker. Macklin took a few long swallows of iced tea.

"What about you, Macklin? You liking it here? I know you must still be grieving for your father."

The farm manager's directness came as a surprise. "Oh well, the whole place is magnificent," Macklin said. "I'll admit I hadn't expected to be working such long hours, but I suppose it's good for me and I've grown to like the horses. And of course my uncle was kind to take me in and send me to college. As for my father"—he paused as his throat tightened—"well, I wish I'd been on better terms with him before he died."

Sorbon held his gaze until Macklin looked down at his plate. "We were very different," he began again as he pushed some greens with his fork. "He was a salesman—that is, when he could find work."

"A difficult job," Sorbon put in. "I tried it for a year." He set down his napkin and went to the stove for seconds. "What did he sell?"

"He sold shoes for a while. He sold insurance. He preferred shoes, he told me once. But a lot of the time, he just did odd jobs, nothing too steady. It was hard because my mother was sick a lot and he would try to help her, but he just didn't know how. He wasn't much of a nurse, he was a terrible cook, and he didn't get along with my grandmother—and she was the only one who could take care of Mama the right way." He took a breath. "I was too young to do much besides fetch the hot-water bottle and read to her. She liked that."

"When did you lose her?"

"My mother? When I was fourteen. My father wasn't around much after that. I stayed with my grandmother. I resented his leaving, of course, but what else could he do? He had to pay the bills, or at least try to pay them, and he had to go where the work was." The words were hardly out of his mouth when Macklin realized what he said was true. He had always resented his father for being away so often, but perhaps he really had no choice.

Macklin ate two helpings of bread pudding before he finally rose to leave. On the way through the little sitting room, he noticed a framed photograph on a table by the door. It showed a serious young man in a sailor's suit. Sorbon saw him pause over it and said, "My son, Daniel." Macklin started to say something, but the older man's eyes told him not to pursue it. Instead he thanked him for the meal and headed across the darkened lawn toward the main house. He knew it would be even quieter than usual with his uncle gone, but after the friendly evening with Sorbon he felt heartened. He was gradually getting to know the rhythms of Red Road Farm.

Uncle Minor called two weeks later to say that he wasn't sure when he would be coming home. His doctors wanted to monitor him, and his friends Furman and Betty Shafer had offered to host him in Richmond as long as he needed. In answer to Macklin's blunt question, he said yes, he would send money. In due time, a small check arrived. No one could say he spoiled his nephew. Macklin took to riding into town with Sorbon to save money on gasoline.

On these trips they talked freely, as they had the night they shared a meal. One morning, a month into Uncle Minor's absence, the two were in the farm truck on their way to the lumberyard. They talked about inconsequential things and then there was a lull. In that interlude, Macklin was suddenly overcome with the desire to talk about Alice. He began haltingly, but once he got going, everything poured out. He sniffled and sputtered and turned his handkerchief into a sodden mess as Sorbon listened. Finally he stopped, in hopes that Sorbon would say something to make him feel better.

The farm manager remained silent until they came to the railroad crossing in the town of Orange. As a train passed in front of them, he turned to Macklin and said, "Well, you should be ashamed of yourself." There was a censorious look on his face. "You shouldn't have left your wife, but there's no changing that now. If she'll still have you, figure out a way to bring her here." Then he turned his attention back to the train. As the caboose passed, two men in overalls lifted their hands in the familiar way of railroad workers. Both lost in their separate thoughts, Sorbon and Macklin waved back reflexively.

Without further conversation, they rode to the feed store and the lumberyard and finally Sparks's grocery. At the first two stops, Sorbon paid for everything and made sure to tuck the receipts in his shirt pocket. At the grocery, Macklin placed several things alongside Sorbon's purchases on the counter. With a sidelong look, Sorbon pushed those items back toward Macklin. "You pay for your own stuff," he said gruffly, loud enough for Mr. Sparks to hear. Macklin felt the color rise from his neck and radiate out to his ears. He had to pay with nickels and pennies for a drink and a chocolate bar. He couldn't afford the crackers.

They continued to work together in the barn, but there was a layer of silence between them that made Macklin miserable. He avoided Sorbon whenever he could and asked Regina to leave his supper on the stove rather than serving him in the dining room. He had a feeling Sorbon had told her about Alice, and now it seemed she disapproved of him as much as Sorbon did.

One late afternoon, Macklin had finished hosing down the barn floor and was sweeping away the excess water while Sorbon attended to a sleek mare named Goldenrod. She was a beautiful horse, Sorbon's favorite. As they worked, Macklin heard a long, rippling rumble of thunder. A storm had been brewing all afternoon. At last there would be a respite from the intense August heat. Now the wind picked up and began blowing through the open stable doors. Macklin had brought in the horses, though Sorbon said it wasn't necessary. Pretty soon the first drops began to fall.

After a dramatic opening act of wind and thunder, the storm

arrived with a vengeance, the steady patter quickly turning to a ferocious downpour. The wind blew rain into the barn and a lightning bolt lit up the twin mountains as the locals call them. It was a severe storm, sure to bring down tree limbs and cause damage. A couple of the horses snorted nervously.

Macklin let his broom drop to the floor as he watched the storm. Sorbon continued to work on Goldenrod, but suddenly he froze with his hand in midair. "Dammit, Macklin," he exclaimed, "I left all the windows open at the house. Come on and help me."

He hurried toward the barn's back door and yelled for Macklin to follow. Macklin wondered why they had to run out in the middle of an electrical storm when Regina could surely close the windows on her own. But with a sigh and a shake of his head, he took off after Sorbon.

To his surprise he saw that Sorbon was heading to the tenant house. "You do the downstairs," he said over his shoulder as Macklin caught up with him and they hurried inside. After closing the downstairs windows, Macklin found an old towel and began mopping up puddles. He could hear Sorbon pacing around upstairs and grumbling. When he asked whether Sorbon needed help, there was a longish pause and then the farm manager told him to come up.

He mounted the steps quickly and came upon a long room with large windows at either end. Sorbon was on his knees peering at a large canvas, which was flat on the floor and spattered with rain. There were other canvases, about four feet tall and four feet wide, leaning against the walls and stacks of smaller ones all around the perimeter of the room. The air was redolent with paint fumes and turpentine. In one corner sat several cans filled with soaking brushes and in another was an easel with a blank canvas on it. Sorbon had turned on a couple of lamps, but as the storm continued, the lights flickered, and Macklin had trouble seeing the paintings clearly.

Sorbon stood up and turned around. Without preamble, he said, "I just finished this one and now it's ruined."

Macklin decided not to say anything about the wholly surprising scene of a studio tucked away on the second floor of the tenant house. He supposed it made sense that Sorbon was an artist, like his mother before him, but the son was working on a much more dramatic and ambitious scale.

When Macklin proposed blotting the painting with a rag, Sorbon looked at him in exasperation. He said, "I told you, I just finished this one. The paint's still wet. If I touch it with a rag, the colors will smear. It's ruined."

Macklin kneeled down and looked at the canvas as the lamps flickered. It showed a couple dancing: a muscular young man with his arms around the waist of a buxom, older woman, her loosely curled hair flying away from her face. Both dancers had their heads thrown back in seeming ecstasy. Even in the dim light, he could see the intensity of the colors. The gold and vibrant green of the woman's dress and the red of her lips set off the creamy color of her skin. The rugged man wore black pants, a white shirt with the sleeves rolled up, and red suspenders with gold buckles.

As he stared at the painting, the lights in the room flickered once, twice, and then went out. Just as he rose to his feet, a bolt of lightning struck close to the house. For an instant, he saw the painting in its full glory: behind the dancing couple stood a crowd of onlookers, their faces in shades of pasty gray and white. Then to his horror he saw that the faces were mere skulls gaping with empty eyes at the oblivious dancers. He gasped and backed away. Sorbon, who was standing at his elbow, let out an irritated grunt.

Macklin collected himself and suggested they tilt the painting on its side and let the water run off. To this Sorbon nodded his agreement. As the rain beat on the tin roof and slapped against the windows, they stood on either side of the painting and gingerly lifted the top of it. Together they watched the water slide down and puddle on the floor. Sorbon bent down to inspect the painting again. He muttered something to himself, but he didn't sound as aggrieved as he had earlier.

The storm was moving fast. Huge clouds tumbled above the

Blue Ridge as the rain fell in sheets. Standing near the one window that remained open, Macklin inhaled the rain-sweetened air.

Sorbon headed down the steps and Macklin followed. He turned down the farm manager's offer of a raincoat.

"By the way," Sorbon began awkwardly, "I may have been too hard on you before. A marriage is no one's business but the people in it."

"No, you were right." Macklin attempted a conciliatory smile. "I'm going to try to do better. Maybe someday Alice will come here."

They stepped outside. It was still raining, but there was sunlight on the mountains. Sorbon headed to the barn, and Macklin knew he expected him to get back to work as well. Trailing after him, Macklin said, "Have you sold any of your paintings? You're really good, you know."

Without turning around, Sorbon replied, "I sold a few in New York City in 1928."

Macklin wanted to know what happened after that. Sorbon, still walking ahead, lifted his voice to the windy, rainy sky. "Nineteen twenty-nine happened, that's what."

2

In his room late that night, Macklin held the letter he had received from Alice earlier in the week but had not yet opened. He had not answered her previous letters begging him to write or call her at the Tipton Home. Recently there had been a long spell with no communication from her. In this letter, he figured, she was probably asking him for a divorce. His long and terrible silence warranted such a request. He would agree to it, of course. But he decided he would write about her while her letter lay sealed before him. In his journal, he wrote:

One day, shortly after we met in freshman biology, I ran to catch up with her between classes. She was in the midst of a rushing crowd of students and all I could see was her hair ribbon bobbing far ahead of me. I dodged in between clusters of students, and got nearly within reach of her, but she didn't hear me call out her name. Finally I reached out and tugged her hair ribbon; it slid off her ponytail and she didn't even notice. People looked at me like I was crazy as I stood there with the purloined ribbon in my hands. I waited outside her class, skipping my own, until she reappeared an hour later. When I showed her the ribbon I had grabbed right off her head, she laughed and asked me to tie it back in place. Doing so, I inhaled her scent and let my fingers graze her long neck. How warm she was, how clean and fragrant! She turned and smiled at me in that deep, candid way of hers. What else could I do but ask her out?

He read over what he had written. There was so much more to say about Alice. Some of it he didn't dare write down. Everything had been so innocent at first. He liked strolling around campus with her, holding her hand, and reading poetry to her, and that would have sufficed for a long time. He had no intention of insulting her honor with a forward gesture. But Alice had made it clear in her looks and her touches that she wanted to do more than hold hands. She had initiated their first kiss, and what a knee-knocking, dizzying experience that was. To his astonishment, she saw no incongruity between her good, churchgoing ways and her lusty cravings. She was quick to say she loved him, and he believed her, but her love of sex was a phenomenon unto itself. Since their dormitory rooms were off-limits, they were constantly on the lookout for places to spend their Saturday evenings. They made love in borrowed cars and borrowed rooms and once, when all else fell through, in a utility closet in the library basement. He was terrified that someone would hear them, but Alice tugged at his belt and told him not to worry. Amid mop pails, the smell of ammonia filling his nostrils, he could not resist her urgent entreaties for long.

Walking back to his dormitory the night of the library escapade, he had thought, *This is who she is, but is this who I am?* Nothing in his lonely and desolate childhood had prepared him for such an intense connection with another person, especially not with this laughing, good-looking, boldly sexual young woman. He thought that what they were doing—and doing so much of—was possibly a mistake. He resolved to back off and concentrate on the studies he had been neglecting. The next morning, however, when he returned to the library and tried to read, the smell of her still clung to his skin. The words blurred on the page, and he felt he would go mad if he couldn't get his hands on her in the next instant. But if his grades fell, he would lose his scholarship, and then where would he be? He hurried back to his dormitory, took a cold shower, and promptly fell asleep facedown on an open book of Keats.

Upon learning that Alice was pregnant, Macklin had initially felt a weird combination of dismay, relief, and fatalism. The last thing he wanted was to get married, but at least this poorly timed development cooled the fires that had been consuming his waking hours. He could think clearly again. He knew he would marry her, even without anyone bullying him into it, and he would drop out of school and take any job he could get to support her and the baby. His reduced prospects were all of a piece with the world he had known before he followed Alice down the sidewalk and plucked the ribbon from her hair. The fog of passion had lifted: he saw that his life was essentially over before it had begun. He would be just like his father. It was a bleak turn of events, but he told himself he deserved no better.

Alice had not pressed him about his thoughts, but in unguarded moments she looked worried and scared. It was only on their wedding day that she seemed more at ease, as if the burden of her uncertainty in him had been lifted. Remembering all of these things now, he buried his face in his hands and then picked up his pen again.

On our wedding day, she reminded me of a peony just about to bloom. She was pink-cheeked and already a little plump around the middle. The image gave me no joy, however. And I remember how the justice of the peace, an oily faced man with dirty fingernails, gave me a sly, knowing look after the five-minute ceremony. He winked at me as we turned to leave, and in that wink, I saw my entire future swirling down the drain.

After the miscarriage he decided the fates were giving him another chance. Whatever it was he felt for Alice—love or lust or some complex mingling of the two—had to be tamped down for a while, maybe forever. He resolved to leave her and walk for a while in the cool air beyond her gaze and grasp.

He had never written to his Uncle Minor before, let alone asked him for help. Just dropping the letter in a mailbox took more courage than he knew he had. In it he wrote only that he desperately wanted to attend college, preferably at the University of Virginia, a school he had read about with great interest, and wondered if his uncle might somehow assist him in this quest. He had not mentioned Alice, and his uncle's reply indicated he had not gotten wind of her existence.

He looked down now at Alice's letter and steeled himself. Reading it would probably keep him awake for hours, but he couldn't ignore it any longer. With trembling fingers, he slit it open with a sterling silver letter opener. There was her familiar rounded script on Tipton Home letterhead:

August 23, 1939
Dear Macklin,

Word has reached me late and through odd circumstances that your father died. I am so sorry. You must be wondering how I found out. Well, news does travel in strange ways. A church group in Tulsa sends us used clothes and toys for the children. I opened a box that contained a handsome set of toy soldiers. They were wrapped in newspaper. After unwrapping them, I began piling up the sheets to throw away. I just happened to notice a story about a man who collapsed and died in Tulsa. It said the man, a stranger to town, was Terrell Macklin Williams of Perkins, Oklahoma.

Mackin, you are in my prayers. Again, I'm very sorry about your father.

With love,
Your wife Alice

P.S. I'm about to go play softball with the children. You'll be pleased to know I'm wearing my green ribbon, your favorite.

It was the only sympathy note that Macklin had received. Chagrined that he had waited so long to read something so kindly meant, he placed it in the back of his journal. No matter that he had discarded all of Alice's other letters; this one he would keep.

The day before fall classes were to begin, Uncle Minor called Macklin to say that he was still feeling poorly and planned to remain in Richmond until spring. He was tempted to close up the farmhouse for the duration, but if Macklin wanted to stay there and continue to have his education paid for, Minor would allow it, on one condition.

"What would that be?" Macklin asked in a small voice.

"Paint the house," his uncle said.

Macklin waited for elaboration on this terse directive, but none was forthcoming. He was about to say that he had never painted anything and would surely need help with such a large house, but he thought better of it. "Yes, sir. I'll get started on it right away."

"Good. I'll come up sometime and have a look." He paused and then added ominously, "And don't neglect your studies."

After hanging up the phone, Macklin fretted for a while and then hurried over to the tenant house. In response to his knock, Sorbon appeared in paint-splattered undershirt and dungarees. It was the first time Macklin had seen him in his artist's attire.

They sat down on the front stoop and Macklin recounted the conversation with his uncle. Sorbon looked across the yard with his chin cupped in his hands and his elbows on his knees. He said nothing for so long that Macklin began to get nervous. At last the older man sat up straight and began to speak. "Macklin, your uncle told me that he was disappointed in your grades. I think that's why he's making you paint the house—to see if you're serious about being here."

Flames of anger rose up within Macklin only to be tempered by rainy feelings of humiliation. His first year at the University of Virginia had begun promisingly, but his grades had plummeted after his father's death. He had actually failed his astronomy class.

When Macklin said nothing, Sorbon went on, "I guess he figured you'd go to summer school and show him you could do better."

"It never occurred to me," Macklin said. "I didn't know the future of my education depended on it." Then he wheeled on Sorbon. "Why didn't you tell me all this sooner? And why haven't you painted the house? You're the big painter around here." He looked pointedly at a blotch of red paint on Sorbon's pant leg.

An imposing frown formed on the farm manager's brow. "I'm not your keeper, Macklin. It's your responsibility to talk to your uncle and find out what's on his mind. You're his blood kin, and you expect me to tell you what's going on?" He turned his head and spat in the bushes. "If you'd spent a little time getting to know him, you'd know his son flunked out of that school. The last thing Mr. Williams needs is another blot on the family name." He eyed Macklin coldly. "And I don't have time to paint the house—I have my hands full keeping the books on this farm and running the stables."

Drawing on all of his willpower, Macklin resisted the urge to point out that Sorbon apparently still had time to paint pictures during the middle of the day. He got up and paced around the yard. Gradually his head cleared. Sorbon's use of "Mr. Williams" had reminded him that the farm manager was still in a subservient position, even if Uncle Minor treated him as a friend and confidant. They both needed to stay in the old man's good graces.

He returned to the stoop and stood before Sorbon. "I'll paint the house if I get paid a fair wage every week, not just the odd check from Uncle that barely covers gasoline."

Sorbon regarded him skeptically. "You got a nice big house to live in, my wife to cook for you, and a free college education if you don't mess up. I'm not sure what you're complaining about. But fine, I'll pay you out of the farm account. Just make sure you do a good job and don't flunk out of school."

His face lit with anger and frustration, Macklin nodded briefly and walked away.

The next day when he came home from classes, he discovered that Sorbon had already bought the painting supplies and left a ladder and some scaffolding propped against the house. It wore him out just looking at it. Once he started, he found that just scraping the old paint from a window frame took forever, and there were dozens of windows. Sorbon was not pleased with his slow progress and refused to pay him until he picked up his pace.

Macklin began to despair. Along with painting the house, he still had to exercise the horses, muck out the stalls, and attend classes. One day, however, his luck changed.

He was having a late lunch at The Virginian when Chippers showed up. His friend slid into the seat across from him and with barely a greeting launched into a tale of woe. His Sweet Briar crush had dumped him unceremoniously for someone else. To make matters worse, he was dangerously low on funds. His father and mother had run through their respective inheritances and had recently moved to a smaller house so they could make ends meet. He feared he would have to drop out of school.

At this point in his monologue, Chippers lowered his head to the table and openly sobbed. Macklin signaled to the waiter to bring a pitcher of beer, and Chippers raised his head and regarded him with bleary gratitude. They drank in silence for a few minutes. With his friend humbled before him, Macklin decided that the time had come for him to be candid. He admitted that he, too, was short on cash these days. Chippers listened sympathetically and seemed not to mind that his turn for talking was over. Macklin then worked his way to Uncle Minor and allowed that they were not particularly close. Chippers poured another beer for each of them and nodded for Macklin to continue.

Between gulps of beer, he told Chippers that he had felt bad for months after his father died and could barely do his work. But that was not all. Taking a deep breath, he revealed his status as a married man. Topping himself, Macklin told his friend about the pregnancy, the hasty wedding, and his dull prospects in the wilds of Oklahoma. It was, he said, just a few weeks before his school-teaching job was to begin that Alice lost the baby. He was on the train to Orange as soon as he could make arrangements with

Uncle Minor.

Chippers gawked at his friend in open-mouthed wonder. When Macklin spread his arms wide and said, "That's it," Chippers asked whether he wanted to walk around and continue talking. He said he would pay for their beer, but Macklin waved off the offer and tossed a handful of change on the table. He had just pawned the cufflinks he had bought with his great uncle's money and had money to burn.

Out into the crisp afternoon they headed. Chippers wore his white V-neck tennis sweater and flannel trousers, and Macklin was in his light wool suit with navy blue tie. To the casual observer, they would have looked like the very ideal of collegiate life: two handsome young men, tall and well dressed, Macklin carrying his books and Chippers his tennis racquet, both of them ready to meet the world. No one would have guessed that they were both perilously close to dropping out of school.

Having set aside weightier topics, he and Chippers commented on the crisp fall weather and greeted classmates as they strolled toward the Rotunda, which gleamed in the late-afternoon sunlight. Macklin was beginning to know more and more young men from the best families up and down the Eastern Seaboard. That day, their friendly smiles revealed that they liked him. He silently vowed to stay among them and get his degree, no matter what it took.

They climbed the marble steps on the Rotunda's south side and sat down at the very top. Shadows were falling across the terraced lawn. Clusters of students were walking along the colonnades to late-afternoon classes while others were heading to their rooms or to the Corner for an early supper. A couple of the campus's stray dogs were frolicking and nipping at each other in the distance, near the statue of Homer. All in all, it was a peaceful scene. Macklin and Chippers stretched out their legs on the steps and took it all in.

Suddenly Chippers piped up. "Won't your uncle buy Alice a train ticket here?

Macklin shifted uncomfortably. "Well, Uncle Minor is out of town—very ill in Richmond, as it happens. I don't dare tax him with my own problems right now."

"You could get a job, you know, and buy her a ticket yourself."

A sigh escaped Macklin's lips. He had a job, and he was still broke. Worse, Chippers didn't seem to understand that Alice was part of his past, not his future. "Alice is working at an orphanage in Tipton, Oklahoma. Maybe it's best that she stay there for a while."

Chippers paused before replying. "Maybe she needs you, Macklin." He put his hands behind his head and lay back. "Boy, what I wouldn't give to be in your shoes. I can't imagine anything nicer than being married and having a girl to come home to."

This burst of sentimentality caught Macklin off-guard. Never had it occurred to him that his untimely marriage was something to be envied. He would think about this later. For now, he would change the subject. "So, Chippers," he began, "tell me more about your career plans."

Chippers sat up and regarded him enthusiastically. "My father has an old friend who runs an art gallery in Chicago. He's promised me a job if I'm willing to specialize in contemporary art—and I am." Chippers picked a piece of lint off his trousers. "But of course I'm studying everything, from antiquity to the present. It's great fun." He smiled at Macklin in his earnest manner.

Macklin began to direct the conversation in a more focused way. "Well then, you just have to raise enough cash to finish up, is that it? And then it's off to Chicago and a fine career in a field that you love?"

Chippers nodded, his smile gone. "My scholarship doesn't cover much," he said mournfully. "If I don't figure out something soon, I'll have to go home."

Barely daring to look his friend in the eye, he asked Chippers if he had any interest in painting the house at Red Road Farm. It was a big job and he thought Chippers could live at the farm for free if he would just help with the painting.

Without any hesitation or a single question for Macklin, Chippers said it was a capital plan and he could start immediately. They stood up and shook hands to seal the deal, and then Chippers pointed out the bronze eagle affixed to the underside of the Rotunda's porch roof. "We're going to fly just like that eagle, Macklin!" With his optimism restored, he grabbed his tennis racquet and hurried on his way.

A week later, Macklin rushed through his reading assignments so he would have time to write in his journal. He wanted to record exactly what had happened in recent days:

My plan has succeeded almost too well. I told Sorbon I had a well-connected friend who could help him sell his paintings. He was careful not to look too interested, but I could tell he was curious and hopeful. When I said that Chippers was broke and needed a place to live, Sorbon got my drift. He agreed that Chippers could move in and even receive a small salary if he did a good job painting the house.

Last weekend, Chippers rode home with me and talked the entire way about his ex-girlfriend, the highly annoying Edith Langborne. Sorbon was puttering around in front of the barn, no doubt waiting for us to arrive. When it came time for introductions, I presented the testy farm manager to the penniless young scion and then went inside to change clothes. When I rejoined them, Chippers clapped me on the back and said, "Sorbon tells me you've been working on this side for weeks, and you've only managed to scrape the paint off a few window frames."

My temper rising, I pointed out a window frame I had painted the day before. It looks terrific, if I do say so myself (and why not say so, in my own journal).

After that, we got to work and I tried to forgive Chippers for his rudeness. By the end of the weekend, we had made real progress. In truth, he did much more than I did—it turns out he really knows how to paint. I took frequent breaks and, on

Sunday afternoon, disappeared for a much-needed nap. It seemed that Chippers didn't even notice. Sunday evening, to my delight, Sorbon wrote each of us a check.

On the drive back to Charlottesville the next morning, I told Chippers about Sorbon's art and went into some detail describing the painting of the dancers and the skull-head spectators. He waited patiently until I finished and then said, "Yes, it's tremendous. 'Swing Low' he calls it."

Naturally I wanted to know how he knew about the painting. He said Sorbon had taken him up to his studio while I was napping! Then he told me that Sorbon's mother had named him after the Sorbonne, where she had once dreamed of studying art. This was news to me. Although I had wanted Sorbon and Chippers to hit it off, I confess to being irritated that they have become fast friends. However, I'm getting paid regularly and I may yet graduate from the University of Virginia.

Macklin felt his eyelids growing heavy. Dropping his journal to the floor, he rolled over on his side. The cool October air coming through the open windows washed over him, and his worries slipped away until morning.

By December, Chippers had become a fixture at Red Road Farm. His activities went beyond scraping and painting the house, and sometimes Macklin got irritated just watching his friend take so much pride in the upkeep of the Williams family home. Whistling under his breath, Chippers washed windows and polished the brass doorknobs. After a heavy snowstorm, he rose early to shovel the long driveway. He seemed to have a hard time sitting still.

But despite Chippers's boundless energy, the house was still not painted. It had been his idea to remove every flake of old paint, on all sides, before starting with the new. He said, rather grandly, that he wanted a completely blank canvas before starting fresh. Macklin thought this was silly and said so, but Chippers had taken charge and would not be dissuaded. The house was now scraped raw and looked awful. Chippers said they could do nothing further until the weather improved. Macklin worried that Uncle Minor would get a bad report from Sorbon and kick both of them out. Already Sorbon had stopped paying them regularly.

Chippers's thoughts were elsewhere, however. One day they were passing through Orange on their way home when he cried out, "Stop! Stop the car, Macklin!"

Thinking an animal had darted in front of the wheels, Macklin hit the brakes with a screech. They rocked forward and backward and then Chippers said, "My apologies, Macklin. I didn't mean you should stop right here. Just pull over and park. There's Edith."

Macklin saw the back of a young woman wearing a plaid wool coat and a blue beret. Walking swiftly on high heels, she disappeared inside Merton's Men's Shop, where Macklin had purchased his wardrobe nearly a year and a half ago. He had not been back to the store since. It was just too expensive for him without Uncle Minor footing the bill.

Chippers was out of the car and on his way inside before Macklin had even turned off the engine. He hurried after his friend and found him already in conversation with Edith, a petite young woman with pretty brown hair and porcelain white skin. Ever the gentleman, Chippers made introductions. Macklin noted Edith's lisp—she had a comical way of saying "Chipperth."

She was speaking very softly to her old beau and suddenly the reason for that became clear. Little Merle, in topcoat and scarf, came bustling in from the back. His face lit up when he saw Edith. He slipped his arm around her waist as she turned to him nervously. "Guess who just walked in—Chipperth Hebblethwaite. You remember hearing about him, right? The tennith player?"

Chippers and Merle, their faces blank, shook hands. Merle acknowledged Macklin with a quick nod. He wanted to know why Chippers was in Orange, and Chippers explained that he was living and working at Red Road Farm. Conversation seemed in danger of flagging after that. When Little Merle began steering Edith to the door, Chippers stepped in front of them and blurted out, "Say, why don't you two come to our Christmas party? We're having a party at the farm on Christmas Day, and it would be super if you'd join us."

Edith giggled and said, "We'd love to. Thank you, Chipperth!" while her boyfriend pursed his lips in displeasure.

Macklin walked to the back of the shop to inspect a rack of handsome neckties. Out of the corner of his eye he noticed the elder Merton bustling toward him, no doubt hoping he was about to go on another spending spree. But he didn't have a dime to spare and was merely extricating himself from the awkward conversation Chippers had created for himself.

The bell tinkled above the door as the two lovebirds escaped, with Edith calling out goodbyes to one and all. Chippers stood with his hands stuffed in his pockets and watched them walk down the street.

Back in the car, the two young men rode silently for a few miles until Macklin could not restrain himself any longer. He asked about the alleged Christmas party.

"I'm sorry, Macklin. It just popped out of my mouth. I guess I figured it would be a way for me to see Edith again. Her family lives in Culpeper. It won't be hard for her to come over for the afternoon."

"But you also invited the odious Little Merle."

"I didn't realize you knew him."

"Well, I know him slightly—as a shopkeeper. I didn't realize he was the one who stole away your sweetheart."

"She never mentioned his name. I just knew he was from Orange and worked in his family business." Chippers sniffed loudly and wiped his nose on his sleeve. "It looks like a nice store. Under different circumstances, and if I had the money for it, I might have bought a sweater."

Macklin nodded distractedly. "Well, they're not coming, are they? Needless to say—or perhaps I do need to say—I hadn't planned on a Christmas party."

Chippers chuckled. "It's not clear whether he's coming, but

I think she is. They had a little spat when you stepped away. He said his parents were expecting them on Christmas afternoon, and she said they'd still have time to come to our party. I think she really wants to see me again, Macklin. Maybe she's ready to break up with this fellow and give me another chance."

When Macklin didn't respond, Chippers took a different tack. "Come on, Red Road Farm needs a party! We'll get a big cedar tree from out back and decorate it, and Regina will cook. And maybe your wife could take the train, get here in time for the party, and move back with you once and for all. Think how great that would be."

The mention of Alice struck Macklin as patronizing. Red Road Farm was his family home, he told himself; it was for him to decide whether they had parties or not. Still, he was not opposed to the idea and, in fact, wished it had been his own. With Uncle Minor away, there was no reason not to raise a glass of cheer with friends.

"Oh, all right," he said, sounding more reluctant than he felt. He wanted Chippers to know he had veto power. "Alice can't come, since the orphanage will need her to help with the children. But we could ask Dudley and Poppy."

By the time they got home, Chippers had expanded the guest list considerably. He was going to invite everybody on his tennis team, the coach and the coach's wife, his parents, and his sister and her husband. The party would be at four o'clock on Christmas Day, and they would use the large formal dining room, the room Uncle Minor always called the ballroom, for the festivities.

Macklin didn't look forward to telling Regina about these plans. If all the guests, including Edith and Little Merle, attended, there would be twenty-two people to feed and look after. He knew Regina was not impressed with him, though she continued to prepare truly excellent meals for him and Chippers. He vowed to put off the conversation with her as long as he could.

With the party as his beacon, Chippers got interested in the painting project again. Although the weather was a problem, he insisted they do what they could so that the house would look its best. On the rare mild day, he was on the ladder with brush in hand and determination in his eyes, yelling for Macklin to join him.

One late night, Macklin heard a bumping and rustling in his bathroom. Half asleep, he fumbled his way into the room and switched on the light. Nothing, not even a mouse. Then the sound started up again, and he realized it was coming from just outside the window. Pulling up the shade, he yelled out in alarm when he came face to face with Chippers on his ladder, flashlight in one hand and brush in the other.

"For the love of God, Chippers!" Macklin said. "What are you doing out there at this hour?"

"We don't have much time left!" he shouted through the glass. "We have barely a week before the party."

A sudden realization made Macklin's temper flair. "Chippers," he said, "why are you painting that window frame anyway? That's the one thing that was already done. I painted it before you started working here."

"You didn't do it right. There are places you missed and lots of drips, and this side is very important—Edith will see it when she comes up the driveway."

So, Macklin thought angrily, this was all about impressing Edith. He shook his head in an exaggerated fashion so Chippers would be sure to catch the gesture and lowered the shade in one quick motion. It was not until after he heard the ladder being lowered—a muffled clanging sound—that he was able to calm down and fall asleep.

The next morning Macklin awoke in a cold sweat, aware that he absolutely had to talk to Regina. Between tending to the horses, writing papers for class, monitoring Chippers, and polishing silverware, he had managed to delay the conversation with her for two weeks.

He found her at the kitchen table drinking a cup of tea and

reading a newspaper. Setting down the paper, she regarded Macklin over her reading glasses with the unblinking gaze he knew well. With a tremor in his voice, he announced the number of guests he expected on Christmas day. In recent days, the count had risen to fifty-five, including various girlfriends and family members of the tennis players. To that Regina merely raised her eyebrows and kept them raised. He took a deep breath and told her he and Chippers would need three roasted turkeys, a baked ham, large quantities of stewed tomatoes, green beans, mashed potatoes, Indian corn pudding, and pickled peaches. They also wanted her Sunday-best yeast rolls, pumpkin pie, fruitcakes and pound cakes, and six platters of sugar cookies and lemon bars. It would be ideal, Macklin said, if she got everything ready by Christmas Eve.

Regina was silent as he pressed his hands to the kitchen table and leaned toward her expectantly. Then she tipped her head back and laughed so loudly and disdainfully that Macklin could only gape in astonishment. She rolled up her paper and slapped it against the table before rising to her feet and eyeing him with frigid merriment. "You go on and have your party, Macklin," she said with rare animation, "but it won't be on my back. Sorbon and I are leaving for Raleigh and won't be back until New Year's Day." With that she spun on her heel and went out on the back porch. He watched her grab her coat off a hook and take off at a brisk pace through the slush and snow.

3

That evening, for the first time, Regina simply didn't bother to cook for him. After an unsatisfying meal of cold leftovers, he retreated to his room to work on a poetry paper. When he could think of nothing more to say about John Donne, he pulled out his journal. His face hot with worry, he wrote:

I dread telling Chippers. We agreed I would handle the refreshments and he has shown great restraint, given his obsessed state of mind, in not asking me about it. At least I have some time to plan what I'll say. He's staying at Dudley's fraternity house tonight so he won't be late to his early a.m. exam tomorrow. I'm planning to drive over to turn in my final papers and then head home, with Chippers in tow, around noon. I expect it will be a very long ride once he finds out about Regina's mutiny.

He knew he wouldn't sleep well. When he finally dozed off, bits and pieces of his childhood filled his dreams along with odd cameo appearances by Chippers, Uncle Minor, Regina, and Sorbon. He woke up before his alarm rang and decided he might as well get up and get on with things.

His regular duties came first. Just as he was finishing with the horses, Sorbon asked if he had figured out what to do about the party. Macklin could only shake his head. With a purposeful look in his eye, Sorbon beckoned for him to sit on the bench outside the barn.

"I hear you're having fifty-five people on Christmas Day. That's a crowd."

Macklin waited to see where the conversation was going.

Sorbon placed his hands on his knees and turned toward him. "Here's what you need to do," he said in an avuncular tone. "Go to Sparks's Grocery and order two Orange County hams, the good, salty kind. If you pay them extra, they'll cook 'em for you. And buy all the ginger ale they have in stock. Then go over to Culpeper to the bakery on Main Street and order twelve dozen biscuits and ten pies. Get fruit pies and coconut cream for the men and chocolate pies for the ladies. You'll also need whiskey, lots of it."

Macklin nodded his agreement and asked him to go on. "Make ham biscuits and set them at one end of the dining room table and put the whiskey and ginger ale at the other end. Put the pies on the sideboard. Let people serve themselves. Keep it simple. No one will expect a couple of college boys to host a formal Christmas dinner. Oh, and borrow a record player and have some music playing. That will keep things lively." At the mention of the record player he raised his index finger in the air and made a few quick circles—to signify liveliness, Macklin supposed.

Though he knew Sorbon's wife could solve everything just by staying at the farm and doing what a good and loyal cook was supposed to do, he nonetheless felt a whimper of gratitude rising in his throat. He had begun to think Sorbon had forsaken him in the months since Chippers arrived. Chippers was Sorbon's favorite, no doubt because he hoped Chippers would help him sell his paintings. Yet now he was offering a plausible solution, and he was speaking to Macklin man to man without condemnation or criticism.

Macklin had to mention one lingering problem, however. "How will I pay for all this? I'd counted on Regina using supplies she already had on hand."

Sorbon raised his eyebrows and held them high, just as his wife had done the previous day. He let Macklin hear his own words before he replied. "I can advance you the money from the farm account, but you'll have to pay it back by continuing to work on the farm, now that the house-painting is almost done."

He paused. "We'll need a new fence around the pasture, and the fishpond should be drained and thoroughly cleaned. That's the kind of thing you can do in the spring." He regarded Macklin hopefully. "You want it to be a nice party, don't you? You'll work off the expenses in no time."

Feeling like Sisyphus, Macklin looked down at his bare hands, which had grown hard and callused during his time on the farm. It seemed he would never be done with the manual labors for which he received so little recompense. How, he silently asked himself, was a man supposed to keep body and soul together at Red Road Farm? Still, he had already committed himself to the party. "All right, Sorbon," he said heavily. "You have a deal."

His wallet stuffed with bills—Sorbon had actually come up with cash—he hurried off to do all his errands in Orange and Culpeper. With barely a minute to spare, he drove to the university, turned in his papers, and then went to the Chi Phi house in search of Chippers.

Dudley met him at the door with a surprised look on his face. "You didn't get word?" he asked. "Chippers is at the infirmary. I took him there after his exam. He had a fever of 103."

Although Dudley offered to come along, Macklin bade him a quick goodbye. At the infirmary a nurse confirmed that Chippers was there, laid up with the flu. He would have to go home or to the hospital, since the infirmary was about to close for Christmas recess. When Macklin asked to see the patient, she led him back to a little room where Chippers lay dozing on a cot.

At the sound of Macklin's voice, Chippers opened his eyes and sat up abruptly. "Oh hello, Macklin. Let me get my things and we'll leave immediately." He staggered to his feet and would have collapsed on the floor if Macklin hadn't caught his arm. His body radiated a sickly heat and drops of sweat poured down his face. He turned his head and coughed heavily into his sleeve.

Insisting he would be fine in a couple of days, Chippers refused to go the hospital. Out of the corner of his eye Macklin saw the nurse glance at her watch. He retrieved the car and parked in front of the infirmary. Then he gathered up his friend's duffel bag and tennis racquet under one arm and took Chippers by the other. The nurse called after them, "Be sure to give him plenty of liquids, and merry Christmas!"

With Chippers safely deposited in the backseat where he could stretch out, Macklin asked him, "Do you want ginger ale or whiskey? The Red Road Farm ambulance is serving both today."

Chippers laughed weakly and said he would start with ginger ale. Thus fortified, he fell into a woozy slumber and Macklin didn't hear another word from him until they got home.

Coming up the driveway, they nearly ran into Sorbon's car. He honked his horn in warning and Macklin braked in time. He expected Sorbon to stop and say something, but instead he merely waved. Regina, seated next to him, dug in her pocketbook and kept her head down. Sorbon did a double take when Chippers sat up in the backseat, but he barely slowed down. His tires spun on the slushy gravel as he turned onto Rapidan Road.

Over the next several days, Macklin puttered around the house when he wasn't tending to Chippers. His friend slept most of the time and then roused himself to drink a cup of tea or a glass of ginger ale. Macklin felt bad that he begrudged him the latter, but he had bought it for the party. The sound of spasmodic coughing bounced off the walls and Macklin heard it no matter where he was in the house. Sometimes when he peeked in Chippers's room, he was shivering beneath a thick pile of blankets. Other times, his face was flushed and he had only a sheet pulled up to his shoulders. He had placed a pillow over his head and turned away in the middle of Macklin's tale about Regina's rebellion.

Sunday morning, after barn duties, Macklin tramped through the snow and stared up at the house. Miraculously, Chippers had managed to put a coat of paint on the front and the sides, and it looked good. As he inspected things, however, his eye lit on the front door. Neither he nor Chippers had touched it, and the old black paint looked dingy and out of keeping with the shiny white front and the freshly painted green shutters.

He went to the tool shed to see what kind of paint was left. There was an unopened can of a shiny holly red that was perfect. He scooped it up and looked around for a fresh brush. With newspapers spread carefully below the front door, he applied a flat white paint, let that dry, and then painstakingly added a coat of the red. The day was bright and windy, and it dried quickly. The second coat looked good, but the third was the charm. The door sparkled in the sun. He stood back to admire his work and wondered if the satisfaction he felt were anything like what Sorbon experienced when he completed a painting.

With a lightened heart, he put away the painting supplies and dug out a few gardening tools. He took a pair of shears down to the garden and cut holly and pine boughs. The wreath he made was lopsided but pretty. There was a hook already on the door—a relic of many Christmases past, he presumed. Once again, he stood back to admire his handiwork. He was getting into the Christmas spirit almost in spite of himself.

As nice as the wreath looked, it was missing something. He puzzled over it for a minute and then his mind flashed on the boxes of Christmas decorations stowed on the third floor. While Chippers slept on, he brought down the boxes and once again found just what he was looking for—a roll of luxurious red velvet ribbon. He cut a generous length and fashioned a bow for the wreath.

It was shaping up to be a very different Christmas from the previous year. On that occasion, Uncle Minor had given him a card with five dollars in it, and Regina served a turkey dinner and mincemeat pie on Christmas Eve. For Christmas Day, they ate ham. There had been no mention of going to church, though Macklin would have gone, had his uncle asked him to. Macklin had spent most of Christmas day sleeping in his room.

These recollections now inspired him to change out of his work clothes into a suit. Since Chippers was fast asleep, he could go to Purcell Presbyterian Church for the morning service. For some time now, he had been curious about the church on the other side of the pasture. He admired its graceful spires and liked listening to the church bell on Sunday morning. He had heard the members of the congregation talking and laughing from a distance and had wondered if the people there might welcome him into their midst.

On this day there were about sixty people present. He arrived right as the bell stopped ringing; the last vibrations seemed to hang in the sharp blue sky. Accepting a bulletin from an usher, he slipped into a back pew and nodded shyly when a few people turned around to smile at him. The sermon was not too long and he was glad that the songs they sang were Christmas carols rather than dry old hymns. During the first silent prayer, he prayed that the party would be a success. During the second one, near the end of the service, he remembered to pray that Chippers would get well soon.

Afterwards, the minister made a beeline for him. His name was Joseph Noel Braswell, and he was a South Carolinian. He had joked about his name during the sermon—truly, Christmas was his middle name. Not a very deep mind, Macklin decided, but a decent fellow. His wife, Harriet, was loud and he moved away from her quickly. The others he met were neighbors who lived in Rapidan or nearby dots on the map. They were pleased to meet "the Williams boy," as they referred to him.

There was a luncheon in the fellowship hall. Since he had brought nothing to share, he tried to beg off, but the Reverend Braswell wouldn't hear of it. He ended up seated between a man named Arnold Radius, who introduced himself as a church elder, and Arnold's wife, Annette. Mr. Radius had shifty eyes and fat hands that looked too soft for a man. Both he and his wife wanted intelligence on Uncle Minor. At first Macklin answered freely, but he was irritated when his inquisitors asked how many acres his uncle owned, how many he leased out, and finally, who would inherit the farm. Even as Annette Radius inhaled to ask the first of these, Macklin felt himself drawing back. Her mouth full of food, she eyed him in an unfriendly way. He thought it was quite possible to read people's motives in their expressions, and her doughy face was a book not to his liking.

Still, it was Arnold Radius who asked the damning question about inheritance. The matter has passed through Macklin's mind on occasion, but he had no idea who would inherit Red Road Farm, and said as much. Mrs. Radius tried to put it another way: "Does he have any other descendants besides you?" To that he snapped, "I'll be sure to relay your inquiry to my uncle the next time I talk to him."

Husband and wife traded a glance. With a swift goodbye, Macklin was up and out the back door. From there he cut across the cemetery, ducked between fence railings, and hurried home. He had on his good shoes and regretted that they were getting soaked with snow. Back in his room, with his shoes off and a drink by his side, he wrote in his journal:

I have developed a craving for ginger ale, just as Chippers has. Tomorrow I will buy more when I go to pick up the hams. I'll try to forget all about Arnold and Annette Radius, and hope that God was listening to my prayers in church. Chippers is looking and acting more like himself today, so maybe good things are happening already.

His words ran over onto the last page of his leather-bound notebook. He had filled several since moving to Rapidan. It pleased him to have a record of his thoughts, and he carefully stored the filled-up journals in his desk, safe from any prying eyes.

The next day got off to a fine start. Chippers came downstairs and was able to eat a normal breakfast. He looked thin and pale, but his eyes had some of their old luster, and he wanted to talk about the party. He approved heartily of the red front door and the wreath and said that the only thing missing was a Christmas tree.

In the field behind the house, they found a nice tall cedar, and after some diligent sawing, got it down and dragged it back to the house. Macklin was finally able to tell the whole story of Regina's mutiny and absence. Barely allowing Chippers to respond, he said he was off to Orange that afternoon to pick up a large order from Sparks's Grocery and would go to Culpeper the next day for the biscuits and pies. Even without Regina around, they would have a feast.

The question of where to set up the tree was quickly answered. Chippers said that at the house he grew up in, they always put the tree in the corner by the entrance staircase, and they could do the same thing here. The boxes of old decorations that Macklin had found in the attic came in handy. Climbing the stairs so they could reach the high branches, they covered the tree in delicate little Victorian globes of many colors, metal Santas, clip-on red and gold birds with sparkly feathers, and various hand-sewn quilted ornaments shaped like dogs and cats and angels. Chippers unwrapped a large silver star from its tissue paper and, using pipe cleaners, attached it to the top of the tree. There was some ancient, crinkly tinsel, but Macklin decided against that. The tree did not need one more thing: it was beautiful as it was.

After they finished, Chippers made a quick trip to the kitchen. Declaring that it would keep the limbs from drying out, he poured half a bottle of ginger ale in the pan beneath the tree and drank the remainder in several long gulps. Then he steadied himself and said he had overdone it and was going back to bed.

With a heavy feeling, Macklin watched his friend drag himself upstairs. An hour later, Chippers announced that his fever had returned. "Call my sister," he said. "She'll come down early if you ask her. Remember, she's expecting a baby, and I don't want her getting sick. But she'll help; she's a whiz at giving parties. And Andy—her husband—will help, too." With Macklin hovering in the doorway, he pointed at his address book and then rolled over. He was too sick to talk a minute longer.

Chippers's sister, Julia, answered the phone on the first ring. She had been a nurse before she married and had a nurse's efficient way of asking questions. Based on Macklin's answers, she decided her brother didn't need to go to the hospital but would benefit from a strong cough syrup, which she promised to bring the next morning. Then she asked about the party. Macklin appreciated the fact that she didn't second-guess the decision to hold it in Uncle Minor's absence. The menu sounded good to her, and she offered to bring roasted peanuts and butter mints to round out the refreshments.

On Christmas Eve morning, Macklin left immediately for Orange after barn duties and a quick breakfast. Mr. Sparks helped him load the wonderfully pungent hams into the car, along with another stash of ginger ale. From there he went to the bakery in Culpeper. The girl at the counter had the order ready. When he asked if he could take a peek, she opened up box after box to reveal the still-warm pies: apple, peach, lemon meringue, chocolate meringue, and mincemeat. The fluffy golden biscuits were equally thrilling. With the girl's help, Macklin carried everything to the car. When he told her about the party at Red Road Farm, her face broke into a broad smile. She said she knew Mr. Williams. It turned out Uncle Minor used to stop by her family's bakery every week on his way home from business in Culpeper or points north. He would buy two cream-filled chocolate éclairs, one for his wife and one for himself, and always said they were the tastiest he ever had.

It gave Macklin pause to think of his uncle making such friendly overtures, to say nothing of sinking his sharp teeth into an éclair. The girl asked how Mr. Williams was and then froze as if she were afraid the old gent might be dead. Macklin told her that his uncle was living in Richmond while receiving medical treatment there. She gave him a sympathetic look and said, "My mother and I are going to Richmond this afternoon. Do you think it would be all right if we took him a box of éclairs?" She paused as Macklin's face registered extreme surprise. "We wouldn't stay but a minute. I'd just run up to the door." Her voice trailed off in embarrassment.

"Oh, by all means," Macklin said, recovering. "I'm sure he'd be delighted to see you. He's staying with Furman Shafer, an old friend, and his wife Betty."

"Oh, we know them," the girl said, her confidence restored. "They're on Kensington Avenue, aren't they?"

Macklin nodded and smiled uncomfortably as a whole new problem unfolded. He could hardly say, "Please, I beg of you, don't tell Uncle about the party!" or "If you promise not to visit him, I'll buy all the éclairs you have in this place!" He made a quick exit and drove off in the car laden with party food. There was no point in worrying about Uncle Minor, though of course now he was worried.

The day was not half over and there were adventures still to come. When he got back to the farm, he saw an unfamiliar car in the driveway. He had barely emerged when Chippers's brother-in-law came running out to help him unload the car. Andy Mallory was an affable fellow, a Washington and Lee graduate, with red hair and wind-chapped cheeks.

Macklin walked inside and set several of the baker's boxes on the table by the Christmas tree. Julia, a pinafore apron covering her little round belly, came hurrying around the corner from the kitchen. She met him with a hug and then stood back so she could look at him. She was a raven-haired young matron, taller than her husband, with a creamy complexion and preternaturally sharp gaze. "So this is the famous Macklin. How grateful we are that you've given my brother a job and a place to live as well as your friendship." She beamed at him and in her wide smile he could see the resemblance to her brother. He was just relaxing into the role of benefactor when she briskly told him to take a tray to Chippers and then report back for instructions on how to set up the ballroom.

She didn't like Macklin's plans for arranging the food and drink. Under the new regime, the ham biscuits were to be made ahead of time, and Macklin would take a tray of them around to groups of guests. Andy was in charge of the bar. She set about re-polishing the silver that Macklin had polished the week before.

In the afternoon she dispatched him to the garden to clip small branches from the magnolia trees. These she used to decorate the mantelpieces. After doing this, she sent him back outside for holly. When he returned, she and Andy had just finished covering the tree in tinsel; he saw that they had brought their own supply. "A Christmas tree can never have too much tinsel," she said with a flash of the familiar Hebblethwaite smile. *Au contraire*, Macklin thought, looking up at the silvery tree.

Andy stooped down beside it and suddenly it lit up with bright lights. Julia clapped her hands in childlike delight and gave her husband a kiss on the cheek. She turned to Macklin and said, "We found the lights on the third floor. I knew you'd have them somewhere."

He took his load of holly into the kitchen, plopped it on the table, and headed straight out the back door and to the barn, where he knew no one would follow him. He felt like crying out, after Regina's fashion, "You can have your party, Julia Mallory, but it won't be on *my* back!"

Chippers continued to sleep. His snoring sounded pathetically labored. He woke up to accept food and drink and then left his tray on the floor outside his room, as if he were in a hotel. He insisted he would be fine in time for the party, and Julia said she thought so, too. Macklin was not so sure.

Late that afternoon, Julia summoned Macklin downstairs to take a telephone call. The caller was none other than Furman Shafer, who said that the baker's daughter from Culpeper had been by that afternoon and let slip that Macklin was hosting a party at Red Road Farm. To that he could only gulp and reply, "Guilty as charged, sir." Mr. Shafer chuckled in a way that suggested a complete lack of amusement and said that he and his wife and Uncle Minor all planned to attend and stay over for the night, and would Macklin be good enough to inform him what time they should arrive? He was tempted to say some late hour, well after the party has ended, but with Julia hovering nearby, he was compelled to tell the truth.

After he rang off, he turned to his eavesdropper and said with false gaiety, "Well, excellent news. Uncle Minor and his friends will be here for the party!"

Julia shot him one of her penetrating looks. "I know. Mr. Shafer told me, but I thought you would want to talk to him. I'm glad to know your uncle is well enough to make the trip home. You must have missed him all these months that he's been away."

Uncle Minor's absence had not made Macklin's heart grow fonder. The old man was a sort of apparition in his mind, a specter that imbued his life with status and meaning on the one hand and aggravation and anxiety on the other. To Julia he said, "I'm sure he'll enjoy meeting you," and bowed out of the room with a good night to her and her husband, who was pretending to read a book while sunk deep in the poodle-scented horsehair sofa.

4

On Christmas morning, everyone except for Chippers was up early. After exchanging perfunctory Christmas greetings, they began flying past one another with arms full of platters and cutlery and glassware. Julia assigned her husband to carve the hams so she could put the ham biscuits together. She ordered Macklin to set up the bar, and then, when it was not to her liking, took Andy off ham duty and told him to take over. She didn't like the whiskey decanters Macklin had chosen and said the ginger ale should be kept in the icebox until five minutes before four o'clock. She said the drinks should be served with cloth cocktail napkins (she had found a box of them in the linen closet), not paper ones. The tablecloth Macklin had wanted to use for the bar was wrinkled and too short.

Andy offered a fraternal wink when Julia told Macklin, in her measured and melodious voice, to go fetch the coasters she had washed last night. He appreciated Andy's tacit acknowledgment of her tyranny, but that didn't make it any easier to follow her orders. She was just impossible. For lunch, he took two ham biscuits and a handful of peanuts to his room so he could eat alone and in peace. As he climbed the stairs, he heard Julia exclaim, "He's going to eat all the food before the party even starts!"

In the midst of all this, Macklin had lost track of Chippers. Around three o'clock he heard his ailing friend call his name. Chippers sat hunched over on the side of his bed. Red-faced, in pajamas, with his hair sticking up, he looked up at Macklin imploringly.

"I'm going to rally, Macklin. After a bath and a shave, I'll be in good shape—I know I will." He rose unsteadily to his feet and began trudging toward the bathroom. "A bath will work wonders," he muttered over his shoulder, as if Macklin had suggested otherwise, and shut the door behind him. As Macklin turned to leave, however, Chippers called out suddenly, "Could I borrow a tie? Just leave it on my bed, if you don't mind."

Macklin returned to his room and swung open his closet door knowing he would find exactly two neckties besides the one he was wearing. One was a red and gold tie, an early gift from Alice. The other was the blue silk he had bought at Merton's. He was wearing the other Merton's tie, the expensive blue and gold one he reserved for special occasions. There was, he knew, an egg stain on the blue silk. With a sigh he took off the blue and gold, and swung the red and gold around his neck. Chippers could wear the Merton's tie in honor of Edith and Little Merle Merton, and he would wear the other. *Thanks, Alice*, he murmured to himself.

By 3:57 Macklin thought he would pass out from anxiety. It was a brisk, bright day, and the house was gleaming in readiness. Julia had thoroughly polished all the mirrors and tables early that morning, lit the Christmas tree, and directed him to turn on every lamp in the house. He could find nothing else to do after scurrying to get the ginger ale from the icebox.

At 3:58 he heard a car rumbling up the driveway, with another close behind it. He and Julia froze in place and exchanged a frightened look. Then her mask slid back into place and she smiled radiantly. "Here we go," she said and began gliding toward the front door.

To his relief, the first guests were Dudley and Poppy. Dudley was carrying his fraternity's portable record player and Poppy clutched a stack of records to her chest. This was the one remaining piece of Sorbon's party plan—the plan Macklin had tried to follow to the letter until Julia intervened—and he was pleased that Dudley had come through for him. After Andy took their coats, Julia gave the well-dressed and smiling couple a quick once-over. Knowing his job without being told, Andy took the record player and led the way across the house and down the steps to the ballroom. Soon the sound of Benny Goodman's clarinet filled the air.

Right behind Dudley and Poppy came Henry Richards, the University's number-one tennis player. He was of medium build, with broad shoulders, a noncommittal handshake, and an extraordinarily aristocratic bearing. Chippers had been very excited when Henry accepted the invitation. Apparently the number-one player didn't go to just anyone's party.

To Macklin's surprise, Henry had brought along his grandmother, a tiny old lady who was not even five feet tall. Her hair was very fluffy and very white. She had an elfin face, bright red lips, and a handshake much firmer and friendlier than her grandson's. She assumed that Macklin was Chippers, and when he tried to correct her, it became obvious she was deaf.

Smiling up at him, she proffered a round tin. "Merry Christmas, Chippers! I made you some chocolate drops."

Macklin peered inside the tin. There, indeed, were the chocolates, two generous layers of them. The proud candy maker urged him to try one. "You need to keep your strength up when you give a party. Have one now and save the rest for later, after the guests leave."

Here, to his glad amazement, was a new friend who seemed to like and understand him even if she had no idea who he was and couldn't hear a word he said. Macklin popped a chocolate drop in his mouth. It was as delicious as it looked and the little lady could read the pleasure on his face. Then Andy reappeared and whisked her and the tennis ace down to the ballroom.

The pattern continued like this, with Julia and Macklin greeting the guests and Andy taking over from there. After a while, people were arriving so steadily that Andy remained below to tend the bar. When the coat rack could hold no more garments, Julia began dispatching Macklin upstairs with armloads of overcoats and mufflers and mink jackets. On one of these trips he nearly sideswiped Chippers, who was looking very presentable in suit and Merton's tie. Clutching the banister, he was still shaky on his feet.

"She's not here yet," Macklin said in answer to the question in his friend's eyes. "Don't breathe on anyone and try not to shake any hands. I don't want people saying they caught the flu at our party."

Chippers took the warning without offense. "I'll just have a drink in each hand at all times," he said, and continued unsteadily down the stairs.

By now everyone was down in the ballroom, and Macklin had met the entire tennis team and all of their assorted girlfriends and family members. Chippers's teammates were a cheerful bunch, peppy and gregarious, quick to eat a ham biscuit and quicker still to quaff a drink. The coach, Ronald Morrison, looked to be about thirty-five. All smiles and manly dimples, he proudly introduced his wife, a shy mouse named Mathilda, and their twin sons—four-year-old redheads who went tearing across the ballroom and dived under the dining room table. Julia shot Mathilda a look that sent her flying after them.

Julia seemed to control everyone within range of her electric gaze. After a couple of drinks, Macklin began to enjoy her company. She had apparently forgotten her desire to have him circulate with tray in hand like a waiter, and he was flattered that she seemed to view him as an ally now that the party was underway. But of course, it was his party to begin with. While she nibbled a biscuit and he sampled the pumpkin pie, they stood together as people formed small groups in various parts of the room. She asked him if Poppy was one of the Popkins of Richmond, and he said he didn't know. She furrowed her lovely brow, still trying to place this particular Popkin. Macklin turned his attention to Chippers, who had settled in a wing chair by the sideboard. His teammates stood around him talking with great animation. Every few minutes they tossed their heads back and laughed uproariously.

On a sofa near the middle set of the French doors leading out to the patio, three middle-aged women sat chatting and daintily devouring their slices of chocolate meringue pie. They were mothers of tennis players: Mrs. Kennedy, Mrs. Wiley, and Mrs. Darling. Macklin was especially pleased with Mrs. Darling, a little countrywoman with gentle eyes and flyaway curls, who regarded him with the same warmth that Grandmother Richards had shown. Unlike the diminutive candy-maker, however, Mrs. Darling was able to distinguish between him and Chippers. She had grown up at Batton, a farm halfway between Orange and Rapidan, where her father was the farm manager. She knew all about the wonderful horses of Red Road Farm. When Macklin told her the farm had nine horses, several of them former racehorses, her eyes shined with pleasure. It was all he could do not to reach out and kiss her hand.

Her son, Hubert Darling, was less prepossessing. Stocky, with a space between his front teeth, he had a way of popping up suddenly to ask for things he couldn't possibly need, like a butter knife or lemon wedge. When Macklin turned on his heel for the kitchen, resigned to helping him, he would wave his hands and say, "Oh, don't go to any trouble. I'm fine, I'm fine!" and skitter back to the table for more food. Macklin could well imagine him winning tennis matches simply by annoying his opponents to distraction.

A handful of the tennis players had found their way to the sunroom with their girlfriends close beside them. Standing among the potted plants, the girls looked lovely in their fancy dresses, yet the boys, shuffling their feet, seemed to be talking mostly to one another. They soon broke into two groups, the boys at one end of the room and the girls at the other end. Macklin shook his head at the foolishness of it all.

A few of the tennis players had brought impressive entourages—their parents, younger brothers and sisters, and the odd grandparent or two. These auxiliary guests wandered about, liberally sampling the refreshments and then returning to their inner circles. After a while, the tennis player siblings decided to join forces. A boy who looked about eleven came over and shyly asked whether it was all right if he and several others played in the front yard, and Macklin gave permission with a benevolent smile. He thought it was better to get the children outside before their good manners gave way to boredom and boredom's sidekick, mischief. Before too long, four boys and a couple of girls were frolicking in the snow and tossing around a football.

Near the fireplace stood several distinguished-looking fathers of tennis players: Mr. Raney, Dr. Prince, and Mr. Wiley. Macklin imagined they were discussing matters of great import—politics, the draft, the war in Europe. When Mr. Wiley shifted to one side, he saw that Dudley was also part of this group. Dudley was dressed the same as the older men, in a subdued but expensive looking suit, and he had a very precise haircut. From across the room Macklin could see that when he spoke, the others all turned and listened attentively.

The scene raised the gooseflesh on Macklin's arms. He had an intuition that Dudley would be very important one day and that he had witnessed the beginning of his friend's career as a statesman. He had never thought of himself as prescient, but in that moment he could see an aura around Dudley's neatly clipped brown hair. Senator? Ambassador? He turned away so Dudley wouldn't catch him staring.

Soon Julia left his side for Poppy, who was gazing at an oil painting above the sideboard. She seemed to find it fascinating or else looking at it was just a way to occupy her time while Dudley mingled with his future constituency. When Julia touched her on the elbow, she turned around with a glad smile. The two of them launched into what Macklin suspected was a mutually pleasing conversation about their respective ancestries.

Somehow he heard the telephone ring above the din of the guests and the record player, which was now playing Louis Armstrong. He hurried up the dining room steps, across the first floor, and into Uncle Minor's sitting room. A high-pitched voice answered his greeting: "Hello, may I speak to Chipperth?"

He knew who it was but decided formality was in order. "This is Macklin Williams speaking, and Chippers Hebblethwaite is busy right now with guests. May I tell him who's calling?"

A nervous giggle. "This is Edith Langborne, Macklin. Merry Christmas!"

"Merry Christmas to you, Edith."

"I'm so sorry, but Merle and I can't make it to your party after all." There was a pause, and then he heard an intake of breath. "We just got engaged, Macklin! Merle asked me to marry him. It happened this afternoon. The engagement ring was my Christmas present."

"Wonderful."

"We're at his parents' house in Orange and all his relatives are here. It wouldn't—it just wouldn't be appropriate if we left and came to your party right now."

Her lisp had vanished, except for "Chipperth"—perhaps she thought that really was his name—and she sounded newly matured, as if her betrothal to Merle had transformed her.

"I understand completely, Edith. I'll tell Chippers that you send your regrets."

"I had wanted to come— "

"No need to say another word. Congratulations to you and Merle. I'm sure Chippers will be delighted for you."

After setting down the phone he heard Andy calling for him. The front door was wide open and Andy looked wild-eyed. "Your uncle is here and we can't get him up the steps." He beckoned for Macklin to hurry.

A dyspeptic octogenarian was pacing on the porch. "Macklin, I'm your uncle's best friend. My name's Furman Shafer and this is Betty!" He stuck out a hand for Macklin to shake, and his wife opened and shut her mouth, as if that were greeting enough.

Mr. Shafer continued in his exclamatory way, "Macklin, we got a problem on our hands! Your uncle uses a wheelchair now. He can still walk a little bit, but we forgot his cane. How're we going to get him up all these steps!"

Andy was standing nearby, nibbling the cuticle on his thumb.

Macklin laced his fingers together, cocked his head to one side, and pretended to assess the situation. He had no idea what to do. The Shafer vehicle was parked under the carport beside the house. With his face pressed close to the glass, Uncle Minor scowled up at everyone from the car. The side steps were steep and narrow, and the wrought-iron railing was wobbly. The front steps couldn't be reached without a difficult slog through mud and snow.

Suddenly Dudley appeared. "Here's what we'll do," he said in a decisive voice. "Andy, how about if you and one of those boys bring the wheelchair up on the porch, and Macklin and I will take care of Mr. Williams."

A flicker of resentment crossed Andy's face, but he had no better ideas. Calling out to the tallest boy playing in the snow, he went to the Shafer car where a wheelchair protruded from the trunk. Macklin watched while they carefully lifted it out and carried it up to the porch. Only then did Dudley beckon for Macklin to come over to the car.

Dudley opened the door and introduced himself to Uncle Minor, who looked noticeably frailer than the last time Macklin had seen him and only nodded a greeting.

"All right, Macklin," Dudley said, "grab my right wrist with your left hand and grab your left wrist with your right hand. And I'll do the same thing in reverse. We'll make a seat for your uncle to sit on."

Uncle Minor shifted his bottom toward them and slung one arm around Macklin's shoulders and the other around Dudley's. Dressed in a sweater and wool shawl, he was less formally attired than Macklin was used to seeing him. He had become an invalid and looked the part. Macklin sagged under the bony weight of the old man's long body. When they got him safely on the porch, he and Dudley eased him into the waiting wheelchair. Then the chair wheels stuck on the doorsill, so they had to lift him up and get Andy to move the chair inside.

By now Julia had joined them. "We'll just move the party up here," she whispered to Macklin after a quick glance at Uncle

Minor. Soon, Andy hurried in with a tray full of food and drink. Behind him came Julia and a straggling parade of partygoers. As she and Macklin tried to introduce everyone to the patriarch, the tennis contingent suddenly began preparing to leave. It was as if Uncle Minor's arrival had rung a bell signaling the end of the party. Macklin ran upstairs for their coats.

In the space of half an hour, practically everybody departed amid a flurry of Merry Christmases and Happy New Years. Poppy and Dudley were the last to leave in the darkness of Christmas night, Dudley carrying the record player and Poppy the records, just as they had when they arrived.

After Macklin had closed the door behind them, he heard Dudley greeting people on the front porch. He figured someone had forgotten a hat or scarf, but when he opened the door, there stood a handsome middle-aged couple flanked by none other than Arnold and Annette Radius, his tormentors from the church luncheon. They stood back a step while the unknown couple came inside.

The question of their identity was quickly answered when Julia welcomed them in. "Mother! Dad!" she cried and embraced them one after the other. "I thought you weren't coming."

"Oh, we wouldn't have missed it, honey," said Mr. Hebblethwaite, looking around the room. "This must be Macklin. My apologies for our abominable lateness, young man. We ran out of gas down the road a ways, and these good folks stopped and helped us out. Took us to their home, then back to the car with some gas, and then led us straight to Red Road Farm so we wouldn't get lost." He gestured to Mr. and Mrs. Radius, who by now had edged inside the house and were looking all around. "They say they know you from church."

Suddenly Uncle Minor raised himself up from his wheelchair. He was scowling at Arnold Radius, muttering in his direction, and then, to Macklin's astonishment, feebly rising and shaking his fist. This last effort caused him to fall back in his chair with a thud. During this display, Radius's piggish mouth formed a small, wet smile. His eyes never left Minor's. Macklin felt the hair stand up on the back of his neck.

It was then that Mrs. Hebblethwaite forever endeared herself to him. Tall and statuesque like her daughter, she has shoulder-length hair and warm brown eyes. She and her husband both smelled of gasoline, an unprepossessing scent, especially for party guests. Moving slowly and deliberately, she handed her coat to her daughter and revealed a lovely if old-fashioned red wool suit beneath. Stepping in front of the enemy to block him from Uncle's line of vision, she said, "Thank you so much for helping us find our way here. Let's see if Julia"—she turned a meaningful look on both Julia and Macklin—"will fix you a plate of food as a small show of our gratitude. We won't keep you an extra minute."

Julia disappeared into the kitchen and returned with the round tin that Grandmother Richards had given Macklin. He almost cried out, "Don't you dare give them my chocolate drops," before he saw that the tin had found a new service. It was so crammed with ham biscuits that Julia couldn't shut the lid. She thrust the offering into Mrs. Radius's greedy hands.

With one hand on the evil one's back and the other on Annette Radius's elbow, Macklin propelled the couple out the door. "Merry Christmas!" Julia called out before shutting the door firmly. Macklin turned the bolt lock. In the split second that followed, he and Julia traded a look that said, "Job well done." He was really starting to like her.

By now Chippers, who had changed into casual clothes and was oblivious to recent events, had joined the group. He greeted his mother, who clucked worriedly over his health, and his father, who drew him close. There were hugs all around. If his parents were concerned about catching the flu from him, they didn't act like it.

After the Radiuses took their leave, Julia conferred with her mother. They decided a light supper was in order. After that the whole Hebblethwaite family would go home to Winchester. There seemed to be a wordless agreement that no one would mention

Uncle Minor's reaction to Arnold Radius—it was as if the rising and the muttering and the shaking of the fist had simply not happened.

Uncle Minor and the Shafers were settled in the living room with drinks and snacks. How the Shafers could find anything to talk about with Minor after so many months of tending to him, Macklin didn't know. This was not a group he wanted to join, so he slipped away to find Chippers.

Chippers was tossing clothes into his duffel bag. "I can't believe she didn't come," he said as soon as he saw Macklin in the doorway. With his parents he had put on a brave face, but now, with Macklin, his guard was down. "I painted the whole house, I planned this party, and all my friends and my family were here, and she didn't even bother to come. She didn't even call." He slammed his fist against the bed.

Macklin sat down in a chair and watched him gather up books and notebooks and toiletries. He could feel the anger rising in him. "It was not just your party, Chippers, and this is not just about you," he said levelly. "This is my family home, and I paid for every slice of ham, every swallow of ginger ale, every ounce of whiskey. And for the past couple of days, your pregnant sister and your saintly brother-in-law and I have worked ourselves silly making sure the party goes well. Yes, you've been ill and we're all sorry about that, but a little gratitude would be nice. And for the record, you didn't paint the whole house. You painted three sides. And I painted the front door."

Chippers sat down heavily and bowed his head. When he looked up, his cheeks were blooming with yet another fever. "You should've used black paint."

"Well, all I could find was the red, and the door looks wonderful. You said so yourself."

"I changed my mind about that." He dropped a tennis ball in his duffel bag and then wiped away the sweat beading on his upper lip.

"Chippers, there's something I have to tell you. Edith

telephoned near the end of the party, right before my uncle got here and everybody else started leaving." Macklin saw the startled look of accusation forming on Chippers's face. "Hold on a minute. You'll be glad I didn't call you to the phone when you hear her message."

Sitting on the bed with his hands on his knees, Chippers listened stoically to the news. "I see," he said when Macklin finished. "Well, his family must have a lot of money, and I know that's important to her." He began distractedly pulling items from his bag, inspecting them, and stuffing them back inside. Then he stopped and glared at Macklin. "You really should have let me talk to her. I shouldn't have to hear this from you."

Macklin was so angry that he stood up to leave. He took a breath and continued in the level voice that hardly sounded like his own, "There was no time. I was the one who answered the phone, you were down in the dining room surrounded by your friends, and she just burst out with it. If she'd wanted to tell you directly, she could have done so."

Chippers didn't try to detain him when he left. In the kitchen he came upon Andy scrambling eggs with bits of ham while Julia sliced some cheese. She told Macklin to find a plate for the cranberry walnut bread that Mrs. Darling had brought. In a few minutes everyone was seated at the table in the family dining room, a much cozier place than the cavernous ballroom. Uncle Minor was at the head of the table, Mrs. Hebblethwaite was at the other end, and Julia, Andy, Chippers, the Shafers, Mr. Hebblethwaite, and Macklin filled up the sides. No one besides Macklin seemed to notice that Chippers said not a word. Uncle Minor, equally silent, ate hungrily. The Shafers and Mr. Hebblethwaite concentrated on their whiskey.

The meal was brief. Macklin offered pie for dessert, but there were no takers. The visitors from Winchester cleared the table and prepared to leave in their two cars. After Macklin said goodbye to the parents and to Andy and Julia (who gave him a firm, sisterly hug), those four headed outside while Chippers lagged behind.

On the front porch he told Macklin he would not be coming back to Red Road Farm in January. One of Dudley's fraternity brothers had enlisted in the army and said Chippers could have his room at the Chi Phi house free of charge. Though not a dues-paying member, Chippers was friends with many of the brothers, thanks to Dudley. He had saved the money he earned at the farm and it would cover, he hoped, his tuition and books for the coming term.

Macklin had a strange feeling in his stomach and throat as Chippers chattered on. He felt a little sick and like he might cry, a terrible combination. It had been such a long day. When Chippers finally stopped talking, Macklin told him he understood. He wished him all the best with his tennis season and said he would try to catch a match or two. This last seemed to catch Chippers by surprise, though Macklin hadn't meant it as a reproach, and he saw a flicker of the old friend whom he had suffered gladly, for the most part, for so many months. Chippers hoisted his bag on his shoulder and scooped up his racquet. "Tell Sorbon I'll be in touch. I think I can convince Mr. Altschuler to represent him. I'll certainly try."

Macklin followed him outside where they paused to look at the red door and the lopsided wreath, both shining under the porch light. "You missed a spot," Chippers said, jerking his head toward a tiny black patch at the top, and then laughed weakly. His own pettiness had finally embarrassed him. "I'm sorry, Macklin, for the things I said earlier. I feel terrible about losing Edith, but that's no excuse." He paused to wipe his nose with his sleeve. "Thanks for letting me live here—and thanks for hosting the party. It was great."

He picked up his bag and trudged off to his parents' car, which was idling in the driveway. Macklin called out a bleak Merry Christmas before going inside to deal with his uncle and the Shafers. His day was not over yet.

5

Uncle Minor was nowhere in sight. Furman Shafer beckoned to Macklin to join him in the living room, where he sat with a half-empty highball glass and a bowl of mints. He explained that his wife had found blankets and pillows in the linen closet and made a bed for Minor on the sofa. Macklin could hear snoring—a high-pitched whinnying sound—emanating from behind the closed door to the sitting room.

He sat down in an armchair and looked at Furman Shafer, a lean, nervous fellow, nearly bald, with strands of silver and brown hair arranged on the top of his head. The man wore rimless spectacles that sat low on his nose and flexed his fingers while he talked. Pointing toward the sitting room where Uncle Minor slept, he spoke in a quiet voice that didn't seem to come naturally to him.

"Your great uncle has been my closest friend for over sixty years, and he was best man at my wedding," he began. "He's too modest to talk about it, but every chance I get, I tell people how Minor Williams saved my life when I was eighteen."

His eyes shining, Furman Shafer told Macklin that Minor had invited him home to Rapidan during their first year at the University, back in 1874. At that time, Red Road Farm didn't yet exist and Minor and his family lived next door, at the farm closest to the Rapidan River. The two new friends went fishing in the Rapidan River and decided to take a quick swim at the end of the day. Furman was not a strong swimmer, but true to his careless nature at the time, he thought nothing of stripping off his shirt and shoes and hopping out of the boat and into the water.

He and Minor swam off in opposite directions. "Before I knew it," Furman said, "I got caught in a current and was sliding down river at a good clip. I was flailing about and fighting the current, which only made things worse." Unable to stay afloat, he yelled for Minor. Just when he thought he was a goner, Minor swam up, grabbed him by the hair, and pulled him to safety.

Furman had coughed up a large quantity of water on the riverbank and then lay on the ground with Minor sitting beside him. All of a sudden, Minor burst out laughing. Furman sat up and saw their boat float by and disappear around a bend in the river. "Oh, someone will find it when it runs aground," Minor had said in reply to Furman's groan of dismay. "Don't worry about that old boat." Sure enough, they got the boat back before the weekend was over.

"And you know what I did, soon's I got back to University?" Furman asked, his eyes fixed on Macklin, who shook his head. "I signed up for swimming lessons! The instructor took a group of us boys out to the lake every day and taught us everything—crawl, backstroke, butterfly, breast, sidestroke." He paused. "My favorite was the sidestroke, still is. I like a clean, quiet stroke where I can keep my eyes out of the water."

He picked up his highball glass, peered into it, then set it down and looked at Macklin again. "You know how to swim?"

"I can dog-paddle."

"You go back to University and sign up for swimming lessons, young man."

"Yes, sir."

He picked up his glass and finished off his watery drink in a single swallow. "And you know what I did soon's I got my law practice going, and I had enough money to afford it?" Again Macklin shook my head. "I joined the Country Club of Virginia. I told myself, 'Furman, you swim every chance you get.' And I made sure my children learned soon's they could walk. We're all swimmers, even Betty. My son Thomas is the swimming coach at Clemson, and my grandson Bobby is a lifeguard in Atlantic City.

He saved a hundred lives last summer—pulling poor devils out of the ocean left and right!"

A vein bulged on his forehead as he talked. It seemed that his near drowning in the Rapidan had set the course of his life and shaped the whole family dynasty. Macklin smiled encouragingly. "A whole family of swimmers—wonderful."

"Well, you should learn how to swim, young man." He squinted at Macklin.

"I will, sir. I just haven't gotten around to it yet."

"Well, get around to it." As Macklin squirmed, Mr. Shafer suddenly changed the subject. "Much as we love him, Betty and I can't take care of your uncle much longer."

Macklin jerked to attention. "Is he coming home to Red Road?"

Mr. Shafer shook his head wearily. "He would very much like to, and he insists that he can and will, but I just don't see how. The doctors aren't very good around here," he said bluntly, "and this house"—he gestured to the large room they sat in—"has all sorts of impediments to a wheelchair, including that staircase leading up to his bedroom."

These were problems Macklin couldn't solve, and there was something else on his mind. "Mr. Shafer, why doesn't Uncle Minor talk anymore? He said hardly a word at the party and over dinner."

"He's just conserving his strength." Mr. Shafer said, with an edge of defensiveness. "He's not doty, if that's what you mean."

"Doty?"

Mr. Shafer tapped his temple with his forefinger. "You know, senile. He's as sharp as he ever was."

"Well, that's good," Macklin said doubtfully. He plunged on with his questions. "Why did he react the way he did to Arnold Radius? I was afraid he was going to have a heart attack when that fellow walked in."

Mr. Shafer cracked his knuckles and rearranged himself on the sofa. "Radius is your uncle's mortal enemy, Macklin," he said.

"They feuded over a right-of-way issue a long time ago when Minor's son Thatcher—your father's uncle—died in Oklahoma. Minor, you see, was planning to leave Thatcher a parcel of prime farmland behind Red Road Farm. He was waiting until his son made something of himself and could handle farm management. But Thatcher couldn't keep his attention on anything for very long," Mr. Shafer paused, eyeing Macklin significantly. "He flunked out of University and moved from city to city, scheme to scheme, and woman to woman. He didn't deserve that land. He would've been better off staying home and listening to his dad."

Macklin nodded uneasily. He wondered how much Furman Shafer knew about his own situation.

"So," Furman continued, "after Thatcher died, Minor decided to sell seven acres in the very back to a family that would rent an adjacent parcel of land and graze cattle on it. They wanted a stake of their own, and your uncle didn't see any harm in it. The problem was, those seven acres stuck off the back like a boot on a big fat leg. The Radius property has a narrow strip of land running all the way across the boot. It was never a problem before, because no one was farming those seven acres or living back there. But with the Teagles buying the land, building a house and all that—that caught Arnold Radius's eye.

"Do you know why he despises your uncle? No? Well, it's because Minor's never given that little smudge of manure the time of day. So when Radius had a chance to deny the Teagles access to the land they expected to farm *and* the dirt road that leads out to Old Rapidan Road, he must've been thrilled. It was a legitimate way to mess with your uncle.

"The Teagles sued Minor for selling them a piece of land they couldn't get to without Radius firing his shotgun and calling the sheriff on them for trespassing. The case dragged on for years, and finally ended up in the Supreme Court of Virginia. The whole thing caused your uncle no end of worry, even though I was his attorney and promised him everything would turn out all right. In the end, Minor won because an old survey showed an easement across that little strip—a spite strip, is what surveyors call it—and that meant the Teagles had the access they needed and your uncle was within his rights to sell them the land.

"After that, Radius left the Teagles alone, but he went after Minor every chance he got. He hunted on Red Road without Minor's permission; he tried to slander your uncle's good name; and when he had a chance to become an elder in the church your ancestors built"—here Mr. Shafer swung his head in the direction of Purcell Presbyterian Church—"he jumped on it. Who knows what he's told that preacher about Minor, one of the kindest men who ever walked the face of the earth!"

That last was high praise indeed, and in Macklin's experience, a bit of a stretch. But Furman had his life, and a whole family of swimmers, to show for Minor's good offices, so he supposed the man could be excused for his hyperbole. And Arnold Radius made Macklin's flesh crawl—he understood his uncle's and Mr. Shafer's aversion to him.

"Well," Macklin said, "I don't think he's poisoned Uncle's name at the church. The minister and the others were all friendly and nice to me."

Mr. Shafer shot him a dark look. "Just be careful with that crowd," he said.

At that moment they heard a scuffing sound on the staircase. Betty Shafer, in fuzzy red robe and slippers, came into view on the landing. Squinting at her husband, she called out in a stage whisper: "Furman! *Fur.*"

"What is it, Betty?"

"It's time for bed, Fur. Come on up here and get some rest. It's after ten o'clock."

Macklin knew his time with this fount of knowledge was running out and he still had important questions to ask. "Mr. Shafer, what about me?" he said. "Does my uncle ever talk about me? When I came here, I thought that if I took care of the horses, he'd pay my bills, and then he said I had to paint the house"—he paused for a gulp of air— "and now I don't have a dime to my name, and I owe Sorbon for advances he gave me from the farm account."

Mr. Shafer froze while his wife remained on the steps near the Christmas tree. "Sorbon gave you advances from the farm account?" he parroted in slow and incredulous tones, as if Macklin had confessed to firing a load of buckshot into President Roosevelt.

Macklin's heart began to race. "No, I meant he paid me from the farm account for the work I did painting the house. The only advance I got is for the party food. I'll work that off this spring, by cleaning out the fish pond and—." There was no point in going on. He knew a lost cause when he heard one coming out of his own mouth.

Mr. Shafer placed his hands on his knees and stood up stiffly. He glared at Macklin before stepping away. "Betty's right. It's time for bed. We'll get this settled in the morning."

After he heard the guest room door shut behind the Shafers, Macklin laid his head on the armchair and closed his eyes. The sounds of the party and its endless aftermath reverberated in his brain. He craved a glass of water, but he was too tired to move. The room had cooled off considerably by now, and he felt a chill creep over his body. He feared he was coming down with the same thing Chippers had.

A jarring sound jolted him out of his woozy exhaustion. Behind the sitting-room door, the phone cried out for attention. Without thinking, he staggered to his feet and hurried inside, but Uncle Minor was already propped on his elbow with the telephone to his ear.

"Yes, I'll accept the charges," he said. He listened, grunted, and then gave the receiver to Macklin before turning to the wall.

A familiar, husky female voice greeted him. "Hey, sweetheart. Is it too late to say Merry Christmas?"

It was Alice, and she wanted to chat and flirt. Macklin was sure she was drunk. With Uncle Minor in the room, there was little he could do but listen and keep his responses short. Finally, he told her his uncle was trying to sleep and he had to go. She went silent and he knew he had hurt her feelings. After a pause he said, "Well, Happy New Year." She echoed his words sadly and then the line went dead.

A call from Alice! His head ached as he made his way out of the room and wearily climbed the stairs.

The next morning Furman Shafer gave him a stern lecture. Among Macklin's transgressions: not finishing the house-painting project; getting bad grades when Minor expected him to uphold the family honor and do well; worming money out of Sorbon, via the farm account, when he was expected to work in exchange for room and board; and holding a party without Minor's permission. As he listened to this litany, Macklin sat slumped at the kitchen table. His head was pounding, his throat was raw and burning, and it was all he could do not to fall forward onto his plate of dry toast.

Pacing around the kitchen as if he were arguing before judge and jury, Mr. Shafer said he had even more damaging things to discuss. He knew Minor had paid for Macklin's father's funeral and given him a ticket home for the sad occasion. He and Minor, and Betty, were astonished that Macklin had done nothing to help Cousin Ned clean and close up his father's little house. Even worse, they knew Macklin was secretly married and that Alice was languishing in an Oklahoma orphanage. Her recent letter to Minor had been forwarded to the Shafer household in Richmond, and Furman understood that she was waiting for Macklin to send money so she could come to Red Road Farm. Macklin's protracted silence about Alice—a sin of omission, Mr. Shafer called it—indicated that he had failed as a husband and provider.

The truth of his harsh portrait was not to be denied, though it was a caricature in Macklin's estimation. He was surprised only that, given all this anger and mistrust, Furman had spoken so freely the night before. But Furman was a lawyer, garrulous by nature and hungry for an audience, and perhaps all the highballs had mellowed him.

When it came time for Uncle Minor to leave, they were again faced with the problem of the doorway and steps. The only solution was to repeat what Macklin and Dudley had done the day before. They got him to the front door and then stood him up and practically dragged him out to the porch. Macklin propped him up while Mr. Shafer got the chair over the doorsill. They wheeled him to the side of the porch, grasped one another's wrists to make a seat for him and carried him down the steps to the car.

Macklin's heart was thudding—the more so because he was sick—and Mr. Shafer looked dangerously spent as he leaned against the car to catch his breath. He was a swimmer, fit and trim, but still a very old man. His wrist felt thin and bony where Macklin had clasped it when they carried Uncle Minor down the steps. Though Mr. Shafer was hardly a friend, Macklin felt a sudden burst of compassion for him. Panting and seemingly embarrassed by his frailty, the old man turned away from the young man's scrutiny.

After they loaded up the wheelchair, Furman said he would confer with Minor and let Macklin know whether he would be allowed to stay at Red Road Farm. He thought Macklin's prospects were doubtful. On that note, he climbed in his car. Betty and an unsmiling Uncle Minor lifted their hands in farewell as the car trundled off.

The hammer came down just a day later. Furman called from Richmond to say that Macklin could finish out the school year, but after that he would have to live elsewhere and pay his own bills. In the meantime, he was to finish painting the house and complete his other assignments around the property, including the dredging of the fishpond.

To Macklin's surprise, Furman reported that Uncle Minor said there was a chance Macklin could return to Red Road Farm at some later date, perhaps when Minor was living there again. Minor's health would likely preclude that return, Furman said, his voice growing strained, but it was his duty to relay exactly what Minor had said. The slim possibility came with a directive and an implied criticism: "It's never too late to straighten up and fly right. Make your uncle proud." Macklin started to say something, but Furman cut him off: "And while you're at it, learn how to swim!" With that he rang off, and Macklin was left alone with a deep sadness in his heart.

He continued to do his duties, even though he was ill with the flu. The sickness was a strange blessing, because it prevented him from fretting about the future. One evening, a couple of days after the terrible phone call from Furman Shafer, he sat down at his desk and took out his journal. As usual, the words flowed quickly:

It is so cold in the morning that I have to crack the ice in the troughs with a mallet. The sound is explosive and satisfying. And on these frigid nights, the stars are astonishing, so high above Red Road Farm's magnolias and walnut trees, lindens and tulip poplars. I stand with my cap pulled low and my hands on my hips, and stare up at them. The constellations tell ancient stories that intertwine and overlap and leave me shaking my head in wonder. I'm alone here—the only human, that is—and quite sick, yet I feel a kind of otherworldly exultation as I trudge from house to barn and back again. Tonight I found Orion's Belt in a mostly cloudy sky. Would it be strange to say that I feel the very presence, the very essence, of God? But when I look up into the sky, the questions forming on my lips are not worthy, maybe not even in the right language, for the depths of truth hiding behind those stars.

He set down his pen and rubbed his head. The writing had drained him. He knew he needed to conserve his strength. Sorbon and Regina were still away, and there was so much to do. The house needed cleaning after the party and the coal furnace in the basement needed tending. He knew that Chippers would borrow a car and come help if he asked him to, but their friendship was frayed and he would not impose. Somehow he would make it to New Year's Day of 1940.

There were a few blank lines left at the bottom of the last page he had written. Macklin picked up his fountain pen and chewed the end. Then he wrote:

My God, why did I leave Alice behind? What purpose is ever served by running from love?

The words stared up at him. He went in the bathroom and washed his face. When he came back, he shut the journal and stuck it in his desk. It had many more blank pages, but he could add no more to this particular volume. It would be a long time before he started another.

Neighbors

Regina Carleton Carter

They think their world is the world. They think
they own the days and wind and sunlight on maple leaves.
They think they own the night.
Their eyeballs send out long wires with little hooks at the end—
to reel it all back in, to possess and squat on and put their
thumbprints on.

Next to me in bed, Sorbon is blue and yellow and shiny red.
I fall into his smell and we paint the night with our love.
Our squabbles matter not.
Son Daniel's in the white man's navy.
Coming home, he stands up hard and straight,
then his eyes change. He comes back to our arms.

I have made my peace with Rapidan.
I have a son with soft eyes and a husband who smells like purple
and gold.
No wires, no hooks.
We are our own kingdom. Those others are far from our world.
Praise heaven, our world.

Arnold Radius

It was my father found that boat in the mud.
He brung it back, on his back, all the way up Rapidan Road.
"Leave it dar!" was all Minor's daddy said.

Not a word of thanks. Just leave it dar.
All the women on my ma's side cooked and cleaned for them.
For so many years, all those wars, so many lives.

When my ma got sick, they let her go without a word.
Went down to Mine Run and rounded up the local talent.
Them Carletons, they think they white.

But we clung on, outlasted Old Minor.
The son's the same, though, the same clenched fist.
He's a old man now, like to die soon.

Way I tell it, I got the right and he got in my way.
Sometimes I go out to that strip of land and toe it with my boot.
Even the earthworms are mine. Even the toads.

The nephew's not so highinmighty's he thinks he is.
Rough hands, shabby collar—poor relation.
I hear he got kicked out. No wonder. No wonder.

I'm a Christian man with a interest in the unrighteous,
the unjust. Some days the Bible ain't enough.

Lenore Thompson Darling

I like that Williams boy. He loves his family place
the way I love mine.
He's traveled some, has an accent far from Virginia.
But when he spoke of horses, I could see the ancestors
crowding his eyes.
His uncle must be proud—and his parents,
God rest their souls.

I wonder about Hugh, my son: all those summer days
hitting balls against the side of the barn, did he ever imagine
that someday Hawk's Hill would be his, and Chester and I,
just a cloud of seedpods blowing across the family plot?
Did he dream of a farmwife, a yard full of Darlings?

He moves so rapidly through his days, talking,
always talking, tapping his foot, bouncing that ball.
The only time he settles down is when I show him family albums,
then he blinks and yawns, leans back and sleeps.
Chester and I worry about this boy, we worry a lot.

How do I tell him: my beloved son,
none of us has much time, what with old age and a war coming.
Put your racquet down and let me see something else in your eyes
besides reflections of this wintry flower,
my own pure and breaking heart.

Daniel James Carter

When I left, I already knew the agony of the world.
I'd seen the shot-down dreams in my mother's eyes, the blood
stains in my father's oils.
My friends took up their historic places in the alleys of Orange.
The young girls turned white with flour and
shrugged away their smiles.
It was all I could do not to run into the creek bed
and give up my breath to the stars.

No one told me to head for the ocean.
I didn't believe it was any more right for me
than the smell of carrion is right for the dirt road
or the crawl of fungus is right for the leaves.
But it was a reason to get dressed, a reason to go on.

Every night on shipboard, I lie awake listening to my wristwatch
below the waves.
It is a kind of heartbeat, a way to hear or not hear God.

When I come home, Mama breaks out the dandelion wine,
we sit on the stoop,

and I try to read her lips
as her actual words get lost in the roar
of the water, the wind, the sea in my soul.

Faithful Hearts

1

They left the morning after the boys went off to become soldiers. The rain had stopped and the sky, before daybreak, was soft with stars.

After Alice rose in the dark stillness of the new June day, her last at the Tipton Home, she pulled on a pair of white cotton shorts and a sleeveless blue blouse embroidered with seashells. These were her summer clothes, things her aunt said were too casual for a housemother to wear. On her feet went a pair of huaraches, the old sandals she loved. With her flowered nightgown stuffed in her side pocket, she tiptoed down the back stairs, down the hall, and out the side door.

In the short time she took to get ready, the sky had begun to lighten. The apple trees on the hill above the Home were silhouettes in the pearl-gray air. Alice paused just long enough to take them in and notice the drowsy murmur of birds awakening. Then she walked purposely around to the driveway. Anna had loaded up the Packard the night before while the children and Mr. and Mrs. Jenkins were safely asleep. Now Alice saw that Anna's kerchief partially covered her face, and she smiled to think that it was an attempt at a disguise.

As planned, Anna put the car in neutral and together they pushed it down the long driveway toward the road. This way, no one would hear them leave, and they would be long gone before Uncle Dale discovered she had stolen Ross's file. Then they were in the car, Anna was starting the engine, and they were leaving Tipton at last. Anna pulled off her kerchief, and the two talked excitedly and congratulated themselves on their undetected escape.

"Oh, no," Alice said, clasping her hands to her mouth. She tilted back her head and laughed in loud gasps.

"What is it?" Anna cried. "Tell me."

"Did you notice I had something in my pocket? It was my nightgown," She laughed again. "I was in such a hurry that I never put it in the car."

"You dropped it?" Anna filled in. "Oh good lord, you left it in the driveway?"

"Yes!" Alice shouted. "Aunt Muriel will think I ran away naked!" Anna joined in this time, and their twin peals of laughter carried them the next couple of miles.

After a while they settled down and found the calm rhythm they needed for a long car ride. They listened to the radio and chatted about sights along the way. Alice paid little attention to the road signs as they journeyed through Oklahoma. Though it seemed they were going farther north than they needed to, she decided not to comment. She had traveled very little in her life, whereas Anna had been many places and was a confident driver. Much to Anna's credit, she had not thrown a fit when she discovered that Alice had damaged the car. She simply got it repaired the day before they left the Home. With all that in mind, Alice trusted her to get them to Virginia safely and speedily.

Neither of them had been away from the Home for a couple of years, and both were hungry for new sights and experiences. Though they had quit their jobs without notice and only Kathleen O'Shea knew they were leaving and that Alice's mail should be forwarded to Rapidan, Virginia, these matters didn't come up as the blue Packard carried them along the road. On this day, they had an unspoken agreement not to let any regret about their abrupt departure dampen their enthusiasm for the days and weeks ahead.

Yet talk of the future held its own perils. Alice had noticed that Anna, just like Ross, grew impatient whenever she mentioned Macklin's name. Most of the time, it was easier just to keep her own counsel. She would be back with her husband soon enough. Anna would see that he was a good man.

They arrived in Missouri in mid afternoon and found a little restaurant outside Joplin, where they sat in a sunny booth and ate sandwiches and ice cream. The waitress eyed them curiously, as if she couldn't figure out what two young women would be doing traveling on their own. Back on the road, Alice grew sleepy. She propped a pillow against the door and quickly dozed off. When she awoke, Anna had stopped at a filling station. The sun was still shining but the shadows were long. Alice got out and stretched her limbs. She could see Anna inside talking to a man behind a counter and consulting a map. After a few minutes, she came out carrying two condensate-covered bottles and a package of peanut butter crackers. She said rather sulkily to Alice, "If you need to use the bathroom, this is an opportune time. We still have a long way to go."

"Shouldn't we find a place to stop for the night? You must be getting tired."

"You're right about the second part. I took the wrong road about half an hour ago, so now we have to backtrack. But it's too soon to stop. I want to keep going and get closer to Chicago. I got you a drink and a snack, and we'll press on."

"Chicago!" Alice exclaimed. "Who said anything about Chicago? I thought we were driving straight to Virginia."

"Change of plans, my dear. I didn't want to tell you in advance, for fear you'd put up a fuss, but we have to pay my parents a visit. As you know, I just turned twenty-one, and that means I have a trust fund coming my way. I need to go to the bank, sign a few papers, and then we'll be back on the road in a day or two. The last thing I want to do is overstay my welcome with Mummy."

Alice sighed. She had always considered herself the leader in this friendship, but things were looking different now. Without Anna and her car, she would be in Tipton at this very minute, changing sheets or washing windows or baking pies in an overheated kitchen. She reached for the soft drink in her friend's hand and took a few long swallows before handing it back to her. "All right, Anna, when I get back in five minutes you're going to tell me all about this."

Anna talked at length as they continued north to Chicago. Alice had always known her friend's family was affluent, but this was the first she had heard about a trust fund. Anna's wealthy great-grandparents had not been pleased with their son's choice of a wife and decided, spitefully, that a large share of the family fortune would skip two generations before being divided among the biological heirs when they reached adulthood. As fate would have it, Anna was the only child of an only daughter.

"I decided not to complain about being sent to Tipton when my mother turned on me. Why rock the boat?" Anna waved her hand for emphasis. "As soon as I get all the paperwork taken care of, you and I can go wherever we want and do whatever we please. We could move to New York and get an apartment in Greenwich Village, and enroll at NYU. Or Barnard—we'll be able to afford it now." She paused as her bold suggestions hung in the air.

Alice said nothing. She looked out the window as dusk darkened the Missouri plains. Visiting New York had long been a dream of hers, but she had always thought she would go there with Macklin. "Well, we'll see," she said at last. "Have you told your parents we're coming?"

If Alice's noncommittal reply hurt her feelings, Anna didn't say so. "I'll call them tonight." Then both young women fell silent and Alice tried to sleep again, but she was alert and hungry, and no longer at ease with Anna, whose plans were so different from her own.

Outside St. Louis, Anna announced they would be staying in a hotel she remembered from two years ago, when the family chauffeur drove her to Tipton. He had deposited her at the Mirador Hotel while he went off on his own. "When he picked me up the next morning, he smelled *rank*," Anna said with a haughty chuckle. "I rather liked him in spite of that. He drove fast, but I never felt scared. I wonder if he still works for Mummy and

Daddy?"

The Mirador Hotel was lovely. When Alice saw how elegant it was, she reached in the backseat for a raincoat. This was not the sort of place that would appreciate a guest wearing rumpled shorts and sandals. Anna got them a room while she hung back, feeling shy and out of place. In a few minutes they were alone in a spacious room with two large beds. The bellman who helped with their bags had left smiling after Anna tipped him generously. Alice was impressed with her friend's knowledgeable ways.

Anna headed into the bathroom after calling room service and ordering them dinner. When she emerged, freshly showered and with a towel wrapped around her hair, Alice took her turn. She ran a warm bath and lay soaking for a long time. She heard a muffled commotion when the food arrived, and the aroma drifted tantalizingly under the door. Anna called out that, with war rationing in effect, they were lucky to get roast beef, but Alice couldn't rouse herself from the tub even for that.

When she finally came out, wrapped only in a towel, she saw Anna glance up expectantly from the bed where she sat cross-legged reading a book and holding a glass of red wine. She had finished eating and her tray was already gone from the room. Alice's food was covered and waiting on a side table. "You want to borrow a nightgown?" Anna said.

Alice felt Anna's eyes following her across the room. "I'll just wear a shirt or something." She dug into her suitcase and found a long-sleeved blouse, and ducked back into the bathroom to put it on.

"No need for such modesty, you know," Anna sang out, fully revived and cheerful now that she was off the road. "You're not a housemother anymore."

"Don't forget to call your parents," Alice called through the door. "I can get dressed and go down to the lobby if you want some privacy."

"Oh, I'll call them in the morning. I wrote Daddy a week ago that I'd be coming home soon."

Alice came out of the bathroom for the second time and settled down on the other bed with her dinner tray. The meal was cooked just right and she ate ravenously. The wine left her feeling relaxed and dreamy as she toyed with the yellow cake with chocolate icing that Anna had ordered knowing it was Alice's favorite dessert. A couple of bites were enough. All she wanted to do was sleep and forget about the difficulties that had begun to crowd her head. She set the tray on the floor and slipped under the covers. It had been such a long day. Without even a goodnight for Anna, she turned off the light and rolled over on her side.

In the gray light of dawn Alice awoke to soft rustling sounds. She had barely moved since falling asleep and still lay facing the wall. Anna had climbed into bed with her and was drawing close. She could feel the other woman's breasts grazing her back and Anna's breath warm against her neck. Then Anna slid her hand along Alice's side and caressed her bare thigh.

Alice felt she was in a dream. She could not believe her friend was doing these things. She lay still as Anna touched her. Gradually the touching became more insistent. She felt Anna's lips on the nape of her neck and a hand slipping inside her blouse. *This is not supposed to be happening*, Alice told herself, but it was, and it felt good. It had been so long since Macklin had held her and made love to her. For too many nights, she had lain awake craving the pulse and excitement of another strong young body, but she had never imagined that body would be a woman's, let alone Anna's.

She turned slowly toward Anna and let herself be kissed. Anna murmured with delight and unbuttoned Alice's blouse. *Okay, now we've crossed a line*, Alice thought. After a few minutes, they found a rhythm that could not be stopped. Alice was no longer thinking; she was just letting her body fill to the bursting point with pleasure. When the time came for release, she cried out and so did Anna. Then they fell back and lay close, panting and laughing. After a while, Anna turned on her side and threw her arm possessively across Alice's waist. They fell asleep curled together.

In the morning, when the sun was dappling their faces, Anna slipped out of bed and dressed. Drifting in and out of sleep, Alice dimly heard her bustling around the room. Then Anna whispered that she was going out to run some errands. She told Alice to be ready to leave by eleven. As Alice regarded her through half-closed eyes, Anna bent down to kiss her cheek before slipping quietly away.

She got up as soon as Anna left and wandered over to the window. Far below, she saw a man in a hotel uniform flagging down a taxi for Anna. Just as Anna moved toward the curb, she stopped to look up at the hotel as if she knew Alice would be watching. Before stepping into the car, she grinned and raised her hand in a big wave. Alice had never seen her friend looking so happy.

"Well, *that* will never happen again," she murmured to herself as she turned toward the bathroom. It had taken her only a minute to decide she was not "that way," as she put it to herself. Anna would be disappointed, but she would have to understand that Alice was still married to Macklin. A few kisses in the dark of night meant nothing. Not with Macklin waiting in Rapidan.

Her face shining, Anna returned to the room an hour and a half later with several boxes in her arms. She had been to a department store. Two of the boxes contained presents for her parents—a hat for her mother and a crisp striped shirt for her father. The third box, white and beribboned in pink, she set down shyly on Alice's bed. "For you, my dear," she said, her cheeks burning with spots of color.

"Oh," said Alice, hesitant but curious nonetheless. Inside the box she found an exquisite silk negligee. She ran her fingers along the material and felt how slippery and soft it was.

"I thought you'd look pretty in that."

"Thank you."

"You don't like it?"

"It's lovely. It must've been expensive."

"It was." Anna laughed happily. "Well, we should go. You had breakfast, didn't you?"

"No, I—I just stayed in. I ate the rest of my cake."

Anna regarded her curiously and then nodded in understanding. "They just charge it to the room, you know. You don't have to pay the fellow who brings the food."

"I didn't know what to tip him."

"It doesn't matter. A quarter, that's all."

Soon they were back on the road. Anna chattered excitedly about her favorite places in Chicago—a restaurant here, a museum there, the lake. She wanted to show Alice all of these places. Her good mood was finally impossible to resist, and when a song came on the radio that Alice loved—"This Time the Dream's on Me"— they both sang along with it.

It was late when they finally turned onto the wide boulevard leading them to the Boyer home. "You did call them, didn't you?" Alice asked.

"Of course. I called from a pay phone before I came back to our room this morning. Mummy was her usual unreasonable self, but then I called Daddy at work and we had a nice talk. He's glad I'm out of Tipton." She concentrated on the road before resuming. "You'll like my father, but Mummy—well, Mummy is a challenge."

Anna had occasionally alluded to trouble at her finishing school, a scandal of some sort that resulted in her exile to Tipton, but Alice had never heard the particulars. Whenever she asked, Anna just looked down and shook her head. Alice knew Anna didn't get along with her mother.

"And they know I'm with you?" Alice felt worried as she looked out at a row of impressive buildings. Anna had said the neighborhood was called the Gold Coast.

"Oh, I told them you're with me, but they don't know we're *together*." Anna tossed her dark-gold hair. "Let's see how long it takes Mummy to figure it out, the nosy old thing."

By the time they arrived at the Boyer home, it was nearly

midnight. They took the elevator to the top floor of a stately brick apartment building and soon found themselves face to face with an attractive woman in her mid forties. Anna's mother was a leaner, sleeker version of Anna herself: her blonde hair held back with a plaid band, she was about the same height as her daughter but with a more regal and brittle bearing. Where Anna's eyes were a pale blue, her mother's were a deeper shade with a hard crystalline sparkle. To go with her dressing gown and slippers, Mrs. Boyer wore tastefully small diamond earrings. The scent of a somehow distancing perfume surrounded her as she hugged her daughter lightly around the shoulders and then fixed her with a penetrating gaze.

Touching Alice on the elbow, Anna said, "Mummy, this is my friend Alice Williams. She was my accomplice in escaping from the Tipton Home."

After giving Alice the once-over, her sharp eyes taking in the younger woman's wrinkled dress and enormous, tattered suitcase, she extended a cool dry hand. Alice was aware that her own palm was damp with nervousness and gritty with cracker crumbs.

"Your father's gone to bed, Anna, so you'll have to be quiet. I had Nancy prepare you a snack, which I suggest you eat in the kitchen. We can talk in the morning. Your companion will sleep in the second guest room." Her eyes held Alice's. "You'll have your own bathroom."

"Daddy's gone to bed? He didn't wait up for me after I've been away two years?" Anna said as she moved around the living room, touching objects as she went. She paused to regard a large abstract painting and then turned to a grandfather clock that ticked insistently. Alice thought the clock face looked like a stern old general rather than a kindly grandfather.

"He was in meetings all day. Let him sleep."

When Alice woke up the next morning, the apartment was quiet. The clock in her room read ten a.m. She was surprised at how late she had slept in this unfamiliar home.

Bars of sunlight slipped between the heavy curtains. Alice

rose and went to the window just as she had the previous day, but this time she didn't see Anna hopping into a taxi. Below her, cars slid along the boulevard and people made their way along the sidewalk. Several of them were walking dogs. Businessmen hurried along in their summer suits with briefcases swinging by their side. And there, Alice observed, swaggered a soldier with his arm around his girlfriend. The girl tilted her head back and laughed at something the soldier said.

Alice stretched her arms and yawned. She felt groggy after her long sleep. From the depths of the apartment she heard Mrs. Boyer's voice and a higher voice, not Anna's, in reply. Then there was a rap at the door. It was Nancy, the housekeeper, asking if Alice was ready for breakfast.

After a hurried shower, Alice emerged from her room wearing a blue skirt and flowered blouse that she hoped Mrs. Boyer would approve of. Neither Anna nor her parents were in sight. Nancy guided her to a table laid out for one in a sunny dining room. Her trepidation vanished once she saw the steaming plate of scrambled eggs and sausage. She ate rapidly, pausing only to gulp down fresh-squeezed orange juice or sip the delicious coffee, sinfully laced with heavy cream. The only sounds besides the clink of her own silverware and china came from the kitchen, where Nancy was working.

Just as she finished her meal, Mrs. Boyer appeared. She wore a pale green linen suit with her hair swept back in a matching green headband. Once again her eyes traveled over Alice's clothes and found them wanting. "Good morning, young lady. Shall we have a second cup of coffee in the living room?"

Alice followed her into the next room. Nancy, her eyes cast down, brought them coffee on a silver tray while Mrs. Boyer arranged herself on the edge of a velvety sofa. Alice chose a straight-backed wooden chair.

In answer to Alice's question, Mrs. Boyer said that Anna and her father had gone out and would be back after lunch. An uncomfortable silence fell between them as Alice listened to the ticking of the grandfather clock. The two women regarded one another over their coffee cups. Finally Mrs. Boyer set cup and saucer down with a small clatter. Before speaking, she looked down at her long-boned, manicured hands as if gathering strength from them.

"You know that your aunt is quite upset, don't you? She had to call your mother and tell her"—she paused, and her direct, furious gaze made Alice quake—"you'd run away with my daughter."

"Aunt Muriel talked to my mother?"

"She said she was going to. It's really not my concern."

"I told one of the girls to tell my aunt I was sorry to leave in such a rush. I told Kathleen O'Shea—"

"That doesn't matter to me. What matters is my family's reputation." Mrs. Boyer spoke icily, her anger swallowing all the air in the elegant room. "I want you to leave right now, before Anna gets home." To Alice's amazement, there were enraged tears in the corners of Mrs. Boyer's eyes. "Philip will drive you to the station. I'll give you bus fare."

Alice rose hurriedly to her feet. "I think there's been a misunderstanding, Mrs. Boyer," she said, her voice rising and shaking. "I'm on my way to Rapidan, Virginia, to reunite with my husband, Macklin Williams. Your daughter kindly agreed to drive me there. But if I'm not welcome in your home, I'll leave immediately." She turned on her heel and hurried away.

Back in the guest room, Alice closed the door, her heart pounding. There was little to pack other than the new negligee Anna had given her, a hairbrush, and a few things she had left in the bathroom. But in her rush to get her aged suitcase closed, she jammed a latch. The suitcase would now neither open nor shut all the way. She pulled at it frantically. Suddenly the latch broke and Alice's belongings spilled onto the floor. Kicking the bag with disgust, she gathered up her hairbrush, the negligee, her toothbrush, her shorts, and the blouse embroidered with seashells and stuffed them into her pocketbook.

Taking one last look around the bedroom, she felt an

inconvenient sensation. Although her mother had never offered her much guidance or advice, one of her sayings popped into Alice's head: "There's always time to go to the bathroom." And so there was, even now. A few minutes later, she felt a tiny bit more in control of her own destiny.

The grandfather clock ticked ominously as Alice made her way to the front door. The living room was empty, but she caught one last whiff of Mrs. Boyer's chilly perfume. Outside the apartment, Alice went to the elevator where a bespectacled young black man, a teenager, stood shifting from one foot to the other.

"You Miss Williams?" he called out as she approached. His face was soft, open, and nervous.

"Why, yes, I am," said Alice.

"I'm Philip. Mrs. Boyer said I should take you to the bus station—or wherever it is that you need to go."

Alice and the young man boarded the elevator together. The elevator operator, an old man, smiled at them, but neither Alice nor Philip mustered much of a response. The boy kept his hands laced behind his back and looked at Alice out of the corner of his eye. It occurred to her that she could send him back for her suitcase, but it contained only a mountain of thoroughly worn-out skirts and dresses and undergarments. Such things would only weigh her down.

On the sidewalk Alice and Philip turned and stared at each other. Alice could not hold back anymore. Tears filled her eyes and with a sob she said, "I don't know what to do!"

To her amazement, Philip's eyes, magnified behind thick glasses, also filled with tears. "I don't know what to do, either," he said. "I just started working here two weeks ago, and I hate it. I hate *her*!" He gestured toward the building behind them and Alice knew he meant Mrs. Boyer.

Wiping her eyes, Alice began walking down the sidewalk with Philip hurrying to keep up.

"I've got to get to Virginia, but it's so far away, and I don't know if I have enough money to get there," Alice said.

"Well, I could drive you to the bus station, like she told me to, but I don't want to go back there ever again, not even to get the car. As far as I'm concerned, I'm finished with her. I don't care how much I need a job."

Alice turned to look at Philip. He was a scared boy with an accent she recognized. "What part of Oklahoma are you from, Philip?"

His face broke into a grin. "The dusty part! Turpin, in the Panhandle."

"*I'm* from the Panhandle, Philip." Alice touched his sleeve. "Boise City."

They knew a handful of people in common, and as Alice thought about it, she remembered hearing about a Negro family in Beaver County, where Turpin was. They walked along contemplating the coincidence of their common origins.

"Listen, Philip," Alice said, as they stopped at a crosswalk and waited for the traffic light to change. "You know Chicago better than I do. Point me toward the bus station, and I guess I'll figure out what to do from there."

"I've only been here a month and I'm ready to leave, too," Philip said. "We can take the El to the bus station together." When Alice gave him a baffled look, he explained about the elevated trains.

At the bus station, Philip waited outside while Alice talked to a ticket agent. She had just missed a bus headed to Washington, D.C. Another was leaving soon for Philadelphia, and the ticket agent told her to take that one. In Philadelphia, she could get on a bus to Virginia. Fretting over every dime, Alice counted out the money and bought the ticket.

Philip turned to her with questioning eyes when she rejoined him. She told him her plans and began to say goodbye. "Hey," he said suddenly, "how about if I go to Virginia with you?"

Alice let out a startled laugh. "You aren't on the run from the law, are you, Philip? Why don't you just go home to Turpin?"

Philip hung his head. "My mother died and my brothers are in the army. No one's left in Turpin for me."

"You're an orphan?"

"My father's still alive, somewhere. But if being an orphan means having no one to turn to, then yes, I guess I am."

"Have you ever heard of the Tipton Home in Tipton, Oklahoma?"

"No."

"Well, you could go there. It's a home for orphans; it's where I used to work." As she spoke, Alice studied the boy in front of her. He was thin and very brown beneath his neat blue jacket. His ears stuck out from his head of close-cropped hair, and he had an intense, earnest gaze. There was something about him that touched her heart. "How old are you, Philip?"

"I just turned eighteen," Philip said, his eyes steady on hers. "But I don't see too well, so Uncle Sam has no use for me."

He was too old for the Tipton Home. Alice hesitated as she realized she didn't know what to tell him. She knew white women weren't supposed to be friends with Negro men; it wasn't considered proper. This was just a fact, though she couldn't remember who taught it to her or why it was so. She had never had a real conversation with a Negro until she met Abe Walker at the Home. Abe seemed nice enough, and Ross and the other boys liked him. Aunt Muriel and Uncle Dale had welcomed him to the Home along with the other children. Philip was an orphan just like Abe and Ross and all the rest she had tended to in Tipton. *He's just another person on this Earth*, Alice thought. And since she was nervous about traveling alone, he could help her get to Rapidan.

"Well, go on then, and get a ticket," she said gruffly, "if you've got the money for it. I don't have an extra nickel."

Philip gave her a serious look. "Understood."

"Oh, and my full name's Alice Williams, by the way."

"I'm Philip Williams. How do you do, cousin."

She laughed as he turned and went inside the bus station.

The ride to Philadelphia was long, hot, and exhausting. Alice dozed fitfully, her face pressed to the dirty window and her body turned away from the large, sour-smelling woman next to her. She bought only crackers and soft drinks when the bus ground to a halt in one little town or another. Philip sat in the back with the other Negroes. He seemed to know it would cause trouble if he talked to her during rest stops, so they only exchanged nods at a distance.

In Philadelphia they met on the sidewalk to discuss their plans. Alice quickly filled him in on her determination to reunite with her husband at Red Road Farm. Without spelling out the reasons for the long separation, she let him know the reunion would come as a surprise to Macklin and involved some risk on her part.

Philip looked as bedraggled as she felt. They were both gulping soft drinks from bottles as they stood in the shade of a newsstand. He suggested, to her surprise, that they take a train to Virginia rather than continuing by bus. "A train is more comfortable," he said. "And even if it costs more than the bus, it'll be worth it." He paused. "You want to rest up and look good for your husband, don't you?"

She smiled wearily. Under the circumstances, looking good would be quite a challenge. But she couldn't stand the bus. And after checking with a ticket agent, she discovered there was a train station in Orange, a small town just a few miles from Rapidan.

The train went to Washington, D.C., and then continued south into Virginia. Even though it was crowded with soldiers and recruits, it was much nicer, Alice thought, than the fetid bus. She splurged on a real meal in the dining car. An hour before arriving in Orange, she washed up as best she could in the tiny restroom, changed into her favorite blouse, the one with the embroidered seashells, and tied a green ribbon around her ponytail. She smiled bravely into the mirror. Macklin would be grateful, she told herself, that she had traveled more than a thousand miles to be with him. Whatever problems they had would vanish as soon as they fell into each other's arms.

2

It was late afternoon when the train stopped in the town of Orange. Alice and Philip met on the station steps and commented on the overcast, humid day. With no bags to carry, they considered walking to Red Road Farm. An old man sitting on the steps told Philip the farm was six and a half miles up the road.

"Or if you wait a few minutes, one of them farmers might come along and give you a ride," the old man said. "S'least they could do on a hot day like this."

Dazed from their travels, Alice and Philip swatted at mosquitoes and looked around. A few vehicles were pulling in and out of the station parking lot. Although two or three men walking by regarded them curiously, Alice couldn't imagine asking for their aid.

Just then a large blue car pulled up sharply and the driver, a young woman, got out in a hurry. To her astonishment Alice saw that the driver was Anna Boyer, her dark-gold hair shining even in the dusty, humid air. Alice watched in stupefaction as Anna put her hands on her hips and scanned the parking lot. Then her face lit up and she called out Alice's name.

Anna swept up Alice in a long, tight hug. Alice could smell the other woman's skin, which was a little too fragrant for her liking. She disengaged herself from Anna and held her at arm's length. "How did you find me?" she said. "What are you doing here?"

"Mummy told me what happened—well, her version anyway. I knew if you left without me, there must've been an awful row. I got on the road as soon as I could." She paused for breath. "You forgot your suitcase, you know," she said, chuckling with fond amusement. "What a broken-down mess that old thing was. I threw it out and got you a new bag." She bobbed her head toward the Packard. "It's in the trunk along with all your clothes."

"You just got here, Anna? This very minute?"

"I got here yesterday," Anna said with satisfaction, "and took a room at a little hotel around the corner. But I didn't know whether you'd be on a bus or the train, or when you'd come in, and so I kept driving back and forth between here and Culpeper and Charlottesville." Her face lit up with a radiant smile. "I knew about this train coming to Orange. I just got lucky, I guess, because here you are."

Alice smiled back weakly. She had thought about Anna on her long trip. She had also thought about Mrs. Boyer, the well-manicured monster she suspected would linger in her memory for a long time. Anna's reluctance to talk about her mother finally made sense. But they were in Virginia, so close to Macklin at last, and Alice didn't know what to do about this young woman gazing at her with unabashed love.

She released her hold on Anna and turned toward Philip, who had retired to a bench on the station porch. "Philip is here, too," she said. He raised a hand and waved uncertainly at Anna.

"Oh, my lord. Then what Mummy said is actually true." Anna stepped away, her smile giving way to a shocked expression that nearly made Alice laugh. "Don't tell me you ran away with the chauffeur!"

"Philip, come here," Alice commanded. If she didn't take charge now, all would be lost. "You tell Anna your side of things. Then we'll all be on our way to Rapidan." Without a backward glance, she left the youth and his former employer's furious daughter to sort things out for themselves.

She lingered inside the station as long as she dared. When she came back outside, Anna and Philip were sitting at opposite ends of the bench.

"Mummy always did have trouble keeping the help," Anna said by way of reconciliation. "But you realize this"—she turned toward Philip—"makes things even more complicated than they already were."

"Well, maybe he can get a job around here," Alice said. "With most of the boys off to war, there must be jobs available for a hard-working fellow. And Anna, guess what, Philip's from Oklahoma! He's from Turpin, near Boise City."

As they walked toward the Packard, Anna pulled her aside. "I hardly know what to say about Philip"—she said his name grudgingly—"but you do realize this whole trip to Virginia is an absurd mission, don't you? Unless, that is, you're going to work out details of your divorce." Her lips trembled. "I assume you're going to divorce him."

Alice turned Anna away from the car so Philip couldn't overhear them. "Anna, you have to understand," she began, "that I have no intention of divorcing Macklin. Our marriage got off to a rough start, but there's no reason we can't begin again, now that Macklin's finished college—I think he's finished—and he doesn't have to worry about paying my way East."

Anna's chin sank to her chest and two tears slipped down her cheeks. "Do you mean to say our night together—to say nothing of all the time we spent together in Tipton—was just a diversion?"

Alice resisted the urge to say, *That's exactly what I mean.* She did not want to be hurtful, but after two years and a hard trip to Virginia, she was impatient to get to Red Road Farm and find Macklin. She consoled her friend as best she could. After a minute, Anna collected herself. "You may yet change your mind," she said in a shaky voice.

"Come along," Alice said, guiding her toward the car. "We've come this far; we may as well go six more miles."

"Six and a half," Philip called out from the backseat.

Rapidan Road picked up where Main Street in Orange left off. The road wound through the Piedmont countryside between large farms set back from the road. They passed one called Batton and another called Hawk's Hill. At one curve, there was a striking American elm, its limbs spread out in a bounty of green leaves.

Alice noted this tree and the blossoming magnolias with approving eyes. As they drew closer to Rapidan, tall trees formed a canopy over the road. Everything was so pretty and green.

After a few miles they passed a sign to Clark's Mountain Road on the right. Soon they saw a little church with tall wooden spires, a sign identifying it as Purcell Memorial Presbyterian Church. The next driveway was for Red Road Farm. The farm's wooden sign was weathered and the iron gate, hanging open, was covered in ivy. Flowers bloomed along both sides of the gate. Alice felt her heart soar. The long driveway led them between a sloping pasture on the left and a formal garden on the right. The garden was shaggy and overgrown, but in the middle there was a brick-bordered fishpond with a sundial near it. It was obvious a lot of work had been put into landscaping, even though the place needed sprucing up.

Then the house loomed into view. It was imposingly large and white, with a wide front porch and a red front door.

"Oh!" Alice said.

Philip whistled softly.

"Reminds me of my grandparents' summer place," Anna said.

The driveway ended in two overlapping loops, one that went along the pasture near the barn and another that came along the side of the house. Anna slowed the car. The three travelers noticed a young man standing next to a horse at the far side of the pasture. Though he was turned away from them, they could see that he was tall and muscular and wore a riding cap. Alice's heart thudded in her ears: it had to be Macklin.

He turned at the sound of the car and began leading the horse toward the fence near the driveway. Alice saw that under his cap he had dark wavy hair and a square jaw. A smile filled his face when he noticed everyone craning to look at him.

"It's not Macklin." Alice said in answer to the unspoken question from the others. "I don't know who that is, but it's definitely not Macklin."

Anna stopped the car and called out across the expanse of the field, "Good afternoon. Could you please tell us where we might find Macklin Williams?" Her voice had assumed the haughty politeness that Alice remembered from their stay in St. Louis.

The young man, one hand on the horse's golden flank, lifted his voice in reply, "You just missed him. He left yesterday for Texas. But maybe I could help you. Or you could speak to his uncle."

Alice groaned. Anna clucked her tongue before murmuring, "Well, how about that."

As they turned toward the house, they noticed a middle-aged Negro man emerging from the barn. An orange cat walked close by his side.

"Let me out here, please," Philip said. "I want to talk to him."

Anna complied and then drove another ten yards before stopping the car. "I can't do this," she said to Alice. "Go find out about your husband and let me know when you're ready to leave. I can't imagine you'll be staying long." She turned off the engine, hopped out of the car, and set off to meet the young man loping toward them across the pasture.

Her heart in her throat, Alice mounted the porch steps and hurried to the front door. She was afraid if she slowed down she would lose her nerve. First she rang the doorbell and then, when no one answered, she opened the screen door and tapped on the red door's large window. Suddenly the door swung open and Alice was face to face with a young woman holding a sleeping infant. The baby's head was nestled against the woman's shoulder and Alice could see only a halo of feathery red hair.

With an excited, grateful smile, the woman greeted Alice. "Thank goodness you're here. We were so afraid no one would be able to come at such short notice. Let me take you into the sitting room, where Mr. Williams is waiting." She shifted the baby to her other shoulder. "I'm Edith Merton. Chipperth asked me to help out until he could get a nurse. He'll be thrilled you came so quickly. Maybe you saw Chipperth when you drove up?" She looked inquiringly at Alice.

Nervous and uncomfortable, and unable to process the woman's burst of conversation, Alice gazed at the baby.

The woman offered an encouraging smile. "This is Meredith—we put together my name with my husband Merle's, and got Meredith." She smoothed Meredith's halo of hair and then refocused on Alice. "And you are?"

"Alice. Alice Williams."

"Well, that's quite a coincidence! Come meet Mr. Williams—perhaps you're distant kin."

Easing open a door into a sitting room, Edith Merton led Alice inside. The wallpaper was a faded red. The furniture was old and heavy, and now that the sun had come out, dust motes spun in the light. The centerpiece was an aged sofa covered with brown fur. The room was stuffy. All the windows were closed, and the smell of overcooked food hung in the air.

"Mr. Williams?" Edith Merton called out. They heard a toilet flush, and after a long minute, a very old man in a wheelchair entered from a side door. He looked thoroughly irritated at the sight of the two young women.

"It's a good thing he can still do *that* on his own," Edith said under her breath to Alice. "I couldn't help him with *that*. But of course, you're trained to do that sort of thing without giving it a thought."

Then she made the introductions. "This is Alice Williams—can you believe it, Mr. Williams? Your new nurse has your very own name." She spoke loudly and simply, as if Mr. Williams couldn't understand her any other way, yet Alice doubted the old man was as far gone as Edith seemed to think he was. She knew this was Uncle Minor, who provided Macklin with room and board and financed his education at the University of Virginia. She had dared to send him a couple of letters. One Christmas night, he had accepted her collect call to Macklin.

Her head jumbled with thoughts and emotions, Alice murmured a few words of greeting. When she spoke, the old fellow sat up straight in his chair. His eyes widened and then narrowed.

He cleared his throat and spoke in a raspy voice: "You come to find your husband!"

Edith Merton turned to Alice. "You're not the new nurse?"

"No. Though I did my share of that back in Tipton—well, for the children, that is—I'm not the nurse. I'm here, as Mr. Williams said, to find my husband."

Edith furrowed her brow as baby Meredith stretched and gurgled. "Your husband?"

"Yes, my husband, Macklin Williams. He lives here, or he used to, with Mr. Williams. He goes to the University of Virginia—or he used to," she finished, her voice fading.

"Oh!" Edith said. "*Macklin*. You mean *Macklin*."

No sooner had Alice nodded that Edith's face clouded again. "*I* didn't know he was *married*. He never said he was married." She seemed to be talking to herself. "I wonder if Chipperth knew?"

Just then, they heard footsteps on the front porch and the sound of mingled voices. Alice turned to see Anna entering the house along with the tall, wavy-haired young man and another young man, this one portly and red-haired and wearing a natty seersucker suit.

"Hello, darling!" Eddie Merton practically skipped to the portly man's side. She placed a towel on his shoulder before transferring the baby to his arms. No spittle will ever mar that seersucker, Alice thought, noting how fastidious these two were, and how well matched.

Alice learned that Merle Merton had come to fetch his wife after his workday at the men's clothing shop he and his father ran in Orange. When Edith announced that Alice was married to Macklin Williams, Merle's response was to take a half step backward in surprise. Then he recovered himself and gave her the same once-over that Mrs. Boyer had given her in Chicago. His wife drew closer to him and reached up to smooth Meredith's halo of strawberry blonde hair.

The other young man now came into the sitting room with Anna. He introduced himself as Chippers Hebblethwaite.

Evidently Anna had already told him who Alice was and why she was visiting. He shook her hand warmly and then pulled her in for a hug. "Alice from Oklahoma!" he exclaimed. "Macklin used to talk about you."

"Did he!" Alice said, and immediately regretted her eagerness. Her husband's long absence from her life had left her desperate to believe, despite so much evidence to the contrary, that he still loved and cared about her.

"Well, why's he going to Texas? When will he be back?"

Chippers dropped his hands to his sides. "Oh, Alice," he said, "he left yesterday morning for the army. I was telling Anna that I was hoping Macklin and our friend Dudley and I would all go to New York for officer training school. But Macklin's paperwork got lost, and he ended up having to go to Texas instead."

"He left yesterday? Did he say anything about—" Alice stopped herself; she couldn't bear for this assemblage to hear that her husband had said nothing about her on the eve of his departure for wartime duties. "Could we talk outside, Chippers?"

Sitting on the porch swing with this young man, a close friend of Macklin's, Alice found out her husband had graduated the week before with his bachelor's degree in English. He won an award for his essay on Emily Dickinson's poetry and planned to go to graduate school after the war was over.

Chippers told her, with excruciating gentleness, that Macklin had indeed talked about her but seemed confused and uncertain about a lot of things, including his marriage. Although Chippers allowed that he could never know the whole story, he gathered that Macklin needed time on his own, especially after his father died. Macklin had talked about a journal he kept; it seemed that writing in his journal was his way of making sense of his life.

Alice felt hot tears burning her eyes as the young man went on and on. It seemed that he had lived at the farm with Macklin for a few months the previous school year, and worked on the house, and the two of them had hosted a big Christmas party, and then Chippers moved back to the university and lived in a fraternity house, and eventually Macklin rented a room nearby and worked at a bookstore. Macklin had some trouble with his Uncle Minor and eventually had no choice but to leave the farm and live on his own, but then just a month ago, Mr. Williams's lawyer and caretaker had died, and Mr. Williams had to move out of that man's home in Richmond. Despite his failing health, he insisted on coming back to Red Road Farm and had summoned Macklin to help find him a good, hard-working nurse. Macklin had tried to do his uncle's bidding, but the best nurses were all caught up in the war effort, and the mediocre ones were unwilling to put up with Mr. Williams for more than a week or two. And then, of course, Macklin had to go serve his country like all the other boys, and was worried sick about his uncle and the farm.

Upon hearing all this, Chippers had volunteered to stay at the house until it was time to leave for officer training school. He told Alice that he loved Red Road Farm as much as Macklin did, and wanted to make sure everything was working out and that Mr. Williams was safe. Alice had arrived on a difficult day, since the last nurse, a pathetic creature with a clubfoot, had quit that very morning. To make things worse, the farm manager and his wife were about to leave for Bethesda, Maryland, to visit their son, a wounded sailor just transferred to a hospital there.

Alice's tears were now falling on her lap, onto her skirt. She could not look Chippers in the eye. She felt sorry for everyone Chippers was talking about, including herself. He reached over and patted her hand. "Everything will be all right," he said. "Somehow it will be."

The swing creaked as Chippers fell silent. They continued to rock gently as Alice, the tears drying on her face, looked out at the terraced front lawn and the formal garden in the distance. There were boxwoods and magnolia trees, and between the boxwoods she could see a path leading to a fishpond surrounded by flowers. Sad as she was, she could not help feeling the peacefulness of the place. No wonder Macklin had wanted to live here.

After a while, Chippers cleared his throat and fidgeted until she felt obliged to look at him. "I hope this won't sound presumptuous, and I know my timing is terrible," he began, "but I wondered if your friend Anna is seeing anyone." He looked sheepish as Alice's eyes widened in surprise. "We only talked for a few minutes, but I really *like* her. She told me she's going to college in New York. And *I'll* be in New York for my training. But, well, I was just wondering if she has a boyfriend already." He looked away and shook his head. "A girl that pretty *must* have a boyfriend." No sooner had he said it that he turned back to her and added, "Of course she's no prettier than you are, Alice, but you're a married woman." He patted her arm.

It had been a day of extreme emotions. Even in her sorrow Alice felt laughter bubbling up inside her. "Well, Chippers, you're in luck, because Anna does not have a boyfriend. In fact, I don't believe she's ever had a serious beau. She's very picky."

Chippers sat up straighter, ennobled by the challenge before him. They were silent for a minute, neither of them rocking the swing, and then he said, "I have just one other question. Maybe I shouldn't ask it, but I got this funny feeling about Anna—"

Alice felt her pulse speed up. "It's always better not to pry."

"Oh, well, you're right." He paused and stared into the fishpond. "But I have to ask. It's just a hunch I have."

"What is it then?"

"Is there any chance Anna plays tennis? I bet she does."

Alice laughed with relief. "She was girls' champion at her country club in Chicago. She hasn't played for two years, unless you count batting a ball around with me at the orphanage, but I can't imagine she would turn down the chance to play again."

"Champion of her club in Chicago." Chippers looked like he might weep with joy. "Well, maybe I better go talk to her then."

"I think you should." Alice stood up so abruptly that Chippers lurched on the swing. "And while you do that, I'm going to have a chat with Macklin's uncle."

"He doesn't talk much, you know. I should join you."

"No, you run along and have your fun. You're about to head

off to war, after all."

Chippers shot her a grateful smile.

Once inside, they discovered the Mertons making their exit. "It's nice to meet you," Merle Merton said stiffly. "We got to go on home now and take care of the little one."

"I'm sorry for all the confusion," Edith said as she adjusted a whimpering Meredith on her shoulder. "I thought you were the new nurse."

After they left, Alice turned back to the sitting room to find Anna seated on the brown sofa with Mr. Williams near her in his wheelchair. Anna was examining her fingernails, and the patriarch was staring into space.

Alice took a deep breath. "Anna, I'm going to get us each a glass of iced water, and then I'd like some time alone with Mr. Williams. Would that be all right with you?"

"Oh, let me help. Here, you can have my seat."

When Anna returned with two glasses clinking with ice cubes, Alice accepted them with a nod of thanks. The room was unbearably stuffy after Anna shut the door behind her. Alice opened a window facing the driveway and then put all her muscle into pushing open another that seemed like it hadn't been opened in years. Though no cooler, the fresh air was a relief from the room's stale odors.

Mr. Williams watched her as she moved around the room, and when she sat down on the sofa, he took a sip of water and regarded her levelly.

"What kind of covering is this, Mr. Williams? I've never felt a texture like this on a sofa before." She ran her hand along the nap of the sofa and chuckled. "Is it dog hair? Or possum?"

The old man's mouth twitched. "It's horsehair," he said in his scratchy voice. "My mother brought it back from one of her Continental expeditions."

"Well, for heaven's sakes. I guess it's scratchy enough to be a horse, and I must say, it does ride well." Alice bounced up and down a couple of times.

Mr. Williams said, "That sofa's four years older than I am."

"Well, by my calculations, it must be—hmm—forty-three."

The old man resumed staring into space and Alice was embarrassed. She looked around the cluttered room and saw a folded-up cot, an end table littered with cups and handkerchiefs, a coffee table covered with magazines, mail, and medicine bottles, and a wicker basket overflowing with sour-smelling clothes. Mr. Williams was wearing a long-sleeved shirt and sweater, though the temperature in the room had to be over eighty degrees. The sweater was stained and his shirt collar was a distressing brown.

"Mr. Williams," Alice began again, "I expected my husband to be here, and that's why I traveled over a thousand miles from Tipton, Oklahoma, to Rapidan. But seeing as he's gone off to war, and you need a nurse and I need a job, I wonder if we might work out an agreement."

He regarded her with his level, unreadable gaze. Then suddenly his hand shot out and slapped the arm of the sofa. "He failed astronomy," he said. "Didn't know his stars or his planets! That's what I call dumb."

"Well, I'm very surprised," Alice said. "He was an excellent student at the University of Oklahoma."

After another silence, Mr. Williams continued, "He'll be damned lucky if he comes out of this war alive."

She held her tongue. Looking down at his spotted hand just inches from her own, she could see his bones through translucent, yellowed flesh. There was a line of dirt underneath each brittle nail. She looked up and shivered: with his pale blue gaze, his long nose and high cheekbones, he looked like Macklin—Macklin aged to the brink of death, flesh hanging off his face and neck, his expression terrifying, eyes furious even as his mouth twitched with a ghastly flickering of amusement. Just as she was wondering whether she should run for her life, the old man spoke again.

"Talk to Hebblethwaite," he said, nodding toward the door. "He'll tell you what to do. And don't expect much of a salary. I got a whole farm to take care of, you know."

"Thank you, sir." The moment seemed to call for a pronouncement on her part, and all she could think of was her Uncle Dale's frequent admonition to the orphans. Halfway out the sitting room door, she turned to him and said, "Labor vincit Omnia!" He responded with a dismissive wave and sank back in his wheelchair.

She found Philip sitting on the steps petting the barn cat they had seen earlier. When he lifted his hand, the cat rose up on its hind feet and pressed its round head against his palm. They repeated this several times before Philip turned around to look at Alice.

"Well, Philip. Good news and bad news."

"The bad?"

"My husband left for Texas yesterday and won't be back anytime soon."

"That's what I heard. I'm sorry, Alice."

"Anna told you all the details?"

"Mr. Hebblethwaite told me. They went into town to do some errands, and I helped them unload the car before they left." He pointed to a cluster of bags and a jumbled pile of loose items on the porch. Among the bags was a large suitcase with shiny gold locks that Alice presumed was the replacement Anna had bought for her.

"Do you want to hear the good news? I guess it's good news, anyway." She sat down on the swing. "I'm going to work for Macklin's uncle. His nurse quit, and I figured I may as well stay here and take care of him until Macklin gets home from the war."

"That's swell. And guess what, I got a job, too."

She stared at him in amazement.

"The farm manager's leaving, and his nephew who was doing all the stable work got drafted a few weeks ago. So Mr. Hebblethwaite hired me to take care of the horses, and the farm manager—Mr. Carter—said I could live at his house until he and his wife get back from Maryland."

"Chippers told me the Carters' son is in the hospital there. Is he badly hurt?"

"Yes, he is."

Just then a car rounded the bend in the driveway on the far side of the barn. "Well, there they go," Philip said. "Mr. Williams let him borrow that car. Mr. Carter said he'll bring it back when he can." He stood up and waved as the vehicle went past the pasture. There were several large canvases strapped to its roof. The driver waved at Philip, and then the car disappeared around another curve in the driveway.

Alice went over to inspect the pile of belongings. Along with the new bag, there were Anna's suitcases with her initials, AGB, embossed on them, two tennis racquets in their wooden presses, and a jumbled pile of books and shoes and raincoats.

"Mr. Hebblethwaite—well, he told me to call him Chippers— said you and Anna will be at the end of the hall on the second floor. You'll have Macklin's old room, and Anna will have the one across from it." Philip leaned down to pick up a bag. "Your room is the one with the parrot door knocker on it," he said with a smile.

After two trips, they managed to get everything inside and up the stairs. Left alone in Macklin's old room, Alice looked at the bed where he had so recently slept, the writing desk where he studied, and a large bureau. Above it, a mirror reflected her weary face. She touched the glass with her index finger. Her eyes were now reflected where Macklin's had been, and the floorboards creaked beneath her feet just as they had creaked beneath his.

A pawn ticket for a pair of cufflinks lay on top of the bureau alongside a small, silver-framed photograph of a five-year-old Macklin in a rope swing with his father beside him. They were both smiling from ear to ear, and the father's hand was resting on Macklin's shoulder. Alice knew he had taken this keepsake when he left for Rapidan. Seeing it brought back the sharp sorrow she felt when she discovered, in their Oklahoma shack, that he had left behind a framed photograph of her.

She looked out a window and saw that it faced the driveway;

it was right above the sitting room where Mr. Williams evidently spent most of his time. The other window overlooked a garden, a row of shade trees, and in the distance an open meadow. Alice ventured into the bathroom, which she and Anna would share. With not even an old razor blade or used washcloth in sight, it offered no clue of its recent occupant.

The bedroom, however, had something of Macklin's spirit. Alice stood in the center of the room and inhaled the scent of soap used on the linens, polish on the pine floors, the heavy summer air just outside the screen windows, and what she thought of as "a clean man's sweat." That clean man was Macklin. Alice had not been near him for three years, but his smell was unmistakable.

She rushed to the bed and pressed her face to the pillow. His scent was there, on the pillowcase, as was a single strand of his hair. She held it between her thumb and forefinger before letting it drop to the floor. With a single motion, she pulled the bedspread and sheet back from the bed and then stripped off the fitted bottom sheet as well. She bundled everything inside the pillowcase and then went off in search of the linen closet. There was no sense in sleeping on dirty sheets, even if they were her husband's.

3

Before Anna and Chippers returned, Alice toured the house from top to bottom, tidied up the sitting room, prepared and ate a supper of vegetables and fried ground beef with a silent but cooperative Mr. Williams, inspected the fishpond, fed the goldfish with oatmeal she found in a garden shed, and visited the horses with Philip scurrying excitedly around her. She was still exploring the barn when she heard a car coming up the driveway.

To her surprise, she saw that Chippers was at the wheel of the Packard. The car stopped near the barn and the two occupants climbed out, in the midst of animated if one-sided conversation. "My second serve was right on the line, but my opponent called it wide, and so I lost the set. Oh, I'll tell you the rest of the story later," Chippers said before turning his attention to Alice and Philip. "We had to go all the way to Charlottesville to find a tennis net. I thought we could get one in Orange, but we couldn't, and then we went to Culpeper, and no luck there, either, so we went to Charlottesville, where I *knew* we'd find what we needed. And as a bonus Anna got to see the university, and we ate at The Virginian."

Well, whoopee, Alice thought as she looked at the loquacious Chippers and then at Anna, who was digging inside the car trunk and avoiding her gaze. In her hands Anna held up a tennis net and the requisite poles for holding it in place.

"We're going to set it up in the front yard," Chippers continued, sounding like a proud little boy. "For now, we'll just work on volleys—we won't even need to mark out the court or cut the grass." He paused. "And how are you?" he said to Alice, and then, "and *you*?" by way of including Philip.

Philip answered for both of them. "We're fine. Alice is the new nurse."

"You are!" Chippers beamed. With a nod toward the church on the other side of the pasture fence, he said, "Well, I guess God does answer prayers. I thank you, Alice, for coming here and helping Mr. Williams and Red Road Farm—and for helping Macklin."

By now Anna had circled around the car to stand beside Chippers. She was eyeing Alice uncertainly, the tennis net cradled like a cumbersome baby in her arms. "You are staying here, then?" she said to Alice.

"It looks that way."

"I will be staying here, too," Anna said in an arch, formal tone, "but just for a short visit before going on to New York."

"Should I let you two talk in private?" Chippers asked.

"No," said Anna, "that won't be necessary. Alice and I understand each other."

Though the air was close and warm even at six-thirty in the evening, Alice felt gooseflesh rise on her arms. She stared at Anna: how cool and certain she looked, how tight the line of her mouth. It was hard to believe this was the same friend who had shared her bed in St. Louis, pursued her all the way from Chicago, and rushed across the train station parking lot to embrace her that very day.

"Or at least Anna understands me," Alice said, still holding Anna's gaze. "Now go play your game before it gets dark, while I check on Mr. Williams. I don't like to leave him alone too long." With that she walked around Chippers and Anna and started for the house. Over her shoulder, she called out, "Philip, if you want something to eat, come over in a few minutes and I'll have something ready for you."

An hour later, Alice and Philip sat together on the front steps. On the lawn Chippers was adjusting the tennis net. Anna, wearing a sporty white skirt and blouse that Alice had never seen before, emerged from the house with a yardstick so Chippers could make sure the net was the proper height. After further adjustments, he stood up and looked at Anna. Something seemed to dawn on them at the same time. "You didn't buy any?" Anna said.

"You don't have any in your car?"

"When I left Oklahoma, I didn't realize I'd be playing a tennis match my first night in Rapidan."

The two stood on the lawn, hands on their hips, and looked around them, as if they might see a tennis ball peeking out from the base of a boxwood or magnolia tree. Philip shot Alice a wicked grin.

Finally Anna said, "We'll play tomorrow."

"I know what you can use!" Alice cried out. "You two wait here, and I'll be right back." She dashed into the house and ran up to her room before anyone could respond.

In a few minutes, she was tossing a rolled-up pair of socks to Anna. "It's about the same size as a tennis ball."

Anna looked down at the object in her hand as if it were completely reprehensible, but Chippers laughed and said, "You've rescued us, Alice. Thanks a million." He took the socks from Anna and went to the other side of the net. "Come on, Anna, show me what you can do."

Anna turned to the net and began tapping the sock ball back and forth with Chippers while Philip and Alice watched. After a minute, the ball came undone and the players had to stop. But Chippers rolled the socks up tightly, and the game was on again.

"How'd you think of that, Alice?" Philip said.

"It just popped into my head. I remembered how the boys at the Home were throwing around a sock ball one time. I heard all this commotion one night not long after I started working there, and when I went to check on them, they were just having fun with a sock ball." She paused. "Turned out they were David's socks, red ones his mother knitted for him."

"Who's David?"

"One of the Tipton boys. The sweetest one. Well, one of the sweetest."

"Only one can be the sweetest."

"That sounds like something my husband would say."

"Your husband's a soldier now."

"He'll be back."

Philip gave Alice a sidelong glance before turning his attention back to the tennis players.

"She's better than he is," Alice said just loud enough for Philip to hear. Anna had hit the sock ball low over the net and Chippers had crouched down to tap it back, only to have it teeter on the net cord and fall on his side.

"And he won't like that," Philip said.

"No," she said, "but he'll try to hide it, because he thinks he needs a wife before he goes off to war."

"And she could use a husband."

"Yeah, but I don't know what she'd use him *for*." She stood up from the porch and stretched her arms. "I'm going to check on Mr. Williams one more time before I turn in for the night. I'll see you in the morning, Philip." Chippers and Anna glanced up from their game and bade her goodnight. She wondered how long they would play without an audience to watch them. *It's really not my concern*, she thought, and then remembered those were Mrs. Boyer's words. She felt the weight of the long day on her shoulders as she mounted the steps to her new bedroom.

Over the next few days, Alice and Philip began to fall into a routine. Alice resumed her habit of rising early and working hard throughout the morning. On the first full day, with Philip's help, she removed a couple of bookcases and an end table from the sitting room. They rearranged Mr. Williams's bed behind a screen so he had more privacy when he slept. Then she washed the floor and the windows, and scoured every inch of the adjoining bathroom. In the linen closet she found a lightweight, colorful quilt to brighten up the horsehair sofa. The next day, she washed the curtains and cleaned the kitchen from top to bottom. By the third day, she was in the habit of bringing in fresh flowers for the sitting room and the front living room. The whole downstairs smelled better and looked more cheerful. And when Alice insisted that Mr. Williams take a bath one evening while she waited for him outside the bathroom, he groused and grumbled and then did as she told him to do. When he emerged, he was wearing the freshly laundered pajamas she had left on the towel rack for him.

In the afternoon while Mr. Williams napped, Alice visited Philip in the barn. He was gentle with the horses and full of enthusiasm and affection for them. Sorbon Carter had given instructions and advice, as had Chippers, but when Chippers left in a few days, Philip would be on his own. "I need to go to Montpelier and talk to the people there," he told Alice on Saturday afternoon. "Mr. Carter said they'll tell me what to do if one of the horses gets sick or needs a new shoe."

"All right, we'll do that Monday afternoon. Chippers can keep an eye on Mr. Williams, and we'll borrow Anna's car."

"We can use the farm truck," Philip said. "Mr. Carter said we could."

Alice watched as Philip carefully led the large golden horse out of the barn. This was the one they had seen Chippers tending to when they first arrived at Red Road Farm. Philip had just brushed her, and her flanks were gleaming. "Her name's Goldenrod, but we call her Goldie," he said proudly. "She's Mr. Carter's favorite. He told me to be extra-good to her."

"Are you allowed to ride her?"

"Yes," Philip said, "but first I have to get my courage up. I've never ridden a horse before."

"Well, neither have I. No, I take that back. One time I rode the old horse we had back in Tipton. I rode her bareback and after a lot of coaxing, we worked our way up to a trot."

"They like carrots," Philip said.

"Then we'll grow carrots. We need to work on the garden, by the way."

"If I have time."

"Oh, you'll have time. There's always time on a farm."

Alice started to walk back to the house and then stopped to speak again to Philip. "Do you want to go to church tomorrow?"

"You want to go?" He hesitated. "They're not going to want me there."

Alice thought about that. "Well, it's right here"—she pointed at the church on the other side of the pasture—"so I think we should go. I can't imagine anyone at a pretty little church like that would turn you away."

"Okay," Philip said, "I wouldn't mind going, I guess. I used to go to church back home in Turpin. I could help you with Mr. Williams, if he wants to go, too."

Alice heard a clanging and clattering sound as she approached the house. The noise was coming from the back, where to her amazement she discovered Chippers steadying a ladder as Anna mounted it with a bucket in hand.

"Hey, Alice!" Chippers called out. "Anna agreed to help me finish a project I started two years ago. We'll get this house painted yet."

Anna was dressed in shorts and an oversized shirt that Alice assumed belonged to Chippers. Her mouth set in a firm line, she did not look down as she climbed ever higher.

"You got everything you need, Anna?" Chippers asked before grabbing a bucket and climbing up a ladder a few yards away. As Anna began dabbing the side of the house with tentative strokes, he called out instructions to her. They seemed oblivious to Alice as she watched them work. Chippers was quite the chatterbox. Anna responded to his anecdotes with dry ripostes that made him laugh.

They are becoming a couple, Alice thought. "Hey, you two!" she said. "Do you want to go to church tomorrow?"

"Sure," said Chippers after which Anna replied, "Thanks, but no."

They looked at each other across their ladders. Anna continued, "I went to St. James Cathedral every Sunday growing up in Chicago and then to chapel at the orphanage twice a week for the past two years. I've earned a Sunday off."

"You're Episcopalian?" asked Chippers.

"Correct," Anna said, "And you?"

"Oh, we're Presbyterian. But my mother was Episcopalian before she married my father." He began painting again, more slowly this time. "I never went to Purcell when I lived here, but it might be nice to attend before I start my training. And I've always liked the looks of that church." He glanced at Anna. "It's Carpenter Gothic, you know."

"Actually, no, I didn't know."

Chippers brightened. As Alice walked away, seeing that she was no longer part of the conversation, she heard him telling Anna that he had studied the church in his architectural history class.

When Mr. Williams awoke from his nap, Alice brought him a glass of iced tea and several of the sugar cookies she had baked the night before. She sat on the sofa, now covered with a flowered quilt, and nibbled a cookie to keep him company. Their visits were often nearly silent and Alice could well imagine that the previous nurses had grown lonely.

"Philip and I are going to church tomorrow morning," she ventured to say, "and I'd like to take you with us. Would you enjoy that, Mr. Williams?"

He turned to her, his eyes alert. "No."

"Well, Anna can stay here with you."

"Where is that girl from?"

"She's from Chicago."

"I thought so. Ask her if she's kin to Teddy Boyer, the judge."

Alice stood up and wiped a damp crumb from her cheek that Mr. Williams had accidentally spat in her direction. "I'll do that, sir. Now if you'll excuse me, I'm going to do a little straightening up before it's time to fix supper."

But the old man would not let Alice go. "Furman clerked for him in Chicago."

"Who's Furman, Mr. Williams?"

"My best friend for seventy years." He gazed up at Alice from his wheelchair, his hands clenching the chair arms.

"I hope I'll have the pleasure of meeting him someday."

"You can meet him after church. His grave is right next to where mine will be."

"Oh!" Alice exclaimed softly. "I'm very sorry, Mr. Williams."

The conversation flagged. Just outside the window, Chippers and Anna were still working. The smell of fresh paint wafted into the sitting room. Mr. Williams seemed lost in thought. His skin was a papery yellow, and Alice could see the veins on his translucent temple. When he reached up to adjust his collar, she resisted the impulse to help him. *He's a proud man*, she thought, *and he doesn't want anyone touching him.*

The frailty behind his imperious manner suddenly moved her. She suspected that if he picked up on her pity, he would either lash out at her or turn inward and breathe his last. With these thoughts weighing on her heart, she gathered up his tray and left the room.

After supper Chippers and Anna went outside for their evening tennis game. Chippers had cut the grass and marked off a court with lengths of twine, which he anchored with long nails he had found in the barn. As usual Alice and Philip sat on the porch swing and watched. Their presence seemed to irritate Anna, which Philip commented on with amusement.

"You're not Anna's biggest fan, are you, Philip?" Alice said, passing him a bowl of strawberries.

"She reminds me of her mother, that's all." He popped a berry in his mouth and passed the bowl back. "She thinks she's better than we are."

"Well, maybe she is."

Philip chuckled and then saw Alice was serious. "She's not better than you, Alice, and at the risk of sounding like one of those *uppity* Negroes, I don't think she's a *whole* lot better than I am."

Alice laughed. "Well, we know she's a better tennis player than Chippers, for whatever that's worth."

Her dark-gold hair swinging from side to side, Anna was like an agile cat on the court. She never seemed to get winded and she had an uncanny way of anticipating where Chippers would hit the ball. Just when he had maneuvered a deep shot nearly out of her reach, she responded with a delicate slice that placed the ball just over the net. Chippers lunged for it, popped the ball up, and Anna waited at the net to angle it away from him or hit it authoritatively at his feet. Time and again she dropped the ball lightly over the net, while her disbelieving opponent waited for the long ball that never came.

Although neither Alice nor Philip kept track of the score—and in fact didn't know how—they could see that Anna was winning. And, as Alice pointed out, this was with a real ball, not a pair of rolled-up socks.

"Okay, we agree she's the better player," Philip said. "But which one is sillier?"

"Hmm." Alice propped her chin on her hand and pretended to think hard. "I believe that's a toss-up. What do you think?"

"He's silly for not catching on to that one good shot of hers—or maybe he's just dumb. In any case, she's sillier because she puts up with him."

"He got you a job," Alice reminded Philip.

"Well, true."

Finally Chippers turned to the spectators and said, "How about if you two play? Or one of you takes on Anna? I need a break."

"Finally!" Philip said. "Come on, Alice."

"Oh, if you insist," Alice said. She, too, had been wanting to play.

Chippers showed Philip how to grip the racquet while Anna walked toward Alice.

"What are the rules?" Alice asked.

With a toss of her hair, Anna said, "You already know."

"When you and I played back in Tipton," Alice said, "we just hit the ball back and forth. You never taught me the rules."

"Just play by the boys' rules," Anna said. "That's how the world works."

Alice did not drop her gaze. "I'd rather play badminton."

"Whatever that means," Anna said as she retired to the porch steps and waited for Chippers to bring her a cold drink.

It took a few tries for Philip, wearing his thick spectacles, to make good contact with the ball. But he was quick, and he radiated an energetic joy as he ran around the court. The first time he was able to hit the ball cleanly, he let out a whoop of delight. After a while Alice caught his enthusiasm and they played until it was so dark they could barely see the ball looping over the net.

At last she decided it was time to check on Mr. Williams. Philip said he would come by in the morning. He handed over his racquet and went running back to the tenant house, with the first stars and a rising cloud of fireflies to light his way.

In the excitement of the game, Alice had lost sight of Chippers and Anna. Now she saw that they had left the front porch. The house was dark except for a single light emanating from Mr. Williams's sitting room.

Alice stood in the yard, which was suddenly quite dark, and listened. She had never known such stillness, such quiet, not even in Tipton. The sound of Philip's footfalls had died away. She could hear the murmuring of bugs and, from the fishpond, the rough reassurances of the frogs.

Macklin was here less than a week ago, she remembered. What would he say if he were standing next to her? Would he brush the loose ends of her hair off her forehead, the way he used to do, and run his fingertips along the contours of her face? For a couple of strange moments, she felt his presence. Dropping both tennis racquets to the ground, she touched her cheek and imagined that her hand was Macklin's hand. The air smelled of boxwood and freshly cut grass, but somewhere she detected the scent of Macklin's warm skin and breath, the musky aroma of his bare chest and arms. How long it had been since she last pressed her bare flesh against his. Yet she tasted him in the humid Virginia air and felt a ghostly nearness in the velvety shadows of the boxwoods.

It shamed her to think of how she embraced Anna in the spangled dimness of the Mirador Hotel. But even now the unbidden recollection of Anna's eager hands stirred her. Even if she hadn't sought out such an encounter, on a soft bed in St. Louis, how could she not answer Anna's kisses with her own? Surely their brief interlude wasn't so terrible or wrong, no matter what Mrs. Boyer's suspicious mind imagined.

Walking aimlessly around the front lawn, she wondered if her life would stretch on like this, flowering and withering, bursts of pleasure followed by spells of self-doubt and longing. She was twenty-two. What lay ahead of her? Who was to say the Nazis wouldn't invade the U.S. and fly their evil planes over the hills of Rapidan? She thought of Macklin and Ross and David and Abe Walker and Billy Moxley and Dennis Delmarvin—all of them fighting for the country, all in grave danger.

Despite the warmth of the night, a shiver passed through her body. The stars above seemed to have sharpened their points as Alice, for the first time in her life, contemplated her own mortality. Her steady breath told her she would live a very long time, as long or longer than Mr. Williams, but oh, when her time came, what would that be like? Would she be surrounded by children and grandchildren, their eyes wet with tears? Or in the hospital with only a night nurse coolly checking her pulse? Or lying in a field of rubble bombed by the enemy?

If I have to die, she thought impulsively, *I want to die here. I want to die at Red Road Farm on a night like this—not tonight of course, but a warm summer night with all the world's wars far away. Maybe I'll just walk into the garden and lay my head down.*

As these notions came to her, Alice's heart slipped out of its usual slow rhythm and thudded with dire urgency. A feverish heat flooded her body, and she grew terrified that her musings had provoked a heart attack. In the morning, she fretted, Philip would find her dead on the tennis court, facedown in the grass. Walking toward the row of magnolias and looking up at the dark ocean of stars, she prayed, *Please, God, don't let me die. Not tonight, not anytime soon. And don't let Macklin die or Anna or Philip or any of the children in Tipton. And please protect all the soldiers.*

She turned and walked back toward the house. Then, as the stars and fireflies swirled around her, she whispered into the night, *Dear God, please bring him home to me. Bring Macklin home to Red Road Farm. And if Macklin doesn't love me anymore, bring me someone who does.*

The sound of full-throated laughter startled her from her reverie. She saw the silhouettes of Chippers and Anna, hand in hand, rounding the bend in the driveway. Before they could notice her, she hurried up the front steps and went inside.

Mr. Williams had gone to bed. His rhythmic snores reassured her that he would live to see another morning. She turned off the lamp and closed his door so Chippers and Anna wouldn't wake him when they came in.

Alice was in bed, with her door closed, by the time Anna and Chippers tiptoed upstairs. Outside Anna's room, across the hall from hers, the two whispered their goodnights. Alice lay motionless on her side and listened to their muffled giggles. Then they grew quieter except for a few sighs and murmurs. The floorboards creaked; there was more whispering and a flurry of sighs, and then Chippers's footsteps retreated down the hallway. She heard Anna in the bathroom that adjoined their two rooms, running water and humming cheerfully. Alice rolled over on her stomach and pulled the sheet over her head. Her face turned to the wall, she realized that all of her muscles were tightened up. She rolled over again and sighed. And then she slept.

4

The next morning Philip came over as promised. He was in his Chicago clothes, and his shoes were freshly polished. Anna had agreed to stay within shouting distance of Mr. Williams while the others went to church. Hurrying out the front door, Alice remembered the question she was supposed to ask. She found Anna sitting on the porch swing, with a book on her lap and coffee cup in hand, and said, "Mr. Williams wants to know if you're kin to Teddy Boyer."

Anna looked up. "Who?"

"Teddy Boyer, the judge in Chicago. Mr. Williams's best friend clerked for him."

"For heaven's sake." Anna closed her book and stood up from the swing. "He was my great-grandfather." She shook her head in wonder. "I haven't thought about him in a long time."

"Well, Mr. Williams was thinking about him just yesterday."

"I will talk to him," said Anna decisively, as if their hour had finally come. She headed inside just as Chippers was rushing out. His wavy hair was slicked down, and his tie swung loose around his neck. He looked sleepy. Alice watched him bestow a deep, meaningful smile on Anna before asking for the keys to the Packard.

"We're not driving to church, Chippers," Alice said. "It's right next door."

"But Alice, you don't want to get your shoes all muddy," he said. "And we'll be late if we walk. It's almost eleven o'clock."

Rather than argue about the absurdity of it, Alice turned and headed to the car with Chippers and Philip behind her.

The church bells were ringing as Alice and Philip trotted up the steps ahead of Chippers, who had parked so close to an old pickup truck that he could barely squeeze out of the car.

A pudgy man in a tight black suit held the door for Alice. He looked at her in a speculative, not particularly welcoming way, and his eyes turned cold when he saw Philip. "And who might you be, young lady?" he asked.

"I'm Alice Williams. I just moved to Red Road Farm from Tipton, Oklahoma. What is your name, sir?"

The man's eyes shifted back and forth from Alice to Philip. "My name's Arnold Radius. And who is *this*?"

Alice glanced at Philip. "This is Philip Williams."

"I didn't know they allowed *white* girls to marry *niggers* in Oklahoma," Radius spat out. "But I'm afraid you two ain't welcome here. You might try one of the nigger churches in Orange."

"I can sit in the back if that's the way you do it here," Philip said tensely. "But, for the record, Mrs. Williams and I are not married. We just happen to have the same last name."

A woman was playing the organ at the front of the church, and the minister was already standing at the altar, but the service had not yet begun. Some of the worshipers swung their heads around in curiosity at the sound of Philip's voice.

"What's going on?" Chippers said to Alice as he came up behind her.

Before she could answer, a little lady came bustling down the center aisle. "Chippers!" she said. "I'm so glad to see you." She smiled at him and then her face grew serious. "You haven't been drafted yet?"

"Mrs. Darling!" Chippers cried out. "I haven't seen you since the Christmas party." He paused to give her an affectionate hug. "I'm going to officer training school. I have to be in New York in three days. How is Hugh? *Where* is Hugh?"

Mrs. Darling's eyes sparkled with a sudden film of tears. "He's in the Pacific, and he's doing okay so far as we know. We get a postcard from him every now and then."

While this exchange took place, Alice stood by in silent fury.

Arnold Radius had been joined by a dour-faced woman, presumably his wife. They were glaring at her and Philip.

Mrs. Darling turned to Alice. "Forgive my manners," she said, and then, with hopeful eyes, to Chippers, "Is this your—?"

"Oh, no, no," said Chippers. "Mrs. Darling, I'd like you to meet Alice Williams. Alice is—well, Alice is married to Macklin. You remember Macklin?"

"Of course I remember Macklin. You and Macklin gave the best Christmas party Orange County has seen in twenty years." She extended her hand to Alice. "Welcome to Purcell. I'll want to chat with you after the service and find out how that wonderful young man is doing. I trust he's an officer, too?"

"Well—" Alice began.

"I just asked these two to leave," Arnold Radius interrupted.

"Why on earth would you do that?" Mrs. Darling asked. To Philip she said, "I'm Lenore Darling. Welcome to Purcell."

"Thank you. I'm Philip—"

"We don't allow no niggers in Purcell." Radius hissed through clenched teeth.

Mrs. Darling shot a jagged look at her fellow parishioner. "Well, in that case what are *you* doing here?" With that she tucked her hand into Chippers's arm and said, "Follow me. We're going to sit in the Williams family pew, all four of us."

With Arnold fuming and muttering behind them, the group marched to the front. As the organ intoned a solemn Presbyterian hymn, the newcomers fumbled their way to their seats, with Alice between Philip and Chippers, and Mrs. Darling on the aisle.

For Alice the next hour passed in a blur of anger and mortification. During prayers she did not pray. When it came time to stand and sing hymns, she stood but did not sing. Beside her Philip sang in a clear tenor, his voice rising to the rafters of the old church. On her other side, Chippers shared a hymnal with Mrs. Darling and both of them sang off-key.

During the sermon, Alice had no intention of listening to a single word. Rather than look at the florid minister, who seemed oblivious to what had transpired earlier, she gazed out the open windows at Red Road Farm. Birds were chirping and bees were buzzing. The pasture was covered in sunlight, the horse named Goldie and a spotted mare were grazing near the water trough, and Red Road's white clapboards were shining in the distance. The makeshift tennis court beckoned. She began to relax.

When the time came for the deacons to collect the offering, Philip dropped a quarter in the pewter plate. Alice's anger and shame rose again. She was sorely tempted to remove the coin and return it to Philip later, but instead she watched Chippers dig in his pockets and come up empty. With a sheepish glance at her, he handed the plate to Mrs. Darling, who tossed in a tithing envelope.

At the end of the service, Chippers and Mrs. Darling moved to the center aisle and were quickly surrounded by people who wanted to talk to them. Alice turned to Philip. "We can take a shortcut." She pointed to a door propped open near the pulpit. Beyond that, Alice could see another door that led outside.

"I want to talk to the preacher," Philip said.

She quaked at the thought of another scene. "I just want to get out of here. Don't you?"

"He'll tell me where the Negro churches are. And when I leave, I'm going out the same door I came in."

Just then Mrs. Darling beckoned to them.

"I've got to go," Alice said, her voice tight. Trading places with Philip, she hurried away and slipped outside without a backward glance.

The noontime sun was dazzling. She stood and blinked as her eyes adjusted to the light. Just being outside made her feel better. The ground was not as muddy as Chippers had feared, but she knew the red clay in the pasture would stick to her shoes. She slipped them off and let her bare feet sink into the lush grass.

From where she stood, she could see several of the cars parked in front of the church. There was her new nemesis, Arnold Radius, on the far side of Anna's Packard. He was walking slowly while looking down at the car. One of his arms seemed tensed as if he were dragging something beside him. Then he made a quick movement as if tossing something inside the Packard's open window. When he looked up, he saw Alice and scowled at her yet again before climbing into the old pickup beside the Packard. Alice glimpsed his unpleasant wife in the seat beside him. They appeared to be the first ones leaving. Their old truck belched smoke as it turned onto Rapidan Road and labored up the hill toward Orange.

Alice shook her head in disgust. She was about to duck under the fence and walk across the pasture when she heard voices. An old man and an even older woman were talking earnestly in the graveyard behind her.

"I don't know why he had to be buried here, so far from home." The woman was staring at a large, fresh headstone.

"Well, Daddy always said he'd be buried in Rapidan." The man knelt down and pulled up a few dandelions near the grave. "He loved it here."

"That he did," the woman said bitterly. "That he did."

"Mama, don't fret over it. Just because he didn't want to be buried in Richmond doesn't mean he didn't love you." The man stood up and wiped dirt from his pants. "Let's go see Minor and take care of our business with him. We'll be in Charlottesville by two o'clock, I promise." He extended his arm and the two of them were about to leave when Alice called out to them.

"You're friends of Mr. Williams?"

The pair turned toward Alice. "Why, yes, we are," the man said. He was trim and well built with a bright pink complexion and a fringe of white hair around his nearly bald head. "I take it you're a friend of his, too?"

"Well, I'd like to be if he'll let me." Alice, still carrying her shoes, advanced toward the two and met them in front of the fresh headstone. "My name is Alice Williams and I work for Mr. Williams as his nurse." She paused and looked from one to the other. "I'm Macklin Williams's wife. He's gone off to war."

The man and woman traded a look before the woman extended

a small, blue-veined hand. Her name was Betty Shafer and the man was her son, Thomas. She asked whether Mr. Williams was well enough to have visitors.

"He'll be glad to see you, I'm sure," Alice said. "Here, let me help you." She took Mrs. Shafer's arm and the three of them made their way around to the front of the church where Thomas Shafer's car was parked.

Though they offered her a ride, she declined, sensing their unease. As Thomas Shafer started the car, she noticed Mrs. Shafer's somber expression. "Forgive me," she said and reached out to touch the woman's shoulder. "I should have said earlier how sorry I am for your loss. Mr. Williams told me just yesterday that Furman Shafer was his best friend for seventy years." She paused in sudden wonder. "That's a long time."

Her lip trembling, Mrs. Shafer nodded in reply.

"We'll see you at the house," Thomas Shafer called out.

By now other people were leaving church. After ducking under the fence to the pasture, Alice hesitated. She wondered if Arnold Radius had done something to Anna's car—it would take just a minute to go back and check. But no, she had to meet Mrs. Shafer and Thomas Shafer, and make sure Mr. Williams was awake.

Slipping her shoes back on as she reached the driveway, she saw to her surprise that Mr. Williams was sitting on the front porch and Anna was standing beside his wheelchair. Betty and Thomas Shafer were talking to them.

When Alice reached their side, the introductions had already been made. Now Anna was offering chairs to the guests. Several wicker chairs were at the far end of the porch.

"I'll move!" Mr. Williams suddenly barked. With a burst of energy, he propelled himself forward. Alice let out a small cry, afraid his wheelchair would roll right off the porch, but he stopped himself in time.

Anna turned to the Shafers. "Would you like something to drink?"

"Some iced tea, no sugar, would be grand," Thomas Shafer

said. He paused and looked from one young woman to the other. "This is a business call, and it won't take long. My mother and I have a luncheon reservation in Charlottesville." He seemed to want time alone with his host.

Mr. Williams piped up. "If it's business we're talking, I want *her* here."

"I'd be glad to sit with you, Mr. Williams," Alice said, "and I can get the three of you something to eat while you talk."

"Not you!" Mr. Williams croaked. "The other one. The one from Chicago."

Alice swallowed hard. "Anna, you mean."

"That's it." He paused to cough into a handkerchief. "You— bring me a cup of coffee and a sandwich." His voice softened a little. "I liked what you fixed me yesterday. Bring me another one of those, if you please."

As she prepared the tea and coffee, and sliced roasted chicken for Mr. Williams's sandwich, Alice wondered how much humiliation she could bear in a single day. After she assembled everything, she stood over the tray of food and took a breath. Although she had not prayed during church, she now felt, for the second time in twenty-four hours, a sudden urge to communicate with God. Bowing her head, she closed her eyes and whispered, "Dear Lord, I am being tested. Please help me pass the test. Please give me strength, and give Philip strength, too. And please don't let me drop this tray. Thank you, and amen."

The group on the porch fell silent as Alice fumbled with the screen door and made her way toward them. The Shafers accepted their tea with nods of thanks. Anna did not look up as she took a glass of iced water. Mr. Williams said nothing when Alice set the tray on his lap.

"Anything else?" Alice asked, her hands on her hips and a drop of sweat sliding down her nose.

"This is lovely, Alice. Thank you," Anna said.

"All right," she said. "I'll be out here, if you need me." With that she headed down the side steps to the driveway with no intention of returning anytime soon.

She had passed the barn when she heard a car approaching. Chippers rolled down the window and asked what she was up to.

"I'm going to find Philip and apologize to him," she said. "It was terrible what happened over there."

"I know, Alice. I want to talk to him, too. But the other folks were nice. Don't let one bigot spoil the whole church for you."

Alice looked at the Packard. "By the way," she said, "I saw that creature—that Arnold—acting very suspicious after church. It looked like he was doing something to Anna's car."

"Well, it seems fine," Chippers said. "Say, did you lose a quarter? There's a quarter on the seat."

She shook her head. "I'll see you in a little while. Oh, and be careful up on the porch. We have visitors, or I should say, Mr. Williams does. Anna was invited to the party, but I wasn't. Proceed with caution."

He laughed in his genial way and drove off.

At the tenant house, she saw Philip sitting on the stoop eating a bowl of beans with some cornbread. He offered her some, which she accepted. After settling down beside him, she found that she had no appetite.

"What's wrong, Alice?" Philip asked. "It's a pretty day, we've both got jobs. What's there to feel bad about?"

His willingness to overlook the episode at the church made Alice feel even worse. He handed her his napkin to use as a handkerchief when she began to cry.

After a few minutes, she composed herself. Still sniffling, she said, "I just feel so bad about what happened at the church. I can't believe I didn't speak up. I'm so sorry, Philip, I really am." She wiped her nose. "That horrible man!" she said. "I'll never go to that church again."

Philip leaned back on the steps and stretched his legs. He seemed to be measuring his words before he spoke. "I didn't expect you to defend me, Alice," he said. "I'm on my own now, and I can take care of myself. And *I* spoke up, remember? I didn't let him keep me—keep *us*—out. And Chippers's friend, that little old lady—she got him good." Narrowing his eyes, he gazed at the far field and fell silent.

She ate a few bites and waited. The birdsong in the nearby trees and in the fields grew more noticeable. A single puffy cloud floated across the high blue sky. The orange cat rounded the corner by the barn and began making his way toward them. Suddenly he stopped and swiped at a bug too tiny for her to see. It looked like he was shadowboxing. Alice's spirits lifted slightly.

"I know all about Jim Crow," Philip resumed. "Arnold Radius didn't teach me anything new."

She nodded. "You ran into this sort of thing in Oklahoma?"

"Of course. We were the only colored family in Beaver County. But there were more Indians there than colored folks. My mother and brothers and I went to a little country church, a lot like Purcell. Usually we sat in the back, sometimes we didn't. Nobody seemed to care. We weren't close friends with anybody, but nobody badmouthed us, at least not to our faces. I guess they had better things to do." He turned to Alice, his mood shifting. "I like to sing. One of the good things about church is, you get to sing."

"You have a nice voice. I wish you'd give Chippers some singing lessons. That boy is hard on the ears."

"I heard him." Philip chuckled. "I'm not sure he's teachable."

"He's leaving this week, you know."

"And what about his tennis partner?"

Alice looked down at her lap. "I guess she's going with him. She wants to go to college in New York."

The cat had joined them by now, and Philip petted the animal on the head. "She's a funny one. She acts like she's interested in Chippers, but I don't believe it."

"Now, whatever would make you say that?"

"Oh, I don't know, Alice." He shifted his legs and sat up. "I get the feeling you're the one she cares about. She's just showing off with him."

"Is that what you really think?"

"That's what I said."

"There's nothing between us." Alice said. "Or I should say—well." She stopped herself. "I didn't know people even talked about things like this."

"I guess we can talk about anything we want to."

"That's true. If we want to."

"You don't want to?"

"All I can say is, I came to Rapidan to find my husband, Macklin Williams." A sudden wave of laughter rose in her throat as a nonsensical phrase came to her mind. "Holy Macklin!" she exclaimed.

Taking his cue, Philip lifted his arms to the skies and rose to his feet as if he were back in church, a more free-spirited one than Purcell. "Macklin! Macklin! Holy Macklin!" he sang in his fine clear tenor. "*Mack*-lin! They called him Holy *Mack*-lin!"

"*Mack*-lin, *Mack*-lin!" Alice sang out. She also stood up and waved her hands high in the air. "Holy Macklin! They called him Holy *Mack*-lin!"

Startled, the cat ran full-speed back toward the barn. This just made Alice and Philip sing louder and laugh harder. Alice thought she had never heard anything as funny as her husband's name.

When their laughter was spent, she bade goodbye to Philip and went back to check on the others. The Shafers' car was gone and Mr. Williams was no longer on the porch, but Alice saw Anna and Chippers standing beside the Packard, deep in conversation. As Alice drew closer, she heard her friend say, "What do you mean, you think somebody at the church did it?"

Alice came up alongside the car. There was a long narrow scratch in the blue paint that ran nearly the length of the passenger's side.

"You drove to a church that's not even a five-minute walk from here, and now look at it!"

"Here's Alice," Chippers said. "She can explain."

"You can?" Anna whirled around. "I'd like to know just what

happened to my car over at that church."

It was then that Alice noticed that Anna was dressed for an excursion. Instead of the culottes and blouse she had on earlier, she was wearing a crisp blue dress and expensive looking sandals. Chippers was still in his church clothes, and Alice saw him glance worriedly at his watch even as he waited for her to rescue him from this crisis.

"Where are you going?" Alice asked him.

"Mr. Shafer invited us to join him and his mother for lunch at Farmington. We'll be late if we don't leave in the next few minutes."

"What is Farmington?"

"It's a country club in Charlottesville. I used to play tennis there—when I got invited, that is. You'd love it, Alice. Hey, you should come, too."

"The car," Anna interrupted. "Tell me what happened to my car."

"A truly despicable man at church called Philip a nigger and tried to keep us from attending the service. We went in anyway." She took a breath. "Afterwards, I saw Arnold—that's his name— loitering near your car. He threw something in the window, and then he jumped in his truck and took off in a hurry."

"What did he throw in my car?" Anna asked, peering inside.

"Maybe it was this quarter I found on the passenger's seat," Chippers said, pulling the coin out of his pocket. "I guess he used it to make the scratch. Look, there's a flake of blue paint on it. I wonder why he threw it in the car."

"I know why," Alice said. "Arnold collected the offering, and he saw Philip put a quarter in the plate. That's Philip's quarter."

"Oh, good lord," Anna said. She was looking at Alice with a mixture of concern and exasperation. "He called Philip that?"

"Yes. And he said some other things."

"Chippers," Anna said, "go inside and call the sheriff."

"I don't think we can have him arrested for calling Philip a name."

"The car, Chippers, the car! We'll have him arrested for vandalizing my car."

He turned the palms of his hands toward Anna as if to fend off further rebukes. "Fine. But I think getting the law involved could be awkward for Alice and Philip, since they just moved here. And that fellow will just say he didn't do it, that the scratch was there before."

"Well, it wasn't there before," Anna said, glaring at Chippers.

"He'll say Philip did it." Alice said. "Oh, I think we better not call the sheriff, Anna." She thought back to the day, not long ago, when she rammed her friend's car into a tree at the orphanage. The Packard had been taking its lumps lately.

Chippers stood with his fists jammed in his pockets. Finally, he said, "We could take it to a garage in Orange tomorrow, and I could pay you back—at some point."

"Oh, for heaven's sake," Anna said. "Let's just go to lunch." She got in the car while Chippers went around to the driver's side. To Alice, she said, "We'll talk tonight. I worked things out with the Shafers. As of today, you're not just Minor's nurse. You're the new farm manager."

"I am?"

"You are indeed," said Anna drily. "Until Sorbon Carter gets back. I have lots to tell you, but it'll have to wait until later."

"Sure you don't want to come with us, Alice?" Chippers called out.

"She can't go with us. She has to stay with Minor," Anna said.

"Oh, what was I thinking? Well, goodbye, Alice." Chippers honked the horn and the pair drove off trailing a cloud of dust.

Inside, Alice found Mr. Williams snoring in his chair, a newspaper crumpled on his lap. In the kitchen she saw that Anna, fastidious as always, had taken time to wash the dishes. With nothing pressing to do, Alice decided to change out of her church clothes and take a walk.

More comfortable in shorts and calico blouse, she found a straw hat in the coat closet and went back outside. First she inspected the magnolias in the front yard. There were three mature trees of varying heights separating the lawn from the flower garden and fishpond at the front of the property. Their waxy green leaves were shining, and they were in full bloom. Alice stood on tiptoe so she could sniff a creamy blossom. The delicious scent brought a smile to her face. When she reached up a finger, the petal quickly turned brown where she had touched it. *Well, I won't do that again*, she thought.

Her next stop was the fishpond. Several toads and frogs hopped in the water when she drew near. By her count, there were eleven goldfish. After retrieving the old metal canister from the shed, she tossed oatmeal into the water and the fish glided rapidly toward the flakes. In the grass she nearly stumbled over a box turtle making its way toward the water. She stooped down to admire it and touch its shell.

From Red Road Farm it was a short walk to the Rapidan River bridge. A sign just before the bridge marked the border between Orange and Culpeper counties, and Alice stopped and stood with one foot in each county. There was a flourmill next to the river, the source of the mill's electricity. No one was working there on a Sunday and Alice passed by it with barely a glance. She was more interested in the river. The water, high and reddish brown from the region's clay soil, flowed swiftly over the dam. Alice walked to the center of the bridge and peered down. There were several Negro men with fishing poles standing on the riverbank. She waved and yelled, "Hi!" Without quite looking at her, they raised their hands in response before turning their attention back to the water.

Upstream, a blue heron stood very still on the riverbank. When it lifted its wings and flapped across the river, Alice let out an exclamation of delight. The bird was enormous and stately. Until now, she had only seen a picture of a heron in a book her uncle kept at the Tipton Home.

She crossed the road to the other side of the bridge. There were several children with a couple of inner tubes standing at the river's edge. Amid much laughing and merriment, a girl and a little boy squeezed into one tube, and the bigger boy got in the other. They began drifting away and Alice watched them until they disappeared around a bend in the river and their high-pitched voices trailed off.

From there, she continued her walk. Beyond the bridge, she walked a quarter mile or so before coming to a side road she had not yet explored. It had a few small houses and, near the railroad overpass, a general store on one side and a post office on the other. She was glad to know about both of these. Beyond the overpass stretched many acres of farmland, as far as Alice could see. She wondered who lived in the farmhouses tucked away from the road and if she would ever get to know those people. Little do they know, she thought, that Alice Williams has come to town.

Walking home, she wondered what on earth Anna meant when she said that she had gotten her the job of farm manager. That was more than she had bargained for, and she had no idea what it would involve. But she wasn't worried; she wasn't even that interested. Her mind was clear and she was at peace.

There was little traffic, but whenever a car or pickup truck passed, the occupants lifted their hands in a small wave. Alice waved back and looked right into the faces of those who drove by: perhaps these people would be future friends.

One such car had a young man at the wheel. He raised his hat politely and smiled. He was driving so slowly on the narrow road that Alice got a good look at his ruddy complexion and thick brown hair. His eyes were golden brown, and he had a very nice smile. He was portly but not fat and looked about thirty years old. There was a kindness about him, and when they locked eyes, she saw something in him that matched something in her: hopefulness. Then his dusty green Plymouth passed by and Alice forced herself not to turn around and stare.

Now I wonder who that was? she thought, as if she were the old timer in Rapidan and the car's occupant the new face in town.

Anna and Chippers took their time getting back from

Charlottesville. Alice had shared a quiet supper with Mr. Williams, who was clearly exhausted from his lunch meeting with Mrs. Shafer and her son. He ate little and seemed on the verge of dozing off several times. When she offered him a bowl of fruit for dessert, he shook his head and waited for her to take his tray away. By eight o'clock he was in bed, sound asleep, before it was even dark outside.

Alice made chicken salad for the next day, cleaned the kitchen, and tidied up Mr. Williams's bathroom. When there was nothing else to do, she went out on the front porch and settled in the swing. It was nearly the summer solstice and Alice relished the long, slow gathering of dusk. She watched the first lightning bugs blinking near the ground. In the distance came the sounds of frogs around the pond. Occasionally she heard a car rattle down Rapidan Road. In the pasture the horses were gradually turning into silhouettes. Returning from her walk, she had seen Philip tending to them. She wondered what he was doing this evening in his little house on the hill.

Finally, shortly after nine o'clock, the Packard's headlights lit up the driveway. Soon Chippers and Anna emerged, and Alice heard her laugh at something Chippers said.

"Waiting up for us?" Anna called out.

"It's a nice night. I was just watching the lightning bugs." She pointed to the magnolia trees, where clouds of fireflies lit up the high branches.

"Oh!" said Anna. "I've never seen so many."

"Do you still want to talk tonight?"

"Let me change clothes first. I'll meet you out here."

Chippers stopped to talk for a few minutes and then said he was going to bed early. He looked tired but happy. Before following Anna inside, he leaned down and said softly, "I'm going to marry that girl; you wait and see."

"Just don't let anything else happen to her car, Chippers."

He said, "We had such a great time today, I'd forgotten all about that. I'll take it into Orange tomorrow and see about getting it repaired. Oh, well. Good night, Alice."

When Anna reappeared on the porch, she was barefoot in a sleeveless nightgown. Her hair was wet and she smelled of soap. Scooting over on the swing to make room for her, Alice said, "I feel overdressed."

Anna chuckled. "My apologies for keeping you in suspense all these hours. I'm sure you've been waiting all day to find out about your new job."

"Let's just say I'm ready to listen."

"Well," Anna began, "as Minor may have told you—or perhaps not—his old friend Furman Shafer managed his affairs for him in recent years. When Furman died, those duties fell to his son, Thomas. But Thomas can't take on the responsibility of overseeing Red Road Farm and supervising Minor's care." She shifted her legs so that she could give the swing a gentle push. "Until last year, Thomas was the swimming coach at Clemson, but after his father died he retired and moved back to Richmond to take care of his mother, who had tended to both Minor and Furman as long as she could."

"She doesn't look like she's doing very well."

"She's not," Anna said. "In any case, they came up here to visit Furman Shafer's grave and tell Minor they couldn't do any more for him. The question was, who would run the farm with Sorbon Carter out of town? Chippers would've been a logical candidate, but he can't, of course."

Alice listened silently. It was the first private conversation she'd had with Anna since their escape from the Tipton Home. She was surprised that her friend was so absorbed in Mr. Williams's affairs and the operation of Red Road Farm.

"So I recommended you." Anna looked very pleased with herself. "I told them you briefly attended the University of Oklahoma and that you're a diligent worker."

No one, Alice thought, could accuse Anna of extravagant praise. "Well, what—"

Anna put a hand up so Alice wouldn't interrupt. "Thomas said he'd never heard of a lady farm manager, but his mother reminded him that they didn't need a permanent replacement, just someone to do the job until Sorbon gets back. And she said there was no reason a woman couldn't run the place just as well as a man could. I have a feeling Mrs. Shafer's the real boss in that family. The fact that you're, technically at least, a member of the Williams family also argued in your favor."

"What do you mean, technically?"

"No one heard Macklin Williams talk longingly about the beloved wife he'd left behind in Oklahoma, my dear."

Alice fumed inwardly. "I have a feeling he and his uncle didn't talk a lot about much of anything."

"You're probably right about that. To his credit, Macklin did try to help out before he left for the war. But now he's gone, and there's no reason to expect him back anytime soon. Happily, Minor and Thomas are willing to give you this important job. You have quite an interesting opportunity here."

"You figured I'd be thrilled about this."

"I got you a raise," Anna continued. "You'll make fifteen dollars a week."

"What was my salary before the raise?"

"You're asking me?"

"Mr. Williams said Chippers would tell me, but I hadn't gotten around to asking him about that. He's usually off somewhere with you." She paused, aware that she sounded aggrieved. "No one's paid me anything yet."

Anna looked down at her hands. Weariness seemed to come over her. "Well, I hope it's a raise, then. Thomas Shafer suggested the amount, and I assumed it was more than you're making now."

"It's more than nothing."

"You don't sound very grateful for my help."

"Oh, Anna!" She stood up abruptly from the swing. "What's happened to you? What's happened to my old friend who helped me escape from Tipton? My friend who was always on my side. I thought you—"

"You thought I what?"

"I thought—" Alice stopped herself again. Then she remembered her conversation with Philip earlier in the day; he had said people could talk about whatever they wanted to. "I thought you cared about me."

"I thought you cared about me," Anna said. She remained in the swing, her face turned up to Alice's.

"You knew, the whole time we were in Tipton, that I was planning to get back together with Macklin. You knew I was in love with my husband. I never pretended otherwise."

"You didn't seem very in love with him the night we spent together." Anna's eyes burned brightly in the starlight, and Alice inhaled the scent of her damp hair.

"You started that," Alice said. "And I didn't—"

"You didn't want to stop."

"Shh, Anna," Alice said, sitting back down on the swing. "You'll wake Mr. Williams."

"Do you have any idea," Anna said, her face glistening with tears, "how long I stayed in Tipton just to be with you?" She paused to wipe her eyes with the back of her hand. With a sob in her voice, she said, "You were the only reason I stuck around so long."

The two young women gazed at one another. "I'm sorry, Anna. I didn't know." In the lull that followed, Alice asked herself, *Or did I?* Anna had followed her around the orphanage and hung on her every word. She never expressed a word of interest in boys. When Alice suggested running away together, Anna was ecstatic. But when Alice thought about their night at the Mirador Hotel, she hardly knew what to think. Looking into Anna's eyes, a part of her wished she could keep her friend enthralled.

"Well, say something," Anna demanded, and Alice could hear in her friend's voice an echo of the imperious Mrs. Boyer.

"I can't think of anything else," Alice said at last. "I guess I should thank you for the farm manager job." She tried a small smile. "Maybe my first act will be to hire a new nurse."

"Don't do yourself out of that part just yet. Once Sorbon Carter comes back, he'll be the farm manager again."

"You're full of instructions and advice, aren't you?"

"I'm trying to look out for you, that's all." Anna's eyes blazed. "I care a lot more about you than your imaginary husband does."

Not for the first time that day Alice felt her heart pound with anger, but this time she was prepared to speak up. "You're being mean, Anna. I'm disappointed in you."

"Oh, so *I'm* the mean one and *you're* disappointed." Anna's voice dripped irony.

They sat for a while and Alice listened to the incongruously gentle creak of the swing. She thought how quiet it would be after Chippers and Anna left. Mr. Williams wasn't good company, and Philip probably wouldn't visit as often without the others around. She felt a stab of loneliness as her old friend seethed by her side. "What about Chippers?"

Anna shifted restlessly. "I've been a welcome distraction for him just as he has been for me."

"How nice for both of you."

"Sarcasm doesn't become you, Alice."

"He told me he wants to marry you someday."

Anna's mouth dropped open in surprise. She turned to look at the magnolias, still lit up with lightning bugs.

Alice twisted sideways in the swing. By now Anna's dark-gold hair was nearly dry. Since leaving Tipton she had lost a few pounds, and her high cheekbones stood out in the starlight. Alice imagined that someday, perhaps someday soon, her friend would be beautiful.

"Would you marry him if he asked you to?"

"He's just a boy."

"He won't be a boy when he gets back from the Pacific, or wherever they send him."

"If he gets back."

Alice looked down at the gooseflesh rising on her arms. "Anna, how can you even say that?"

"Well, no one knows what the future will bring."

They sat quietly for a few minutes, and then Alice started up again. "I heard you last night. I heard you kissing him."

"You had your ear pressed against the door?"

"It seemed like you wanted me to hear."

"He's very attracted to me." She turned toward Alice in a friendly way. "And he's quite a good kisser. I wouldn't have guessed that."

Though she knew it was wrong, Alice leaned forward impulsively and kissed Anna on the lips and ran her fingers through Anna's thick hair. When she pulled back at last, she said, "Is he better than me?"

Anna rose unsteadily from the swing and smoothed her hair where Alice had tousled it. "You shouldn't have done that." She again looked like she might cry. "You're cruel."

"No crueler than you are to him."

Just then the porch light blinked on. Chippers, in pajamas, stepped outside. "You two all right?" His eyes bleary, he looked from one to the other. "It's getting late."

"I was just coming up to bed," Anna said. In a cold, clear voice, she added, "Good night, Alice."

Alice watched Chippers hold the door as Anna disappeared inside without a backward glance. She could hear their footsteps on the staircase and then all was quiet except for the night sounds of Red Road Farm. A deep sorrow filled her chest. She rose at last and walked to the edge of the porch. The sky was a haze of stars. She stared up at them until, to her amazement, she saw one shoot across the sky. It tumbled out of place so rapidly that she wondered whether she had really seen it. But she had. And then inexplicably the image of the man in the dusty green Plymouth appeared in her mind. She thought of how he tipped his hat and smiled as he drove past her on the bridge. *No one knows what will happen*, she thought, before going inside and letting the long day end at last.

5

From then on, Alice saw little of Anna. Her car was gone the next morning when Alice came downstairs for breakfast. Chippers agreed to keep an eye on Mr. Williams while Alice and Philip ran errands in Orange. With Philip at the wheel of the farm truck, they drove to Montpelier, where he met the men who worked with the horses. Several of them were colored, and from her perch in the truck, Alice could see them welcoming Philip. Rather than join him on a tour of the stables, she lay down on the front seat. With the windows open and the truck parked in the shade, she quickly dozed off.

She awoke to the sound of Philip laughing as he opened the door. "Wake up, sleepy head!" Alice sat up and looked at her watch. It was ten-thirty; she had slept for nearly an hour.

Beside Philip stood a young colored woman wearing a bright red smock. Her skin was very dark and she had a brilliant smile. "Alice, this is Rosa Washington. She works in the kitchen at Montpelier and helps with the horses, too."

"Hello, Rosa," Alice said. "Come see us sometime at Red Road Farm. We've got lots of horses there."

"Rosa's looking for an extra job, something she could do on weekends," Philip said, his eyes resting steadily on Alice's.

She was fully awake now. "You like to cook?"

"Yes, ma'am," Rosa said.

"Are you good with old people?"

"Yes, ma'am. I helped my mama take care of my granddaddy for two years before he passed."

"Well, I may have something for you. Let me think it over, and I'll get back to you pretty soon."

Their next stop was the feed store, where Alice introduced herself and Philip to the clerk and cast a wondering eye on all the supplies. She would have to learn exactly what to buy and how much she was allowed to spend. From there they went to the hardware store and then Sparks's Grocery. Their new acquaintances regarded them with curiosity, but no one spoke to them the way Arnold Radius had. They drove around Orange until they found the A.M.E. church the preacher at Purcell had told Philip about. "That's where Rosa goes," he said.

"She seems nice," Alice said. "You think I should hire her?"

"You do what you want to do, Alice," he said. "But I think you'll get worn out pretty fast if you never take a day off."

"She can cook *and* she's good with old people?"

"And she'll help with the horses." Philip laughed. "Everybody wins."

They took the back roads home, and stopped at the post office on Route 614. To her surprise, there was mail waiting for her. Stuck among several bills for Mr. Williams she found a postcard from Ross Gentry and a letter with a military return address forwarded from the orphanage.

"Well, this is interesting," she said under her breath. Deciding to savor both of these missives in private, she held the mail on her lap as Philip drove her back to the farm.

As they came up the driveway, she saw Anna and Chippers sitting on the porch steps. When they spied the truck, they immediately stood up and headed to Anna's car.

"Uncle Minor's doing fine, Alice," Chippers said. "We gave him his lunch and now he's taking a nap. See you tonight."

Anna barely glanced in her direction. She was in the car with Chippers before Alice could do more than say goodbye. There was nothing to talk about anyway. She told herself she would be glad when Anna was gone—and Chippers, too. He wasn't a member of the Williams family, yet he acted as if Red Road Farm were his. *But it's not*, she thought. She wasn't quite prepared to think, *It's mine*, but she had already begun to think of it as home.

212

Chippers and Anna returned late that night. Alice was in bed when she heard the car pull up. The front door opened and there was some muffled conversation, but this time, Chippers didn't follow Anna to her room to say good night. The two seemed to be making every effort to be quiet, and Alice fell back to sleep quickly.

She got up at seven and served Mr. Williams breakfast in the kitchen. He ate well but wanted to return to his room afterwards. After shutting the door to his room, where he was staring fixedly at an open ledger, she was surprised to hear the doorbell ring. She wondered who on earth would be calling so early in the day.

At the door stood a smiling young man in a light blue summer suit and an attractive young woman who looked, Alice thought, like she had just stepped out of a bandbox. Though the day promised to be hot and humid, the young woman was exceptionally well turned out in a pink and white sundress and a little matching jacket. Her brunette hair was pulled back in a knot at the nape of her neck.

Introducing themselves as Dudley and Poppy Douglas, they said they had come to meet Chippers and Anna. The four of them were driving to Winchester, to see Chippers's family, and then Poppy would return home to Richmond while the others went to New York. Dudley, it turned out, was going to officer training school with Chippers.

Alice invited them inside. Just as Poppy was asking whether she was Mr. Williams's granddaughter, Chippers and Anna came clattering down the stairs. Anna was wearing a gray linen dress with little roses embroidered on it, and Chippers was in his church clothes, which were in need of pressing. His wavy hair was slicked down on his forehead and his tie, as usual, was slung around his neck. Alice caught a whiff of aftershave as he joined the group. Dudley and Poppy declined coffee. They were anxious to get on the road.

"Well, we're ready to go, aren't we, Anna?" Chippers said.

"Yes, certainly," Anna said, her gaze shifting from him to

Alice. "We just need to get our bags."

While Dudley and Chippers followed Anna upstairs, Alice turned to face Poppy. The two young women sat down on the sofa together. Her hands folded in her lap, Poppy seemed to be waiting for Alice to speak.

"I'm not Mr. Williams's granddaughter," Alice resumed as if there had been no interruption. "I'm Macklin Williams's wife. Macklin's gone to Texas to join the service, and I'm taking care of his great uncle until he gets home."

Poppy's eyes widened. "Did you—did you just get married?"

Gazing at the young woman's open, friendly face, Alice decided to trust her. "We got married in Oklahoma, and then I stayed behind when Macklin came out here for school. Money was tight, and we drifted apart because, well, we *were* apart. I gather Macklin didn't tell too many of his new friends about me. When I finally got here, he'd already left for Texas. I just missed him."

"I'm sorry to hear that," Poppy said, her eyes resting on Alice's with quiet compassion. She waited before speaking again. "It sure is hard having our husbands go off to war. Dudley and I got married the day after his graduation and a week after mine. It was supposed to be a big wedding, but with the war going on, we decided to keep things low-key. We had a three-day honeymoon at Sandbridge, and now he's leaving. Who knows when I'll see him again."

"You couldn't go to New York with him?"

"He won't be there very long, so we decided I'd stay in Richmond, where my family is." She smiled slightly. "It'll be all right. I got a job as a commercial artist at Miller and Rhoads."

"What kind of business is that?"

"It's a big department store. I'll sketch models wearing the latest fashions. My drawings will be in the *Times-Dispatch* and the *News Leader*."

With much bustling and chatter, the others came downstairs and headed outside, each of them carrying suitcases. There was a flurry of activity as Chippers and Dudley loaded everything into the Packard and Anna supervised. Alice saw that the car was pristine again; the long narrow scratch on the passenger's side could not be detected. Freshly washed and waxed, it gleamed in the morning sunshine.

When they were ready to leave, Chippers and Anna said goodbye to Mr. Williams, who had just awakened. Dudley and Poppy got in their car, and Poppy wrote her phone number on a scrap of paper and handed it through the open car window. "Come visit me in Richmond, and we'll go out to lunch." Alice slipped the paper in her pocket just as Chippers hurried down the porch steps.

He gave Alice a bear hug and a kiss on the cheek, and said he would be in touch. In a flash he had started up the Packard. She retreated to the porch and stood awkwardly as the two cars idled their engines. At last Anna appeared. She stopped next to Alice and looked her in the eye for the first time since their conversation two nights ago. "I just left something for you in your room," she said. "It's a present—actually, a couple of presents."

"Well, thanks. I guess this is goodbye, Anna."

"I don't know if—" Anna's voice trailed off.

"If what?"

"I don't know if we'll ever see each other again."

"You'll know where to find me. I'll be here, at Red Road Farm."

Anna's face looked drawn, as if she hadn't slept well. She touched Alice lightly on the cheek. "They're waiting for me. Goodbye, Alice." With that she walked away.

Chippers leapt out of the car to open the door for Anna, and Alice watched as first the Packard and then the other car drove off. Chippers honked the horn and waved, and Dudley and Poppy waved as well. Only Anna stared straight ahead. Alice kept her arm aloft in farewell until the two cars were gone.

6

After the others left, Alice sat on the swing and looked out at the front yard. Everything was still and quiet except for the usual chatter of birdsong. Her face felt hot, but her mind was calm.

Her eyes scanned the lawn, which was growing shaggy. It was then she realized the tennis net was gone, as were the lengths of twine marking the makeshift court. A single grass-stained ball caught her eye. Jumping up, she ran inside to look for the racquets Chippers and Anna kept near the umbrella stand. The racquets, too, were gone. She paused indecisively and then went to the door of Mr. Williams's room. Her hand on the doorknob, she listened to his steady snoring. She had never known anyone who slept so much.

She thought of seeking out Philip to tell him the others had left, but then she remembered Anna's last remarks. Curiosity drew her up the stairs to her room.

There, on her bed, she found a large paper bag and a bulging cream-colored envelope. From the bag she slid out a badminton set: a net, four racquets, and a birdie, along with a page detailing the rules of the game. Shaking her head in bemusement, Alice set this aside and opened the letter. Pulling out a single sheet of heavy stationery with Anna's initials engraved at the top, she saw that the envelope was stuffed with ten- and twenty-dollar bills, a handful of which slipped to the floor. It took her a minute to collect and count the money: three hundred dollars altogether. She looked at this in amazement and then read the letter from Anna, whose large slanting script filled the page:

Dear Alice,

You said you liked badminton better than tennis, so here is a badminton set. Use it in good health. And here is something else, which I suggest you deposit in a bank. Every girl needs a rainy-day fund.

 We have disappointed one another, and I am sorry for my part in that. For whatever it is worth to you, I remain—

Yours,
Anna

 She stared at the note before putting it back in the envelope and storing it, along with the scrap of paper bearing Poppy Douglas's telephone number, in the top drawer of the writing desk. In the drawer she found an empty fountain pen. A wan smile flickered across her face as she remembered Macklin's fondness for pens of this kind. With a rubber band she secured the thick wad of money and stowed it in her pocketbook.

 Out the window she could see Philip refilling the water trough in the pasture. For a minute she watched him go about his chores. The orange cat was trailing behind him and rubbing against his leg. The tractor was parked in front of the barn, so today was a mowing day. Maybe later that afternoon she could get Philip to sit with Mr. Williams while she walked to the general store and the post office; she didn't yet trust herself to drive the big old farm truck.

 "Oh my goodness!" Alice hopped up from her chair. Her feet flying, she hurried downstairs to the table where she had left yesterday's mail. Somehow, in the confusion and tension surrounding Anna's departure, she had forgotten to read the card from Ross and the mysterious letter.

 The letter was just where she left it, but the postcard from Ross was nowhere to be found. She looked under the table and scanned the living room floor. She looked in the kitchen and dining room, though she didn't think the card would be there. Wondering if she had dropped it on her way inside, she made a quick, fruitless search of the porch and driveway.

It has to be in the truck, she thought. Thus reassured, she sat down on the front steps to read the letter. The unfamiliar handwriting on the envelope was precise and male. Inside a thin sheet of tablet paper revealed a brief letter:

Dear Alice,

I'm about to go back to sea, but with my few remaining minutes of shore leave, I promised myself I would actually mail this letter rather than tossing it away, as I have all the others I've written to you.

I have two weeks of leave coming up in September. May I visit you?

I miss you!

Yours truly,
Dennis Delmarvin

P.S. I am 6 foot, 3 inches. Still growing. Hope you are fine.

Alice chuckled as she read the letter. She had always suspected Dennis had a crush on her, and here was confirmation. He wasn't one of her favorites at Tipton—how could he be after he beat up Ross—but he was good-looking. She remembered his broad shoulders and long, muscular legs and the way he looked at her. Sometimes his bold attention made her pulse leap.

Their conversations about his father had always left her feeling troubled and worried for him. Back in Tipton, Dennis was confused and full of simmering anger. But all that was absent from his letter. *I guess the navy agrees with him*, she thought.

September was a ways off, but it would be nice to have his visit to look forward to. If he could find his way to Rapidan, she would welcome him as an old friend.

With Dennis Delmarvin's letter clutched in her hand, she dashed toward the truck. She could hardly wait to read the card from Ross.

The rest of June passed swiftly. Thomas Shafer called Alice with instructions regarding the running of the farm. The farmers who rented land from Mr. Williams mailed in their checks and were rarely heard from otherwise. Philip was in touch with Sorbon Carter about the horses and general farm upkeep. Between Sorbon's instructions and the advice from the horse trainers at Montpelier, he was learning quickly and doing a good job. Thomas Shafer approved of Alice's request for a weekend cook and caretaker and seemed uninterested in her selection of Rosa Washington for the position; he would leave such things to her, as he had no desire to play an active role in running Red Road Farm. He told her about the farm and household checking accounts, which Alice needed to balance at the end of each month.

She was relieved to learn that Mr. Williams had a broker who handled his investments and other holdings. She wasn't responsible for anything other than the farm, and even that would revert to Carter Sorbon's management when he returned. The word from Philip was that the Carters' son was still in the naval hospital. It was unclear when Sorbon and his wife would return to Rapidan. When Alice told Thomas Shafer that she and Philip were maintaining the vegetable garden and planning to get some chickens, that seemed to win him over once and for all. He told her to draw twenty dollars instead of the agreed-upon fifteen dollars for her weekly pay.

With a portion of the three hundred dollars Anna had given her, Alice bought a used Ford. With gas rationing going into effect, she would not drive it very often, but it was good to have her own car. With the remainder of Anna's gift, she opened a savings account at a bank in Orange.

All of these developments gave Alice a new feeling of independence and self-sufficiency. Although Mr. Williams still alternated between gloomy silences and startling bursts of conversation, his health was stable and he ate her cooking with gusto. Most days, she wheeled him out on the porch after breakfast and sat reading a book or newspaper by his side until he was ready to go in. These times felt almost companionable, and Alice, busy with her chores and plans, was less lonely than she had feared she would be.

When Mr. Williams's prescriptions for several medications were about to run out, she decided it was time to meet his doctor in Orange and make sure she was caring for him properly. A phone call to his physician's office revealed that the old doctor had retired and a newcomer, Dr. Perkins, had taken over the practice. She made an appointment for the next morning.

It was now early July and seeringly hot. The grass was so dry and burnt that Philip had stopped mowing for a while. At nine in the morning, the temperature was already eighty degrees. Alice helped Mr. Williams into the passenger's seat as Philip eased the wheelchair out from under him. They used the truck, which had room for the wheelchair in back. With Mr. Williams in the middle and Philip at the wheel, they made their way to Orange.

"I still wonder what happened to that postcard from Ross," Alice said, meditatively looking out the window as the hills and farms rolled by. "I know I had it when we came home that day."

"Well, it's not in the truck," Philip said. "You know we searched every inch of it."

They rode quietly for a while until Mr. Williams spoke up. "The card with the bird on it?"

"Why, yes," Alice said. "I believe it did have a bird on it. Do you know where it is?"

Mr. Williams fixed her with a look. "I threw it away."

"Mr. Williams, why on earth would you do that?"

"Somebody left a glass on it. I don't like water rings."

"But I hadn't read it yet."

"The ink was all blurred. You couldn't read it anyway."

"Well, I could've tried. That card was from an old friend of mine in the service, and I don't know how to reach him."

"If he's really your friend, he'll write you again."

Alice could see that Philip was trying not to laugh. Mr. Williams's irascible ways amused him. When she had told him how the old man chose Anna over her the day Thomas Shafer and his mother visited, Philip had held his side, he was laughing so hard. A couple of days later, he came to the door and asked, in an arch tone, if he could speak to the lady of the house as he peered over Alice's shoulder. Baffled, she asked what she could do for him. "Not *you*," he crowed. "I want the one from Chicago!" She was mad at first, but then she couldn't help chuckling.

They arrived at the doctor's office on Madison Road. After Philip unloaded the wheelchair and got Mr. Williams inside, he went off to do errands. The office was in a modest storefront with a waiting area on one side and examination room on the other. The nurse, a woman named Molly who looked to be about sixty, said the doctor was finishing up with another patient. Through the thin wall, Alice heard a querulous female voice followed by a reasonable male voice. As soon as one stopped, the other started up. She couldn't make out the words, but the urgent tenor of the exchange made her uneasy.

After a few minutes, the door opened and there stood Arnold Radius's wife. Her left eye was blackened and she was limping. Although the room was small, she didn't seem to notice Alice and Mr. Williams. Molly told the woman not to worry about paying right then and waved her out the front door. "You two can go in now," she said to Alice.

Inside the examination room, the doctor stood behind his desk looking sad. His mind appeared to still be on Mrs. Radius. When he saw Alice, however, his expression brightened.

She instantly recognized him. When he came around his desk to meet her, she saw that he was just about her height, maybe an inch taller. Ruddy cheeked and brown-haired, he had a firm handshake and a twinkle in his eye. When he smiled, Alice noticed his fine straight teeth. Even the extra weight on his frame pleased her. It made him look prosperous and mature.

They discussed the medications Mr. Williams was on, and then Alice stepped outside while he examined the patient. When Dr. Perkins ushered her back in, he said he would give her several refill prescriptions, and he wanted Mr. Williams to start taking vitamin supplements. To the patient, he said, "To put it simply, you're doing all right. But your muscles are weak and your color is pale. I recommend you get more fresh air and exercise. I'll give your granddaughter a list of exercises for you to do."

The conversation was brief and professional, but Alice couldn't help smiling the whole time. Dr. Perkins had an English accent that she loved. When their business was finished, he asked if he could have a word with her. With Mr. Williams safely out of earshot, he said, "You're the girl on the bridge!"

They fell into easy conversation. Alice learned that Jonathan Perkins had moved to Orange just a few days after her arrival. He had an apartment in town but was looking for a new place where his dog, Winston, could roam around. The day she saw him driving across the Rapidan River bridge, he was on his way to look at a house, which turned out to be nothing but a shack with barely enough room for him, let alone the dog.

"Say," Alice said, "why don't you come to supper some evening? You could bring your dog. We have plenty of space for him to run around at Red Road Farm." Her heartbeat quickened as she waited for his answer.

"I'd love to," he said. "How about tomorrow night? If that's not too soon."

She gave him directions and bade him a quick farewell. Without turning around, she knew his eyes were on her as she wheeled Mr. Williams out the front door.

That evening brought welcome thunderstorms. The next day's temperature hovered in the low seventies all morning. Alice went about gathering flowers and tidying the house. Although she didn't tell Philip about her dinner date, she had him trim the boxwoods around the front porch. By late afternoon, she had the meal ready: a platter of roast beef, a pot of butterbeans seasoned with ham, fresh potato salad, a salad with tomatoes from the garden, yeast rolls, and iced tea. For dessert, she baked molasses cookies, following a recipe in the Fannie Farmer cookbook that Regina Carter had left behind.

With plenty of time to spare, she bathed and put on a light blue checked dress with short sleeves—it was old but fit her well. For her hair, tied back in a ponytail as usual, she had a freshly laundered navy blue ribbon. Though makeup held little appeal for her, she decided the occasion warranted lipstick.

Promptly at six-thirty, the green Plymouth rolled up the driveway. Alice could see a long-nosed dog poking his head out a back window. When Jonathan Perkins emerged and began walking the dog to the house, she stood up from the porch swing and went to meet him.

Dr. Perkins looked freshly scrubbed and a little bashful. A dot of paper was on his cheek where he had cut himself shaving. He wore a crisp summer suit, but the collar of his buttoned-down shirt was frayed. *A bachelor*, Alice thought. Fumbling with the dog's leash, he greeted her and handed her a box of chocolates—a box she recognized from the shelves of Sparks's Grocery.

The dog, Winston, was a golden retriever. He gave them something to talk about as they stood awkwardly on the porch. "He's four years old," the doctor said. "I got him as a puppy when I was in medical school. Winston spent many a night helping me study and seeing me through my residency."

Alice petted the dog, which regarded her with gentle eyes. "He's very handsome. I set out some water for him," she said, pointing to a bowl by the front door. "Would he like something to eat?"

What Winston really needed, Dr. Perkins said, was to run around; the dog had been cooped up in the apartment all day, except for a short walk at lunchtime.

"Well, you can let him off his leash, if you want. All I have to do is close the gate to the driveway. The property around the house and barn is fenced in."

The doctor's face broke into a grateful smile. "That would be lovely. But let me walk down and shut the gate. That's the least I can do."

She went with him and the dog to the end of the driveway. The stroll had a calming effect, and their conversation grew more relaxed. Alice learned that her visitor had followed his parents and younger brother and sister to the U.S. after graduating from a university in England and serving in the British army. His father was a master distiller at a whiskey distillery in Tennessee and had wanted his son to follow him into the business. Jonathan had other ideas, however, and took a series of menial jobs so he could afford medical school at the University of Tennessee.

"I inherited my father's love of chemistry but not his fascination with whiskey. I just don't have the taste for it," he said. "The truth is, my parents were both very disappointed when I decided to become a doctor."

When a favorite professor told him that an old friend, Dr. Dean McDonald of Orange, Virginia, was looking for a young doctor to take over his practice, Jonathan decided this was his chance. He wanted to practice in a small town and see a new part of the country. Dr. McDonald—"a delightful old chap"—was willing to take a fair price. Jonathan was paying for it through monthly installments, and, so long as all his patients paid their bills on time, he expected to own the practice outright within a couple of years. Until then, he would scrimp and save.

Alice absorbed this information with great interest. By now they were back at the house. Jonathan let the dog loose. After a quick look at his master, Winston ran the length of the front lawn, stopped, and charged back toward them. His tongue lolling to one side, he looked like he was smiling. After barking and prancing around, he ran down to the fishpond and disappeared among the boxwoods.

"Should we bring him inside while we eat?"

"Oh, no. I wouldn't impose on you like that. He's a very loyal dog. When he's tired of running, he'll just come up on the porch, have a drink of water, and then go to sleep by the front door—you wait and see."

With that settled, Alice led her guest inside. The table was already set with the Williams family silver, and the goblets of iced water were jeweled with condensate. Crystal vases of flowers were on the table and mantle. Mr. Williams had wheeled himself into the living room and was now heading toward them with surprising vigor.

Dr. Perkins greeted the old man with enthusiasm and complimented him on exercising his arms. Mr. Williams responded with a noncommittal grunt.

Over supper, the doctor asked Alice and Mr. Williams to call him by his first name. "I would like for us to be friends," he said with a smile that included both of them.

His hearty appetite matched Mr. Williams's. The two men cleaned their plates and accepted Alice's offer of seconds. While she was in the kitchen, she overheard the doctor asking a few questions about the history of Red Road Farm. To her surprise, Mr. Williams's voice came back clear and strong.

As she set his plate before him, Mr. Williams looked up at her. "This fellow's got good manners," he said. "He didn't ask me how many acres we got here."

Alice could think of no meaningful reply to this, so she just smiled. When Jonathan said how nice it was that Mr. Williams had his granddaughter around to help him out, the old man shot her a sharp, lucid look but said not a word. This was the second time she had let the doctor's false assumption pass without correction. As she nibbled a roll, she wondered why Mr. Williams hadn't come out with the truth.

After the meal, Jonathan helped clean up the kitchen and then said he wouldn't overstay his welcome, especially since he had paperwork to do that night.

It was dusk. She walked him outside and felt a pang: how she would have loved to take a walk with this good-looking Englishman and maybe catch hold of his hand as they strolled around the fishpond.

The young doctor's thoughts were elsewhere, however. "Winston!" he cried. "I nearly forgot about him."

The dog wasn't curled up asleep on the porch, nor was he anywhere to be seen in the shadowy front yard. Jonathan began whistling and calling the dog's name, as Alice felt a mixture of panic and inappropriate laughter bubbling up in her throat. The disappearance of the doctor's beloved dog would surely ruin the budding friendship.

Finally, after a few minutes, they heard an answering bark. In the distance, next to the barn, Alice saw Philip rounding the bend with the dog by his side.

Dr. Perkins accepted Winston with gratitude and led him to his car. Just as he was starting up the engine, Alice heard Mr. Williams calling out from the sitting room window. Mr. Williams, his face hidden in shadows, said, "We'll see you back here for supper next week. Come a little earlier next time. We like to eat at six."

The doctor expressed his thanks and then glanced at Alice. "I won't hold you to that," he said softly.

"Oh, do come back. There's so much more we can—so much we can talk about."

With a radiant smile for her and a cordial nod for Philip, he made his exit. The dog stuck his head out the back window and seemed to smile at her.

To her relief, Philip didn't linger. They bade one another goodnight and Alice went inside. As she made a final round in the kitchen, pausing for a glass of ice water, she realized she was exhausted. She had spent the entire day preparing for her evening with Dr. Perkins, and it had been, as far as she could tell, a great success. Even Mr. Williams had enjoyed himself. She was too tired to do anything now except go to bed. Dragging herself upstairs, she unbuttoned her dress and pulled out her hair ribbon as she went. Her last thoughts before she nodded off were of Jonathan Perkins's praise for her cooking and his astonishingly warm smile.

From then on, he came for supper every Thursday. It was hard for him to get to Red Road Farm by six o'clock because patients often arrived after they got off work. But when he was running late, he always had his nurse, Molly, call to say he was on his way. Despite his busy schedule, he never missed a week and always brought Alice a little box of candy from Sparks's Grocery—or, occasionally, a jar of black olives. Alice set aside the candy for her own enjoyment. The black olives, which she didn't like, found their way to the dining room table on Thursday nights.

The evenings followed a predictable pattern. Jonathan and Alice would walk around the yard and the flower garden while Winston explored on his own. Sometimes they would play fetch with him before going inside for supper. Alice began preparing the meals the night before so there was less work to do in the anticipatory hours leading up to his visit. She took note of his favorite foods—corn on the cob, fruit pies, and yeast rolls—and made sure to serve those often.

He was always kind and courteous and seemed genuinely interested in her Oklahoma girlhood. When she came to the part of the story where she dropped out of the University of Oklahoma and went to work at the Tipton Home, she said it was because she had run out of support. Jonathan could draw his own conclusions about the kind of support she had lost. She saw no need for the earnest doctor to know about her out-of-wedlock pregnancy or her hasty marriage to Macklin. Nor did she discuss her cross-country journey to Rapidan in pursuit of her errant husband. As far as Jonathan knew, she was a loving granddaughter who had come to an old man's aid just in time.

Before supper, while Alice got everything ready to serve, Jonathan made a point of visiting with Mr. Williams. He would wheel him out on the front porch and engage him in a game of catch or get him to twirl his outstretched arms in ever-widening circles.

Without fail, Mr. Williams would exclaim, "This is stupid!" or something to that effect, and Jonathan would reply with a broad grin, "Quite right you are, sir," or "Beyond stupid, if you ask me, sir." Then they would continue making circles with their arms or stretching their hands high for another minute or two. As a finale, Mr. Williams would walk the length of the porch with only the doctor's arm to steady him. Alice watched from inside the screen door before calling them in to eat.

After supper, Mr. Williams went to his room without assistance and closed the door behind him. It was at this point that Alice hoped her friendship with Jonathan would advance beyond spirited conversation. He helped her clean up and sometimes patted her on the arm as he praised her cooking. Occasionally he would join her on the porch swing and they would talk softly as dusk fell. The dog, having explored the whole property, was now in the habit of returning to the porch and going to sleep as Jonathan had predicted he would. At 8:45, however, Winston would rouse himself and find his master.

"Uh, oh, time to go home," Jonathan said on his fourth visit. "Back to our tenement, right, Winston? We don't want to impose any longer on our lovely hostess."

"You're not imposing," Alice said with quiet urgency. "I always enjoy your visits. Can't you stay a little longer?"

Busy with Winston and his leash, he turned to look at Alice over his shoulder. "You're very kind, but I really must go. Thank you for your hospitality."

"Will we see you next week?"

The doctor looked abashed. "Of course. I wouldn't miss it." He stepped forward hesitantly, the dog pulling him in the opposite direction, and hugged Alice with one arm. "You're such a good friend. Thank you." His lips grazed her hair.

With that, he hurried off, seeming embarrassed. Alice was once again left alone.

Lying in bed that night, she relived their parting over and over. She couldn't fool herself into believing there was great passion in his touch, but still, she reasoned, they were making progress.

With each week, her desire for Jonathan Perkins increased. Macklin rarely crossed her mind except as an impediment, and she thought of Anna only when she noticed the badminton set in her closet. As she went about her daily chores, she imagined telling Jonathan how much she liked him and then brushing her hand against his. Perhaps then he would respond with the intensity of emotion she felt, grab hold of her, and they would—well, only at night did she let her mind wander that far.

In the darkness of her bedroom, she indulged her yearning. She took off her nightgown, kicked the sheet to the floor, and lay naked on the narrow bed. With the humid air barely stirring, she felt she would burst with lusty desire. Sometimes she touched herself as she thought about Jonathan, and if she did that long enough and in just the right way, she was released from the sweet torment. Turning over and clutching her pillow, she stifled the accelerating sighs that meant relief was coming. But before she finally drifted off to sleep, she was always aware of how alone she was.

After five weeks of Jonathan Perkins's regular visits, Alice took him down to the fishpond one evening before supper. She told him she had Saturdays off, now that Rosa Washington was working at the farm. To her dismay, this broad hint elicited little reaction. Jonathan ran a hand through his hair and gazed down at several goldfish nibbling algae at the pond's edge. He asked what she intended to do with her free days.

Go out with you, you dough-head, Alice thought. "Oh, I don't know. I'm still so new to the area. I'd like to go exploring, but I hardly know where to start."

"I hear there's a peach orchard on top of Clark's Mountain. Have you been up there yet?"

Alice's heart leaped. "I've heard about it, but I haven't been." *Now ask me*, she willed him.

"Molly's going this weekend. Maybe you'll see her up there."

"Maybe so." She turned her head away so he wouldn't see her disappointment. Running into Molly the nurse at a peach orchard wasn't high on her list of things to do.

The next day she called Poppy Douglas and set up a lunch date. "I need to talk to you," Alice said. "I need your advice on something important."

With Poppy's directions and a map by her side, she made the drive on Saturday morning. It was the first time she had driven so far on her own, and she felt guilty about using rationed gasoline for a pleasure trip. After a long, quiet spell on Route 33, the traffic grew heavier as she navigated the Richmond streets. On Monument Avenue, she gazed up in wonderment at the statues of Confederate generals on horseback. It was quite an impressive city. Without too much trouble, she found Miller and Rhoads, the large and glamorous department store where Poppy worked as a commercial artist. Stepping inside, Alice smoothed her yellow dress and looked around for the tearoom. She was overcome with bashfulness and briefly missed Anna, who would have gone right up to the perfume counter and asked for directions. After a few minutes of aimless browsing, she finally mustered the courage to approach a benevolent clerk who told her to take the elevator or the escalators to the restaurant on the seventh floor.

It was impossible to resist the escalators. Climbing ever higher, with the milling shoppers below her, Alice began to enjoy herself. *No wonder Poppy wanted to work here,* she thought.

Poppy broke into a glad smile as Alice approached. The tearoom was a lovely and inviting place. A nattily dressed man was playing tunes on an organ, and the cheerful music added to the hubbub in the room crowded with well-dressed women and a scattering of businessmen in tailored suits. Poppy and Alice both ordered the chicken salad special, and then Alice couldn't contain herself any longer.

"Poppy, I have a confession to make."

"What is it, Alice?"

With a stifled sob, she said, "I'm in love with Dr. Perkins and he won't ask me out."

She watched as Poppy's expression shifted from surprise and mystification to calm resolve. There was no sign of judgment being passed. "Well, tell me about this Dr. Perkins. How did you meet him, and what, if anything, have you heard from Macklin?"

The story poured out. To her relief, Alice saw that her intuition about Poppy was correct. Her new friend was wholly sympathetic and, though curious about Macklin, not the least bit concerned about any impropriety on Alice's part.

They spent much of the meal talking about Jonathan Perkins and his enigmatic ways. In answer to Poppy's questions, Alice said he was unmarried and seemed, in his reserved, English way, quite interested in her. But he never stayed late and never asked her out for Saturday, when he knew she was free.

"I've been wondering," Alice said, her eyes steady on Poppy's, "if I just need to fix myself up more for him."

"Oh, Alice. What kind of fixing up do you think you need?"

"This dress is old," she said, picking at the cloth of the dress she had bought before her freshman year in college. "And I never got any help from my mother with clothes or makeup." She tapped Poppy on the arm. "Could you help me? You know so much about fashion. Please take me shopping. I don't have much money, but I need new clothes. Tell me what I could do to get Jonathan's attention."

A flattered Poppy assessed Alice before speaking. "Have you ever thought of cutting your hair?"

By the end of the afternoon, Alice had two new outfits and a new hairdo. Her long honey-brown hair, forever relegated to a ponytail, was now in graceful waves that fell just below her shoulders. Poppy raved over her, and the hairdresser said she looked like the actress Veronica Lake. Alice smiled shyly at her reflection. As a girl, her mother had cut her hair. She let it grow while she was away at college, and at Tipton, her aunt trimmed it for her. The new hairstyle made her look older, she thought, and much more fashionable.

The two young women now stood outside Thalhimer's, another large department store where Poppy had insisted Alice buy one of her outfits, since it had especially good sports clothes. Afterwards, she had taken Alice to the Thalhimer's bakery, where they each bought a small yellow cake with seven layers of chocolate icing. The fresh cakes came in stylish black and white checked boxes tied with string. "The icing will melt on your way home," Poppy advised. "But just put it in the icebox and it'll be fine by suppertime."

With a final hug, they parted and Alice began her journey back to Red Road Farm. She drove with greater ease this time and smiled happily as she thought of Poppy and the hairdresser saying she looked like a movie star.

7

The following Thursday, Alice roasted a chicken, prepared a pot of butterbeans, and baked a peach pie. While things cooked, she polished the silver, gathered fresh flowers for the dining room table, and dusted every surface downstairs. She swept the front porch and filled up Winston's bowl with water. All was ready by four o'clock. She went to her room and allowed herself a nap. After an hour she awoke suddenly, her heart thumping with excitement. There was just enough time to bathe, put on her new dress with the snappy belt, and fluff up her hair, which she had washed and curled the night before.

At five minutes before six, the phone rang and Alice flew to answer it. Molly told her that Dr. Perkins had stayed late with a patient and was just running out of the office to fetch his dog. He wanted her to know he would be at Red Road Farm in twenty-two minutes.

On the dot of 6:17, she saw the familiar green Plymouth rounding the bend in the driveway. As usual she was waiting on the porch swing and rose to her feet when Jonathan and the dog emerged from the car. Winston came bounding up on the porch to greet her. She took a step backward so he wouldn't leap up on her new dress. It took a few moments for Jonathan to join them. He was still in his work clothes, his tie loosened and his trousers wrinkled. His usually neat hair was mussed, and as he approached, she could see from his movements and expression that he was deeply tired. In his hand he carried a jar of black olives.

When he was within a few yards of her on the porch, he stopped and stared. "Why, Alice. Look at you." His weary face broke into a smile. "Aren't you a sight for sore eyes. You look beautiful—but then, you always do."

She accepted the compliment along with the olives and then stood looking back at him and feeling shy. It was as if they had turned back the calendar to their very first supper at the farm. Jonathan's eyes were full of tenderness and that hopefulness she remembered from the time she saw him driving across the bridge.

He shook his head as if to clear his thoughts. "Shall we walk around a bit? I could use some fresh air after the day I've had."

It was an overcast but temperate evening. A slight breeze lifted the leaves and cooled their faces as they walked to the fishpond. He wanted to know what she had been doing in the days since he last saw her, so she told him about driving to Richmond, her first excursion there and her longest drive on her own. Unwilling to divulge the purpose of her shopping trip, she instead told him about Poppy's job at Miller and Rhoads.

"Well, I commend her," Jonathan said. He looked across the fishpond and pointed out a box turtle before continuing. "I've always admired strong, independent women—like you, Alice. It must be so difficult, though."

She drew closer to his side. "What do you mean?"

"I'm treating a very hard case these days," he said, his face suddenly distraught. "As a new doctor, I'm still learning how to handle patients, and this poor woman—" His voice broke off.

The conversation was not going as she had hoped, but Alice was intrigued nonetheless. In response to her questions, at first he said he couldn't reveal too much. But clearly he wanted and needed to talk, and Alice reminded him she was a newcomer so there was little chance she knew the patient in question.

Gradually it came out that the woman's husband was regularly beating her up, and she was afraid to leave him. They were estranged from their children, who had moved away a long time ago. She refused to call the sheriff because her husband, she believed, would kill her if she did. The doctor was the only person, it seemed, she confided in. When he asked his predecessor in the practice, Dr. McDonald, for advice, the retired doctor said,

"They've been going at it for years. She probably gives as good as she gets. Treat her as best you can, but don't worry about her."

But Jonathan did worry. As they walked back to the house, he seemed unable to hold back any details. Talking rapidly, he said he had seen the woman that very day. She, in fact, was the patient who had kept him late at the office. He set her sprained wrist in a splint, gave her a prescription for painkillers, and told her to apply an ice cube wrapped in a facecloth to her blackened eye.

It was this last detail that caused Alice to stop in her tracks. "Mrs. Radius!" she cried out, remembering the woman leaving Jonathan's office before Mr. Williams's first appointment. Everything Jonathan had said about the violent husband was of a piece with what she knew of the despicable Arnold Radius.

Jonathan stared at Alice in astonishment. "Oh, I said way too much," he said. "I've broken poor Annette's trust in me."

Alice tried to reassure him, but he was disconsolate. He sat down on the porch steps and put his head in his hands. She had never seen him so unhappy.

"I haven't been here very long, Jonathan, but if Orange County is anything like the places I lived in Oklahoma, most people already know Arnold Radius is beating up his wife. It's not like you gave away a big secret." She stopped to think. "I wonder if the minister could help her in some way."

"What minister?" He lifted his bleary eyes.

She told him about her ordeal at Purcell Presbyterian Church and how Arnold Radius had insulted both her and Philip and then vandalized Anna's car.

He shook his head in disgust. "I'm sorry you had to go through that."

"But the preacher—Braswell's his name—seemed all right. Maybe he could take Annette in or help her get out of town."

"I suppose I could call him," he said doubtfully.

"Do you want me to talk to him?" she asked.

"Could you?" It was as if the sun had come out on Jonathan's face. "I would be so grateful if you could help her—and me."

It occurred to her that the Reverend Braswell was usually at the church on Saturdays. She had seen him doing odd jobs around the property. Occasionally he was alone, but often there were others, members of his congregation, helping him tend the churchyard. She was in the habit of waving to him, but she had never ventured over for a chat.

"I'll go see him Saturday—on my day off," Alice said pointedly. "Would you like me to call you afterwards and give you a report?"

The doctor's expression clouded yet again. "Normally, I'd say yes, but I'll be out all day looking for a new place to live. Winston is terribly crowded in the apartment, and I can't say I like it much better than he does. There are a few places in town I'm going to look at, and then I'll be driving out to see a house in Somerset, where Winston would have plenty of space, but I fear it's out of my price range."

"You're the town doctor! Back in Tipton, some family would've taken you in for free, so long as you chipped in for food and firewood." Her righteous indignation barely masked her irritation with him. She couldn't understand why he wouldn't ask her out. Surely, when they got along so well, it wouldn't hurt to have her along on his search for new living quarters—or he could stop by the farm afterwards and take her out to dinner.

Jonathan raised his eyebrows in a quizzical, humorous way. What this look meant, Alice couldn't fathom. "Well, let's go in and eat. Mr. Williams must be famished by now." Too late she realized she was still referring to her "grandfather" in an oddly formal manner, but if Jonathan noticed, he was too polite or preoccupied to say anything about it.

Over supper, conversation flagged as Alice sulked and Jonathan fell into an uncharacteristic silence. Finally Mr. Williams set down his dessert fork with a clatter. "You're a damn fine cook, Alice. Where'd you learn to bake a pie like that?"

It was not only a rare compliment from the crusty old man; it was the first time he had addressed her by name. "Why, thank you, sir. My aunt back in Tipton taught me. She taught all us girls how to bake and sew and run a household."

Mr. Williams turned his eagle's gaze from Alice to Jonathan. "It's not often you have a piecrust that good and flaky. You won't find pies this tasty at the Main Street bakery in Culpeper or anywhere on the Eastern Seaboard, for that matter." He slapped his frail hand on the table for emphasis.

Jarred out of his lull, Jonathan began talking to Mr. Williams. As Alice cleared the table, she thought with amazement that the old man wanted Jonathan to see what a good catch she was. Maybe he recognized a perfectly suited couple when he saw one.

Upon returning to the dining room, she found the young man accompanying the old one away from the table. Jonathan was again talking about his difficulties at the apartment. It was awfully cramped; the landlady was nosy; a neighbor had complained about Winston barking while Jonathan was at work. He wanted to take Winston to the office, but Molly reminded him some people were allergic to dog hair and there was enough sneezing in the office already.

By now the two were on the front porch. Alice, her arms folded across her chest, stood a few feet away from the screen door and watched as they tossed an old tennis ball back and forth. Mr. Williams was in his wheelchair and Jonathan was standing about six feet away. Between complaints about the apartment, he urged his host to throw first with his right hand and then his left. He tossed the ball back gently but at different heights, so Mr. Williams had to stay alert and grab the ball out of the air. Then the doctor backed up so the game required more exertion.

Jonathan was talking so much that Mr. Williams couldn't get a word in. He seemed too engrossed in his activity to say anything anyway. Over recent weeks, his reflexes had gotten quicker and he no longer objected to playing catch with their weekly guest. Alice knew better than to join them right now. She had been able to coax her employer to walk with a cane for a few minutes twice a day, but his face turned stony when she produced the tennis ball. If she tossed it to him, he let it fall to the floor and roll under the horsehair sofa. Once, though, she had caught him unawares, squeezing the ball, first with one hand and then the other. It was a strengthening exercise Jonathan had prescribed.

"I'm hoping one of these places will work out. The house in Somerset would be nice, but if the owner isn't willing to negotiate on the rent, I'll be out of luck. And it sounds a bit out of the way. I'm not sure how practical it would be if I got an emergency call in the middle of the night."

Mr. Williams caught the ball and held it. "Enough already. Just move here. The dog can have the run of the place." Then he threw the ball back to Jonathan.

Moving farther away from the door, Alice caught her breath. The sudden prospect of Jonathan living under the same roof made her heart pound.

"What a kind and generous offer, Mr. Williams. I hardly know what to say."

"Then it's settled," Mr. Williams said.

"I should ask your granddaughter—"

"She's not my granddaughter," the old man shot back.

Leaning against a table, Alice thought she would faint. The truth about her marriage was about to come out.

"She's not?"

"She's my niece. My great-niece."

There was a pause as Jonathan absorbed this news. "Well, if your great-niece is agreeable, I would love to live at Red Road Farm. I'm honored you would invite me into your home."

With no words of reply, he turned his wheelchair toward the door signaling that the conversation was over. Alice hurried to the kitchen so they wouldn't know she had been eavesdropping. From her post at the sink, she could see Mr. Williams walking to his room with only his cane for support. Jonathan was pushing the wheelchair behind him. In a few minutes, the doctor was by her side, his face glistening with excitement.

"You'll never guess what your great-uncle just proposed, Alice." He was looking her directly in the eye. "He invited me to live here at Red Road."

She nervously wiped her hands on a cup towel. "Well, that's wonderful, Jonathan."

"I—I don't want to be a burden on you, though. You've got your hands full with all the work you do around here."

She smiled back uncertainly.

"I could help out with your uncle. I work long hours, of course, and get some emergency calls at night. Thursday is the only day I ever leave on time, and that's because—well, you know. I don't know what Mr. Williams would want for rent—or you— or whether it would insult him if I offered to pay. Perhaps his invitation was purely a gesture of friendship. I don't know!" He paused to wipe a drop of sweat from his brow. "Oh, I'm babbling. Please tell me if this doesn't suit."

It suits, Alice thought, *it suits*. She took a deep breath and said, "Jonathan, I would love it if you lived at Red Road Farm. And if Mr.—if my uncle didn't say anything about rent, then you don't have to pay any." She drew close enough that she could smell his peach-scented breath.

He smiled joyfully. Before sweeping her up in a hug and kissing her on the cheek, he chuckled and said, "I'll chip in for food and firewood."

Hearing him repeat her own words, Alice remembered the quizzical look he had given her before supper. Perhaps he had been angling to live here all along, and she was just too dull to pick up on it. With him in her arms at last, she tried to prolong the hug, but he pulled away excitedly. "I'll have to give notice at the apartment, but maybe my dear old harridan of a landlady will let me go before the month is out. When can I move in, Alice?"

"Oh, whenever you want. We've got eight spare bedrooms, five on the second floor, and three on the third, so you have plenty to choose from, and they're all neat and clean. Go upstairs and have a look, if you want."

With another dazzling smile, Jonathan turned on his heel and fairly scampered upstairs to pick out his room.

His momentum didn't last, however. The following week, for the first time, he canceled his weekly visit to Red Road Farm. In a Wednesday afternoon phone call, he told Alice he wasn't sure of his plans. His days were long and suddenly crowded with patients; there was no time to pack; Winston had a thorn in his paw. His voice sounded strained and distracted, but he still asked how she was and whether Mr. Williams was getting exercise and fresh air. She assured him she and her uncle were doing fine. Beyond that, there was little to say.

After hanging up the phone, she took a few breaths and tried to collect herself. It would be hard telling Mr. Williams that Jonathan wasn't coming for supper the next night and harder still if he decided not to move in. They had both grown to depend on his warm heart and friendly ways.

Over the past week, she had begun to daydream about making a life with Jonathan at Red Road Farm. Although it might be awkward dating a man who lived in the same house, it would be merely a prelude to marriage. No matter how busy he was during the day, they would have the long summer evenings to stroll hand in hand to the bridge and stare down at the river. While she dusted and did Mr. Williams's laundry, she imagined an autumn wedding in the flower garden.

But Jonathan's ambivalence made her fantasies feel absurd, and every once in a while, she remembered the pesky matter of her marriage, such as it was, to Macklin. Even if Jonathan returned her feelings, she was not legally available to him, and it might be awkward to divorce Macklin when she depended on Macklin's great uncle for her home and livelihood. The fact that Jonathan's last name was Perkins, which was the name of the town where Macklin grew up, nagged at her as well. After all her years of pining for her absent husband, now she wanted nothing more than to shake him off and start fresh with a new and better mate.

That night she slept fitfully. At two a.m. she was awake and staring at the ceiling. After an hour of this she got out of bed, splashed water on her face, and sat down at the writing desk. Her eye fell on an envelope she had slipped deep into one of the cubbyholes. With a start she realized it was the letter from Dennis Delmarvin asking if he could visit in September. She had written back with directions to Rapidan, but he never replied, and his inquiry had slipped her mind once Jonathan began his weekly visits. *How would I ever find out if something happened to him,* she thought. The newspapers were full of bad news, and she feared for Dennis and all the Tipton boys who had gone off to war. With these worries and Jonathan's change of heart weighing on her, she thought of Poppy, the only person she knew who could understand what she was feeling. There was too much to say in a long-distance telephone call and she couldn't very well call her in the middle of the night anyway, so she decided to write her a letter.

The desk's top drawer contained envelopes but no writing paper. The two middle drawers were empty and the bottom drawer was stuck. After a few determined tugs she managed to pull it open. Inside was a stack of thick leather-bound notebooks. Though she thought she had explored every inch of the room, this was a new discovery. Pulling out a few of the books, she flipped one open and saw that it was Macklin's journal. She paged through it at random and looked for her name. One passage practically leaped off the page at her:

I'll never tell Dudley and Chippers I am married—and that I abandoned my wife after she miscarried our child. I can only imagine their shock! That revelation would, I'm sure, end their association with me. I would be ostracized and, for all I know, kicked out of my beloved University.

Tears of rage and astonishment stinging her eyes, Alice flipped the book shut and stood up. With no clean handkerchiefs to be found, she tore off a long length of toilet paper to manage her streaming eyes and dripping nose. Her head bowed, she wept quietly.

She couldn't bring herself to write to Poppy now. In a minute she was dressed and making her way out the front door. She moved stealthily so as not to wake Mr. Williams. The grass was wet with dew. The birds were still asleep and all was still as she walked past the barn and up the hill to the little house where Philip lived. It was a shame to wake him in the middle of the night, but she needed a sympathetic friend.

With the orange cat pressing against her ankle, she knocked on the door. When there was no response, she called Philip's name and knocked more loudly.

Then she heard a woman's voice: "What could she want at *this* hour?" The door swung open, and there stood Philip, bare-chested and wearing nothing but boxer shorts. The cat saw its opportunity and darted inside. Looking past Philip, Alice caught a glimpse of Rosa Washington in a filmy nightgown. The two women locked eyes for a split second before Rosa disappeared around a corner.

"Oh, I'm sorry, Philip. I didn't mean—"

"What is it, Alice? What's wrong?" Philip stood with his hands on his hips. His body exuded a strong musky scent that made Alice step back a pace. Without his glasses, he was staring at her in an unfocused way. He seemed to be teetering between genuine concern and a mixture of embarrassment and exasperation.

She explained that she couldn't sleep and just wanted to talk, but that it was nothing so urgent that it couldn't wait. Philip didn't try to detain her. With more apologies and much chagrin, she backed off and began walking away. She heard the lock turn, and then the night was quiet again except for the small sounds of her footsteps on wet grass.

Now she understood why Philip had kept his distance lately. It wasn't just because he recognized her need for privacy as she tried to get to know Jonathan Perkins. He, too, was busy with affairs of the heart. Rosa was young and pretty, and had always been pleasant if a little guarded. When Alice tried to draw her out, she chatted about her work at Montpelier and her love of horses. But always she shifted the conversation back to the farm and to Alice, who found herself telling the young woman about Tipton and the children there and Aunt Muriel and Uncle Dale. Rosa listened to these tales as she worked in the kitchen and Alice dawdled, with nothing special to do on her day off.

A few times, she had seen Rosa and Philip together in the late afternoon. Rosa was teaching Philip how to ride. On horseback, the two of them would start out slowly and then, with Rosa leading, pick up the pace to a trot. Once Alice had seen her shake the reins and get Goldie to break into a canter and then a full gallop. Philip had brought his horse to a standstill and watched as Rosa raced toward the road and then brought Goldie back at the same exhilarating speed. A bouquet of freshly picked daylilies slipping from her hands, Alice, too, had watched. Rosa's fluid grace astonished her. It seemed the golden horse was an extension of this young woman with the shining dark skin.

As she walked back to the house, these memories competed in her mind with what had just happened. She thought of how Rosa said, "What could she want at this hour?" and then held Alice's gaze before vanishing into the back of the house. The flash of hostility in her eyes was unnerving. Alice wondered if Rosa frequently criticized her to Philip or maybe she thought Alice, knocking on the door so presumptuously, had designs on her man. Or perhaps as the employer she was nothing more than a mote in Rosa's eye—a passing annoyance she thought of only when she had to.

How long, she wondered, had their affair been going on? She tried to tell herself it hardly mattered one way or another, but she still felt foolish. *I practically caught them in the act*, she thought with an embarrassed shake of her head.

By the time she reached the driveway, a couple of doves had begun sleepily cooing. Weariness overcame her.

She slept late and upon waking couldn't recall any of her dreams. Sunlight was streaming into her room and across the leather-bound covers of Macklin's journals. The first thing to do, she resolved, was put those back in the bottom drawer where they belonged.

It was then that the telephone began ringing. She heard Mr. Williams's muffled voice as he answered. Then he yelled up to her in his raspy way, "He's coming after all. Tonight for supper and then to stay. Bake a pie!"

8

It took Jonathan Perkins three weeks to move in. Week by week, toting bags and boxes, he began to fill up the little bedroom behind the guest room, at the opposite end of the hall from Alice's quarters. Finally, on a hot Sunday afternoon in August, he said he had emptied out the apartment at last. Declining Alice's offers of help, he brought in several suits on hangers and an armload of shirts. Then came his framed diplomas, one from his college in England and the other from the medical school in Tennessee. Returning to his car, he dug into the trunk for Winston's supplies, including bowls, leashes, brushes, and rubber balls of various sizes. He returned to his car one last time. From the backseat he lifted a forlorn houseplant in a too-small pot with long trailing stems nearly bereft of leaves. "I've had this plant since medical school," he observed as he carried it past Alice, who was sitting on the front porch with the dog by her side. "It's been a constant in my life, just like Winston."

She laughed, but his backward glance told her he wasn't joking. "It'll look better once I water it," he said as the screen door slapped shut behind him.

As much as she adored him, Alice had to admit that Jonathan was not quite what she had thought when they first met. His emotions were very close to the surface, more so even than her own. Whenever the subject of his parents came up, his shoulders drooped. His lack of closeness with them, especially his father, weighed heavily on him. Beneath the radiant good humor that originally attracted her was a great deal of nervousness and self-doubt. A bit like his dog, he had a way of bounding forward and then veering off course. One night in the flower garden he had told her, his face lit with anguish, that he should have accepted an apprenticeship in the whiskey distillery in Tennessee. That was what his father wanted him to do—*what his father expected.* When Alice stroked his arm in compassion, he leaned toward her and rested against her shoulder. But there had been no kissing and not even a hug when he left that night. His feelings of loneliness and regret seemed deeply engrained in him. She longed to unbutton his shirt, run her hands up and down his chest, and tell him how much she loved and wanted him. But she feared her natural assertiveness would scare him away. In his own time, she decided, he would come to her. And now, perhaps, their new proximity would be the charm.

Progress continued to be slow, however. Jonathan rose at dawn and was gone before Alice awoke. He always washed and dried his dishes, so there was no extra work for her to do in the morning. He came home late most evenings and maintained his routine of joining her and Mr. Williams for supper only on Thursdays. He and Mr. Williams continued to get along well. Once or twice a week, Jonathan contributed a bag of items from Sparks's Grocery: flour, sugar, crackers, and chocolates and black olives if he could get them. When Alice asked if she could pack him a lunch, he said he liked going to the drugstore's soda fountain; it was his way of getting to know people outside his office.

On the evenings when he returned home late, Alice got in the habit of preparing him a plate and leaving it in the icebox. Jonathan ate the food cold, at the kitchen table, while reading a newspaper. When Alice joined him, he talked politely but didn't prolong the conversation. She learned to leave him alone unless he sought her out.

Every now and then he got an emergency call at the house. In a rush, he would gather up his doctor's bag, put on his suit jacket, and resolutely head out to his car. After his first week at the farm, he offered to pay for a telephone extension in his bedroom. Alice agreed this was a good idea and Mr. Williams had no objection.

Once the new phone was installed, she occasionally heard

him talking late at night. From the upstairs hallway, his voice was a muffled purr. Tiptoeing into the bathroom between the guest room and his room, she tried to make out his words. But even with her ear pressed to the door, she could hear only his elegant cadences, sometimes rising in urgency, and nothing more. One time, he ended his call abruptly and moved toward the bathroom so swiftly that she barely had time to back out and flee to the hallway. Heart pounding, she ducked into her bedroom and shut the door.

After that, he seemed increasingly distant. Alice tormented herself thinking that he had caught her spying on him, but she was afraid to ask him about it. He was as kind as always, but his smiles were scarce and he spent more and more time at work. Where in the beginning he went in for only a couple of hours on Saturday, now he spent all day there.

One such Saturday in mid September, a breathtakingly clear and golden morning, Alice walked to the post office. Alone except for Winston's amiable company, she remembered her first glimpse of Jonathan as she crossed the Rapidan River bridge. The water was sparkling in the late summer sun, and the river breeze lifted her hair away from her neck and shoulders. How surprised she would have been, just a couple of months ago, to know that she would soon be sharing a home, and a dog, with the handsome man who had smiled at her and tipped his hat. The news would have made her slightly younger self so happy, yet the new situation was depressingly ordinary. It was Winston rather than his preoccupied and rather diffident master with whom she spent most of her time.

The postmaster greeted her cordially as he handed over the mail. Sandwiched in among the usual bills and other business correspondence for Mr. Williams was a letter for her. Tipton Home was the return address, but the handwriting was unfamiliar. Ripping the envelope open, she sat down on the bench outside and read:

Dear Alice,

This is Louise Moore (David's sister), and I'm writing to you from the Tipton Home. Or I should say, what's left of it. There was a terrible fire here two weeks ago, and the wing I was in with the other older girls burned to the ground. It was so scary. No one was hurt, but we girls lost everything, not that we had much.

For a week everybody stayed with families all around Tipton. Now we've moved back. We have to double up in the little girls' wing. It is stuffy and crowded and there aren't enough beds. Kathleen O'Shea (she says to tell you hi) and I have to sleep on the floor. Mr. and Mrs. Jenkins say they'll shift things around so that the girls don't have to double up every night, the boys will take their turn. They hope to rebuild by next spring.

Alice, I can't wait that long. I want to come live with you in Virginia. My brother told me you went to Rapidan to rejoin your husband and live on a farm. Is there room for me? I am a hard worker, just like David, and I will cook and clean. (I would also like to finish school.)

Everything is all turned upside-down after the fire. The little kids cry off and on all night and some of the big kids cry, too.

If you can't help me, I understand. But David told me to write to you. By the way, he is fine (in France) and sends you his love, please pray for his safety.

I hope you and your husband are well. Thank you and please let me know if I can come to Virginia!

Sincerely,
Louise Moore

P.S. I have enough money for a bus ticket.
P.P.S. Have you heard from Ross Gentry?

Alice read the letter a second time before walking Winston across the road to the general store. Without giving Louise's request more than a few seconds of thought, she purchased a postcard with a picture of the Rapidan River on it, wrote a brief affirmative reply, and walked back across the road to mail it.

On her way home, she decided Louise could have the room with the twin beds opposite the guest room. That would put her halfway between Alice's room and Jonathan's but on the other side of the hall. She didn't think Mr. Williams would mind. After all, he had welcomed Jonathan into his home, and Louise could help around the house. She remembered David talking affectionately about his sister: how pretty she was and how smart. He had written a few weeks after she arrived at Red Road Farm to say his mother had died and his sister had gone to Tipton. He was still in boot camp and hadn't made it home for the funeral. His note was broken-hearted. Alice wrote him a sympathy letter right away. Seeing no point in describing her circumstances, she had said only that all was well at Red Road Farm. It was evidently based on this bland report that David encouraged his sister to seek her aid.

The thought of the fire at Tipton made gooseflesh rise on her arms. She remembered what it was like the morning she left: everything tidy and calm, the sun rising peacefully over the Tipton Home. Although she had been eager to leave, and fearful of what would happen if she stayed and her aunt and uncle found out she had stolen Ross's file, there was so much about Tipton that she loved: the good, sweet children, the wholesome work routines that kept her strong and fit, and her friendships with several of the older boys. The naughtiness of her nights out drinking beer with Anna had added a dash of excitement and showed her pious aunt and uncle that she had a mind of her own. She had no regrets about Tipton, she thought now, a little surprised by the truth of it.

There had been at least a dozen girls living in the wing that burned down. She could well imagine how cramped and uncomfortable it was for these teenagers to share space with the little girls, some of whom were only four and five years old. How terrifying the fire must have been for all the children, the housemothers, and Aunt Muriel and Uncle Dale. Alice could only hope that the people who lived in and around Tipton would rally around the Home as they always had in the past. She decided to send her aunt and uncle some of the money Anna had given her. It would be a way to show that she cared.

On her way up the driveway, she glanced over at the church. There, at last, was the Reverend Braswell alone in the churchyard. For weeks she had been waiting for an opportunity to talk to him about Annette Radius. The first Saturday after Jonathan had responded so gratefully to her offer, there had been a wedding at Purcell. She watched from a distance as the young bride and groom, hand in hand, came outside. They stood looking at the world as if it were completely new to them. Then the wedding guests began flowing around them, and Alice never even glimpsed the minister. The next Saturday, a brutally hot day, there was a funeral service in the morning and another in the afternoon. Clusters of mourners, baking in their black suits and dresses, had wandered around to the graveyard and stood by the newly dug graves with their heads bowed as the preacher said his prayers.

A few days later, Alice had run into Annette Radius at the grocery store. There was no splint on her arm, and her eyes were not blackened. *Maybe the crisis has passed*, Alice thought, but then she saw several mottled bruises, shaped like handprints, on the woman's upper arms.

Without giving herself time to change her mind, Alice walked across the pasture. She needed to get Winston home to his water bowl, but this conversation wouldn't take long.

The minister looked up in surprise when Alice called his name. A heavyset fellow with a big belly, he was on his hands and knees with a trowel in his hand and a small burlap sack by his side. Drawing closer, she saw that he was planting tulip bulbs. Standing up with some effort and wiping his hands on his pants, he approached the fence. The look on his face was decidedly neutral.

Alice introduced herself and reminded him that she had attended a service at Purcell back in June. Did she plan on attending tomorrow morning, the minister asked with a challenging smile.

"No," she responded. "I came over because I wanted to talk to you about Mrs. Radius."

The man's face grew still. He waited to hear more.

Without identifying Jonathan, she told him she had heard from a reliable source that Arnold Radius was regularly beating up his wife and that Mrs. Radius was afraid to move out and get away from him. "Can you help her? Can you take her in for a while until she finds some other place to live?"

"The Radiuses have lived in this community a lot longer than I have," he said. "As a newcomer to Rapidan, I can't presume to know what's best for them."

"How long have you lived here?" Alice asked, curious to meet another new arrival.

"Seven years," the man said, his eyes steady on Alice's.

"Reverend Braswell, she needs help." Alice said, feeling her pulse quicken and her temper rise. "What do you suggest we do?"

"Young lady," he said, thrusting his belly forward and sticking his hands in his back pockets, "I suggest you mind your own business." That was all he had to say.

Alice stared at the man in astonishment. "Well, goodbye, then." She turned away and joggled Winston's leash. Together they made their way across the pasture and back to the house.

With Jonathan keeping increasingly long and unpredictable hours, Alice saw little of him for the next several days. When she did have a few minutes with him, the time never seemed right for discussing her conversation with Reverend Braswell. Finally, when Thursday rolled around, she resolved to tell him after supper.

Both men were quiet during the meal. While this was common for Mr. Williams, whose epic silences Alice had grown used to, it was not Jonathan's way. Whereas he usually chatted happily about England or his military service or the people he was meeting in Orange, tonight he pushed his food around on his plate and kept his eyes down. The few times he looked directly at her, his expression was bleak. His one-syllable answers to her questions left her frustrated and worried.

After the meal he got Mr. Williams to walk back and forth across the living room, but he skipped their usual game of catch. If the old man noticed the oversight, he didn't say so. He sank back in the wheelchair and went to his room.

Alice hung back in the kitchen for a while before coming into the living room. To her alarm she found Jonathan sitting on the sofa with his head in his hands. "What's wrong?" she cried, rushing to his side.

When he looked up, tears of sympathy stung Alice's eyes. She had never seen anyone look so upset. "Tell me, Jonathan, what is it?" She covered his hands with her own.

"Oh, Alice," he said and abruptly stood up. "I can't tell you in here. I'm afraid I'll disturb your uncle."

Taking his arm, she led him outside and down to the driveway. Several times he tried to speak, but he wasn't ready yet. His face was haggard and there were tears in the corners of his eyes. Her gentle coaxing made no difference.

They made their way down to the road and headed toward the bridge. He seemed to grow calmer then. To her amazement, he put his arm around her shoulders as they walked. When a pickup truck came barreling down the road, he pulled her close in a protective way.

Having reached the center of the bridge, they stopped and gazed down into the dark river. It had been a mild day, but now the breeze had a little snap to it. The dull roar of water rushing over the dam was comforting. Soon the stars would come out. Slipping her arm around Jonathan's waist, she turned to look at him. His noble profile was unutterably sad. Willing herself not to rush him, she drew nearer and thrilled to the warmth of his body.

Finally, he was able to speak. "I have to go back to Tennessee, Alice!"

Alice stared at him. "Why? For how long?"

His eyes bright with trepidation, he said, "Alice, I should've told you a long time ago. I'm engaged to a nurse."

Hearing the word "nurse," her confused mind could conjure

only the gray-haired woman in his office. "You're engaged to Molly!"

"Oh, no," he said with a weary chuckle. "Not Molly. I'm engaged to a girl in Tennessee—Velma. Her name is Velma Reilly. I met her while I was in medical school. She's a nurse at the hospital there."

Her feelings of humiliation and disappointment were so profound that Alice feared her knees would buckle. Steadying herself against the bridge railing, she said, "I'm surprised you never mentioned her before."

"Well, I didn't want to burden you with my personal troubles, that's all. Velma is a Tennessee girl, and she was very upset when I told her I wanted to live in Virginia. I asked her to move here with me, and for the longest time, she resisted. She didn't want to live so far away from her family, and for a few months she broke off our engagement and I hardly heard from her. But now, well, she's had a change of heart. She says she misses me, Alice. She wants to come to Virginia after all."

Even in her embarrassment and confusion, Alice detected a strain in his voice. She gave him a hard look. "When's the wedding?"

The direct question seemed to wound him, and he swallowed before answering. "Well, before all the trouble started, we'd been planning on the fall. Now I suppose we'll be married in the spring."

Now it was Alice's turn to feel wounded, yet again. Without asking any more questions, she began walking back across the bridge with Jonathan trotting to catch up with her.

He didn't try to hold onto her this time. They walked quickly and silently beneath the rising moon. When the occasional car or pickup truck passed them, Alice kept her head down and didn't wave. It was all she could do not to burst into tears.

Once they were back inside the house, Jonathan fumbled in his back pocket for his wallet. He pulled out a small photograph and thrust it at Alice. "Here she is. Here's a photograph of Velma."

Curiosity won out, and Alice took the picture from his hands and held it under a lamp. The face she looked at was not attractive: the girl had a low forehead and thin lips. Her lank hair was pushed behind her ears. If she hadn't felt so terrible, Alice would have been inclined to laugh.

"She's lovely," she said.

"Well, I think so," Jonathan said loyally, as if he could read her mind. "And she's a smart girl. She graduated second in her class at nursing school."

She repressed the urge to say, *But she wasn't smart enough to graduate first.* She wanted nothing more than to escape to the privacy of her room. "Well, I'm happy for you," she said, with one foot on the staircase.

"Alice, I know it's late and you need to get some rest. But just one more thing."

She waited.

"I'm taking the bus tomorrow night for Tennessee to visit Velma and see my family as well. I'll be gone two weeks and Dr. McDonald has agreed to cover for me. I was wondering if—well, if you—"

"What, Jonathan?"

"If you might be willing to keep Winston while I'm away." He smiled tremulously. "He loves it here so much, and I can't take him on the bus."

"Sure, I'll keep Winston," she said. "By the way, I'll be out tomorrow night, so I won't see you when you leave. If you need a ride to the bus station, ask Philip to take you."

"You'll be out tomorrow night?" He sounded surprised.

"That's right." She was halfway up the stairs.

"Well, goodbye, Alice, I'll see you in a couple of weeks, and thank you, thank you for everything."

"Good night." She couldn't look at him again.

It wasn't until she was in the bathroom, splashing cold water on her face, that she remembered her conversation with Reverend Braswell. She had missed her chance to tell Jonathan that Annette Radius was still defenseless against her brute of a husband. And at this point, she had no desire to speak to Jonathan about anything, ever again.

The next day, a half hour before Jonathan was due home, Alice went to the barn in search of Philip. They had talked little since their uncomfortable encounter the night she had caught Rosa Washington with him at the tenant house.

"Could you help me load Mr. Williams into my car?" she asked Philip. "I'm taking him for a drive and we're going out for dinner afterwards."

"Sounds like a date," Philip said with a sidelong smile. "Why aren't you taking your doctor friend instead?"

Alice made a small sound of disgust. "I'm not sure he's ever been a friend of mine." Saying these harsh words made her want to confess everything, even though she was afraid she might break down and cry. "Jonathan's going back to Tennessee to retrieve his fiancée."

Philip was quiet as they walked across the grass. At last he said, with no trace of teasing in his voice, "I'm sorry, Alice. I know you liked him."

"And I thought he liked me. He acted like he did. And now this."

"Well, he's a fool for passing up a chance to be with you."

Alice saw the sincerity in his eyes. "You're kind, Philip. I appreciate that."

With some effort, they got Mr. Williams into Alice's car. Philip wedged the wheelchair in the trunk while Alice helped the old man into the passenger's seat. She had made sure he bathed and dressed neatly that morning. When she told him they were going out, he was pleased. He was so frail that she rarely risked taking him off the property.

She drove aimlessly around Rapidan, aware she was wasting rationed gasoline just to avoid Jonathan. A couple of times, Mr. Williams pointed out the window, his way of indicating he wanted her to turn down this road or that, and she obeyed. Then, lost in her thoughts, she circled back onto Rapidan Road. She didn't want to drive by the farm since Jonathan could be coming or going at any time now, so she turned onto the road next to the flourmill. She had often walked along Old Rapidan Road, which was dirt with occasional patches of gravel, when Mr. Williams was safely napping or Rosa was covering for her. It wended along the river and looked especially pretty in the late afternoon light. As they came to a bend in the road, she saw a man locking a sturdy metal gate across a weedy driveway. His head was lowered, but there was something familiar about him.

"Stop the car!" Mr. Williams commanded.

Alice hit the brakes. The car skidded toward the man and stopped just short of the gate in a dramatic swirl of dust.

At the sound of all the commotion, the man whirled around, and Alice saw that it was none other than Arnold Radius. "Let's not talk to him," she said quietly but firmly as her passenger squirmed in his seat.

"He's not allowed to block that road," Mr. Williams said. "Furman and I went to court to keep him from doing that. I'm going to set him straight."

Glaring at Alice, Arnold Radius advanced toward the car. "What the hell you mean, drivin' your car at me like that? You tryin' to scare me? I'll call the sheriff on you."

Mr. Williams raised his fist in a feeble gesture of rage. Her hands tight on the steering wheel, Alice maneuvered the car away from the gate. With Arnold Radius still yelling at them, they drove back the way they came.

As they approached the entrance to Red Road Farm, her heart sank. There was the farm truck, with Philip at the wheel and Jonathan beside him. In hopes of avoiding them, she slowed the car as much as she dared without coming to a dead stop. Philip honked the horn and waved before pulling out of the driveway. Jonathan turned around to lean out of the passenger's side and wave at her at well. Alice stared ahead grimly.

She drove up the driveway, turned off the engine and then, unable to restrain herself, put her head down on the wheel.

There was a shifting beside her. "What's wrong?" Mr. Williams asked in his raspy voice.

She couldn't yet answer.

"Where's Jonathan going?"

The painful truth was all she had to offer, and she told it as briefly and simply as she could.

Mr. Williams was silent for a long minute. Then he said, "I don't think we've seen the last of him."

"Well, he'll still be your doctor. Philip will take you to see him."

"I didn't mean that."

"I didn't think you did."

The old man cleared his throat before speaking again. "Didn't you say we were going out to dinner? Let's go."

They drove to Orange and went to the James Madison Inn on Caroline Street. It was the first time Alice had been there, and she liked the look of the elegant old building with its white columns and gracious dining room. Once seated, Mr. Williams received several visitors from nearby tables—friends and business acquaintances he had seen infrequently in recent years. Alice knew these exchanges took real effort; he was exhausted midway through the meal. By the time the check arrived, his eyes were drooping. He had left his wallet at home so Alice, an ironic smile tugging at her mouth, paid the expensive bill.

As they drove home, Alice couldn't stop thinking about Jonathan Perkins. She pictured him leaning his head against the bus window and trying to sleep. Or maybe his seatmate would find out he was a doctor and pester him with medical questions all night long. She wondered whether he would give any thought to her. Or would the prospect of seeing Velma Reilly consume him? *I will not think about him*, she told herself, but she knew she would.

On Monday morning, she received a business phone call. The caller was Fred Teagle, who owned a house behind the Williams estate and rented land for cattle grazing. Alice had met him soon after she took over Sorbon Carter's job. He was a raw-necked, uneducated fellow in his early forties with big eyes, thinning hair, and large nervous hands. On the earlier occasion, after sizing up Alice and learning that Sorbon was due back eventually, he seemed more at ease.

Now, on the telephone, his voice was strained. "That gall-durned Radius is up to his mischief again, Miss Williams. He's put a gate across the driveway connecting my property and Old Rapidan Road. It's open during the day, but he locks it up at night. I told him it was illegal to keep me and my family penned in like that, and he just cussed me up, down, and sideways."

At Fred Teagle's request, a sheriff's deputy had come out, but the gate had been wide open then and Radius claimed that it always was. When Fred asked the deputy to come back that night, the man said he had better things to do.

Alice told Fred that she and Mr. Williams had seen the gate, and Mr. Williams was furious about it. He had said something about a lawsuit involving a property line dispute.

Fred Teagle interrupted to say that the lawsuit had resolved an earlier dispute. The latest indignation was something new. "Me and my wife and kids need to get in and out of our property just like everybody else. We ain't stayin' in all night long, just because Radius thinks we should be penned up like a bunch of cattle."

Before she had time to mull over this worrisome phone call, there was a loud knock at the front door. An unusually tall, beefy man in a brown uniform was peering in. He had a full head of white hair, a handlebar moustache, and a pistol protruding from the holster on his belt. *Well, if that's not the sheriff, I don't know who is*, Alice thought.

Her assumption was correct. Sheriff Waller had a report of harassment with a motor vehicle over at the Radius home on Old Rapidan Road, and now it appeared someone had tampered with Mr. Radius's new gate. He had come to get her fingerprinted, and Mr. Williams, too.

"You'd fingerprint a ninety-year-old man in a wheelchair?"

Alice asked incredulously. "Are you out of your mind?"

The sheriff gave her a severe look. "Remember who you're talking to, young lady. My job is to keep order in this county, and your job is to be a law-abiding citizen. And who's to say that a man in a wheelchair couldn't tamper with a gate? Or a headstrong young gal who's new to town? Where there's a will, there's a way."

Her hands trembling with fury and indignation, Alice allowed herself to be fingerprinted. Mr. Williams had been in the bathroom when she got the call from Fred Teagle, and now he was back in his room, slumped in his favorite armchair. He blinked at her blearily when she patted his arm and spoke to him.

Looking abashed, Sheriff Waller entered the room. His heavy boots squeaked as he approached Mr. Williams's chair. "How're you, sir?" he said. When no reply came, he sat himself down on the horsehair sofa with some effort. There was barely room behind the coffee table for his big haunches. With a glance at Alice, who had decided not to help him present his case, he took a breath. "We got a little problem over at Arnold Radius's place, Mr. Williams. He says you and this young lady went and messed with his gate, so I'm gonna have to fingerprint you." He held up his inkpad and the clipboard with the blotting paper on it.

Mr. Williams gave the man a withering look before extending one frail hand and then the other. Sheriff Waller completed his task with care and then rose heavily to his feet. "Well, thank you, sir, for your cooperation. That's just what I expected from a true Virginia gentleman such as yourself. You can get that ink off your hands with soap and water."

His last words hung in the air. Mr. Williams turned toward Alice, who stood protectively beside him. In an unusually clear voice, he said, "Tell this cretin to get out of our home."

"You heard my uncle," Alice said between gritted teeth.

Sheriff Waller's pompous face fell. Quickly recovering, he stood his ground before making his way to the door. "No man is greater than the law, Miss Williams," he said, eyeing her coldly. "Good day."

"Goodbye," Alice said, closing the door swiftly.

She tried to talk to Mr. Williams about what had just happened and the telephone call from Fred Teagle, but the encounter with the sheriff had exhausted him. When she paused to take a breath, he said, "Call Furman. He'll take care of it," and turned his head away.

Though Furman Shafer was dead and buried next door, there was still his son Thomas Shafer in Richmond. After lunch Alice went upstairs to make the call. It was the first time she had used the telephone extension in Jonathan's room. Early in his stay, she had dusted and straightened up his room one afternoon when he was at work. After that one and only time, he kept his door shut. He said he didn't expect her to clean up after him.

Today the room was messy and cried out for a thorough cleaning. Alice made up the bed before sitting down on it. On the nightstand, beside the telephone, was the photograph of Velma Reilly that Jonathan had shown her. *Oh well, now he'll be with the real thing*, she thought crossly. Without premeditation, she flicked the picture off the table. It landed facedown in a dusty corner and she left it there. Arranging the pillows behind her, she readied herself for her important phone call.

Betty Shafer answered the phone. Then a minute passed while mother and son whispered loudly back and forth. Thomas barely listened to her report before launching into a lengthy saga Alice could barely keep track of. The tale involved a long-ago right-of-way dispute, Fred Teagle's lawsuit against Mr. Williams, something called a spite strip, and a tangential narrative about Mr. Williams's no-count son Thatcher. Thomas was incensed that his father's best friend had been fingerprinted. In the background she could hear Betty Shafer talking excitedly.

Alice hung up knowing Thomas would be no help. She was on her own dealing with Arnold Radius and the sheriff and Fred Teagle.

When she discussed everything later that day with Philip, he said, "Alice, you can be sure Fred Teagle was the one who tried to break the lock. All he wants is to get his access road back. He's grazing his cattle on Williams family land, and he has his house and his family back there. You're not the one with the problem. Teagle is the one who has a problem with Arnold Radius who, as we both already know, is completely nuts."

"Well, what should I do?"

"Nothing," Philip said emphatically. "Just leave it alone. These old white guys—" he said before catching himself. "These guys can duke it out on their own. Stay out of it."

She tried to tell him about her efforts in behalf of Annette Radius, but he cut her off. "You think you're helping, but you're not," he said before heading back inside the barn.

The next several days passed without incident, and her thoughts began to turn elsewhere. She realized how she had planned her days around Jonathan's return from work in the evening. The suppers she prepared and the clothes she wore were all designed to impress him. Now, none of that mattered. He was back with his Tennessee sweetheart, and soon he would be completely gone from Red Road Farm. If he had ever liked her—and it seemed that he had—those feelings had been successfully tamped down. His love for Velma Reilly had won out in the end. She shook her head sadly. The memory of his arm around her shoulders came back to her as she wandered around the farm. How warm he was! How good and gentle. He'd had ample chance to consider her, but a homely nurse in Tennessee had the stronger claim to his heart. Her chest swelled with sorrow and disappointment.

9

One morning not long after Jonathan left, she was nearing the end of a leisurely walk around the property. She had gone down to the garden to feed the goldfish and pick chrysanthemums, and then had a short visit with Philip, who was riding Goldie around the perimeter of the pasture. Suddenly the sound of mingled voices attracted her attention to the driveway. A tall, well-built young man and two slender teenaged girls were walking toward her. Their heads bent toward one another, they talked animatedly. Alice stopped in her tracks.

The young man was the first to spot her. "Alice!" he cried out and began jogging her way. He wore a sailor's uniform and carried a duffel bag over his shoulder. When the two girls saw her, they also called out her name and began running to catch up with the young man. All of them were laughing with delight.

The group converged all at once and encircled Alice in a hug, crushing the chrysanthemums against her chest.

"Dennis!" Alice said, a wave of surprised gladness filling her heart. She had hardly expected that Dennis Delmarvin would pay a visit when he didn't reply to her note. "And Kathleen. Oh, my goodness! Welcome." She grinned at the red-haired girl who now stepped back shyly, embarrassed by her spontaneous show of affection. "And you must be Louise." This girl, whom Alice had heard about but never met before, had a startling vibrancy about her. Her springy blonde curls fell past her shoulders, and her dimples showed when she smiled.

"Oh, Alice, thank you so much for letting us come!" Her sincerity brought a lump to Alice's throat: she could see something of David in the girl's lovely face.

Alice gazed at the three of them standing radiantly before her. She was thrilled but baffled. "How did you get here all at once?" As the girls looked at one another, uncertain who should answer, Alice thought, *And what is Kathleen O'Shea doing here? I don't remember anything in Louise's letter about her.*

Dennis took the lead. "Their bus got in five minutes after mine. I was standing there trying to decide whether to walk here or take a taxi when these two rolled off the bus looking like a couple of bedraggled pups." He grinned at the girls. "I recognized Kathleen—and gosh, I could hardly believe my bad luck. I've been sailing around the world trying to get away from Tipton for the past two years, and here she comes, with another Tipton girl right by her side." He was warming to his tale. "I tried to run away, but they caught me—the two of them together are actually very strong—and so I submitted, and here we are." He took off his sailor's cap and ran a hand through his thick dark hair. It was then that his gaze lingered on Alice's face. She felt a shimmering warmth flood her body; there was no mistaking that look in a man's eyes.

Gaily they made their way to the house. Louise took Alice aside and explained that the night before she left, Kathleen had begged to come along. Alice assured her there was room for everybody at Red Road Farm.

The girls had one small suitcase between them and it wouldn't take them long to unpack it in the room Alice assigned them. Dennis made his way past them on the staircase to the guest room. He wanted a bath after the dusty bus ride up from Norfolk. With just thirteen days to spend with Alice, he said over his shoulder, he didn't want her pushing him away because of the way he smelled. Kathleen and Louise traded a look, and Alice turned away.

After unpacking, the girls came downstairs and found Alice in the living room. "What should we do?" Louise asked.

"Well," Alice said, looking at her inquiringly. "I could get you something to drink and fix you lunch. After that, do you want to walk around and see the place, or take a nap? What do you feel like doing?"

Louise smiled. "I should've said, what needs cleaning? We're ready to work."

Absorbing this glad news, Alice suggested they start upstairs. She told them where the cleaning supplies were and directed them to begin with Jonathan's room. "Be sure to sweep up and dispose of all of the trash!" she said, thinking evilly of the photo of Velma Reilly that she had tossed to the floor.

"Oh, one question," Alice said as the two turned to go. "Just out of curiosity, how did you get here? Did you take a taxi? I hope you didn't have to walk."

Louise had already gone upstairs, but Kathleen heard her. From the landing, she said, "We got a ride from one of your neighbors. He had a strange name—it started with an R. Ray something, I think."

"Radius? Arnold Radius?" Alice asked in amazement.

"That's it. He was walking past the station and heard us talking about Red Road Farm, and he said he was going that way."

"He's an odd one, Kathleen. Don't accept any more rides from him."

"He asked us some questions about you, but we didn't know the answers. And I wouldn't have told him anything anyway."

Alice held her tongue. The girls didn't need to know about the trouble Arnold Radius was causing her and just about everybody else he came in contact with. But if they had to meet up with him on their first day in Orange County, she was glad Dennis had been with them. He was tall and strong, and his sailor's uniform carried authority. It was unlikely, she decided, that this disturbing man would do any harm so long as Dennis was around.

When Dennis came downstairs, freshly shaven and smelling strongly of cologne, she invited him to sit down while she made his lunch.

"Lunch can wait. I want to have a look at this place. How many acres you got here? The old man must be loaded." He gave her a sly smile and a nudge in the ribs.

Alice recoiled. She knew what Mr. Williams thought about questions like his.

"Oh, well, there's definitely room to roam," she said. "I'll show you around."

Her second long walk of the morning gave her a chance to size up Dennis. He pranced around her like a frisky puppy and pointed out birds and rabbits as if he were the first to ever see such creatures. When he saw Philip at a distance, he said, "Who's the nigger?"

Alice stopped and grabbed Dennis by the arm. "Don't you ever call him that again. That's Philip Williams, and he's my friend. He used to work for Anna's family—remember Anna Boyer? And now he takes care of the horses here at the farm."

"Well, I beg your pardon," Dennis said in a sarcastic way. "I didn't know I had to be so careful with my language. It must be the old Virginia aristocracy rubbing off on you. Not that those aristocrats ever had any problem owning slaves."

"It's just a matter of common decency," she said. "Come on, you need to meet him."

After a terse exchange of hellos with Philip, Dennis scrambled onto Goldie and rode her up and down the pasture while yelling excitedly to Alice. The horse was nervous and none too pleased with her boisterous rider. Alice could read the irritation on Philip's face.

"He's a real live wire," Philip said. "Where'd you find him?"

"He found me. He was an orphan back in Tipton."

"Whoa, now, horsey!" Dennis yelled as the horse suddenly picked up speed. "Stop!" He yanked on the reins, but Goldie ignored him. Horse and rider went from a canter to a gallop as Dennis cried out in alarm.

Before she could say anything, Philip had mounted the gentle spotted horse they called Patches. He caught up with Dennis and Goldie, and soon the two horses fell into an easy trot back toward the barn. When Dennis climbed down, his face was dripping with sweat. "Well, that's enough riding for one day," he said to Alice.

"Let's go back to the house."

Alice served Mr. Williams lunch in his room so she could talk to him privately. Over a bowl of homemade soup and fresh bread, she told him about the new arrivals. It was easy to explain the visiting sailor, an old friend from the Tipton Home, but the presence of the two teenaged girls was another matter. Mr. Williams was silent when Alice said the girls had no place else to go and might be around for a while, maybe even a few years if Mr. Williams would permit it. When she asked if he objected, he looked her in the eye without saying a word.

"Well, it's settled then," she said a little too brightly. "And don't worry, sir, those girls are workers. They'll keep this place shining, even more than it does now."

He silently held up his tray. Alice took it from him and exhaled with relief as she left the room.

The girls quickly set up a routine of cleaning house, canning vegetables, and helping Philip in the barn. They offered to stay with Mr. Williams when Alice needed to go out, and he seemed to like them well enough—at least he had no complaints. Alice began to wonder how she had ever managed without them.

Louise called the high school in Orange, and soon she and Kathleen were catching a ride to school with several other children who lived up the road. They rose early and worked for a couple of hours before and after school. At night they retired to their room to do their homework. *You can take the girls out of Tipton*, Alice thought, *but you can't Tipton out of the girls.*

Dennis was also busy. He was deferential toward Mr. Williams and made a point of taking him out on the porch every morning and chatting with him. He told stories about his voyages and the war, and Mr. Williams listened attentively. Where normally he would be sound asleep after breakfast, now he was Dennis's willing audience.

In the afternoons, while the old man slept, Dennis set about building a ramp alongside the back steps. "This way, he can get outside more," he said to Alice. "You'll be able to wheel him around the yard and get him to the car a lot more easily." He had found some lumber in the barn and spent hours on the project every day. When he was finished with the ramp, he built a hand railing along each side. Though he still needed to sand the railings and paint the whole thing, he called Alice to come and see.

She had to admit the ramp was a very good idea, and she was irritated with herself for not thinking of it on her own. Standing in the yard with him, she complimented his handiwork. He slipped his arm around her waist and pulled her close. "That's not all I can do, sweetheart," he said, giving her a wet kiss on the cheek. Alice pulled away abruptly and went inside without another word. She had been aware of his eye on her ever since he arrived, but he was too crude and aggressive for her tastes, and she had not forgotten the way he'd spoken of Philip.

After the incident in the backyard, however, she noticed a distinct change in him. He spent more time with the girls when they got home from school and redoubled his efforts with Mr. Williams. One night he took her and the girls out to dinner, and she let him drive her car to the James Madison Inn. Unlike Mr. Williams, he paid for the meal. He was a perfect gentleman whenever she spoke to him, and he listened with more than polite interest when Kathleen and Louise talked excitedly about their new school. Sometimes he and the girls reminisced about Tipton, and to Alice's surprise his memories of it were mostly fond.

Reversing her earlier judgment, Alice began to regret he was leaving so soon. Now when she lay in bed trying to fall asleep, she thought of him instead of Jonathan Perkins. Jonathan's ambivalence had always been there even when she most wanted to believe he was falling in love with her, whereas with Dennis, the physical attraction was real and certain. He had backed off, yes. But her instincts told her he was just playing a waiting game. He still wanted her; he had to. Because she had always preferred being the pursuer rather than the pursued, his new reserve made him more interesting to her. Thinking about Dennis now, she stretched out her arms languorously and ran a hand down the length of her torso. Maybe it was time to see what he had to offer.

A big rainstorm blew into Orange County a couple of days before he was scheduled to leave. The girls were at school and Mr. Williams was napping as usual, and neither Alice nor Dennis could work outside. With the rain pounding on the roof and slanting against the windows, Dennis settled himself in the living room with a cup of tea and a volume of Hegel he had found on Mr. Williams's bookcase. Dressed in chino pants and a neat white shirt, he had a clean-cut look that Alice found attractive. Winston was asleep on the floor beside him. She went and stood behind his chair and tried to engage him in conversation, but he was engrossed in his reading and had few words for her. In answer to her question, he said he wanted to continue his education after the war ended. She was pleased to hear that he was ambitious.

With no one around to see, she lightly massaged his shoulders as he resumed reading. "Mmm, that feels good," he said and leaned his head forward. "Do it harder." She obliged and soon her hands were sliding down his back. The scent of his cologne filled her nostrils, and she expected him to stand up and pull her into his arms. When that didn't happen, she bent down and ran the tip of her tongue along his ear. Though he murmured his pleasure, he didn't make a move. She moved her lips along his neck and nibbled his earlobe. Soon she was leaning awkwardly over the chair so she could stroke his legs. She gave a little gasp of delight when she felt the length of hardness beneath the cloth of his pants. Still he read his book, or pretended to.

Footsteps and voices on the porch signaled that the girls were unexpectedly home. School had ended early due to flooding on the back roads. Alice, having backed away from Dennis in time, stood in the middle of the room as the girls came in laughing and shaking the rain off their yellow slickers. They didn't seem to notice her dazed expression. Dennis greeted them and then, when they trotted off to the kitchen, gave Alice a quick wink before turning yet again to his book.

The rest of the afternoon and evening Alice felt like she was walking in a fog. It dawned on her that Dennis was leaving very soon and this was her chance to be with a very virile man who clearly wanted her. Having sex with him would help her put the infuriating Jonathan out of her mind. Late that night, she dressed in the silky negligee Anna had given her and sat on the edge of her bed. The house was still. There was just the sound of the endless rain beating against the roof and windows.

Without giving herself time to reconsider, she stole down the hall and entered Dennis's room without knocking. When she said his name, he responded groggily. She was disappointed that he hadn't been lying awake thinking of her. But there was no turning back now that she was in his room.

"Do you want to cuddle?" she whispered as she sat down on the bed.

"Oh, Alice," he said, sitting up on his elbows. "I'm leaving. We shouldn't be starting anything now."

She decided he was only teasing her. Playfully agreeing that he was absolutely right, she slipped her hand under the bed covers and discovered he was naked. Further probing revealed that he was as ready for sex as she was. When he made no move to invite her into his bed, Alice found herself growing wild with desire. She kept her hand under the covers and began stroking him first with one finger, then two, and then her whole hand. *He is bigger than Macklin*, she thought. It was obvious he wanted her very much. She scooted closer to him and greedily inhaled his pungent smell.

With a small grimace, almost of regret, he slid his hand under the covers and on top of hers. For a few minutes their hands moved in unison as he tilted his head back, mouth open, and closed his eyes. As she watched him and listened to the rain on the metal roof, the sweet pain at Alice's core was almost more than she could bear. Suddenly he began urging her hand on. His release came quickly and brusquely, in a series of rapid shudders and grunts. His eyes were squeezed shut and Alice had the awful realization he was not thinking of her at all. She let her sticky hand go still.

It was then that Dennis sat up abruptly and pushed her hand away. "You're going to have to leave," he whispered. "I mean it."

She stifled a cry and jumped up from the bed. Without another word, she ran down the hall. Whispers emanated from another room. *So the girls heard us*, Alice thought with deep dismay.

She ran a hot bath and lay back in the tub with her eyes closed. She was too mortified even to weep.

The next morning she and Dennis circled warily around one another. The girls kept their distance, but Alice saw them exchanging glances. At one point she nearly fussed at Kathleen O'Shea for acting strangely but thought better of it. Kathleen and Louise had proven so useful around the farm that she didn't dare antagonize them.

It was a Friday, and Philip showed up at lunchtime to ask whether he could take the weekend off. He stood inside the front door with rain dripping off his coat and shoes and said he wanted to borrow the truck. He was looking at his feet and acting nervous. Finally he announced that he and Rosa were getting married. He said he would be back Monday morning.

When Alice gave her permission, he turned on his heel with a quick nod of thanks. "Be careful," she called to his back. "With all this rain, I'm afraid the river will flood."

"I know," Philip said, glancing at her over his shoulder. "That's why I wanted to leave now."

With that he was gone. Alice stood at the open doorway and looked out at the rain. She thought how irritated Rosa Washington had looked the night Alice had interrupted her and Philip at the tenant house. *Well, at least one woman around here will be getting what she wants*, she thought. There were deep puddles everywhere and the rain was falling more heavily all the time. Suddenly she remembered that her car was out of commission with a flat tire. Both Philip and Dennis had looked at it and pronounced it beyond repair. With war rations in effect, it would be quite a while before she could replace the tire. She wished Philip had picked another weekend to get married.

Over supper that night, in front of the girls and Mr. Williams, Dennis announced he would be leaving early the next day for Norfolk.

Mr. Williams spoke up. "Fix him a lunch he can eat on the bus."

"Will do, sir," Alice said, barely able to keep the anger out of her voice.

The girls cleared the table and did the dishes with their usual efficiency. When Kathleen offered to make Dennis's lunch, Alice shooed her out of the kitchen. Soon she could hear voices coming from the living room. Dennis and the girls were sitting on the floor playing cards, with Winston asleep on the sofa beside them. It was a peaceful, domestic scene, and it made Alice mad. She slapped meat down on a cutting board and sliced it roughly. No special treats for this lunch. After finishing her work, she went up the back stairs so she could avoid the others.

Midnight came and went as she lay tossing in her bed. She was furious at Dennis and couldn't stop thinking of how he had humiliated her. Finally she dozed off, only to be awakened by the sound of loud barking. She wondered what had gotten into Winston. Lying still, she hoped he would stop without her aid. But the commotion only grew louder. She swung her feet to the floor. Then, to her alarm, she heard the front door opening and the sound of voices. "Burglars!" Pulling the negligee around her and taking the only object she could easily find—one of the badminton racquets Anna had given her—she crept out of the room and bent over the stair railing. Wearing nothing but his undershorts, Dennis was already there.

The living room light was on, and they could hear two voices, both male, neither trying to speak softly. To her astonishment, Alice recognized the voice of Jonathan Perkins. Rushing around the corner and halfway down the stairs, she cried out his name. Just as Jonathan and the other man turned toward her, she stopped on the stair landing and brandished the badminton racquet.

There was a split second of silence before Dennis swooped

down and pulled Alice to his side. "What the hell's going on?" he said. His arm around her waist, he and Alice descended the remaining steps. She set down the racquet and distractedly patted Winston on the head. She noted that the other man was Fred Teagle, the farmer who had a home behind Red Road Farm.

Both men were drenched. Puddles formed around their feet and around Jonathan's suitcase and medical bag.

"How did you get here in the middle of the night?" Alice asked Jonathan.

"The bus was running late because of all the rain, and then I couldn't get a taxi in Orange," he said, wiping a hand through his wet hair. "When I finally found a driver crazy enough to take me, he got stuck in the mud about three miles from here. We both got soaked to the skin fooling with his car, and in the end I had to walk the rest of the way here. I ran into Mr. Teagle"—he nodded at his companion—"just as I reached the front porch."

With this exchange out of the way, Fred Teagle began talking. "Miz Williams, we got trouble with that gall-durned Radius again!" He paused to let this register on everyone. "I heard him come home in that noisy old truck of his, and then I heard a scream," he said, his voice trembling, "and I ran out in the rain, and there come the preacher—Braswell's his name—running out of the Radius house. He tripped and fell, and Arnold Radius was yelling at him. Then the preacher was up on his feet and he got away, and Arnold went back in the house. It was quiet for a spell after that."

"What does any of this have to do with us?" Dennis asked, drawing Alice closer as Jonathan continued to stare at her.

"I'm getting to that part, young feller," Fred said, narrowing his eyes at Dennis. Then he turned back to Alice. "So Radius goes back in his house, and like I said, it's quiet for a while and then I hear more yelling and screaming. And this is screaming like I've never heard before—and the Radiuses are a fighting couple, so I've heard 'em yelling before." He paused for a breath. "But not like this. And then I heard gunshot!

"I run to the kitchen to call the sheriff, but the phone's gone out in this rainstorm. My wife's awake and the kids are crying, and I says to my wife, I gotta get the sheriff, and she says, 'Well, don't think you're going nowhere in this storm tonight. The car's stuck in the mud, you know that, and Arnold Radius got us locked in, besides.' So's I says to her, I'll run over to the Williams place, and they'll help." He took another gasp of breath. "And that's what I done."

Jonathan found his voice again. "Are you saying someone may have been shot?"

Fred Teagle wiped the rain and sweat from his brow and looked at the doctor incredulously. "That's what I'm saying, man. One of you people's got to call the sheriff."

Dennis made a move toward Mr. Williams's room, where the phone was, but Alice stopped him. "Don't wake up my uncle. Use the phone upstairs."

"I'll make the call," Jonathan said, shooting a daggered glance at Alice as he passed by.

"Since the rest of you seem to have this under control, I'm going back to bed," Dennis said, "but first, Alice, tell me who's this guy going upstairs." He jerked his head toward Jonathan's back.

"That's Dr. Perkins. He rents a room—he used to rent a room here." She was standing so close to Dennis she could see the pores in his skin. "He's a friend of my uncle's. And a friend of mine."

Dennis gave her a quick, cynical look before sidling upstairs.

Left alone with the farmer, Alice saw that his face was gray, and he was steadying himself against a chair. "You don't look well, Mr. Teagle. Would you like a cup of tea? Why don't you sit down and I'll bring you a towel so you can dry off."

"Don't mind if I do, ma'am," he said. "But can I use your facilities? I feel sort of sick to my stomach."

Fred Teagle disappeared into the bathroom while Alice set the teapot on the stove. Shivering in her negligee, she hurried upstairs to fetch the promised towel and get dressed. Coming out of her room, she ran into Jonathan, still in his sodden clothes and overcoat. "Did you reach the sheriff?" she asked.

"The phone's not working. Must be the case all over Orange County," he said with a woeful shake of his head. "I suppose I should go over there and check on Mrs. Radius. Can you give me directions or should I ask our visitor?"

"You go to the flourmill and turn left onto Old Rapidan Road, and then it's the first road on your left. But Arnold Radius keeps the gate locked, and I expect Old Rapidan Road is flooded."

"Well, I've got to try."

"I think you better check on Mr. Teagle before you go. He's feeling sick."

Jonathan raised his eyebrows and turned to go downstairs.

"I didn't think you were coming back for a couple more days," Alice called after him.

"I came back early to see if you would have me, Alice," he said, pausing to look up at her. "I broke up with Velma Reilly."

"Oh!"

"But I see I'm a bit late, since you've obviously hit it off quite well with your new gent."

Before she could stop herself, Alice blurted out, "He's no gent."

Dennis stuck his head out of his room. "I heard that." He sounded more amused than angry.

Jonathan continued to gaze up at Alice, his hand on the banister. "I'm surprised at you, Alice, but of course you owe me no explanations. I was just a boarder here."

A groan interrupted their conversation. Jonathan ran down the steps with Alice close behind him. Together they found Fred Teagle collapsed against a table. Jonathan grabbed him under the arms and pulled him to the sofa. He checked the man's pulse and then retrieved his medical bag. As Alice hovered, he pulled out his stethoscope and told her to bring a glass of water right away and then fetch a pair of pajamas, a bed pillow, and a couple of blankets. Mr. Teagle wouldn't be moving from the sofa anytime soon.

Having done all these things, Alice hung back and watched from a discreet distance. Jonathan had given the man a pill and now was helping him out of his wet clothes and into a fresh pair of Mr. Williams's pajamas. Mr. Teagle's face was ashen, but she sensed that the immediate crisis was over.

Suddenly she snapped to attention. "What about Annette Radius? Somebody has to go check on her."

"Well, I can't in good conscience leave this man alone, Alice," Jonathan said. "He just had a heart attack." He paused. "Wait until morning. By then, hopefully the phones will be working again, and the sheriff can address whatever troubles the Radiuses are having."

Fred Teagle tried to sit up and speak. "My wife—" he began before slumping back on his pillow.

"His wife will be worried sick when he doesn't come back," Alice finished for him. "Jonathan, I'm going to go. I'll tell Mrs. Teagle her husband is staying here for the night. And I'll look in on Mrs. Radius."

Jonathan shook his head in silent disapproval before turning back to his patient.

When Alice went upstairs to get a sweater and a flashlight, she noticed a light was on in the girls' room. Louise and Kathleen, looking pale and scared in their long nightgowns, came out to ask what was going on. It was too much to explain right then. Sizing up the two, Alice made a quick decision. "Come on, Louise," she said. "Get dressed in warm clothes and grab your raincoat. You're coming with me."

When Jonathan learned that Alice's car wasn't running, he fished his keys out of his pocket and tossed them to her. He would no longer try to stop her, but his expression revealed his displeasure. He and Louise traded a baffled glance—neither had any idea who the other was.

Outside, the rain was cold and hard against their faces as Alice and Louise ran for Jonathan's car. The Plymouth lurched to life and then stalled out. This happened several times. "It's nearly out of gas," Alice said, "and now I've flooded the engine."

"Well," Louise said, "the roads probably aren't passable anyway."

Alice turned and gazed at her while she thought hard. "I know," she said, "we'll take Goldie. That way, we can cut through the fields and avoid the roads and the locked gate."

With that plan in mind, they took off for the barn as fast as they could. The horses were snug in their stalls, and Goldie snorted in surprise when Alice approached her in the darkness. "You know how to ride, don't you, Louise?"

"Well, I rode the old mare at Tipton once or twice."

"Good. You have as much experience as I do."

They led the horse out of her stall and put an old leather saddle on her. Alice felt around in the dark until she found the reins hanging on a hook. She adjusted them as best she could. She got on first. Louise climbed up behind her and clutched Alice's waist. Alice pointed the flashlight ahead of the horse, and off they went.

The way across the field was treacherous, and Alice wondered aloud whether they should have walked instead. But the horse's bulk beneath her was reassuring, and Goldie seemed to trust her as they moved steadily through the night. The horse carried Alice and Louise above the brambles that would have torn their clothing and slowed them down even more.

The flashlight's thin beam wavered in the rain. As they rode along, Alice told Louise as much as she knew about Arnold and Annette Radius, and explained at some length about Jonathan Perkins. Louise asked only a few questions. When their conversation flagged, Alice's thoughts turned to the Reverend Braswell. What on earth, she wondered, was he doing at the Radius home on this most unpleasant of nights? She recalled how resistant and unfriendly he had been when she asked him to help Annette. And yet something about Mr. Teagle's story nagged at her: he had heard Arnold come home and then the preacher ran out the door. A sudden intuition told her Arnold had caught his wife and the minister doing more than praying together.

When they finally reached the back of the Williams property, they climbed down and tethered Goldie to a tree with a rope Alice had thought to bring at the last minute. They ducked under a decrepit wooden fence, made their way through a dense stand of pine trees, and then stood blinking in the rain, which had tapered off to a fine, needle-sharp drizzle. It was a landscape of utter darkness. Neither the Radius house nor the Teagle home had any lights on. "I wonder if the electricity's gone out along with the phones," Alice murmured.

"Or maybe everyone's asleep," Louise said hopefully.

The stillness of the two houses made Alice deeply uncomfortable. It crossed her mind that they could turn back now, and no one would ever know they had been here. But turning back was not her way. She took a breath and faced Louise. "Tell Mrs. Teagle her husband is at Red Road Farm for the night. Say he took ill, but Dr. Perkins is with him and she can come see him in the morning."

"What are you going to do, Alice?" Louise said. "You're not going into the Radius house by yourself, are you?"

Alice compressed her lips into a thin line. "Somebody has to help that poor woman," she said. "It might as well be me." She leaned forward and hugged Louise before they went on their separate missions. The girl, whimpering, made her way toward the Teagles' front door without looking back.

She had let Louise keep the flashlight and now it was too dark to see a path to the Radiuses' house. Finally her feet found a brick walkway. With trepidation she walked to the door and knocked.

There was no answer. She knocked again, louder this time. When there was still no response, she banged on the door with both fists, and cried out, "Anybody home? I'm here to see Mrs. Radius!"

The door was solid wood. She walked across the sodden grass and pressed her face against a window, but curtains prevented her from seeing inside. Moving around to the side of the house, she tried to look in one window after another. She could see nothing in any of them. There were no sounds other than the light rain pattering on leaves and her footfalls. The near silence was beginning to make her flesh crawl. Having made a full circle, she stood before the front door and knocked again. It was no use, though. She was about to turn away and rejoin Louise at the Teagles' house when something made her try the doorknob.

The knob turned easily and suddenly Alice was inside the Radius home. She fumbled for a light switch but, as she had feared, the electricity was out. Moving forward into the house, she called out softly, "Mrs. Radius? Annette? It's me, Alice Williams."

From the entrance hall, she found her way into the kitchen. In the darkness she glimpsed an ashtray on the kitchen table and next to it a book of matches. Seizing on this, Alice struck a match and used it to light her path. A sense of dread rose in her throat as she fell silent, no longer wanting to call out Annette Radius's name.

The downstairs was tidy, everything seeming in its rightful place. She used up two matches, then a third, peering in room after room. Steeling herself, she climbed the stairs. The whole house seemed to weigh on her, and the air on the second floor was close and sour. Her chest felt tight, and the image of Mr. Teagle collapsed against the table flickered through her mind. *I need to get out of here*, she thought, *right now*.

But curiosity pushed her on. She lit the last match and turned into an open doorway. First she saw Annette, a lumpy shape sprawled across an unmade bed, and then Arnold, who was lying impossibly still on the floor. There were two bullet holes in Annette's chest and one in Arnold's forehead. The gun was in his hand. His lifeless eyes stared up at Alice.

The match had burned down to her fingertips. She backed out of the doorway and ran downstairs. She did not scream or cry out or even swallow. Outside again, she took a deep gasp of the wet night air and began running toward the Teagles' home. Louise was calling her name.

She cried out, "Don't come this way, Louise!" Grabbing the

girl's coat sleeve, she pulled her toward the fence where Goldie waited. Though Louise kept asking her questions, Alice barely spoke on the ride back. What she had seen would stay with her the rest of her days, but she would not speak of it at length to anyone besides Sheriff Waller, who did not even bother to take notes as she told him her tale, and later Philip, who listened solemnly. She wanted him to tell her she had been brave and done the right thing, but in his expression she could see that he thought otherwise.

It was not long after the traumatic night that she heard that the Reverend Braswell had moved on rather suddenly to another church, one back in South Carolina where he was from. A new minister arrived at Purcell Presbyterian in November and came over to Red Road Farm soon thereafter to introduce himself. Fresh from the seminary, he was a plainspoken man with a firm handshake and a forthright manner. He talked quietly with Mr. Williams and left before the old man got tired. Alice instinctively liked him.

On Christmas Eve, with Louise and Kathleen trailing after her, Alice went across the field for this new man's midnight service. The brilliant stars lit their way as they walked in silence. There was a war going on, and Alice had decided there was no reason anyone should have to fight it all alone.

Women

Annette Radius

I search my past for family or kind friends warning
about the pain accompanying my walk through life,
and nothing comes but the tilted-back head of my sister
the night she got caught at the colored fairgrounds
with a man not her own and the sheriff brought her
home bruised and after Mamma slapped her,
she turned to me and tilted her head back and made
such an odd sound, not of laughter nor weeping nor explanation.

Having just learned the word, I thought her *pathetic*,
yet in my later years, I also made that sound.
In time, I told the young doctor everything, but I could tell
when he stopped listening because his eyes went far
away from me, then came back with the utmost
reluctance and a strange kind of delicacy.

Elizabeth Chapman Shafer

Can a man divorce his wife after he's dead?
That's what I asked the day the will was read.

I hadn't known he would lie apart from me
in a grave seventy miles north of our family.

In all our years, there'd been no talk of this divide.
For the whole of our marriage, he took my side.

And now I must make the drive to Rapidan
with only my aging son to hold my hand.

If the air is sweeter there, I cannot say.
If the grass is softer, I cannot say.
If his friends are dearer...

I am a widow, now and to stay.

Kathleen Margaret O'Shea

When I saw him again, it was as if the dream of living
had come true for me at last: the sleep of my childhood ended
when he gathered me in a rough hug outside the train station,
his sailor's uniform pressed against me,
his lips grazed my cheek, and
I could smell his fragrant hair, the tousled head of a wayfarer,
a man intimate with high tides
and churning oceans I'd never seen.

He was to be mine, I believed it, prayed it, and then
when I heard the commotion from his room that night—
instantly recognizable as love in the making—
I made myself giggle along with Louise
and praised the darkness that hid my tears.

The next day I walked into the fields and nearly gave myself up
to the cloudy sky, but I was and still am too young
to leave the small gift of my slim chances behind.

Sidney Jane Adams

When I spied her in the library nibbling a pencil tip
and said, "You can do better than that," she looked up
in irritation that gave way to the slowest of smiles.
We made our way from provocation to conversation,
and in time, the syllables that began in her mouth
ended in mine. By day, we spoke the language

of Lenox and Gorham, finishing schools and family trees.
By dusk, my bare arm brushing hers, we were wind
and wildlife, snowfall on secret trails. How many times
we pushed aside my Coleridge and her chemistry and let
our tongues meet in a sky of keen constellations.
I used to say, "Anna, did you ever guess?"
And she'd say, "I wanted to, yes—"
But who could predict this dizzying world—these stars!—
and both of us truly and finally loved?

Sky Dance

1

Ross stood outside at the filling station. "Are you done, honey?" he asked. "Be sure to wash your hands." Sam was hopping up and down beside him, and he was afraid Sara would accidentally lock herself inside.

There was the sound of a flush, and then the little girl emerged, smiling happily. Sam ran in, and then Ross took his turn.

It was a still, clear morning. The small rocks along the road were sparkling in the light. The dewy sweetness in the air was just yielding to a steady midsummer warmth. After boosting the children into the front seat, Ross paid the attendant and then rested for a moment beside his truck. He was grateful he had found a filling station open on the Fourth of July. Both the twins had needed to use the bathroom many miles back, and his pickup truck was perilously low on gasoline. His wife had warned him the trip would be hard, and her words echoed in his head as he imagined being stranded with the twins halfway between Fort Bragg and Rapidan, Virginia. Perhaps he shouldn't have taken these back roads—another thing Tracy warned him against—but his old truck groaned when he pushed it past thirty-five or forty miles an hour, and he didn't like driving on the highway when he had the children with him.

But now all was well again. The children curled like kittens against the pillows he had brought, and it wasn't long before they fell asleep. With the long flat road stretching before him, his mind calmed and he allowed himself to think once again about Alice Williams. How often he had thought of her over the years, though he had heard nothing from her since the rainy day he left Tipton in the back of Mr. Jenkins's pickup truck. He had sent a long letter thanking her for the personal file that she had taken from her Uncle Dale's office, but the letter came back marked "addressee unknown." He suspected she hadn't yet arrived in Rapidan, and he intended to re-send the letter in a week or two. But in the end he just sent a postcard showing a picture of a bright red cardinal; it was as close as he could come to a scissor-tailed flycatcher. Alice never responded and he had turned his attention to boot camp and surviving the war.

When he arrived at Fort Bragg, he asked everybody about David Moore, but no one had heard of his Tipton friend. After one terrifying attempt, he realized he didn't have the heart or the stomach to jump from planes the way David did. In truth, he had always known that. He was glad David wasn't around to witness his failure of nerve. With his old objective set aside at last, he resolved to be the very best soldier possible. He spent four years as an infantryman slogging through battlefields all across Europe. He stayed on course as men around him dropped to their deaths, sometimes immediately, sometimes with agonizing slowness. No matter what happened, he pushed on. Miraculously he escaped harm.

He made a few friends. One of them, a nice guy from New York, said he thought his sister and Ross might hit it off. Ross accompanied him home to Brooklyn when they both had leave time and quickly fell into a romance with Tracy Stone. She was small-boned and quick moving, with green eyes that stood out against her olive complexion. Her Brooklyn accent made him smile. Everything with her was relaxed and easy, and he loved the way she pressed close to his side when they walked around Manhattan in search of a cheap Italian restaurant. They began corresponding. On his next leave, he impulsively proposed, and on his third, they married. She moved to a little apartment near Fort Bragg and got a job as a waitress. After a lifetime with no family to call his own, he was proud to tell his platoon buddies he had a wife waiting for him in Fayetteville.

During the early months of their marriage, he and Tracy

relished their time together. On his infrequent trips home, they took long walks and talked for hours about her childhood in Brooklyn and his at the Tipton Home. Some nights they went to movies and she giggled when he dozed off and snored in the theater. Their intimate life was wonderful, and Ross smiled in the darkness of their bedroom when he thought of how Alice had warned him against using the same rubber twice. He and Tracy were already trying for a baby and had no need for rubbers.

If at times she seemed moody, a little glum, he attributed that to the war and the loneliness of her days and nights when he was away. She told him she had suffered from depression off and on ever since she was fourteen. Marriage, she hoped, would vanquish that gloom forever. Ross didn't allow himself to think too deeply about these disturbing remarks. He couldn't bear to think of his wife being so deeply sad. When they were together, he reminded himself, she seemed fine.

When he received her excited letter announcing she was pregnant, he had done a little dance of joy. He immediately wrote her back to express his elation. No matter that he was in the midst of a war; he was in love and about to become a father. He managed to be home for the birth of the twins. With their silky dark hair, round cheeks, and bright, intelligent eyes, the babies radiated the glory long missing from his life. The mere thought of them made his chest swell with love and pride. He carried a picture of Tracy and the twins in his wallet and kept another in David's old cigar box where he still stored his most precious belongings.

To his alarm and dismay, Tracy fell into a depression soon after the babies were born. Her mother visited for six weeks and did everything she could to help, but Tracy still seemed unshakably sad. Her sister took the next shift and visited for a couple of months. During that period, Tracy wrote infrequently to Ross. The letters she did send were short and rather general. Their powerful connection as a couple was clearly slipping away. Then, after her sister left, she wrote to say she had hired a girl to watch the babies and was returning to her waitressing job. After a month of working part-time, she went back to fulltime, and a teenager Ross had never met was raising his children.

The next time he was home, they argued late into the night. He said they didn't need what little money she was earning. She said she couldn't stand being cooped up in the apartment all day—what's more, she had just been promoted to assistant manager. If Ross didn't want to live in Brooklyn near her family, she was going to do what she could to occupy herself in Fayetteville. Her face livid with anger, she added that she would keep her salary in case she decided to leave him.

Ross drank a few too many beers that night. When he lay down heavily beside her in bed, she hissed through her teeth, "Don't you touch me." That was the last thing on his mind, but her tone made him so mad he punched his fist through the thin wall above their bed. She leaped up and let out a frightened cry, and immediately the babies began wailing in the next room. "It's your turn, Ross!" she shrieked. "You take care of them for a change." After pulling on her clothes and grabbing her pocketbook, she flung herself out the door and didn't return until the next day. He was too angry to ask where she had gone.

Her absence gave him time to patch the wall and apologize to the couple next door. The landlord told him over the phone, "If it happens again, I'm calling the MPs and they'll haul you out of there." Ross had no doubt that they would.

Now the war was over, and his marriage brought no joy to his life. He had a desk job at Fort Bragg that gave him a reason to put on his uniform and leave the apartment early in the morning. In what she said was a concession to his wishes, Tracy stayed with the children all day. But she left the apartment promptly at 5:45, a few minutes after Ross got home, so she could work at the restaurant until it closed at one in the morning. Most nights he was asleep when she came in and awoke only briefly when she slipped into bed. He could smell cigarette smoke in her hair and sometimes, if she turned toward him in her sleep, a whiff of alcohol as well. She didn't seem either angry or sad anymore, just uninterested in him. He thought she might have fallen in love with someone else, perhaps the restaurant manager. The suspicion was not as painful as he felt it should have been.

When he got home one day and found a letter from Alice Williams, he was happy for the first time in months. Tracy had left the letter, forwarded from the Tipton Home, lying on the kitchen counter. She didn't bother to ask him who was this Alice Williams, whose name was in the return address. On her way out, she merely said there was some leftover meatloaf he could heat up for himself and the children.

The meatloaf would have to wait. Sam and Sara were hugging his knees and begging him to come play with them. They were building a tower of blocks in their room and needed his help. He promised to come as soon as he washed up and read his mail. Reluctantly they let him escape.

He took his time in the bathroom so he could draw out the anticipation of reading Alice's letter. How he had missed her! Now he could admit that to himself.

After he got married, he had decided it was wrong to contact her, but he still yearned to know where she was and what she was doing. Six months after his courthouse wedding, he sent a Christmas card to the Tipton Home and casually asked about her as well as David. The card he got back from Dale Jenkins said Alice was still in Rapidan, Virginia, as far as anyone knew. David's sister, Louise, had lived at Tipton briefly after her mother died and then followed Alice to Virginia after the big fire at the orphanage. They hadn't heard from Louise in quite a while and had no idea where David was.

Now, sitting on the edge of the bed, he looked at Alice's handwriting on the envelope. He still had the scrap of a note she had enclosed with his personal records from the Tipton Home. Considering how many countries he had been in and all the buses, planes, and ships he had traveled on, it was a wonder the note hadn't gotten lost. But every time he moved, he wrapped the red woolen baby's blanket, the one keepsake of his true family origins, around David's cigar box holding his few other special things and packed that bundle first, no matter where he was going or how much of a hurry he was in. These days, he kept his old treasures in a locked metal box tucked in the back of his pickup truck. This letter would go there as well, but first he had to read it.

Alice had used the letterhead stationery of Red Road Farm in Rapidan, Virginia:

May 24, 1946
Dear Ross,

It has been so long since we've seen one another, and I pray to God that you are well and safe. You have been in my thoughts, and though I don't know whether this letter will reach you, I have a good feeling it will. There has been very sad news of the Tipton boys lost in the war, and though each name brings me to my knees in pain and sorrow, I rejoice that your name is not on any list that I have seen.

In case you wondered, I'm still in Rapidan. But so much has happened—too much, really—that I can't tell it all in a letter. You will have to come visit. And just so you know I mean it, I'm writing to invite you to the First Annual Fourth of July Party at Red Road Farm. Come at four o'clock or really any time you want, and plan on staying a while. We have plenty of room and you will meet new friends and see old ones from Tipton days.

OK, I will end here in hopes of greeting you in person on July Fourth. Call me for directions. We need to catch up, old friend.

With love,
Alice

She had scribbled her telephone number at the bottom of the page. His heart singing, he stuffed the letter in his pocket and went to play with his children.

A week before the party, Ross finally mentioned it to Tracy.

She asked how long a drive it would be. He shrugged and said seven hours or so. At that she screwed up her face and said, "Forget it!" The day before the party, he announced he was going whether she came along or not. Without hesitation, she told him to take the twins; she could use a good rest on her own. Then, her voice quavering, she said she wanted to have a talk with him when he got back from his trip. He nodded his agreement as a strange wave of relief flooded his body. He would grant her a divorce and pray she wouldn't try to keep the children away from him. But she was always so glad to hand them off to him that he doubted she would put up that kind of fight.

Now, trundling toward the Virginia border, he glanced down at the twins. Sara was awake and leaning on him. Sam was just starting to stir. He reached over and tousled his boy's head and then pulled Sara a little closer.

That morning he had called the number written beneath Alice's name. A woman answered, but it was Kathleen O'Shea, not Alice, and she said Alice was out running errands. When he asked whether Kathleen had arrived early for the party, she said she lived at Red Road Farm. Aware of the expense of a long-distance call, Ross decided not to press her for details. He got the directions and quickly rang off.

It was about two o'clock when he reached Gordonsville, Virginia. He stopped at a roadside diner and waited while first Sara and then Sam used the facilities before ordering them a snack. A waitress watched them while he went in the men's room and freshened up. He changed into a short-sleeved plaid shirt, washed his face, and ran a comb through his hair. It had been a long hot trip, and he wanted to look nice for Alice.

From Gordonsville, it took them about twenty minutes to reach Orange, and from there it was another ten minutes before he saw Purcell Presbyterian Church on the left side of Rapidan Road. Just beyond the church and a little ways before the bridge Kathleen had told him about, there was an open gate on the left. A small wooden sign identified the property as Red Road Farm.

A sheet of paper taped to the bottom of the sign read "TIPTON" in big bold letters. And there stood Alice, in a green sundress and large straw hat, with pruning sheers in her hands. She was snipping honeysuckle vines on one of the brick pillars holding the gate in place. When Ross slowed the truck and began turning toward the driveway, she lowered her shears. In the moment before she recognized him, Ross saw that the pretty girl he had known was now a gorgeous young woman: her skin had a buttery tan, and her honey-brown hair was loose around her shoulders. The sundress fitted her slim figure perfectly. But her eyes looked sad, and to his dismay as he pulled the truck alongside her, he saw that she was crying. There were tear streaks on her face and a couple of fresh tears clung to her eyelashes.

"Ross," she said and dropped the shears to the ground. She was beaming through her tears and tugging at the door to get at him. He turned off the engine and nearly knocked her over in his eagerness to step down and greet her. They laughed awkwardly as they hugged one another and Ross inhaled the sweet but somehow also spicy smell that was Alice's alone. His lips brushed her cheek before she stepped back to take a good look at him.

"You're taller," she said. "And—" She paused to find the right words as her eyes searched his. "The war was awful, wasn't it?" Without giving him time to answer, she hugged him again and he could feel her tears dampening his collarbone. "Oh, Ross, you don't know how I worried about you. About you and all the Tipton boys."

When she looked up, Sara and Sam caught her eye. In a flash she composed herself. "Well, well," she exclaimed. "Who have we here?"

Ross made the introductions and his children smiled shyly when Alice reached across him to shake one little hand and then the other. "Their mother couldn't come," he said in answer to the question in Alice's eyes.

"Your wife, you mean?" she prodded him.

"Yes, my wife—Tracy."

"Ah! You'll have to tell me all about Tracy, but first, let's go up to the house. I bet these young ones would like some lemonade—and maybe you would, too."

Alice rode with them to the top of a circular driveway. Sara and Sam let out yelps of delight when they saw horses grazing in the pasture. As Ross parked, a little girl came running out of the house. She bounded across the porch, practically flew off the steps, and barreled toward Ross and Alice. "Look, I have on my party dress!"

In one swift motion Alice leaned down and caught the child in her arms. She was almost absurdly cute looking. Her pale blonde hair and radiant cheeks brought a smile to Ross's face. Her dress was white with green polka dots, the green matching Alice's outfit.

Alice set the child down beside the twins, who stood rubbing their eyes and looking all around.

"Hi, I'm Minnie!" the little girl declared to the newcomers. It dawned on Ross that this was Alice's daughter. Because he had long nurtured a tiny, secret hope that she might fall in love with him, he felt the smile drop from his face.

"Minnie, I want you to meet my old friend Ross Gentry," Alice said. "And these are Mr. Gentry's children, Sam and Sara. They're going to be your playmates. Isn't that wonderful?"

The girl grinned broadly at the others. "It *is* wonderful," she said. "Come on, Sam and Sara, let's go down to the fishpond." She tugged at Sara's hand and then pulled at Sam for good measure. The twins looked up uncertainly at their father, but Ross nodded at them. "You can go. So long as Mrs. Williams says it's okay, that is." He glanced at Alice.

"They'll be fine," she said. "It's right down the hill, and Minnie won't let anyone fall in the pond." She started walking toward a path where the children were already heading and then stopped abruptly. "Do they need to use the bathroom?"

"We took care of that earlier. But don't you need to get ready? Can't I help you with something?"

"Thanks, but we have things under control. How about if you bring your bags inside, and I'll show you your room." She paused again and he could see her making a decision. "Ross, I'll rearrange a few things and put Sam and Sara in the room right next to yours."

"Oh, I should've told Kathleen I was bringing the kids. I'm sorry."

"I'm thrilled you brought them, Ross. It's just that I'll have to find another room for Anna and her friend. But I can move those two to the third floor. It's a little hot up there, but they'll manage." A mischievous smile crossed her face.

"Anna Boyer?" Ross said incredulously. "I'd almost forgotten about her."

"Well, she hasn't forgotten about you. She asked me just this morning if you were coming."

"What about David?" he asked.

Alice turned a distressed face toward him and put a hand on his arm.

Ross felt his knees turn to water. "What is it, Alice? Is he dead?"

"Oh, no, thank God. But he was badly injured." She held his eye as if trying to gauge how much bad news he could take.

"Tell me!" he begged.

"He's lame, Ross. He shattered the bones in his left leg. That's the risk he ran when he became a paratrooper." She dropped her hand from his arm and looked at him hard. "I'm glad you didn't do that." When he didn't reply, she continued. "It could've been a lot worse. He's been living here at the farm for almost a year now." Her face brightened. "You'll see him soon. He and his sister— you remember Louise?—are both living here, and they'll be at the party."

Ross bowed his head and said nothing. Except for a few lingering pains in his knees and back, his body was sound. His heart broke to think that David, such a fine athlete, would never run again.

"There's so much to tell," Alice said, taking his hand and

leading him up the porch steps. "I'm glad you're here early."

The old house was surprisingly cool inside. The living room glistened with cleanliness. The tables were decorated with small bowls of mints and peanuts, and there were vases of flowers everywhere. The vases on the mantel had little American flags mixed in with zinnias, and the small vases on the end tables were filled with bright yellow and orange marigolds. Beyond the living room Ross spied a sitting room. It was furnished with tall bookcases, a couple of easy chairs, and a brown, rather strange-looking sofa that appeared to be an antique. The room's curtains were drawn against the afternoon heat. With his sensitive nose, he noticed a powdery scent as he walked by—the smell made him think of old people.

Ross followed Alice upstairs and set down his duffel bag in a room around the corner from the staircase. She went in the bathroom and rapped on a door leading to another bedroom. "Anna, I'm going to have to move you and Sidney Jane up to the third floor. Ross needs your room for his children."

"Oh, he does, does he?" came the arch reply. There was the sound of footsteps, and then Anna Boyer stuck her head into the room from the hallway. "Hello, Ross," she said, looking him up and down, "and welcome home. Alice told me you were coming."

Ross moved toward Anna and she met him halfway, offering the briefest of hugs. Then she stepped back and crossed her arms across her crisp blue and white dress. She was slimmer than he remembered her. With her dark-gold hair coiled at the nape of her neck, she looked stylish and urban.

Before either of them could say another word, another young woman squeezed into the doorway next to Anna. She was short with a pixie haircut and bright brown eyes. In white culottes and a sleeveless red blouse, she had an artless, casual look about her. "Hi," she said to Ross in a friendly way. "I'm Sidney Jane Adams. Happy Fourth of July." Then Anna told her they were moving upstairs to accommodate Ross and his children.

"Sure thing," said Sidney Jane. "I'll get our stuff."

"I'll see you at the party," Alice said over her shoulder with a flicker of a smile.

Alice winked at Ross after the two left. "They came down from New York for the party and Anna has been acting like the grand dame. Her girlfriend is actually pretty nice." She glanced in the mirror above a chest of drawers and grimaced. "Good grief, look at me." She went in the bathroom and began dabbing at her face with a washcloth.

Ross stood in the doorway and watched her. "Alice, when I first got here, it looked like you were crying. What's wrong?"

"Oh, Ross," she said, coming toward him. "I was crying because we just lost Uncle Minor, Macklin's great uncle. He died ten days ago. I almost canceled the party and maybe I should have, but I thought Minor would want us to go ahead and celebrate the end of the war." She stopped when she saw his pained expression.

"I'm sorry, Alice. Was it sudden?"

"He'd been in poor health ever since I met him, so I can't say it was unexpected. But I just can't believe he's gone." Her eyes welled up.

Ross sat beside her on the bed and drew her close. "You really cared about him."

Alice leaned her head on his shoulder. "I really did care about him, but what I didn't realize was how much he cared about me."

"What do you mean?"

She pulled back to look at him and said, "Ross, he left me Red Road Farm!"

"That's great," he said, dazzled as always by Alice's rapid revelations. "From what I've seen, it's a beautiful place."

"Well, he left me a life trust in the farm, but that's as good as leaving it to me, or almost." She read the confusion in his eyes. "A life trust means I don't own it. I get to live here my whole life, but I can't sell it and I can't leave it to anyone in my will."

"Well, who owns it if you don't?"

"Macklin owns it."

"But you're still married to him—" He was about to say,

and you have a daughter, but something in Alice's troubled face stopped him. "Where is Macklin anyway?"

"I haven't seen him in seven years." Her eyes stayed on Ross's. "He'd just left when I moved to Rapidan. That's when I moved here with Philip." Again Ross could see her realizing she had more to explain. "Philip was Anna's mother's chauffeur back in Chicago. He and I—oh, Ross, don't look so shocked. I didn't sleep with him if that's what you're thinking. He wanted to get away from the Boyers as much as I did. So we came to Virginia together, and Anna followed us, but that's another story. Philip and I both got jobs at the farm." She paused to flick a ladybug off her dress. "You just missed him. He and his wife and two little boys moved away about a week ago. He got a job in Winchester working for Julia Mallory. You'll meet her at the party and her brother, Chippers Hebblethwaite. He was Anna's boyfriend for a while—a short while."

"But you and Macklin...." He still wanted to ask about Minnie, but then the telephone rang, a loud echoing sound that made him catch his breath.

"There's so much to tell you, Ross," Alice said as she stood up. When she smoothed her hair, he noticed a small diamond ring glistening on her left hand. "I'll tell you everything later. You wouldn't believe how complicated things are." She turned to leave and then glanced back distractedly. "Oh, Ross, I never even got you or your children anything to drink."

He waved her away, and she hurried through the bathroom to the room Anna and her friend had recently vacated. Through the wall he could hear her answering the phone. Rather than wait for her, he decided to go look for the twins. Their innocent ways would be a relief, he decided, after the excitement and confusion of talking to Alice.

2

By four o'clock, the open space in front of the barn had filled up with cars and pickup trucks. More cars were parked all along the driveway. Ross marveled at the ever-growing crowd. There were dozens of people milling around in the big living room and dozens more on the front porch. All were talking and laughing and availing themselves of the refreshments that Kathleen O'Shea and a Negro woman named Mrs. Carter had brought out right after Ross came downstairs. He and Kathleen had exchanged greetings when the first wave of guests arrived. She accepted his offer of help before rushing back to the kitchen with Mrs. Carter close on her heels. The three of them carried ice buckets and pitchers of lemonade to the long tables on the front porch. After that, Kathleen told him to enjoy the party; he didn't need to work the whole time.

His old shyness having returned, he would have gladly spent the day doing the bidding of this brisk and grownup Kathleen, no longer the giggly, blushing young girl he remembered from Tipton. Instead, he filled a plate with salted peanuts and little cucumber sandwiches for Sam and Sara. The two of them sat cross-legged on the porch eating and talking to each other about the goldfish and frogs they had seen in the pond. Ross stood awkwardly above them tilting a cup toward his mouth even though nothing remained in it except a few melting ice cubes. He knew he should try to mingle with Alice's other guests, but he wasn't ready yet. He looked out at the front yard filled with little children racing around. Several of their mothers were moving among them, talking to one another while keeping an eye on the children's random games. Ross watched as Minnie commandeered a couple of these women to set up a badminton set. As they did her bidding, she swatted wildly at the birdie and broke into peals of laughter when it bounced off the head of a prim-looking young matron staking a net pole in the ground. Ross turned away to hide his smile.

It was right then that Ross felt a hand clapped on his shoulder. He turned around, startled, to face David. They embraced, and Ross felt tears welling up in his eyes. David had been his first close friend, his best friend, and at night during the war he had prayed that David was safe and that they would someday meet again.

David had grown tall. His blond curly hair was cut short and he had a deep suntan. Despite his crutch, he looked strong. He wanted to know everything Ross had done during the war and where he lived and what he was doing now. Ross gave a brief account and then indicated the twins still sitting at his feet. With a grimace of pain, David set aside his crutch and sat down on the porch swing. When he spoke to Sam and Sara, they responded to him as the little children at Tipton always had—with immediate trust and affection.

Sam asked what had happened to David's leg, and David responded that he had jumped out of a warplane in France and had a very rough landing. And yes, the leg hurt, but he tried not to think about it too much.

Ross sat down on the edge of the porch and watched as Sara shyly offered David the last of her cucumber sandwiches. "Thank you, Sara, don't mind if I do," David said with exquisite politeness. He took a tiny bite and then, holding the little girl's steady gaze, popped the rest of it in his mouth and chewed with exaggerated delight and a noisy smacking of the lips. She and her brother broke into giggles. Sam cried, "Do it again! Do it again!" With no sandwiches left, they scampered off to get more.

"Hey, I could use some food, too," Ross called after them, but they were caught up in a sea of adults and didn't hear him. The screen door opened and they disappeared inside.

Ross asked where David had been all these years and what kind of action he had seen in the war. In response, David turned to look at the front lawn. "I was in the army for a year and a half before I got to be a paratrooper. I did fine with that until my best friend got shot and killed. After that everything got a lot harder for me, and I don't mean just the jump that nearly cost me my leg."

Now it was Ross's turn to look away. He felt terrible for David. Yet it embarrassed him to realize he was upset that someone else, even someone now dead, had been David's best friend. "I'm sorry," he said.

David waited until Ross looked at him again. He met Ross's gaze with the impossibly sad smile that Ross had seen on so many soldiers' faces over the past several years. "My best friend in the war, that is. You must've lost friends, too."

"I lost a few. But I didn't have many friends—same as in Tipton."

"Oh, you had plenty of friends in Tipton." David's face changed. It seemed he wanted to stay upbeat. "Everybody liked you."

"I had friends, I guess. But there were just two who meant the whole world to me," Ross said. "You and Alice." He looked down at his lap. "Say," he began again before David could respond. "Alice wrote me that some of the Tipton fellows died. Did she tell you who?"

"Oh, man. She told me." David winced. "Do you remember Ronnie Campbell?"

At first Ross couldn't picture anyone, and then he remembered the boy. Ronnie was the only one who noticed Dennis Delmarvin's absence the night Dennis ran away. "Yeah, sure. Ronnie died?"

"Early on, in an accident at boot camp," David said. "And Harry Foote."

That one hurt more. Ross clasped his hands together tightly and felt his eyes sting with tears. "Hairy Feet," he murmured. "He was a good kid."

"He was," David said. "He died in the Pacific somewhere."

"Did Alice say anything about Dennis Delmarvin?"

David laughed. "She didn't have to tell me anything about him that I couldn't find out on my own. He lives here. I see him every day."

"Are you kidding me?"

David grasped Ross's shoulder as he shared the news. "You didn't know that he and Kathleen got married?" Ross stared at him. "He came to visit Alice and fell head over heels for Kathleen, who was living here. I guess she'd grown up enough for him by then. They got married as soon as she graduated from high school. He's going to seminary now, believe it or not, and she's raising their daughter and helping Alice around the farm."

Ross was amazed that Dennis, the great non-believer, had decided to go to a seminary, but he had something else he was more curious about. "Which one's their daughter?" Ross said, glancing at the yard full of young children.

"That one," David said, pointing. "Minnie. The one waving the badminton racquet."

So the child was not Alice's after all, though she seemed to have something of Alice's irrepressible spirit. Maybe that spirit was somehow also Dennis's, Ross thought. It was the first time he had ever considered that those two had anything in common. Instead of asking David for further details about his old nemesis, Ross said, "What about Billy Moxley?"

"Gone. In 'forty-three. Alice said he died a hero, in a fire. She didn't know much more than that."

"Abe Walker?"

"He made it!" David's voice rose with the happy news. "He's fine. Alice invited him to the party, but he couldn't get off work."

"Where does he work that a veteran couldn't take off the Fourth of July?"

"He's a bellman at a hotel in D.C."

"Oh." Ross remembered how impatient Abe was to go into the army and serve his country. "Seems like he deserves a better job than that."

"Well, he's enrolled in night school. He told Alice he's going to be a doctor—a surgeon."

Again Ross felt tears stinging his eyes, this time with admiration. "Glad to hear it."

They sat in silence. Then David spoke up. "So, you're a married man. Is your wife here in the crowd somewhere? Tell me about her." He poked Ross lightly in the ribs.

Ross saw the throng of adults parting as Sara and Sam made their way toward them with a fresh plate of food. "She didn't want to come to the party. I'll tell you more later," he said, nodding his head toward the approaching children. "Let's just say I married too young and too quickly. I might be getting divorced."

David's face sagged with sympathy.

"Do you have a girlfriend?" Ross asked.

"Not yet, and not for a while," David said as he reached for his crutch and rose awkwardly from the swing. "I don't have much time for dating."

Ross stared up at him. "What do you mean?"

"I'm going to school, Ross. I'm in my second year at the University of Virginia. Since my sister was living here, I figured I'd go to a school near her."

Ross stood up and asked what he was studying.

"Anything I can pass." He paused and Ross could see him deciding to give a serious answer. "I'm studying history. I want to know about all the wars there ever were, and after I graduate I want to—well, I don't know how else to say it, but I want to work for peace." He paused again and a new resolve filled his face. "There are good, kind people everywhere, Ross. Despite all the horrors I saw—and you saw, too—most people want to do what's right. I just know they do. We've got to learn how to be at peace in this country and all over the world." He gazed at Ross earnestly. "I just want to make things better."

Just then a young man came outside and called David's name above the hubbub of party chatter. He had a bright, sturdy look about him and wore a moustache. Ross looked at David for an explanation.

"That's Victor—he's a friend of mine from the university. He's got a crush on my sister so I invited him to the party. I better go see what he wants." Before leaving, he paused to accept a half-sandwich from Sam and another from Sara. After carefully inspecting and sniffing the food, he stuffed both little wedges in his mouth and gobbled them down with furious pleasure. The twins laughed and leaned against him and allowed him to leave only when he promised he would visit with them later. To Ross he said, "We'll talk more tonight after the party's over. Hey, you should think about moving here. You should be going to college, too, you know."

The twins had no interest in the food now that David was gone. They tugged at Ross's hands and said they wanted to go play with the other children. "Go ahead," he told them. "Just mind your manners."

They scrambled down the front steps just as Minnie saw them and yelled their names. He watched them start up an anarchic game of badminton which involved hitting the birdie over the net, under it, and at it. Four of the children had racquets and three were using their bare hands. The watching mothers had retreated to the shade of the magnolias or come back to the front porch.

One of them, the prim young woman who had sustained a blow from Minnie's errant birdie, made her way toward the table laden with pitchers of lemonade just as Ross arrived there. She gave him a little smile and waited for him to introduce himself after he poured her a cup.

Her name was Edith Merton. She pointed out her husband, Merle Merton, and Ross turned to see, at some distance, a pudgy fellow in a summer suit. His tie was loosened around his neck, and he looked hot and uncomfortable. "I told Merle he didn't need to dress up," Edith confided, "but he said, 'It's the Fourth of July, we won the war, and I'm wearing my seersucker.'"

"Well, that's the spirit," Ross said and began edging away.

"Are you a friend of Alice's from out of town?" she persisted. "I don't believe I've seen you around before."

"Yes," he said. "I met Alice a long time ago, back when she was a housemother at the Tipton Home."

"Oh, the Tipton Home. I've heard her speak of it." Edith lifted her eyebrows significantly. "I can't imagine how terrible that must've been, being stuck in an orphanage in the middle of nowhere."

"It's in Tipton, Oklahoma," Ross said, "and I was one of the orphans."

Edith's eyes registered her blunder, and she had the grace to apologize for her remark.

After an awkward pause, he said, "Those two are mine," and pointed out Sara and Sam. They were chasing after a somewhat older girl with long strawberry blonde hair. She was running around the badminton net and clutching a tennis ball, which the twins seemed to want. The girl, it turned out, was Edith's daughter, Meredith.

Ross's eye lit on a tall young man who had suddenly attached himself to the group of children. He was weaving among them, interrupting the flow of their overlapping games. Minnie suddenly whirled around to face him. They exchanged a few words and then the man scooped her up and began walking toward the porch with Minnie on his shoulders. It was then that Ross felt his stomach drop as if he were once again in a transport plane bouncing over the Atlantic. The young man was Dennis Delmarvin.

When Dennis reached the porch steps, he set the child down beside him. Ross watched them talk animatedly before Minnie pulled away and ran back to the other children. Without her, they had quickly broken up their games and were heading toward the fishpond.

Oblivious to Edith Merton, who remained beside him, Ross gazed at Dennis. He was standing alone and glancing around, his face blank. He looked strong and muscular and as handsome as a movie star villain.

When Dennis saw him, he yelled "Injun!" and bounded up the steps to gather Ross up in a bear hug that nearly knocked

Edith Merton into the refreshment table. Gripping Ross tightly by the shoulders and looking him in the eye, he said, "You made it. Thank God!"

Ross said, "Yeah, we got here a few hours ago—"

"Gentry, you idiot," Dennis said, laughing. "I meant you made it through the war." He let Ross go and stepped back, again jostling Edith. With a murmur of displeasure, she took her lemonade and went to the other end of the porch.

Out of the corner of his eye, Ross saw Kathleen and Mrs. Carter emerging from the house with platters of fried chicken. The aroma wafted toward him, and he wanted to eat, but when Dennis said, "Let's have a beer. I have a stash in my car," he followed without protest.

They crossed the yard and the driveway together. In the trunk of Dennis's car Ross saw an ice chest filled with bottles. Dennis opened a couple and handed one to Ross. They leaned against the car while Dennis asked Ross a series of rapid-fire questions about where he had served and what rank he had risen to. When Ross volunteered that he was married with twins, Dennis nodded but said little in reply.

Finally Ross ventured to say, "I hear you married Kathleen and I met your little girl. Congratulations."

"Yes, I have a family now," Dennis replied.

Ross set his beer bottle on the ground. "Alice hadn't told me that. And Kathleen didn't say anything about it when I called for directions, but we only talked for a minute. I had no idea. But hey, good for you." He clamped his mouth shut so he would stop babbling.

Dennis drained his bottle and went for another. "Well, it's a funny story, Injun. I thought Alice was the one I wanted." He flipped the bottle lid onto the ground and then kicked it across the yard with his toe.

Curiosity overcoming his reservations about what Dennis might say, Ross said, "Well, start at the beginning."

Between gulps of beer, Dennis talked. Early in the war, he had written to Alice, who invited him to Red Road Farm. By chance, he arrived on the same day as Louise and Kathleen. Though he initially pursued Alice, her mixed signals put him off. The younger girls were easier to handle. He had considered Louise, but she reminded him too much of her brother. Kathleen, however, was prettier than he remembered her from Tipton days, and she obviously had a crush on him. It had not taken him long to realize she was a much better bet than Alice, steadier and less prone to predicaments.

They leaned against the car as Dennis rolled the beer bottle between his hands. Ross said, "I noticed Alice was wearing a ring. She never wore one back in Tipton."

"You're a quick one, Injun," Dennis said with a short bark of laughter. "I guess that's how you got promoted to sergeant."

Ross turned to look at Dennis sharply. He waited for more information and when it wasn't forthcoming, he decided he'd had enough of Dennis. He waved away the offer of another beer and said he was going back to the party. Dennis suddenly began asking more questions about his military service. It seemed he wanted to prolong the conversation, but finally Ross was able to break away.

"I'm leaving for a while," Dennis called after him. "Tell everybody I had a hell of a good time, and I'll be back tonight in time to tuck Laura into bed."

Ross turned to look at him questioningly. He wondered if Dennis had yet another child.

"Kathleen wanted to name our daughter after the old man—Minor Williams. But when she had a girl, I said you can only use Minor as her middle name. You have to give her a normal first name."

"Whatever you say, Dennis."

"So we named her Laura after Kathleen's mother—Laura Minor Delmarvin. Kathleen and Alice insist on calling her Minnie, after the old man."

"Kathleen's mother," Ross said meditatively. He couldn't remember if he had ever heard how Kathleen had lost her parents.

"May she rest in peace," Dennis replied, lifting his bottle to the sky.

Ross walked off. He could hear the car door shut, and by the time he looked back, Dennis's car was moving down the driveway. Dennis stopped and leaned out the window. "Hey, Injun, you should move up here!" he yelled. "We could go to seminary together."

"When did you start believing in God?"

"Aboard the *Oklahoma*!" Dennis yelled. "I could've died four and a half years ago—but I didn't. I lived. That must mean something." When Ross stayed silent, he continued, "I'm not really sure what I think about God. I'm just curious about Him, that's all." With that he drove off, his tires kicking up a cloud of dust.

Ross walked back across the lawn. David and Abe, and even Dennis, had begun planning for the future while he was toiling away at a trivial desk job in North Carolina. His marriage to Tracy was essentially over, and only his children gave his life meaning. He told himself he would find a way to go to college and make something of himself. Sam and Sara needed a father who had goals and a plan, and those were things he also wanted for himself.

As he mounted the steps, suddenly everybody wanted to know who he was. In rapid succession, he met a friendly young man named Chippers—Ross remembered that Alice had said he was Anna's ex-boyfriend—and one of Chippers's former teammates on the University of Virginia tennis team. Henry Richards was a reserved, elegant fellow, accompanied by his fiancée, a rail-thin blonde who smiled and said not a word. As the couple moved off the porch and toward their car, Ross heard someone murmur, "The last time he came, he brought his grandmother." Another voice piped up, "She died a couple of years ago, didn't she?" And another: "Henry was a hero in the war, but he's too modest to talk about it."

Then he met another friend of Chippers's—Dudley Douglas, a self-assured young officer now in law school. He was with his wife,

Poppy. She was holding a whimpering baby boy, and a toddler, another boy, was pulling at her skirt. Despite these distractions, she regarded Ross with sincere interest. Alice had told her all about him, she said.

Just then, Alice made her way through the crowd and put her arm around Poppy's waist. "Ross, I'm so glad you two have met. I've begged Poppy and Dudley to stay here tonight. But they have to go home to Richmond because Dudley has a golf date with the governor early tomorrow morning." Alice raised her eyebrows in a knowing way. "Give him a few years, and Dudley will be running for office; I just know it."

"Oh, Alice," Poppy blushed charmingly.

Ross looked from one young woman to the other, and his eyes lingered on Alice. Evidently Dennis wasn't the only one who'd had a few beers. Alice's cheeks were pink and her voice was a little too loud. Before he could say anything, Poppy began to draw away. "I'll be back soon. We're coming up for Minnie's birthday, remember?"

Alice's eyes grew shiny. "Ross, Poppy came to the hospital when Minnie was born. Dennis couldn't get home from the navy, so Louise and I drove Kathleen to the hospital in Charlottesville, and Poppy came up from Richmond to meet us there." She moved toward Poppy and kissed her on the cheek. "Go on home before I make a spectacle of myself."

Dudley picked up the older boy, and the young family departed. Others were leaving, too. In a flurry of departures, Ross met the University of Virginia tennis coach and his wife and their large brood, a few more tennis players and their wives, and a fragile little woman named Mrs. Darling, whose son, Hugh, had died in the war. Her hand was warm in Ross's, and she looked up at him with a mixture of exquisite pain and grief. He wasn't a demonstrative person by nature, but seeing the look in her eyes, he gathered her in a hug and she clung to him briefly before pulling away and joining the tennis coach, who was giving her a ride home.

Though it was after six o'clock, the sky was still bright. Ross saw his children sitting on the front porch steps with a large golden dog between them. Minnie was standing on the step below them, with one hand on the dog's back. There were several other children gathered around them. They were occupied and at peace, so Ross decided not to disturb them. He looked to see whether there was any fried chicken left. His hand closing in on one remaining wing, he felt someone's eyes on him and glanced up.

The young woman standing a few feet away was tall and slender with a cascade of rippling dark blonde hair. Her pink dress set off her suntan and her blue eyes, and a little gold locket shimmered in the hollow of her neck. She was regarding him in open-mouthed wonder, a smile spreading slowly across her face. He didn't think anyone, even Tracy in the early days of their courtship, had ever looked at him with that sort of marveling interest.

"Ross," she said, and moved toward him. "I'm sure you don't remember me. I'm Louise Moore, David's sister."

He wiped his palm on his trousers awkwardly before accepting her handshake, and she laughed. "Oh, Ross. You haven't had a proper meal. Let me fix you a plate."

He followed her inside the house. Kathleen was in the kitchen, tidying things up, and she chatted with Ross and Louise until she saw Louise's eyes on her. Giggling in the old way that Ross remembered, she said, "Let me see if anybody needs anything outside." She hurried out, tossing a smile over her shoulder at both of them.

Ross and Louise sat down at the kitchen table. She wanted to know all about his time in the service and hear about his plans now that he was about to be discharged. When he talked about Sam and Sara, she complimented them and said she had met them earlier. She didn't ask about his wife, and Ross decided not to volunteer anything about his crumbling marriage. She said she was going away to college in the fall. David would help pay her tuition, and Alice had promised she would always have a home at Red Road Farm.

After a while it seemed like time to rejoin the others. Just as they reached the front door, Louise paused and turned to him. "I know this will sound strange, Ross, but I have to ask you if you ever got my letter—" She stopped herself and he could see her face coloring.

"You wrote to me, Louise?"

She collected herself and began again. "A long time ago. I sent you a letter right before I moved to Tipton. My mother had just died."

Just then, the screen door swung open, and Victor, David's friend, appeared. "Come on, kids," he said. "Alice wants to take pictures. We need everybody on the porch, pronto." He placed a hand on the small of Louise's back. "Ladies, first," he said as he propelled her out the door.

She said to Ross, "We'll talk later."

After a few moments of perplexity, he remembered the letter he had left on the bus station bench in Oklahoma right after he enlisted. That was the letter he used to dream of finding. Through the screen door, he watched Victor press close to Louise's side. His mind flashed back to his first meeting with her, when she was just a little girl who had come with her mother and mean old stepfather to fetch David from the Home. He had liked her and sensed that she like him, too. Then she wrote to him, wanting to be pen pals, and he had given her letter to Kathleen, a girl her own age. What made her keep reaching out to him? He looked at her slender back through the screen door. She had wanted so much to talk to him. Something dawned within him then, a knowledge that defied words but brought joy to his heart.

She seemed to sense him staring at her, and when she turned around, he pushed open the screen door and wedged himself between her and an irritated Victor. "There's room," he said firmly. Then, pushing aside Louise's hair so he could whisper in her ear, he said, "I lost your letter before I had a chance to read it. You'll have to tell me what it said." They stood quietly after that, their arms touching.

Alice and Chippers were looking up at the group and directing everyone to line up by height. The children were sitting on the grass, and several of the young mothers, including Edith Merton, stood above them. Chippers's sister, Julia, insisted that Victor come down and join her row, since he was half-hidden in the back. David took Victor's place beside Ross. Then, a bald-headed man and his ancient mother, a Mrs. Shafer, made their way down the steps to stand between Victor and Julia. Mrs. Shafer was leaning heavily on her son's arm and murmuring that they would have to leave as soon as the picture-taking was done; she didn't want to drive home in the dark.

The screen door wheezed open behind Ross, and several more people came out to join the group. Sidney Jane and Kathleen moved down to stand next to Edith Merton while Anna found a space below Ross, and a very pleasant fellow named Jonathan Perkins appeared on Louise's other side. It turned out Jonathan owned the dog that Sam and Sara had been playing with earlier. He spoke with an English accent that Ross liked; he had always gotten along well with the English soldiers.

With Alice hovering, Chippers held the camera up and gestured for everyone to move closer together.

"Come on, Alice," Jonathan called out. "You have to get in the picture, too."

"I can't believe I forgot to take pictures when all the others were here," she said fretfully. "What will Poppy and Dudley think? And Henry Richards?"

"Oh, good lord," Anna murmured under her breath. Two rows down, Sidney Jane responded with a trill of laughter.

Now that Alice was seated on the ground surrounded by children, Chippers backed up and held the camera to his face yet again. It seemed that the group was ready at last. "Wait a minute!" he cried out and lowered the camera. "Where's Regina? We can't take this picture without her."

"I never heard of posing for photos with the maid," Mrs. Shafer said.

"She's part of the Williams family," Chippers said.

"No, she's not," Victor murmured, just loud enough for everybody to hear.

Kathleen made her way back up the steps and opened the door. She called for Regina to come outside. Everyone else stood squeezed close together and awaited the reply. After a few unheeded calls, Kathleen said to Chippers, "She's not answering, and it would take too long to go find her."

"All right, then," Chippers said. "Maybe she's helping Sorbon get his paintings ready for me to take back to Chicago." Without further ceremony, he kneeled down and the camera clicked.

"Hold on!" Edith Merton said grouchily. "I swatted a mosquito right when you snapped the picture."

A ripple of laughter ran through the group on the porch. Ross was so glad to be among these people, all so comfortable and blunt with one another. Suddenly he thought of Tracy, but he couldn't hold her image in his mind for long. He instinctively looked for his children, who were sitting with Alice and the large golden dog.

Chippers took two more pictures, each time counting out *one, two, three* with exaggerated slowness. After Kathleen took a photo with Chippers in it, the guests began to disperse. Mr. Shafer and his mother said their farewells, and the Mertons gathered up little Meredith and made their exit. Julia and her husband Andy disappeared inside for a few minutes and then came out with a box of leftover chicken. "We're taking this to Philip and his family," Julia announced to the group at large, but no one seemed interested. She called out a goodbye to her brother, who had taken up a racquet and was playing badminton with Anna. They moved with a natural self-assurance that filled Ross with wonder; he suspected it had something to do with their social class.

The only guests remaining were the ones staying overnight and Jonathan, who now had his dog on a leash. Ross petted the dog and asked Jonathan where he lived.

"As the crow flies, about a half-mile away, directly behind Red Road Farm," he answered. "But if you're not a crow, it's about a two-mile drive." He paused. "Until recently, I lived here."

"Here, on this farm?" Ross didn't bother to hide his puzzlement.

"Indeed." The man's face turned serious. "It's a long story, Ross." He stroked the dog's head as he spoke.

"I'll listen," Ross said. There was something about the doctor that he intuitively liked and trusted, and he sensed that Jonathan felt the same way about him.

Jonathan took a breath and began to talk. "There was a tragedy involving some neighbors a few years ago, and after it was all over, Minor Williams, at Alice's urging, bought the property where the unpleasantness occurred. Alice had the structure on the property—a perfectly nice house, actually—torn down. In the meantime, I'd moved back to Red Road Farm. You see, I had lived here when I first began my medical practice in Orange." He paused. "I had to move out—it's too much to tell you about right now— but later Alice invited me back. The timing was quite fortuitous because Mr. Williams needed frequent medical attention by then, and well…I missed Alice."

Ross nodded and waited for Jonathan to continue. It seemed that another piece in the puzzle was about to fall into place.

"Then one day, Alice called me to Mr. Williams's bedside. The dear old fellow had something to tell me." He paused and Ross could see that he was trying not to cry. Jonathan composed himself and went on. "He wanted to give me the land where that house in the back had been."

"That was very generous of him."

"It certainly was." Jonathan held Ross's gaze. "In many ways, I was closer to him than I am to my own father. He said the land was his engagement present to us."

"His engagement present!" Ross echoed. The tiny diamond winking on Alice's hand flashed across his mind. "I didn't realize—"

"She didn't tell you we're engaged? Well, maybe she was just being discreet, though that's not usually her strong suit." Jonathan smiled briefly before resuming. "It's an absurdity, but Alice is still married to Minor Williams's nephew. It's been quite an ordeal trying to find him and get everything cleared up. And since Minor has died, we have even more things to figure out." He paused to pat the dog on the head yet again. "Now Alice says she wants to stay at Red Road Farm and rent out the other house. No matter that I just spent a year and a small fortune building it, and the farmhouse is getting, as you may have noticed, rather crowded."

Ross thought about all the orphans from Tipton who had followed Alice to Rapidan. He was tempted to say, "*Once a housemother, always a housemother*," but then Alice and Sara appeared at his side. Ross's daughter hugged the sweet old dog while Alice embraced the doctor. "Jonathan, we hardly even get to talk," she said in bleary tones.

"I know, Alice," he said, his voice soft. "But we talked yesterday and we'll talk on the phone tonight. Thank you for hosting this lovely party. Minor would be very proud of you."

She pulled back to include Ross in the conversation. "Uncle Minor's right over there, Ross," she said, wiping away tears and pointing toward the graveyard behind the church next door. "He's over there watching out for me and for all of us—and thanking Jonathan from the bottom of his heart for being his doctor and his beloved friend."

"Alice, don't let yourself get upset right now," Jonathan said gently. "You still have guests." He leaned forward to kiss her on the lips before saying goodbye to Ross and Sara and tugging his dog away from the little girl's clutching hands.

Alice and Ross watched him walk off to his car. When he was out of earshot and Sara had trotted back toward her brother and the other children, Ross said with an edge of accusation in his voice, "You're engaged to this doctor but still married to Macklin!"

Alice turned to look at him. "Well, aren't you the detective."

"I'm just surprised, that's all."

"Oh, Ross. You couldn't possibly know what I've been through." She tucked her arm in his. "I wanted to tell you, but there's hardly been time to do anything today except fry chicken and chase children and hug a few people here and there."

"I'm also surprised you let Dennis live here."

"How could I not, Ross? He's married to Kathleen. We all get along as best we can, and Dennis is trying to be better. Kathleen's a good influence on him, and I love Minnie like she's my own child." She turned Ross toward the house and they walked along quietly as they used to do as teenagers.

Then she said, "Remember the Fourth of July back at Tipton? Remember how we'd have the big picnic out on the front lawn?" She picked up her pace and hardly seemed to expect an answer from him.

Ross inhaled the scent of boxwood and allowed his thoughts to travel back to Tipton. During the war, he used to lie awake thinking about his childhood and the file on his origins that Alice had stolen for him. Sometimes it just seemed unreal: a faraway farm in Oklahoma, a crowd of fresh-faced children, each one's story sadder than the last, and a distracted couple running the whole operation on a shoestring. The part about his Indian mother and his "gentry" father had never stopped mystifying him. The knowledge, such as it was, made him shake his head in wonder. He couldn't decide whether it cast a light on his life or created a shadow. Sometimes in the barracks after the others had fallen asleep he would dig out the cast-iron toy soldier Alice had given him and run his finger along its edges. Then he would find the soft red baby's blanket and inhale its scent of pine needles and wilderness. He had lain in this blanket the last night his mother held him in her arms. How could that little blanket still hold that smell, the mystery of a lost lifetime, after all these years? He had kept the file Alice had stolen, of course, but it had been a long time since he read it. He knew its contents by heart.

There were so many questions he couldn't answer, and they baffled him. Had he really spent his whole life in Tipton until the war catapulted him to the other side of the world? How, in just a few brief years, had he gone from the boy he was then to the man he was now? Could the Tipton Home even still exist? He knew there had been a fire, and the Home as he knew it was gone to ashes, replaced by a building he had never seen and probably never would see. In his waking hours, he rarely had time to indulge in remembrances, yet Tipton lived on in his dreams as he walked the long rows of its vegetable garden or ran toward its apple orchard. *The fields of the fatherless*: that was a phrase from the Bible that came to him in one dream. In another, he heard Dale Jenkins telling them all to pray. In another, he faced Dennis Delmarvin yet again and swung punches in his sleep. In still another, he was back in the infirmary looking up at Alice's worried face.

"I remember," he said at last to Alice, who was a few paces ahead of him. "I remember the photos on the walls of the dining hall—the pictures the newspaper photographer took of all the children every Fourth of July."

Alice stopped walking. "Oh, that's right! Let's take one now—a picture just of the Tipton boys and girls." She broke into a run. "Come on, Ross. We'll round up the old gang while there's still enough light. It'll be just like old times."

Ross walked along and then he, too, began to run until he caught up with her. He remembered the other time they had run side by side: holding hands, from the barn back to the Home. That was the night he wept while telling her that David's mother and stepfather had taken David away. That was the night she caught one of his tears with her forefinger and touched it to her tongue. When they had run back to the house, his heart had lifted and he felt like he was running straight into his own future. He didn't know what it would be, but for the first time in his life, he had thought maybe it was worth running toward. Maybe, even now, something good could come out of all his years in Tipton—with its long dusty driveway, cotton fields, the orchard with its sweet aromas of earth and apples, the endless sweep of the sky, the birds colored pink and blue, those scissortails—and the one flashing just for him (or so it seemed), doing a sky dance all by itself. If Alice had wanted to know more about what he remembered, that's what he would have talked about.

But right now she was ahead of him calling out to Anna, who

was still playing badminton with Chippers, and then running inside to find the others. Soon all but Dennis, who had not yet returned, had assembled on the porch steps: David and Ross and Anna in the back row, Kathleen and Louise in the middle, and Alice standing on the ground front and center. Chippers was on the lawn focusing his camera, and he was just about to snap the shutter when Minnie and Sam and Sara came running around the corner of the house.

"We want to be in the picture, too!" Minnie shouted and dived for Alice's knees.

"Well, you're just in time," Alice said and pulled them all close.

Chippers backed up and set about focusing the camera again. It was then that Ross spied a car coming up the driveway. Kathleen called out playfully, "I hope we have enough fried chicken left over for the late arrival, whoever that is."

The car trundled up to the house and then stopped, and everybody heard the expected sound of a door opening and then slamming shut. The newcomer was a young man in an army officer's uniform with several medals on his chest. He was sandy-haired with a slim face, a rather long nose, and a very determined and set expression. Ross watched him walking toward Chippers before Alice exclaimed in a low voice, "Oh, my heaven!" The shutter clicked just as she stood up.

"Hey!" Chippers said.

Ross watched as Alice and the stranger stared at each other. Everyone else, even the children, remained in place. Chippers was still kneeling on the ground and fumbling with his camera. He was the only one oblivious to the scene.

In a hushed voice Alice said, "Macklin."

At the sound of this name, Chippers abruptly rose to his feet. "Macklin!" he cried. "Welcome home." He walked toward the other young man and hugged him. Anna let out a small groan and turned to go inside with Louise following behind her. Kathleen collected Minnie and took her inside as well. Ross's children climbed the steps and hugged his legs; they were tired from the excitement of the day and didn't object when he told them to go inside and rest for a while.

Alice stood facing her husband—the absent Macklin whom Ross had heard so much about back at Tipton. He knew he should leave them alone, but his feet would not move from the porch.

David looked over and said, "It just never ends, does it?"

"No, it doesn't seem to," Ross answered.

Chippers came up on the porch and then, seeing that no one wanted to talk, collected his camera and went inside.

Alice walked with Macklin in the direction of the fishpond. They stopped in the middle of the lawn and faced each other. Ross stared at the handsome young officer and then at Alice, all abloom with emotion and vitality.

"I've missed her," Ross said.

David nodded. He fumbled in his pocket and pulled out a tiny toy soldier. "She sent me this when I went off to war," he said. "I carried it with me the whole time."

He could have said that Alice had sent him a soldier exactly like the one David held in his hand, but he held back. "Your good-luck charm," he said instead.

They sat down on the steps, David resting his crutch by his side. The old magnolia trees and the tulip poplar were casting long shadows, and Ross noticed how quiet everything was now that the party was over. He could hear David breathing beside him. He started to say something and then stopped himself. Alice and her husband were still standing in the middle of the yard, just out of reach of the shadows. She had her hand on his arm. Their voices suddenly rose. Ross caught the words "codicil" and "promise," and then Macklin's voice rang out.

"We are still married!" the young officer said firmly. With that, he took Alice's hands in his and gazed at her. The two began walking down the driveway arm in arm while talking animatedly.

Ross turned to look at David and saw his lip twitch. David began laughing in a wild sort of way. Ross leaned his forehead on David's shoulder and let his own choked laughter give way to tears—tears that had been a long time coming. After a minute, he heard the screen door slap. Louise sat down and gave him a handkerchief. Together, brother and sister held him until his spasm of grief ended as suddenly as it began.

"I'll be all right," Ross said, sitting up straight and wiping his face with the handkerchief one last time.

David patted him on the back. The three of them sat still. Ross listened to the chirping of the birds and felt the warm nearness of the other two. They were breathing softly, almost in rhythm with one another, and he sensed that their thoughts had drifted away from him but not too far away. He looked at the clean line of David's jaw and then at Louise's profile, her lips slightly parted, her hair falling over her shoulders. Neither one was getting up and leaving him behind. Ross closed his eyes and listened again to the birds. He felt a little sleepy. He thought he should go inside and check on his children. For now, though, he would sit with David and Louise. If they all waited long enough, he figured that sooner or later Alice was bound to come home.

Last Words

I am Ross I am Alice I am the shining hills
and these layers of beauty and sorrow, sky and shadows,
are a waking dream.
I tell myself I will write to you. I tell myself I too will live.

We live in the days and wind and sunlight on maple leaves.
We live in the air, shining—we are our own kingdom
and our conversations go on in heaven.
We live in one another's eyes, in a world still shining.
It is all we can do not to run to the water and give up our breath
to the stars.
Our words get lost in the roar of the river, the wind, the sea in our
souls.

These are the words on my tongue.
This is my tongue on these words:
 If the air is sweeter there, I cannot say.
If the grass is softer, I cannot say.
You were to be mine, I believed it, prayed it, and then
I walked into the fields of Rapidan, the shining fields,
quietly breathing, all alone.

Alone then together we took hold of this dizzying world
and inhaled
the same air as the stars above Rapidan above Tipton naming
ourselves
Macklin Dennis Kathleen David Anna Sidney Jane Louise
Dale Jenkins Muriel Jenkins Billy Harry Abe and Earl
Sorbon Regina and James
Minor Williams Furman Betty Thomas
Philip Rosa
Jonathan Perkins
Chippers Julia Andy
Dusty Goldenrod Winston the orange cat
Reverend Braswell Mrs. Darling

Arnold Annette the Teagles—
Austin Pettigrew David's mom
Minnie Sam and Sara
and in the firmament above and below we linked arms
with a hundred thousand soldiers everlasting.

I am Ross. I am Alice.
We are in these shining hills of Rapidan the fields finally and truly
loved forever in Tipton always and forever home in Rapidan.

About the Author

Hilary Holladay has published a biography of the Beat Movement icon Herbert Huncke and a collection of poetry, *The Dreams of Mary Rowlandson*, as well as books on African American literature. She teaches American literature in the University of Virginia's Interdisciplinary Studies Program and lives in Orange County, Va.

CPSIA information can be obtained at www.ICGtesting.com
Printed in the USA
LVOW08*1745171114

414134LV00004B/34/P